S0-AXJ-555

RAVE REVIEWS FOR STAN CUTLER'S *THE FACE ON THE CUTTING ROOM FLOOR!*

"Will leave you reeling!"—*Kirkus Reviews*

"A wonderfully comic novel . . . This engaging duo is definitely the Laurel and Hardy of mystery fiction."—*The Clarion Ledger*

"Well plotted . . . sheer fun with a naughty, saucy edge."—*The Orange County Register*

"An interesting fun read . . . incisive and humorous!"—*Mystery News*

⊘ SIGNET MYSTERY　　　　　　⦿ ONYX　　(0451)

TANTALIZING MYSTERIES

☐ **BEST PERFORMANCE BY A PATSY by Stan Cutler.** "A terrific page turner—a mystery set in today's tinseltown. A treat!"—*Los Angeles Features Syndicate* "This Hollywood novel has everything—memorable characters, irresistible plotting, show business gossip, and a classic murder."—*Clarion Ledger*　　(403592—$4.50)

☐ **KING SOLOMON'S CARPET by Ruth Rendell, writing as Barbara Vine.** A beautiful woman fleeing a loveless marriage takes refuge in a Victorian schoolhouse, where she becomes the tool of terror in a dangerously passionate affair. "A jolting novel of psychological suspense."—*New York Times Book Review*　　(403886—$5.99)

☐ **MORE MURDER MOST COZY More Mysteries in the Classic Tradition by Agatha Christie, P.D. James, and others.** Baffling, intriguing, and wonderfully engaging murder returns to vicarages and villages, boarding houses and quaint seaside resorts. These eight superb stories are the perfect treat for the mystery connoisseur.　　(176499—$3.99)

☐ **TELLING LIES by Wendy Hornsby.** Exposing the truth is investigative filmmaker Maggie MacGowen's business. So, when her sister Emily is mysteriously shot in a Los Angeles alleyway and the evidence shows that it's no accidental street crime, it's up to Maggie to unravel the tangled threads of lies, deceptions, and buried secrets.　　(403800—$3.99)

☐ **KNIGHTS OF THE BLOOD created by Katherine Kurtz and Scott MacMillan.** A Los Angeles policeman is out to solve an unsolved mystery—that would pitch him straight into the dark and terrifying world of the vampire.　　(452569—$4.99)

Prices slightly higher in Canada

―――――――――――――――――――――――――――――――

Buy them at your local bookstore or use this convenient coupon for ordering.

PENGUIN USA
P.O. Box 999 – Dept. #17109
Bergenfield, New Jersey 07621

Please send me the books I have checked above.
I am enclosing $＿＿＿＿＿＿＿ (please add $2.00 to cover postage and handling).
Send check or money order (no cash or C.O.D.'s) or charge by Mastercard or VISA (with a $15.00 minimum). Prices and numbers are subject to change without notice.

Card #＿＿＿＿＿＿＿＿＿＿＿＿＿＿＿＿ Exp. Date ＿＿＿＿＿＿＿＿
Signature＿＿＿＿＿＿＿＿＿＿＿＿＿＿＿＿＿＿＿＿＿＿＿＿＿＿＿
Name＿＿＿＿＿＿＿＿＿＿＿＿＿＿＿＿＿＿＿＿＿＿＿＿＿＿＿＿＿
Address＿＿＿＿＿＿＿＿＿＿＿＿＿＿＿＿＿＿＿＿＿＿＿＿＿＿＿＿
City ＿＿＿＿＿＿＿＿＿ State ＿＿＿＿＿＿＿ Zip Code ＿＿＿＿＿＿
For faster service when ordering by credit card call **1-800-253-6476**
Allow a minimum of 4-6 weeks for delivery. This offer is subject to change without notice.

THE FACE
ON THE
CUTTING
ROOM
FLOOR

Stan Cutler

A SIGNET BOOK

SIGNET
Published by the Penguin Group
Penguin Books USA Inc., 375 Hudson Street,
New York, New York 10014, U.S.A.
Penguin Books Ltd, 27 Wrights Lane,
London W8 5TZ, England
Penguin Books Australia Ltd, Ringwood,
Victoria, Australia
Penguin Books Canada Ltd, 10 Alcorn Avenue,
Toronto, Canada M4V 3B2
Penguin Books (N.Z.) Ltd, 182–190 Wairau Road,
Auckland 10, New Zealand

Penguin Books Ltd, Registered Offices:
Harmondsworth, Middlesex, England

First published by Signet, an imprint of New American Library,
a division of Penguin Books USA Inc. Previously published in a Dutton edition.

First Signet Printing, September, 1993
10 9 8 7 6 5 4 3 2 1

Copyright © Stan Cutler, 1991
All rights reserved

Cover art by Gary Kelley

 REGISTERED TRADEMARK—MARCA REGISTRADA

Printed in the United States of America

Without limiting the rights under copyright reserved above, no part of this publi-
cation may be reproduced, stored in or introduced into a retrieval system, or
transmitted, in any form, or by any means (electronic, mechanical, photocopying,
recording, or otherwise), without the prior written permission of both the copyright owner and the above publisher of this book.

PUBLISHER'S NOTE
This is a work of fiction. Names, characters, places, and incidents either are the
product of the author's imagination or are used fictitiously, and any resemblance
to actual persons, living or dead, events, or locales is entirely coincidental.

BOOKS ARE AVAILABLE AT QUANTITY DISCOUNTS WHEN USED TO PROMOTE PROD-
UCTS OR SERVICES. FOR INFORMATION PLEASE WRITE TO PREMIUM MARKETING
DIVISION, PENGUIN BOOKS USA INC., 375 HUDSON STREET, NEW YORK, NEW YORK
10014.

If you purchased this book without a cover you should be aware that this book
is stolen property. It was reported as "unsold and destroyed" to the publisher
and neither the author nor the publisher has received any payment for this
"stripped book."

To Elaine, because . . . why not?

1

Rayford Goodman

On the face of it—small joke—the body was going to be a little hard to identify. Because the *face* was where the .25 caliber slugs had dotted the eyes and crossed the teeth.

Plus before, during, or after—gotta hope after—an *X* had been burned into each cheek by your basic acid bath. Which would've been spooky enough in maybe old Kampuchea, but struck me a little B movie for Beverly Hills.

Especially in a very expensive suite.

At a four-star hotel.

Sort of almost under my nose.

I was, wouldn't you know, the first person on the scene. On account the reason I was there for openers was make sure nothing like that happened. Funny so far? Actually, old hindsight nudging my ribs, I was really there, pretty sure *now*, to finger the corpse in question.

Naturally, that wasn't the way the deal'd been laid out. Just the way it shaped up after you figured out what an asshole you'd been.

Le Petit Ermitage was an annex of sorts to Beverly Hills's L'Ermitage Hotel. L'Ermie was your basic "exquisitely tasteful, excellently appointed luxury hostelry" (I'm quoting one of those little booklets tells you what's in and what's not and what's out of the question), where people richer than a paroled junk-bond dealer hung out. Opposed to the merely loaded who had to make do with the likes of the Beverly Hills, Bel Air, or Beverly Wilshire. Your basic castle away from castle. That's old L'Ermitage, the grand.

The *Petit* Ermitage was a very small (hence *petit*) couple of suites, separate little build-on where the same too rich, too exclusive got limoed after their Bev Hills plastic surgeons had a go putting the spring back in old Roy's neck. The entire clientele was face-lift rehabs, and L'Ermie was where they hid out till they healed young.

Besides what the pamphlet calls "understated elegance" (like crown jewels are understated) and "fastidious and caring medical supervision" (drop-dead gorgeous nurses), it's also about the only semi-hospital I ever knew the food alone could cure you.

Not to overkill—bad choice of words under the circumstances—it really is "the ultimate in exclusivity." Even fellow celebrities don't know who's next door, they're that discreet. Plus everybody's all wrapped up in about seventy yards of bandages and looks like a cross between King Tut and Claude Rains.

OK, body on the floor, face all bandaged, *bullets* in the face, *X*'s burned in the cheeks, me set up for the fall. Hold that picture.

First, I'd like to set things straight. You shouldn't have to read a hundred and fifty pages to find out if a guy's got a mustache (no). Actually, of course, you'd know all about me if you'd read *Rayford Goodman, Fixer to the Stars*, my autobiography ("As Told to Mark Bradley"—which means I told him the story and he put down the words. Only listen to him, you'd think he actually wrote it. Writers have some ego).

Rayford Goodman, Fixer to the Stars wasn't my choice for a title. I sort of liked *The Man Who Saved Hollywood*. But it turns out you don't have all that much say. Even if it is your life, it's their publishing company.

Anyway, if you *had* read it, you'd know enough about me I wouldn't have to repeat all this back-story jazz. But if not, you wouldn't know I was Ray—for Rayford—Goodman. That I was the wrong side of fifty, heavier side of two hundred, and shorter side of six feet. Plus the poorer side of divorce, unhealthier side of a heart attack, and not leading the pack in the virility sweeps. I understand these days you just plain tell everything, no holds barred. Or holes, for that matter.

But hey, big change. I'm still over fifty, over two hundred, under six feet, divorced, and with the heart thing. But in the old mattress department, happy to say, I'm now hotter than a Szechuan-Mexican dinner. This is largely, or more like totally, due to a fantastic and athletic lady named Francine, who I'm currently and constantly involved with. But I'll get into that in a minute. I give myself straight lines.

Did I mention I'm a private detective? Then and now; was and still. Actually, I'm a private detective *and* sort of celebrity, what with the book's being out and doing so good. I'm starting to get tables with low numbers at restaurants, and now that I can afford to pay, comped a lot. Life's a knuckleball.

Anyway, it was around twenty to one Tuesday morning and I was with the aforementioned Francine celebrating my return from the dread. How do I love thee? Let me count the ways: there's the missionary position; the passionate pony . . . Bill Basie was on the box, Joe Williams wailing "Teach Me Tonight"—what Francie calls my antique music—when our coitus was interruptussed by a loud banging on the door. Segue "Ev'ry Day I Have the Blues." I'd gotten out of bed, trying to suck in my love handles—Francie was a lot younger; everyone was a lot younger—and gone to check who wanted to see me all that bad.

Turned out a couple of "the boys" from Armand (The Dancer) Cifelli, the local warlord in charge of whatever's illegal and/or feels good.

The hood with the power of speech told me, "Our mutual friend would like a little sit-down."

Cifelli and I had exchanged favors in the past. Meaning I did what he told me in exchange for him not killing me. In truth, it was a little more complicated than that, but the way I saw it we were at least even. Only he wasn't the kind of guy you pointed out things like that.

"It's really not a very good time," I tried.

"You wouldn't rather put some clothes on?" he answered, opening his jacket on a gun Clint Eastwood would need help just to lift.

"Won't be a minute," I reasoned.

He followed as I popped back into my bedroom to dress—in case I got dumb enough to try packing heat. I'm not that kind of dumb—or brave. I told a nervous Francie not to worry. No sense both us. And if I wasn't back by dinnertime, finish the leftover meatloaf.

"But it's really all right?" she said.

"Sure, just going for a little talk."

"At one o'clock in the morning?"

"Beat the traffic."

"Right," she said, no more convinced than me.

The guard-dog guy started to get impatient. "Let's move

it along," he said. "Don't want to keep our mutual friend waiting."

I love that—our "mutual friend." My terrific "mutual friend." Which I guess does beat "ruthless killer."

"Just one question," I said.

"No questions," he said.

"Important."

"Well?"

"Is it dress casual?"

The one good thing being kidnapped by Armand Cifelli, you got to travel good. We were in his real super custom Mercedes limo and the Talking One was on the car phone. No big deal, these days you see 'em in Volkswagens and beat-up Chevy pickups. Who're all these people calling—their brokers? He was telling Mr. C. they'd picked up the "package." By calling me the package they fooled anybody might be listening in. That way they'd only think at one-thirty in the morning the guys'd picked up about eleven million dollars worth of dope.

Besides the telephone there was an intercom, a TV, a fax machine, and a bar. I noticed nobody was offering me a drink, or to see what was on TV. But then again, I wasn't being punched around the face, either, which seemed hospitality enough given the current company. I didn't know whether not being bound and blindfolded was a plus. Like if you weren't coming back, they didn't need to hide where you were going . . .

With thoughts like these, time didn't hang too heavy as we left my cozy nest high on one of the bird streets up off Doheny, zapped on down to Sunset, and turned right toward Beverly Hills. At least it wasn't toward the waterfront.

But the more I thought about it, there wasn't anything I'd done to or remotely against Cifelli. Our previous connection, where I'd found out somebody I'd nailed for murder had been framed, ended up with the guy staying framed once it turned out Mr. Cifelli had an interest in it staying that way. Not without some kind of mafia-like justice—the framee being a scuz and a thief. So he couldn't be mad about that. In fact, last I understood, I was aces in his book.

So why wasn't I looking forward to this little sit-down? Maybe it was just when the top capo of the Los Angeles mob sent for you in the middle of the night, he wasn't likely looking for someone to play a little boccie.

When the Driving Hood turned down Bedford in Beverly Hills, I figured maybe Cifelli had a house in the flats there. Which'd be a good sign, taking me to his house. But the car kept on going, all the way down to Santa Monica Boulevard and across. I was a little surprised at that because below Santa Monica all the streets were totally commercial. Everything had to be closed this time of night.

I was even more surprised he stopped in front of 435 North Bedford, being that was a doctor building, one of eleven thousand in Beverly Hills—hands down the doctor capital of the world.

"Out," said the Talking Hood, escorting me by himself, which I took as a plus. We went to the elevator and up to the top floor, where he prodded me out with the baby bazooka, was I getting too comfortable. We continued on down the hall past door after door of doctors specializing in this and that. I kept looking for one said "Practice Limited to Making Money." Then on to another door just like all the others. This one said, "B. T. Sorrento, M.D., a Medical Corporation. By Appointment Only." That was ours. I guess we had an appointment.

The waiting room was done up with some probably fairly expensive but very outdated pieces. There were two real heavy maroon horsehair armchairs, had lace doilies on the arms. The word *antimacassar* came to mind. The god of brain damage had decided to leave me antimacassar and take away my phone number. There was a matching sofa, and one of those two-legged half tables leaning against the wall—the kind always made you feel it went on through and the other half was on the other side of the wall. It had those bow legs that ended in kind of chicken claws holding on to a couple balls—always a favorite. Next to that stood a heavy bronze lamp with a big beaded shade looked like a petrified umbrella. And on the wall was a brown and white etching of Mt. Etna. The whole thing had the feel someone's maiden aunt died and they couldn't get a secondhand dealer to bid on her worldly goods.

The Talking Hood stood me next to the lamp (a strand of beads tickling my ear) and knocked on the door leading inside. Then he opened it, peeked in, took hold my arm, and led me over.

"Doctor will see you now," he said with a big garlicky grin. I took a breath out the other side of my mouth and stepped in.

The always dapper and elegant Armand (The Dancer) Cifelli popped up gracefully from a heavy desk matched the table outside and tangoed over to shake hands.

"I really appreciate your coming at such an awkward hour," he began. "I apologize for any inconvenience." He always talked that way. It was always so good of you to accommodate him on this little matter of some personal importance, taking time out your busy day. Where'd these guys learn to talk like that? Was there a Godfather School of Highfalutin Speech somewhere? Finishing Jail? And the way it still came out was thanks so much, it was so very kind of you to be of assistance, mostly because now they wouldn't have to put up with getting your blood all over everything.

"There's a small service you might be able to render me," he said (see?), indicating I be seated in a chair matched those outside and probably completed the "suite." I was careful not to wrinkle the antimacassars.

I gave him a sincere, I'm listening look, and listened. I always figured with guys like Cifelli, the less said the safer.

"I have an associate," he began. "Mr. G. Deeds, who has recently undergone plastic surgery." Uh-huh. "I guess we're all getting to an age where Mother Nature can use a little help . . ." Ri-i-ight. "Mr. Deeds is recuperating at Le Petit Ermitage, you know it?"

I nodded.

"Well, I got to worrying about Mr. Deeds' . . . security in a situation like that."

"Yeah, I hear it's a rough place."

"You like a little joke."

"I figure it never hurts to look on the bright side," I answered, not all that sure.

He cracked a little lip—I guess a smile.

"Mr. Deeds," he went on, back to business, "as so many entrepreneurial people, has alienated certain . . . factions . . ."

Which answered Mr. Deeds getting a new face.

"And," Cifelli continued, "there are those who would like to, uh—"

"I understand," I said, understanding.

"So, even though, if proper precautions were taken, the, uh . . ."

"Factions?" I prompted.

He nodded. ". . . shouldn't know him by that name, or presumably by his current appearance, there is some slight danger, as always of, uh, uh . . ."

"A fucking slipup?" I helped again.

"Exactly."

"So what do you want from me?"

"My associates, not being exactly the kind who'd've stumped the experts on *What's My Line,* strike me as apt to . . . stand out at the Ermitage."

"Unlike suave me."

"Unlike suave you. I don't know the room, they don't give that information out over the phone."

"Thanks to the *Enquirer.*"

"But I'm sure you'll have no trouble finding him. I'd like you merely to—protect him for a day or two from . . . whatever he might need to be protected from."

So what it was, Cifelli had a buddy holed up at the Ermitage. The guy sure had great style, give him that. He once kidnapped my biographer and held him hostage in a suite at the Bel Air Hotel.

I don't usually do bodyguard work. And I really didn't want to start now.

"I'd like you to think of it as a favor," he continued.

On the other hand, I didn't have any ambitions to become part of a new off ramp for the freeway, either.

"I'd be glad to," I said, showing lots of teeth.

"Thank you," he said, shaking hands again and slipping what I later found to be a thousand dollars into my palm. Which somehow took the edge off my resentment.

"Angelo is waiting downstairs," he wound up, "and will be happy to drive you wherever you wish."

I nodded and started to go, passing the Talking Hood coming in with a container of coffee. Which I guess he put it on the desk, because on my way out I heard Cifelli say, "A coaster, Vincent, stupid asshole! You don't put coffee right on top Aunt Serafina's desk, dumb fuck!" Looked like smooth talk wasn't for the help.

In the elevator down, I couldn't help thinking having an office in a doctor building was a pretty shrewd move. Who'd figure that?

Outside, Angelo was seated behind the wheel, smoking a cigarette. I had just opened the rear door when out the corner of my eye I began to get an inkling maybe somebody *had* figured where Cifelli had an office as a very Darth Vaderish black-windowed sedan slid into view, the windows slowly lowering.

I just finished saying, "Mr. C. said you'd give me a lift home, Angelo," when I caught sight of the artillery poking out the windows. I hit the deck and pulled the pavement over me as enough firepower for a couple Rambo sound tracks let go in quadrasonic Dolby.

It didn't take much of a look at the newly late Angelo for me to add, "Or I could grab a cab."

2

Mark Bradley

Nobody knows the trouble I've seen, nobody knows—barring perhaps Gore Vidal, Merle Miller, and the late truncated Truman Capote. I am an artist, only somehow I can't seem to get to it. Hardly a mystery, the somehow being personified (or thingafied) by Richard (Dirty Dickie) Penny, my publisher and perennial cross to bear.

I'd done autobiography after autobiography for him (in the Hollywood sense, meaning "as told to"—itself a euphemism for "as written by"). The understanding was after four I'd get to write my own book, my *real* book—about my life and hard times, you should pardon the expression. Which Pendragon Press would then publish. And I had every reason to expect even such a drekky dreg as Penny would finally honor his word after the unexpected and huge success of my latest literary prostitution, *Rayford Goodman, Fixer to the Stars*.

Lord knows it hadn't been the smoothest collaboration 'twixt macho man and yours truly. More like intense and abiding hatred at first sight. Nevertheless, it had sort of worked out when, in the course of our collaborative research we'd re-solved a twenty-five-year-old crime he'd initially mis-solved. Though that sort of remained a secret between us, due to pressures neither of us was prepared to resist. These were manifest on the one hand by the terrifying persona of Armand (The Dancer) Cifelli, who with the merest flicker of his barbered eyebrow could have all trace of your existence removed from the earth, and on the other by America's most renowned and beloved patriot-comedian, a man of equally awesome influence whose wife turned out to be the guilty party, precluding successful prosecution anyway. Therefore a negotiated settlement had been reached in deference to reason and cowardice, allowing the original felon to retain his billing of guilty as charged. In exchange, we were to receive some benefits. I was to write a screen-play which my associate, Francine, was to produce and in which my lover was to co-star. (Other emoluments were to accrue to Goodman.)

Alas, no sooner had the deal been struck than the Laughter of America winged off on tour to entertain our military abroad and there came to an untimely end. He succumbed, officially, to cardiac arrest, following the giving of his all in the service of his country. Unofficially, according to my sources, the Great Man met his maker while a buxom Marine nurse vigorously instructed him in the Heimlich maneuver—from the front.

At any rate, that, thank God, was all behind me. I had surely seen the last of Mr. Cifelli, and the others in that misadventure, as well as the dubious pleasure of working cheek by jowl by jowl with Rayford Goodman.

So at long last, I was looking forward to writing *the* book, the novel of my heart, at last to experience that stretch of powers the soul's muse cries out for every artist to attempt, when you mustered your courage and gave it your all.

But as I contemplated this happy and fulfilling prospect, there intruded on my consciousness an awareness that the voice I'd become so accustomed to only half hearing was, with a prototypical disregard for his word of honor—an oxymoron if I ever heard one—saying something rather disheartening.

It appeared that the founder and driving farce behind Pendragon, the aforementioned Dick Penny (Bad Penny to the initiated) was again importuning me to put aside my life's work, my hope for posterity, my sacred artistic commitment. Instead I was to undertake—"Just for a coupla weeks, what's the dif?"—the writing of yet another Hollywood "inside story." This time the "true tawdry tale" of what went on behind the cameras when the director was Claudio Fortunata, the legendary cinema cocksman.

"But, Dickie," I implored, "you gave your solemn word if I just did Rayford Goodman I could do my book next. You promised."

"That's true."

"I can do my book?"

"That I promised."

"Right, and . . . ?"

"And, whatta ya think? First you do the Fortunata thing."

"Give me one good reason why I should."

"Because I got you by the testiculars."

That'd be enough to scare *me* straight.

"Would you care to put that another way?"

For an answer he pulled out a single sheet of printed paper, on which was the fall list of publications due from Pendragon Press, and finger flicked it across the desk to me.

Somewhere after *"And . . . Action! The Autobiography of Claudio Fortunata* (as told to Mark Bradley)" and "*A Nympho's Christmas*" there was a spot penciled in reading, "*Inchoate Yearnings—a first novel by Mark Bradley.*"

"*Inchoate Yearnings*?! Where'd you get that?"

"Or whatever—one of those artsy-shit things you're gonna come up with. The point is, you're on the list."

"In pencil."

"You do Fortunata, and you got *Yearnings* or *Damp of Night* or whatever you want to call it, absolute lock promise."

"You'll have to do better than that, I want a contract."

"We could shake."

"Contract."

"Letter of agreement?"

"Confuckingtract!"

"You're a tough little pederast."

But before we could consummate either a realistic understanding or an absolute rupture, the phone rang. Penny, per custom, didn't excuse himself, or render service to any of the niceties, he merely picked it up and yelled, "Yeah, what?"

Meanwhile, I took a deep breath and mulled over whether I was going to go for his latest manipulation.

It was one of those mullings that took about a minute and a half. Who was I kidding? The BMW in the parking lot—in its assigned place; the condo in West Hollywood—in its choicest location; the Brian Alexander *in* the condo—the inamoratus of choice who, let's be honest, was a roommate only in the sense of occupying room. A consumer of consummate magnitude, there were additionally the costs of his car, his wardrobe, medical expenses—the man had needs. And given the vagueness of his commercial aspirations—"actor—model would be OK, too"—it wasn't realistic to assume Brian would in the foreseeable future be likely to come up with his share. At the rate money was hemorrhaging, it wasn't realistic either to pretend I had any choice but to accept Penny's offer. Besides, he had promised to publish *Secret Good*—and I *knew* his word was his bond.

"Fuck you, too," said Penny, hanging up. His calls all seemed to end with a tit for whatever tat he'd provoked.

"You still here?" he continued. "Got some questions?"

"No questions."

"Get started, then. You know the drill."

The phone rang. Penny snatched it up, "Yeah, what?"

"I'll just let myself out," I mentioned—to the chair.

And with a heavy sigh of resignation—wishing it could be a *letter* of resignation—I trudged wearily to my office.

It was a place bare of personal effects, the better to perpetuate the illusion I could just take off and leave at any impulsive moment. I flopped down at my desk, distressed.

But after a few moments' reflection, my customary optimism prevailed. After all, it wasn't exactly Devil's Island. And there was time. I was, besides, not even thirty yet—though that dreaded millstone loomed barely ahead—still trim of figure and sound of tooth. And if my extravagances were excessive in terms of middle America, I didn't, after all, *reside* in middle America. I could just imagine what middle America would make of where I did live, West Hollywood, with its gay mayor and its strange mixture of old Jews—the early settlers—and the carpetbagging upwardly mobile inhabitants of what had become Boys' Town who now predominated. What a coalition—Yummy Kippur!

I sharpened a few pencils, checked the batteries in my tape recorder, and was just about convinced four-thirty in the afternoon was not the time to start a book—a smidge early for cocktails, but definitely too late to start a book—when into the room ambled Francine Rizetti, my ace researcher, in hand a parcel of Xeroxes and news clips that suggested, as usual, she was way ahead of me.

Francine was my good friend. Bouncy and buxom, button cute, she had the mind of a man—look who's sexist!—and the body of a Botticelli, which for some inexplicable reason she was currently lavishing on my erstwhile literary nemesis, Rayford Goodman. I understood in part. She hadn't been spectacularly successful with regular, reasonable choices—

like good-looking men with a job. She had, in fact, had terrible luck and almost retired from "the guy business"— as she put it—when for reasons comprehensible only to her analyst (if that) she had "taken a hankering" to Goodman and, to my utter disbelief and dismay, actually semi-lived with him. Of course, given her track record, it was only a question of time before balance and order were restored to the world. I say this without gloating. Or minimal gloating— since when unencumbered she had more time and energy to devote in my service.

"Francie, me darlin', what brings you to this nape of the forest?"

"I got started on the Fortunata thing. Lots of print on the man. If you look at the files, you'd be surprised how far back he goes. The guy's been a fixture in Hollywood since Vilma Banky got her first period."

"Ever the delicate flower."

"The interesting thing, considering he's directed nearly a hundred pictures, everybody seems to love him."

"Just one little question, Francine." She gave me her innocent smile. "What made you so sure I'd *do* the 'Fortunata thing'?"

"Give me a break, the way you spend money?"

"How about my integrity?"

"Right. Shall we get on with it?"

At which point, somehow deciding I wasn't provoked enough, she whipped out a joint and lit it.

"Hey," I said, "I thought you promised Goodman you'd give up dope."

"Yep."

"Well?"

"Grass is not dope."

"Who says?"

"Dope is serious business—pharmaceuticals, man-made— whereas grass is something else. Even the Bible says thou shalt partake of the herbs of the earth. The herbs, it says, not some herbs, all the herbs."

"I never read that. Where's it say that?"

"I don't know—Kinky Kings II. Look, I'm smoking a little joint, what's the big deal?"

"You're breaking your word."

"Bending. And didn't it ever occur to you it's none of your business?"

"Not seriously."

"Shall we fucking continue? You *are* going to do the Fortunata book, and I *have* done some preliminary research. He's a good subject, very colorful, full of romance, funny, well liked, as I say, and very talented."

"Well, at least it won't be working with Rayford Goodman."

"Watch it, you're talking about the man I'm smit with."

"Which defies comprehension."

"Which is part two of none of your business. Here's the file I've collected so far. There're a couple of avenues you might like to explore. His female stars, for example, could be a good chapter. Old Claudio seems to have invented leading ladies falling in fuck with the director . . ."

"Good."

She handed me the file, took another. "Then, Academy Award nominations—he got seven, won three. You could do the making of those pictures," handing me that file.

"How about the guys who hate him?"

"They don't." Another file. "Man's man, likes to drink, cuss, gamble, and slaughter innocent animals."

"Sounds like my kind of person."

"Might be at that. I'm telling you, everybody likes him. Go talk to the guy."

"Hey, great idea!"

She didn't even blink. "You notice snideness doesn't affect me? I've become impervious," she said.

"Before you met Goodman, I was under the impression you'd been impervious for the better part of a year. Which may explain your bizarre infatuation."

"I'll thank you not to poke around in my business."

"You really like to live dangerously, don't you?"

"*And* I suggest you get started. You can find Mr. Claudio Fortunata currently at Le Petit Ermitage, where he is convalescing after a surgical attempt to recover his youth, under the nom de scalpel Mr. G. Deeds."

Which is how I happened to arrive at Le Petit Ermitage the very moment Ray Goodman was about to be arrested for the murder of my subject.

3

Rayford Goodman

I will say this, any other city but Beverly Hills there was a murder there'd be lots of black and whites, ambulances, TV press vans, patrolmen yelling get outta there, keep moving. Beverly Hills called for maybe one detective, couple guys to cart off the remains, so smooth might as easy be a pile of laundry, and a press agent to keep it out of the papers.

Which I guess is maybe why it bothered this particular detective, Chief Broward, so much I was there.

Maybe another reason was they have murders in Beverly Hills about as often as rent parties, and here I happened to be in the frame for *two* murders got themselves perpetrated in twenty-four hours.

Add to that Eddie Broward had a hardie for me going back twenty-five years, when I'd thrown egg on his face for busting the wrong person in a famous murder case—the American Beauty Rose. And lately got to rub it in again when my book came out and reminded everybody what a dumb bunny he was. So the odds were this wasn't going to be one of my better afternoons. (Actually, we'd both been wrong, but that was my little secret.)

"Maybe you'd like to tell me exactly what you *were* doing here," he was saying.

"Can't do that, Eddie. Client privilege and all."

"What you call client privilege I call accessory before, during, and after the fact."

"Only if my client had anything to do with putting old Claudio here to sleep. Whatta ya make of the two *X*'s burned in his cheeks?"

"What I make I don't discuss with you. And I'm not Eddie, I'm Chief Broward . . ." Which certainly put a damper on friendly banter.

But the real conversation stopper came in the face and form of a startlingly beautiful young woman now joining us.

She had the palest, flawless white skin, huge gray eyes, and lustrous jet black hair which she parted in the middle and combed straight back. The original "Draw Me!" Completing the picture was a world-class body on which was laminated the kind of power suit said she was seriously working. With the kind of laser seams suggested she got paid a lot for the work.

"Gentlemen, I'm Tiffany Kestner, the corporate executive in charge here. I came as soon as I got word of these . . . events."

"Good-o," said Broward, "I'll want to talk to you by and by. Stay close."

With a sigh suggested she was used to dealing with inferiors, Kestner said, "First, let me close this door," which she did.

"Now just a minute, missy, I'm in charge here!" Broward sputtered—a cross between spit and stutter.

"Next," growled the last person in the world to call missy, ignoring his sputter, "let me remind you this is a medical facility. It is absolutely essential we have minimal disturbance."

"There's been a murder, lady; I call that a large disturbance." With which he crossed the room to reopen the door, and continued, "Which calls for investigation, and certain procedures."

She went and reclosed the door. "And be very quiet and discreet."

"Look, miss, I work in Beverly Hills. I understand the drill. But that doesn't include sweeping murder under the carpet . . . at least when it's a celebrity," said Broward, raising his voice.

"Please, keep it down. That doesn't preclude 'handling.' We shall have no fuss."

"I'll have to question everybody. If that's a fuss, then there's going to be a fuss, and nothing in the world's going to stop me!"

"Other than the police department incurring a lawsuit?"

"Other than that," said Broward, making a soft landing back on earth.

"You do know the people I represent?"

"Naturally," said Broward, not knowing and afraid to, his voice a lot lower.

Figuring she had him checked, Ms. Kestner turned her attention to me. "And you are . . . ?"

"Rayford Goodman," I said. "Here in a private capacity—on behalf Mr. Deeds, Mr. Fortunata."

"Fortunata was registered under a phony name?" asked Broward.

"I wouldn't phrase it exactly that way," said old Tif. "Many of our clients register under assumed names to avoid publicity. One of the prime requisites of our facility is the guarantee of discretion. Please keep that in mind, Mr. Broward."

"I do what's necessary to solve the crime," he said—not exactly the truth, in my experience. "And it's Chief Broward."

"Whatever."

"So for the record," he continued, no gain, "Mr. Fortunata, alias Mr. Deeds, was a patient here in this suite, the Marie Antoinette?"

"That is my understanding," said Kestner.

"I can vouch for that," I added. "When I got here I didn't know which suite was Mr. Deeds'. The lady on the desk was giving me a slightly hard time, wanting to clear with you, I guess, or someone. But when she got called away, I sort of slipped behind the desk. That's when your Miss her name tag said Alicia Blake showed up and asked *me* which was Deeds' room. I figured that gave me almost permission, so snuck a peek at the roster and told her Marie Antoinette."

"Not Fortunata, Deeds?" asked Broward.

"Yeah, well, that's what he was registered as. I didn't know Deeds was Fortunata."

"And you say it was a Miss Alicia Blake?" said Kestner.

"Yeah, brunette, about five eight or nine, killer body, about a hundred twenty-five, large boobulars, perfect teeth. My kind of nurse."

With which she went to a phone, dialed two numbers, and said, "Ms. Kestner here, do we have an Alicia Blake on the floor?" She listened a moment, then informed us, "There is no Miss Blake working here."

Which set me to wondering how "Blake" even knew Fortunata was registered as Deeds. From Cifelli?

"Maybe I wasn't so far off when I said killer body," I said.

"And maybe there was nobody else at all," said Broward.

"What's that supposed to mean?"

"Convenient for you, right? We have a murder on Bedford Drive, nobody else there but you. We have a murder here on Burton Way, whatta ya know, again nobody but you."

"Are you going to do that stupid thing again where you haul me in so you can tell the press—"

"No press," said Kestner automatically.

". . . you've got a suspect in custody, and then when it gets obvious to any dumbo with half a brain it couldn't be me you have to let me go?"

"*After* you spend a night or two in jail and a couple of weeks' salary on lawyers."

"You really are the pits."

"And you really are under arrest. You have the right to remain silent."

"Son of a bitch."

"In fact, I insist on it!"

Which is about when, I didn't have enough aggravation, the one person I really hoped I'd seen the last of, Mark Bradley, my gay collaballero, stuck his head in the door and said, "I guess this wouldn't be the best time to interview Mr. Fortunata."

What happened then, Broward turned his attention to Bradley; Ms. Kestner got on the phone and made several calls; and I wandered off here and there on the off chance I might find a clue or two.

I knew Cifelli was going to be a tad pissed I'd you might say bungled my assignment protecting Mr. Deeds, or Fortunata as it turned out. And I had, actually, since at the time I arrived he was no doubt still alive.

The way I reconstructed it, "Miss Blake" was probably a professional hit person ("You've come a long way, baby"). And while some associate of hers got the regular nurse off on a wild goose chase, Blake showed up. She already knew I would be there and would probably've found out what suite was Fortunata's. Then she got real creative, told me wait outside, she had to change his bandages and clean him up. I figured OK, I was on the job just waiting outside. And when she finished—really finished—she came out, closed the door again, and told me to wait ten minutes more as Mr. Deeds was resting after the strain having his bandages changed. He was resting, all right, from then on. And I went for it. It seemed reasonable, since she had the kind of boobs lent sincerity to her words.

And here we were.

I was frankly a lot more worried how Cifelli would take it than Broward. Although I couldn't help wondering what connection there was between Cifelli and Fortunata. I'd assumed Mr. Deeds was just someone getting his face changed to protect the guilty.

Broward was finishing up with Bradley, taking notes, as Bradley was at the same time finishing up with him, also taking notes. I'd read in the trades Pendragon Press was doing a book on Fortunata. Pretty good timing.

About here two sanitation gents in Armani coveralls showed up, wheeling a dazzling chrome cleaning cart looked like top-of-the-line Hammacher Schlemmer (or Sharper Image to you Kevin-come-latelys).

"Oh, right, in here," said Ms. Kestner, motioning them in.

"Whatta ya think you're doing?" said Broward.

"Cleaning up," she told Broward. "Go ahead," she told the trendy "sanitation engineers."

"Whoa, whoa," said Broward. "This is a crime scene, hold your horses."

"Chief Broward, there are bloodstains on this carpet."

"That'll happen, people pump bullets into other people," he explained patiently.

"You don't want them to set, do you?"

"What I don't want is anything touched."

"Perhaps you don't understand, these are Aubusson carpets, extremely valuable."

"And you don't understand, you're not in charge here, girly."

"No, you don't understand, buddy boy . . ."

It was about then forensics showed up and threw the bunch of us out in the hall.

After tempers cooled down some, we wound up in Tiffany's office. Or museum. Or jewel box. Whatever it was. Start out it cost about eighteen million dollars, everything totally decorator degenerate. For openers, the clock was a nicely laid-back carriage with sixteen bronze horses. Then two midgets in gold armor guarded a marble fireplace, or maybe it was all those eggs laid by Fabergé on the mantel.

For company the tin dwarfs had a skinny china dog I wanted to kick in the ass. The whole thing looked like someplace the dauphin might use to change his knickers in. I really hated it a lot.

"All right," said Broward, not that touchy. "This'll do fine for my interrogations. Ms. Kestner, I'm going to want to question every one of your staff and all your patients."

Ms. Kestner took this news about as well as if he'd nominated her for sweetheart of the Turkish army. "Mr. Broward, I don't seem to be getting across to you," she said, her lovely lips tightening. "You are not going to interview my patients. I have phoned our attorneys, who are en route and should be arriving momentarily. They will apprise you more precisely of the penalties in store and liabilities incurred by anyone interfering with the treatment of patients in a medical institution. In the meanwhile, I suggest you remove your men to some more remote area, and permit me to restore tranquility." Once she got rolling, she talked almost as nice as the mafia guys.

Broward was sputtering again. He certainly didn't like what he was hearing. On the other hand, he knew clout when he saw it. And in Beverly Hills he tended to see it a lot. He also hadn't gotten to be chief of detectives misreading a lot of situations. So he backed off, instead turning to me.

"All right, let me first get something clear with you."

"Me who's under arrest and warned not to speak?"

"We can do this here or we can do it down at the station."

I often wondered why the station was always down. Nobody ever went up to the station—or even over or around.

"You know, that sounds familiar," I said.

"You say you were here on business."

"I wasn't getting a face-lift."

"That's obvious," said Bradley, whose two cents nobody asked for.

"I'll do the talking," said Broward, talking. "What was the business?"

"I can't say," I said.

"You can say, and you will say," said Broward.

I didn't say.

"OK, this doesn't seem to be getting us anywhere. You,

Kestner, don't go in that room till forensics is done. In fact, don't enter it at all till I tell you."

"Except to clean the Aubusson carpets."

"Maybe that."

"You," to Bradley, "just get out. I got no further business with you. You," to me, "let's go."

"Look, Ed—Chief—this is silly. You know I didn't have anything to do with this."

"But I also know you know stuff I *don't* know, and I know from previous experience you ain't about to share it with me."

"Yeah. So the charge is?"

He thought for a moment, then came up with, "Withholding."

"In some quarters that's considered a desirable attribute," said Bradley, about four miles over Broward's head.

He settled for a look, then rose from in back of a second-hand desk previously owned by fourteen or fifteen Louies, scraping it with the badge pinned to his belt. That drew an involuntary, painful "ooh" out of Ms. Kestner, which Captain Klutz also failed to catch. Instead he just herded us all back out the hallway and over toward the elevator leading to the parking level. We were only about a step or two away when the door opened and out walked what you might call the ghost of Hollywood past. What registered first was this helmet of bandages that encased his entire head but for a little piece of face framed at the cheeks. If that wasn't cute enough, add two little bulbs on either side about ear high filled with I guess blood. It was half silly and half unnerving.

"Oh, my *god*," said Ms. Kestner, clearly opting for unnerving. "It's him!"

"Him who?" said Broward.

"Let me," said Bradley, really enjoying himself. "Ladies and gentlemen, I believe this is Mr. Claudio Fortunata."

"In the very tender flesh," said Fortunata. "What's up?"

Mark Bradley

So, it was apparent I wasn't going to get off that easy. There was still a book to be written, and it was still an autobiography—technically. I had to admit it was certainly starting off promisingly.

After the tall, elegant director—if anybody can look elegant in bandages with blood bubbles at the temples—had made his startling entrance, there ensued a lot of wasted motion and energy. This was led enthusiastically and lead-footedly by Chief of Detectives Edward Broward—to the vague bemusement of Fortunata. The latter was as yet unaware he'd apparently returned from the dead and thus did nothing to stop Broward's almost compulsive running off at the mouth. When Broward finally got to "I want answers, and I want them now!" it wasn't the director who responded—both because he had no idea what they were talking about, and second, wouldn't accept that kind of dialogue—but old Rayford Goodman, who apparently did and would.

"I think I got the picture," he said. "While you folks locked horns over what to do about Audubon's rugs, I poked around and noticed a few things. First, what wasn't—no tapes, scripts, dictating machines, or even silver-framed snaps of gorgeous ex-wives. Second, what was—an adding machine, a book telling changes in this year's tax laws, and a list of foods 'not good for you, don't eat' in a note from somebody Sherry or Shirley. And finally, several letters looked to be about accounting matters and one a thank-you from the U.J.A. All addressed to a Mr. Hamilton Cohen—which you take all together gets him my vote for corpse du jour."

At the word *corpse* the noted Chilean director seemed to lose a bit of aplomb, his sangfroid noticeably slipping.

"What corpse, wha' you talking about, man?" he demanded in a bandage-muffled panic.

"Looks like someone's after your bones," replied Goodman evenly. "My guess is you were the target. Whatever reasons, you weren't in your room. Instead, I feel pretty sure old Ham Cohen was. And both your heads being almost totally wrapped in bandages, a logical enough mistake for a hitman—hit person—to figure him for you."

"And while we're at it," interrupted Broward, addressing Fortunata, "just how come you weren't in your room, and Mr. Cohen was?"

"I was off the premises," said Fortunata, resuming the mantle of cool sophistication he'd let slip for a moment, "because there seems to be some kind of company policy against female companions *on* the premises."

"You did not have permission to leave," said Tiffany.

"Exactly why I had to go to all the trouble of sneaking out," explained Fortunata.

"I suppose the lady in question can verify that," said Broward.

"I'm sure she'd remember it," he replied smugly. "But I wouldn't for a moment put her through that sort of embarrassment—or her husband."

"Let me get this straight," said Broward. "OK, you were out, doing—whatever with, for the moment, whoever. And Mr. Cohen was in your room why?"

"Because the window in my room faced the window next to the duty nurse's desk—which kind of got in the way of coming and going on the sly."

"That's the Marie Antoinette suite."

"Right."

"Next to the Venus De Milo suite."

"Right."

"So you got Mr. Cohen to switch with you?" asked Broward.

"Right."

"And wound up in . . . ?"

"The Joey Bishop suite."

I was describing the aforementioned action to my roommate, the preaforementioned cute and costly Brian Alexander, in the living room of our trendy digs on Willoughby at King's Road in the heart of West Hollywood.

Brian was once again between engagements, having relinquished his part-timer at a Beverly Center gift shop in order to pursue a series of auditions for a commercial he didn't get—surprise. This should have had at least one salutary effect, my not having to listen to his day before discussing the more interesting aspects of my own. But apparently not.

"So this poor schnook Hamilton Cohen gets knocked off by mistake, can you believe the luck?" I said.

"The plumber didn't show again," said Brian.

Definitely not.

"Here he probably thinks he's made it to the big time, exchanging liposuction stories with an Oscar-winning director. And when his new best buddy asks him to switch suites, why not? What're buddies for? So what happens—he winds up a stand-in for murder. Hey, there's a title!"

"The cable's out, too," continued Brian with unabated self-absorption. "I called all day and it was either busy or they kept me on hold and made me listen to awful music."

"But I don't want to burden you with all the fascinating details of my extraordinary life—"

"Plus I don't know what's wrong with Bernadine. She didn't show up again, either, and I had to do all the vacuuming myself."

"So much for 'hi, honey, I'm home.' "

Brian was being beastly again. I don't know why it is the more dependent someone gets, the more they seem compelled to prove gratitude works in inverse proportion to debt.

For quite a while now I'd had the sinking feeling our relationship had sprung a slow but fatal leak. More and more he had to be he and the he he had to be seemed less and less the he for me (I think Cole Porter could have done something with that).

I'm beginning to believe the best way to live is in a series of sequential relationships. It seems only with someone new are we willing to make the kind of sustained effort it takes for success. Once you stop holding in your tummy and keeping a smile on your face and trying your damnedest to be a terrifically desirable person, the handwriting's on the wall—that old moving finger. It's sort of like the landlord refusing to paint or recarpet for the old, established tenant, thereby driving him out, only to immediately do those very things to attract a new, unproven replacement.

Evidently I wasn't the only one continuing an inner monologue, as Brian added, "And I'll be damned if I'm going to do the bathrooms, either."

"Why is that, Brian?"

"I'm no maid."

"So who do you think should do them, absent Bernadine?"

"I don't know, you figure it out."

"I think I have," I said. Which seemed to irk him even more (I Get an Irk Out of You) as he gave a that-does-it look, grabbed his jacket, and headed for the door.

"And just where are you going?" I hated myself for asking.

"Don't do that," he warned me. "Don't you be asking those kinds of questions, you're not my keeper."

I even took a moment. I wasn't that angry. I could easily have held back. "Could have fooled me," I still said, an escalation in anybody's book.

Brian reached for a rejoinder, couldn't quite find one—cute ain't necessarily smart—and tried to compensate by slamming the door.

I didn't feel like I'd won anything.

Back at the office I started doing some preliminary work on the book. With Fortunata still at the Ermitage, I'd have a few days to really get going with my interview before he had to resume production on his picture. But first I needed to review Francine's notes and prepare my questions.

I'd just settled down and begun perusing her printout when Francine herself stuck an anxious head in the door.

"Did you hear, they took Rayford to jail!"

"Yeah, I know, but they won't hold him."

"All the same, Broward'll drag it out as long as he can."

"So?"

"Come on, let's go pressure Penny to get his lawyers on it."

"Hey, it's none of my business. You do whatever you want."

"What kind of friend are you?"

"Good enough not to encourage your incomprehensible romance with that man."

"Are you coming?"

"All right, I'm coming."

Which I should have known I was somehow going to regret. At any rate, we shortly found ourselves again face to face with literature's fiercest foe, the publisher and editor-in-chief of Pendragon Press.

Francine quickly recounted the details of Goodman's summons by Cifelli, then I recounted the events which had transpired at Le Petit, concluding with Goodman's incarceration by Broward and the urgent necessity to get a lawyer to Beverly Hills headquarters and spring him.

"Absolutely," said Penny, suspiciously agreeable. "We must do everything we can for Ray."

We exchanged wary looks. Somewhere near that pony was some horseshit.

"Right," said Francine, a touch anxiously.

"Absolutely whatever we can," reiterated Penny.

By which time instinct was screaming. "Why is that again, Dickie?" I asked, half suspecting I didn't want to know.

"Because with what's already starting to happen on the Fortunata project, given Goodman's already involved from another angle, I think the thing to do—I know the thing to do—what we're gonna do—is team you guys up again!"

"Oh, no, no, no, no," I said.

"Sure sure sure," he said. "It's a natural. Look how successful you were last time."

"You don't know what that took out of me. I don't want to work with him. I don't need him."

"You can't tell, you might. I mean, we're talking murder here."

"Of someone named Cohen."

"Of accidentally someone named Cohen, when they meant on purpose Fortunata. I wouldn't feel right leaving you out there all alone with no protection."

"You can't do that to me, Dickie, really."

"Sure I can. Plus it's not only for your own safety, it's also commercially right—not that that's a primary consideration."

Right, no one would suspect Penny of thinking about money.

"Look," I had to try one more time, "we plain don't like each other."

"He likes you."

"He doesn't. He called me a fruit and a fag."

"Words. Fruit and fag; fruit and fiber—words."

"Listen, while you two are breaking in your act, Ray-ford's still in jail."

"Wonderful!" said Penny. "How long do you think we should leave him there? I mean, publicity-wise."

"Call the lawyer," said Francie.

But before Penny could oblige, the phone rang. He took it, threw in a few routine obscenities, finally paused, listened.

"For you," he said, handing me the instrument.

It was Brian, who'd returned home to apologize—I'm such a shit. I said I thought that was really nice and we'd have a lovely make-up dinner together and I appreciated it, even if it was, at the moment, interfering with business, at my place of which we had agreed he wasn't supposed to call. In fact, given his addiction to telephoning in general, we'd made a specific pact that he wasn't to call *ever*, barring the most extreme emergency, for which, for example, the cable fixer's failure to show didn't qualify.

He said he understood all that, and he was really very sorry to disturb me at the office, given especially that he'd agreed not to. And while, since we *were* talking, he did want to apologize for our earlier contretemps and hoped everything would henceforth be all right between us, there was, additionally, another, more pressing reason for the call.

Which was?

"These two guys with guns standing here, wanting your help to do something-or-other for somebody-or-other about someone-or-other."

"Could you narrow that down a little?"

"For openers, I think they're mad at you, and by extension me."

"Because why?"

"Because they have some business with Mr. Fortunata that requires something with Ray Goodman, who they can't seem to locate that they figure you can help them with."

"Did you tell them I'm not in business with Mr. Goodman?"

"My part's been mostly listening. Why don't I put them on? Mister, you want to talk on the phone?" There was a mumble and a bump of some sort. "He doesn't want to talk," said Brian in a thin, reedy voice.

There followed some more bumpy noises, a silence, then

Brian again: "He said just tell you to get your ass over here so they don't do awful things to me." Then added, explaining the bump I'd heard, "More awful things."

"Tell 'em I'm on my way."

"He's on his way," I heard him say. "Don't hit."

With which the line—hopefully the only thing—went dead.

"I knew it! I knew I shouldn't do this," I said.

"What's up, kid?" asked Penny.

"I haven't even said yes yet, and already there're a couple of bent noses over at my place pressuring Brian."

"Wonderful, I love it!" said Penny. "You got a subplot already. Terrific!"

"They are threatening my roommate."

"Marvelous," said Penny.

The man had a heart as big as all indoors.

But even as Francine and I headed for the Beverly Hills bastille to try springing Goodman ourselves, I couldn't help wondering why, with Goodman working for Cifelli, Cifelli's boys didn't just check with their boss if they were looking for him.

I mean, if they were that inefficient, how did they ever get to be called organized crime?

5

Rayford Goodman

First I was going to call "Dr. Sorrento" to bust me out of the joint. Little joke, Beverly Hills jail beating most Marriotts. But even though Fortunata was still alive, it sure wasn't my doing—more poor Mr. Cohen's. So the good doctor mightn't be overjoyed at my performance protecting Mr. Deeds. I decided best cool it asking favors in that area.

I suppose for options I could have called an independent lawyer. I was definitely wishing I had. Because what I did, I called Luana, my ax-wife. It seemed both only fair since I was supporting her and in her best interests for me to be out and earning a dollar. Not my smartest move. But at the time I'd figured since she was co-domiciling with this hotshot lawyer, Ron Tann (don't that sound like a sunblock?), he wouldn't mind laying a freebee on me.

He didn't mind. He was actually glad to help, the shit. OK, he was too good-looking to be a movie star. OK, he made about a zillion dollars a fiscal year. I could even live with he was a scratch golfer and played tennis only a little better than Boris Becker—did he have to also be a nice guy?

I really didn't want to deal with why I would still be jealous over someone gave me such a hard time even when it still counted. Considering the old marriage of inconvenience was long gone, I couldn't for the life of me explain she still had this talent to bug me. Besides, even if Old Paint—who was Old Paint like Christie Brinkley was Old Paint—had given me a bad couple of years, there had been some really good ones . . .

"Rayford, are you listening at all? I'm talking to you!"

. . . which I'd be able to forget real easy in about a minute and a half.

"It's a reflection on me, that's all I'm saying, this constant involvement with lowlifes." You could count on Luana to keep Old English alive all by herself. "Lowlifes."

"I don't deal with lowlifes," I said. "Highwaymen, maybe; the occasional cutpurse."

"You certainly have a right to live your own life," she continued, not meaning it. "But you can't expect me, or Ron, to come bail you out all the time."

"Look, Luana, it's not all the time. It was once and I admit it was a mistake. God, I admit. But the way I look at it now, a lot older and wiser, I'd really rather go pay someone else a ton than listen any more of this shit."

I admit it's possible it was the mention I was willing to pay clued her I was serious. She let loose a big long-suffering sigh. Luana always felt so disappointed when I answered back. When I did that she always said how she'd hoped we could be civilized with each other. Her idea of civilization being she got to be England and I got to be a colony needed fixing.

She sighed again, turned on her at least three-hundred-dollar heel—and headed toward the current knight waiting by his Bentley steed. It kills me to say this, because character is supposed to show on your face, but she looked really great. On top of that, it was on the natch, unlike her friends who'd had so many face-lifts they all looked like dead teenagers.

The thing that really bugged me, I hadn't needed to go through all this at all because it turned out Mr. Penny at Pendragon Press was arranging my release at the same time. And my price to him wouldn't be my total soul, just working with Mark Bradley again. Close.

I didn't much care for that idea, either. But it looked like our paths were crossed no matter what. He was writing an autobio for Claudio Fortunata, and I, figuring I was still on the job, was hired by Cifelli to protect Fortunata. The reason I figured I was still on the job was nobody'd shot me yet.

Bradley and Francine pulled up just after Luana and Ron left, so at least I was spared a whole lot of sarcastic politeness.

"You're out," said Bradley—not one of his brighter observations.

"Yeah, they dropped the no charges. You guys came to rescue me?"

"That's right," said Bradley. "Hop in."

I hopped.

"Looks like we'll be working together," said Bradley, with a lemon-sucking look, as we pulled away. "That your understanding?"

"I guess," I said, finding it hard to get the words out since it didn't exactly thrill me, either. Stuck in my craw's more like it. "I got a call from Penny, who figured we might as well, being we're both working on Fortunata."

"Yeah, now what is it exactly?" said Bradley.

"I'm sort of . . . protecting him," I mumbled, embarrassed.

"For . . . ?"

"Our 'mutual friend,' " finished Francine.

"Ah, so that's what you were doing, back at the Ermitage," said Bradley, giving me a little zinger. "In any case, I'd like you to stop off at my condo and straighten out a few of our 'mutual friend's' minions, who are stirring up some very unpleasant memories for Brian."

Brian had been beaten up once before when he was more or less under my protection, too—by mistake. They'd been out to annoy me by roughing up Bradley, and I guess the job description seemed to fit Brian just as well. But it was beginning to look like protecting wasn't one of my better things.

"I don't see why Rayford should go sticking his neck—" began Francie, but I stopped her.

"I owe him, babe," I said. Living in Hollywood can affect the way you talk from time to time.

Bradley speeded up the BMW, and it was only a minute or two till we were pulling up beside his place in precious West Hollywood. Actually, I'm not one of those people goes around saying he's got no prejudices. What I *will* say, I've got considerably less since meeting Bradley. In a lot of ways he was a stand-up guy, no pun intended. But he was a you-know-what. And I've got to also say while I no longer think gays should be tarred and feathered—definitely not feathered—I don't exactly understand all this pride stuff. I mean, they have weeks now, Gay Pride Week—for doing god knows what. Why not Premature Ejaculator's Week? Impotence Week! Anyway, I'm a lot more tolerant, you can see that.

We parked, got out, crossed to the security panel,

buzzed, posed in front of the monitoring TV so as not to upset anyone by surprise, and got passed in.

The elevator opened on Bradley's floor, and the three of us headed down the hallway, around the corner, and up to the door, which was slightly ajar. I don't guess it could be largely ajar.

Brian was huddled in a big gray chair was shaped like a leaky blimp, looking very vulnerable but not noticeably marked.

"OK, guy?" said Bradley.

"Yeah," said Brian, halfway convincing.

I turned my attention to Moke and Poke towering over the proceedings.

"You guys wanted to see me?"

"You're Goodman?"

"Yeah, I'm Goodman."

"Ray Goodman?"

"That's me."

So, satisfied there was no mistake, they began beating the shit out of me.

Brian, I didn't expect much, he sank deeper in the chair. But Bradley was a big disappointment. Here I'm fighting off these two momsers and not doing too good at it, what's he do? Backs off, wanting no part of it.

"Hey, give me a hand," I grunted between ducks and fattening lips.

Francine jumped in.

"Not you," I gasped, catching a hook.

"Stop that!" she yelled, jumping on top of Moke and swinging her chubby little fists.

This had about as much effect as you'd imagine. He just shrugged her off his shoulder, tossing her more or less on top of Brian. Meanwhile I took a couple more shots weren't going to feel too good. I did get in a nice overhand right oughta give Poke a shiner. But they were pros, and there were two of them, and it wasn't going to go well for me. Which, by now, Bradley wasn't even in the room.

That's what I mean about gays—any regular man would've helped me, no matter the odds—

Which was exactly when Bradley popped back in the room.

"All right, hold it right there, assholes!" he yelled, getting their attention. What got their attention even more was the large gun in his hand.

Like I said, what a guy!

Things settled down quickly after that. Bradley covered the gunsels. I peeled Francine off of Brian. And Brian got useful, bringing me a bag of ice to cut the swelling I was already starting to get.

"I want answers, and I want 'em now," I heard myself saying, and saw Bradley roll his eyes. "What is this shit?" I rewrote.

"Just a little message," said Moke.

I hate that. It's one of the things about gangsters I hate even more than their hitting all the time. Every time they talk to you, it takes a gangsterologist to figure what they mean.

"Message," I repeated, as if I knew what the hell it was all about. "Well, I got a message, too—fuck you!"

It wasn't the wittiest thing I ever said, but it was basic all-purpose. They were the sort of guys could always make something out of a fuck-you.

"Yeah, well, fuck you!" replied Moke.

"Fuck you!"

"Fuck _you_!!!"

"Can we go now?" said Poke, having aloofed himself from this clever exchange.

"No, you can't go now," answered Francine. "I'm going to call the police."

With which she started for the phone. I caught her arm.

"No, you're not, hon," I said.

"Give me one good reason."

"Because they work for the guy I work for."

Moke treated me to an out-of-your-mind look.

"Ask Cifelli," I said. "I work for Cifelli, too."

They'd both lowered their hands, since it was clear they weren't about to get shot. And now they headed for the door.

"We don't work for Cifelli, asshole," deloofed Poke. "We work for Nash."

With which they were gone.

"Nash?" asked Bradley. "Who's Nash?"

"Nash is the boss of what you call your rival gang."

"What does that mean?" asked Brian, taking an interest in our work.

"It means I don't know what it means—besides definitely not good."

I was a little banged up, so Bradley got out a first-aid kit. As he tended to a couple cuts he told me Boy Scouting was good for more than one thing—which I didn't exactly understand but had the notion I didn't want to. I'd forgotten Bradley owned a gun.

"It was a logical extension of knowing you," he said, as if it was my fault he'd been kidnapped and Brian'd been beat up during last time. But his having *gotten* the gun came in handy then, too.

"Anyhow, thanks," I said.

He acknowledged that with a casual nod. Cool.

Then we straightened out our various transportation, Bradley BMW-ing Francie to where her Mustang was— trendy, the girl was trendy—and me back to the Ermitage for my '64 classic Eldorado Caddy convertible. They were off to the office to I guess get started doing the Claudio Fortunata book, me to figure what "the message" was and why it got sent in the first place. They didn't ask me along. I guess not ready yet for the real collaboration.

I would have been normally starting to stiffen up by now, only happened Francine had a Percocet on her. For some-one who'd given up drugs she seemed pretty well stocked. But you can't look a gift drug in the mouth. Anyhow, the Perc'd kicked in and not only wasn't I feeling any pain, I was feeling no pain.

In fact, things didn't look too bad, really. It was probably just some sort of mix-up could be straightened out with a call or two. Sure.

I turned on the radio and got about a minute and a half of some great old Woody Herman. Then Christ, there came the commercials. The whole thing about FM used to be the no commercials. Which, of course, got it popular. Which got it commercial. Which made for as bad as AM. I turned it off and popped in a Bill Watrous tape.

That grooved me. Calmed me right out. Yeah, it would be all right. Hell, it *was* all right. Misunderstanding. Music hath charms. Painkillers likewise.

I turned down Bedford, across Little Santa Monica. There was a line at the municipal two-hour free-parking

building. I couldn't see any open space down the block.
Never an open space down the block.

I was going to have to go to the bandits. Just past 435
there was a lot, part of the doctor building, charged a buck-
twenty every twenty minutes! Ought to have a pill for that.
Well, maybe Cifelli validated.

I pulled in the center lane, a little left of center on the
logic the attendant was going to open only the driver's sides
of the three cars, so what I wanted to protect most was the
passenger side of mine, even if there was a chance he might
chip the edge of my driver's side door, that was a strong
part. The goddamn attendants, for those kind of prices
you'd think they'd guarantee not to dent your car or scrape
the paint—go read the small print back of your check.

Maybe my pill was wearing off. Have to talk to Francie
again, she shouldn't be doing that. Definitely the pill was
wearing off. I was getting mad at the attendants, my girl,
definitely anybody named Nash, and I wasn't too sure I
wanted much more to do with Cifelli, either.

Well, we'd get this thing straightened out in a hurry or
I'd quit the case. I didn't have any hang-ups about having
to finish what I'd started when it wasn't my decision to start
in the first place.

I opened the door, did a dance around a guy with a big
leg cast had a bumper sticker saying, "I'd rather be skiing,"
and caught one of the world's slower elevators.

I went on down the hall, past all the medical corporations
specializing in Tax Dodge, and finally up to Cifelli's suite.

The door was pretty much as I remembered, except now
there were all these little light glue spots where the letters
formerly spelling out, "B. T. Sorrento, M.D." left an out-
line. That sort of gave me a clue. The waiting room was
empty—not even an antimacassar—and I could see inside
the "doctor's office," where a Spanish guy was scrubbing
pizza stains off the wall back of where Aunt Serafina's desk
used to be.

6

Mark Bradley

I'd spent the night catering to the whims (where's your *mind*?!) of my roomie and chief tormentor Brian Alexander, to compensate for the injuries—in this case mostly psychological—he'd sustained as a result of his association with me, me with Goodman, both with Penny. An old story.

However, inasmuch as those whims in the main took the form of various exotic take-out foods (and you thought . . .) and extracting promises of greater care and feeding—my god, the appetite on kids today!—I wasn't too distraught.

I was used to it and I understood it. What I couldn't understand, more to the point, was the twofold involvement of the Cifelli and Nash gangs with my biographical subject, Claudio Fortunata.

I did expect, however, that some of those questions would be resolved when I'd begun to spend time with the aforementioned child of fortune. To that end was I now en route to his home in Beverly Hills.

Taking what I'd laughingly thought of as the direct route, I had managed to enmesh myself in the worst of the morning traffic.

After a three-light wait at Kings Road and Santa Monica, and I don't know how many more through the crawl to Holloway, there was a momentary false hope for the few blocks past La Cienega till I reached Sunset, where it got really awful at the Tower Records turn. Then, finally finally finally through Sunset at le pace d'escargot till I reached the nine thousand buildings and beyond into Beverly Hills, where, for a few blocks anyway, there was an actually perceptible space between cars.

Proceeding past Sierra, Alta, Arden, I was between Hillcrest and Palm when I spotted the imposing figure of my co-worker, Rayford Goodman, plodding along on his two-mile mosey. This in required cardiovascular deference to his—I'd learned from Francine—heart attack of a few years back. At the rate he was shambling, I didn't get the feeling there was much value to it. I speak in smug superiority, having some hours earlier sweated my way through one hundred and four stories on the Stairmaster at my thrice-weekly Sports Connection workout.

I tapped the horn twice as I passed, but Goodman seemed too intent on counting the number of cracks in the pavement for it to register. Even at a glance, he looked dispirited and clearly suffering the aftereffects of yesterday's "message."

Despite this show of lethargy and depression, the thought occurred to me I *was* in something of a collaboration with the man. Plus he did have a responsibility of his own in regard to Fortunata. And Fortunata was to the best of my knowledge unguarded and potentially still vulnerable. Ergo: I ought to take Goodman with me.

You can neither park nor stop on Sunset Boulevard in Beverly Hills. So I circled the block, managing to time my reentry to the thoroughfare as Goodman had passed the old Arab grounds (whence erstwhile—pre-arson erst—had stood the scandalous, genital-enhanced statuary the since departed sheik had found decorous). I allowed him to lead me to the intersection of Rexford and Sunset, at which I again turned, honked, and pulled over.

"Hi, sailor," I said.

"Oh, Jesus."

"I was just on my way to Fortunata's. Thought you might like to join me—in a manner of speaking."

"I'm exercising," he said.

"No, you're not. You're taking a slow walk, kidding yourself. What you really ought to do is come with me to the gym."

"Sure, I can just see that. We'll get matching leg warmers."

"You're right, forget it. So, what do you say, you want to keep up this grueling pace, or you want a good excuse not to?"

That caught his attention.

"OK," he said, opening the door. "Business before health," and piled in. I pulled away, U-turned, and turned right again on Sunset.

"I was surprised to see you walking," I said.

"I'm supposed to."

"I mean, surprised you weren't covering Fortunata. You got somebody else helping with security?"

"No."

"Aren't you in charge of that?"

"I don't think so. At least that's my impression. Firstly, Chief Broward strongly hinted I quit. So we didn't have any more 'coincidences.' "

"What kind of coincidences?"

"Me being wherever bodies get found. It's getting to be like inviting Angela Lansbury for the weekend."

"You never listened to Broward before."

"True. I said that was firstly."

"And secondly?"

"There was Nash's message. The way I figure, the message was 'Drop the case or else.' For whatever reason I haven't the slightest idea."

"And you listen to him?"

"I don't go out of my way not to. I sure *heard* him," he said, fingering his bruises. "Mostly, I'm just adding it all up. We got one, we got two. But thirdly, for whatever reason Cifelli hired me to begin with, the job was protect Mr. Deeds—or Fortunata—at Le Petit. Which he's no longer at Le Petit. And since Mr. Cifelli's no longer doing business at his old stand, either, and hasn't contacted me again, I figure either he or Claudio's hired other security. Or the threat's over. Or whatever. It's just plain not my business anymore."

"So then just one question—why're you coming with me?"

"Because of my job."

"You just told me the job's over, there is no job."

"My detective job. My collaborator and co-writer job's still a go, far as I know."

"Right," I said, wondering if I had any Gaviscon in the glove compartment.

We passed the venerable Beverly Hills Hotel—now the humble abode of the sultan of Brunei, who so far despite apprehensions he would turn it into a private fiefdom, hadn't made nearly the waves of his predecessor, Ivan Boesky. It was there in the Polo Lounge I'd first encountered my Odd Couple co-star when we collaborated on his bio—oh, day of mixed blessings. I turned up Benedict Canyon Drive.

Traffic now flowed easily, since I was heading in the Valley direction. Being morning, the Valley was coming to Beverly Hills—to work. Nobody from Beverly Hills worked in the Valley.

I turned at Tower Road, where the only upward traffic at all was now gardener and poolman trucks. A few blocks later, in short order, we arrived at the gates to Casa Fortunata. These were of a size and bulk sufficient to withstand successive assaults by Saracens, Visigoths, and looky-looks. I pulled up to the window-height console, pressed the button, and presented my face for TV scrutiny.

Evidently passing muster, we were granted safe conduct in. The gigantic gates slowly opened with a somehow incongruous silence. Finding, surprisingly, no moat, we set out to negotiate the incredibly long, tree-lined driveway, which terminated in a large jousting area—or perhaps parking lot—at the steps to the mansion itself. We easily found space amid a profusion of Ferraris and Lamborghinis and such on *down* to Mercedes (for the help?). There we were greeted by two huge, playful Irish Wolfhounds, whose exuberance threatened to exhaust us before they were called off by a single piercing whistle. Reprieved, we proceeded up the marble stairs, where, waiting for us before a pair of massive Ghiberti-like doors—could they actually be?—was the whistler, who surprisingly turned out to be the staid personification of all butlerness. The man actually wore white gloves, in the ninety-degree heat. And looked perfectly comfortable.

Mostly bald, with just a fluff of white curly hair over each ear—not unlike a couple of lamb chop panties—he solemnly bade us enter—a privilege sternly denied the dogs.

As if we weren't already mightily aware this magnificent edifice belonged to one of Hollywood's true royals, in the entryway the impression was immediately reinforced by the display of Fortunata's three Oscars. Each was theatrically mounted on its own pedestal, with its own baby spot—your basic crown jewels.

Arthur Treacher informed us his lordship would receive us in the breakfast room. I'd always considered breakfast rooms one of the genuine measures of true wealth. People doing *OK* didn't have breakfast rooms. The rich had breakfast rooms, with everything in light butter yellows and crisp whites and soft greens—and on the sideboard silver salvers on trivets full of dozens of eggs and rashers of bacon and yards of sausages—most of which would get thrown away, or perhaps fed to the animals. Insensitive, wasteful, and extravagant—I love it.

"Hoo-hoo, breakfast room," chortled Goodman. "As if nobody else ever had a kitchenette."

Among other accoutrements, the "kitchenette" sported a fortune in antique china artifacts, a wondrous and wistful collection of gag porcelain teapots, plus a separate corner for some serious pre-Columbian entries which, surprisingly, didn't seem out of place. On the walls hung several name-brand French Impressionists—a veritable conjugation of Impressionists: Manet, Monet, Money—the whole framed in sparkling beveled glass French doors through which could be seen a sculpture garden, where apparently grew real sculpture. Fortunata, now sans bandages but with considerable swelling and discoloration, was in the garden with a sizable group of people, conducting a meeting of some sort.

Spotting us, he called a break, made some sort of note in his script, and crossed in. With him was a virtually lipless, cheek-boney, skinny person with a modified Mohawk, incongruously wearing a lot of California costly casual suedes and silks, and carrying a drink in either hand. Trailing both was a harried-looking young woman experiencing great difficulty keeping her hair out of her eyes, carrying scripts and notebooks and various clerical impedimenta. With an affable lopsided grin, caused by the post-procedural swelling, Fortunata welcomed us "to my humble home." Mi castle su castle would have been more like it. "So," he addressed Goodman, "Dick Penny tells me you've been added to the writing team. Rayford Goodman, was it?"

"Still is," said Goodman.

"Well, welcome aboard," said the director, extending his hand. But before Goodman could respond to the apparent overture, the obviously more experienced Mr. Cheekbones stuck one of the two drinks he carried into it instead.

Goodman affected to examine a cuticle.

"You with the picture?" he asked, the inspection complete.

"No, this is Billy Zee," said Claudio, as if we should know. Judging from previous experience, my guess was

Billy Zee would turn out to be the sort of flunky Resident Best Friend people like Claudio always seemed to have around.

"Hey, dudes," said Billy, with maybe the trace of an accent?

"Sorry, I'm a little behind the pace here," continued Claudio. "We're running a touch long on our production meeting. My new picture, *One Fell Swoop*?"

We nodded knowledgeably.

"We can wait," I said.

"Or maybe you wouldn't mind introducing us to some of your fellow Fell Swoopers," said Goodman, either being a detective or, heaven forfend, a better reporter than I.

"Sure, come on out."

He still hadn't introduced the woman trailing him. Given her singular lack of grace or beauty, one was willing to bet big bucks not only was she his secretary, but very good at it.

The group in the garden had remained more or less in place, though with diminished intensity, but now reperked on Fortunata's return.

"People," he said, in the manner of directors whose origins had been Broadway, "I'd like you to meet two folks you'll be seeing a lot of, my writers—" At which point a depressed-looking gentleman with bad skin sighed audibly. "Not on the picture," Fortunata responded reassuringly. "On my book. This is Mark Bradley, and this other gentleman is Rayford Goodman."

We howdied and jadooed—guess which.

Claudio continued, going around the table. "Terrence Coyne you know, my star," he nodded toward the fantastically handsome, dark-haired bit of heaven deigning to give me a glance through just about the thickest eyelashes this side of Bambi.

"Terry," I said, affecting the Hollywood first-person familiar. And receiving no noticeable acknowledgment in return. Well, who's available, anyhow?

"Freddie Forbes, our set designer." We exchanged nods, recognizing each other without any special interest even if we were available.

"Laszlo Nagy, my spiritual brother and actual cinematographer, without whom I should be absolutely nothing."

"Come off on it, some nothing, seven Oscars," said

Laszlo Hungarianly, with just a hint of jiggling facial fat reminiscent of the late S. Z. Sakal.

"Seven nominations," corrected Claudio. "Only won three," he qualified modestly. "But on my oath, could not make a picture without this man."

"Don't you to believe him," said Laszlo. "But with such generosity maybe comes now a good time to renegotiate my contract?"

"Or maybe I *could* make a picture without him," said Claudio.

They exchanged ritual chuckles—obviously part of an ongoing bit of badinage. Billy, on the other hand, laughed audibly—suggesting that was one of his functions.

"This gorgeous lady, of course," Fortunata continued, indicating the famous-featured beauty seated closest, "is my co-star." And here he made a kissing sound, somehow and surprisingly not unlike those heard on barrio street corners. "Maurissa Burroughs."

"Pleasure," said Maurissa, whether greeting us or indicating her preoccupation, I wasn't sure.

"Our dressers," whose names I had a feeling he'd forgotten.

Then, indicating a rather unshowbusinessy figure in a shiny silk navy blue suit, so short I was tempted to look under his chair to see if his feet touched the ground, "Our new executive producer, Barry Nash."

"Hi, yuh," said Nash. "Raymond."

"The function of the executive producer is to produce . . . the money to make the picture. That, in turn, makes him Producer di tutti Producer."

Nash's lips smiled at this daring reference to a mafia hierarchy. That is, his lips smiled. His eyes were not amused.

"Is this *the* Nash?" I whispered to Goodman.

"Uh-huh," he mumbled through his teeth. "Barry," he said aloud, nodding, acknowledging both that he knew him and was in receipt of the "message." No wonder he didn't correct the "Raymond."

"Mr. Nash," I said in case I was expected to say anything. The cold eyes flickered over me, seemingly with disinterest. Which I figured was all to the good.

"This gentleman," continued Claudio, unaware of the subplot unfolding, and indicating a man so ordinary-looking he defined average, "is Vernon Charles, our line producer."

Vernon mumbled something suitably unmemorable in greeting.

"The line producer actually produces," added Claudio. I got a picture of a man on an assembly line stamping out negatives one by one. "And finally," indicating a very tall, over six foot, severely tailored "lady"—"my agent, Claire Miller, of Creative Artists and Assassins."

"Ms. Miller," I said.

"So, shall we continue?" said Claudio, having completed casting.

"On page five," said Terry, "Rob says to the broad, 'You know who you're talking to?' I would never say that. I would say, 'to whom you're talking.' He went to college."

"Yeah, Ter," said the pale, depressed guy with the bad skin, "but it's colloquial. Even well-educated and highly articulate people employ colloquialisms."

"Who the hell's that?" said Terry.

"The writer," said Claudio. "You met Harvey?"

"Don't be giving me colloquialistics. I've written twelve pictures, I know what I'd say."

He hadn't, of course, written *any* pictures, but like most actors tended to believe the evidence of his ears. If he said it, he must have "written" it. Else whence?

"Claudio, you hired this guy?" asked Terry.

"We'll work it out, babe, not to worry. A who, a whom, I have to believe between artists of goodwill we'll make the choice that works best. I do think a 'whom' would be good there, right, Harv?"

"Shit," said Harv as Claudio made a notation in his script.

Then Maurissa felt compelled to match complaints with her co-star. "I like have some problems about my like dialogue, too."

"God," said Harv.

"I mean, like, when she says like, 'Please feel free with me,' does she like mean relax or fuck or like what?"

"All in good time," said Claudio, familiar with actors jockeying. He gracefully flicked a cigarette out of a pack lying on the table, and before it was halfway to his lips, Billy had a lighter out and a flame going. Claudio inhaled deeply, then, exuding charm and control, continued: "Let's not get sidetracked on details, people, we're way ahead of ourselves here."

"Are you saying my innermost feelings about my character is or are a mere detail?" said Terry. I was beginning to see he wasn't all that attractive.

"Never say that, Ter. Just it's too important for you and me not to do a one-on-one on it," with which he sipped his drink, perfectly relaxed.

"Or a three-way," mumbled the scribe, experienced in the Hollywood ways of writer-rape.

Fortunata let the moment play out, draining his drink. Billy swept up the empty glass the second it touched the table, laid his lighter on top of the pack of cigarettes in case Claudio should want another, and left to refill the drink.

"Let's stick to our agenda here," said Claudio, after a beat. "Sets was next, let's talk sets. Don't forget, we shot a lot of footage we'll have to match." Then turning to Goodman and me, he expanded: "We had a little shutdown for a bit, till our, er, executive producer produced some additional funding." During which hiatus, I guess, he had his face-lift. "OK, sets. And costumes!" he seemed to remember, addressing a note to himself in his script. "I don't know that this sort of technical stuff would really interest you," he said to us.

"Then, wait a minute, here on page twelve," Terry continued with that monomaniacally narrow focus typical of his calling, "the other guy says, 'Trouble is my middle name.' "

"Yes, Ter?" said Claudio.

"And I say, 'Mine's Victor.' "

"Yes, Ter?"

"Why would I be telling him my middle name?"

"It's a joke," said what's-his-name, the writer.

"I know it's a joke, I just want to know why I would be doing that."

"Why don't we wait till we're there," said Claudio.

"I could say, '*Big* Trouble's mine.' I like that, that's much better. 'Big Trouble's mine,' " he reiterated, marking the change in his script.

"When we get to it," said Claudio. The writer took out an asthma reliever, pumped it into his throat, his eyes rolling back in his head. "Right now, we're going to talk about sets."

Miffed, Terry took one of Claudio's cigarettes, lit it, and slipped the lighter into his pocket.

"You don't like want to talk about like interpretations?" said Maurissa.

"Sets!" snapped Claudio, sensing a need to exert greater control. Then softer, "Sets." He also renewed his invitation for us to excuse ourselves. But before we could, an extremely attractive young woman, brunette, about five eight or nine, with an outstanding figure, made an entrance from the pool house.

"Before we get into sets," said Nash, apparently rising, though he seemed to remain at the same approximate height as sitting, "I'd like to introduce my associate executive producer. Mr. Goodman, Mr. Bradley, say hello to Miss Heather Hansen."

"How do you do," I said.

"Miss Hansen," said Goodman. "I believe we've met."

"I don't think so," she said.

"I'm pretty sure."

"Absolutely not."

"Well, then, did anyone ever tell you you're the spitting image of a nurse named Alicia Blake?"

7

Rayford Goodman

Oh, boy. Oh, wow. Oi vey.

It didn't seem to register on Bradley. He said hello, how ja do, nice to meet you. And headed off toward the pool.

What the hell was I going to do about this one?

"Things're getting a lot more complicated than I expected," I said, catching up.

"How's that?"

"Well, I'm not here as a P.I., I'm here as a writer, right?"

"Right," he said, I thought a little hesitantly.

"So what'm I supposed to do I just said hello to the one killed Hamilton Cohen?"

"Heather Hansen?"

"That was Alicia Blake."

"Blake like in Miss Blake the nurse at the Ermitage?"

"That Miss Blake."

"Can't be."

"Bradley, I'm a detective. I've got years and years' experience. Hansen is not an ordinary-looking woman I saw for a minute, across a crowded room, at night, after ten drinks. Hansen is Blake. And Blake is who shot Cohen."

He could see I had my sincere look on.

"I believe you," he said. "I don't want to, but I believe you. So?"

"So the question is, what do I do about it?"

"Well, my advice would be to act like you believe you made a mistake."

"And if that's not good advice?"

"Then you get killed."

"Catch on?"

At which point Hampton (neither East, South, or Lionel, but it turned out the butler's name) came out and asked was there any service he might render us. Since he was about a hundred and eight, and looked like he'd been fixed,

I didn't think it was a pass either one of us had to deal with. I allowed as how a Bloody Mary might not be a bad idea.

Bradley said he'd have a Virgin Mary.

I told him to give me Bradley's vodka, too.

He left at that pace made you wonder how they ever put the British empire—or got through the day. I watched as he Tim Conwayed out and looked past him to sneak another peek at Hansen/Blake.

"So look," I said to Bradley, "you've had some experience at this by now, does it make any sense to you?"

"You mean Nash wanting Fortunata killed? Assuming Cohen was a mistake?"

"Right. Angelo I can figure. Some sort of bad blood between Cifelli and Nash, so it's a gang killing. That's the way they get each other's attention. But with Nash having money in Claudio's picture, why would he want Claudio killed? Assuming again that's who Hansen was after at the Ermitage when she offed Hamilton Cohen." At which point I could see the object of our conversation whisper something in Nash's ear, then quietly leave.

"Doesn't make sense," agreed Bradley, also watching her go. "Claudio's an essential component of the picture. Why damage an asset to his investment? For that matter, what's he got against you? Talking about the 'message.' "

"You know, maybe I can understand that. Suppose, for the sake of argument, Cifelli's the original investor in the picture. Maybe it's like the Cotton Club thing with rival guys wanting a piece of the action. Maybe Cifelli's laundering some mob money. Here comes Nash, muscling in—and we know he must have done something, since he's openly got a position."

"The position of new executive producer," said Bradley. "Right, Claudio said *new* executive producer."

"You heard that, good. So, say Nash wants Cifelli out. To make the point, Nash hits Angelo. For another, his goons warn me off."

"Yeah," said Bradley, a little tentatively.

"Cifelli reads the signs," I went on, "thinks it over, and throws in his hand."

"How do you know that?"

"I don't know that, I'm figuring. One thing, Cifelli closed up shop at the Bedford address. Another, I haven't heard from him again. So my guess is he decided this one just wasn't worth going to the mattresses over."

"Except then why did Nash want Claudio killed—hitting Cohen by mistake?"

"Except that," I allowed, which stopped the conversation very nicely.

The midday sun was coming on fairly strong, so after a bit we took ourselves over to a poolside table had one of those big umbrellas over it, the kind say Cinzano on them. I couldn't help wondering why anybody this rich had to swipe an umbrella.

The pool was a little lower than the sculpture garden, so we had to look up—and past some statuary looked like petrified dinosaur do-do—to see the group sitting around the table. Occasionally bits and pieces of conversation would drift our way.

I could see Terry's hand under the table groping toward Maurissa's home base. Terrific actors, neither changed expression.

"Well," said Bradley, eyeing the same thing, "I guess I can cross Terry off the if list."

Along about then, old Hampton grass-skated over with the Bloodies, Mary and Virg. I should have asked for a couple; there was a reasonable chance he wouldn't be able to make it back again. I took a gulp.

Terry, meanwhile, with his free hand, started pounding the script. ". . . fucking piece of shit," wafted over clearly, the left hand still busy on its own.

". . . -othing carved in stone," said Claudio.

"Just once," said Harvey, the writer, ". . . stand up for . . . theater . . . tistic integrity . . ."

"What's he saying, autistic integrity?" I asked Bradley.

"I don't think so," he said as we watched Harvey angrily toss his script in the air.

Still, the right hand not caring what the left was doing to Maurissa, Terry continued, ". . . Robert Towne, hundred writers." At which point the wind shifted both for Harvey and for us, who could now hear clearly.

"Not going to put up with it, the script stands," said Harv.

"Now, I wouldn't take such an arbitrary stand," said Fortunata. "I think there's a lot of merit in what Terry says."

"You think this little asshole shit knows what he's talking about?" screamed Harvey. "I've written five pictures."

"Among them *Teenage Swamp Tramps*, *Perverts from Pluto*, and *Lust Junkies*," said Fortunata.

"I shared credit on that. You're forgetting *Song of Sonora*, which I wrote for you."

"Well, Harv, you sort of wrote it. Basically, I improvised; wouldn't you say?"

"No, I would not say."

"Then I guess you don't care much for the truth," Fortunata went on. "Which is somewhere between you have this small talent and I took you on for old times' sake."

"Well, you can twirl on this, for old times' sake," said Harvey, giving him the finger. Which even I knew didn't prove his point about being much of a writer.

"You got the wrong finger, Harvey—it's this," said Fortunata, showing him the thumb. "You're out."

Harvey, not even knowing a curtain line when he heard one, jumped up, knocking over his chair. "Improfuckingvise? You don't even direct!" he said, which I didn't understand at all, and stomped out. In a huge rage he halfway stumbled across the garden, tripped on the step to the breakfast nook, lost his balance completely, and partly lurched, partly lunged through the French doors and into the cabinet of antique china, which he knocked over with a monster crash.

"And that," said Claudio, holding back his temper on our behalf, "is what is known as 'creative differences.'"

But it was clear all this had taken the heart out of the meeting. When Fortunata made no effort to reconvene, Vernon Charles—the one really produced—said, "I guess that'll do it for today. We'll reschedule and let you all know." Then he took off his plain round glasses, pinched his nose, and sighed. "Barbara," he went on, "note to business affairs: find a way to terminate Pitkin's contract, no pay or play, get around it."

Everybody got up and started drifting off. Among the last were Terry and Maurissa, it taking them awhile to sort out all their parts.

"The ego on those people," said Terry as they drifted off.

The set designer, Freddie Forbes, who for some reason seemed to wear the tightest, highest collars, rolled up some sketches, put them in a long alligator-skin tube, and he took off.

Laszlo Nagy had a final word with Vernon, which involved a little jowl jiggling. "I'll check with Silverman," said Vernon, "if Claudio wants to sue for the art. Though I can probably fix the vitrine myself. But in any event, it can't be charged to the picture." This last with a flick of the eyes in Nash's direction.

"As they say, not on my table," said Nagy.

"First day back and already over budget," concluded Vernon in his dull monotone, more or less to himself.

Nash had something or other to say to Fortunata—which involved a lot of looking up. The tall agent, Claire Miller, after a word with someone I couldn't see, looking down, was next to go. Then the set dressers together, like bookends, or sconces, or whatever. And finally the whole gang heading off, either around the side of the house, or through the breakfast room—stepping over broken china. By which time Fortunata turned his attention to us, coming over with the woman juggling papers and files while constantly brushing her hair back. Billy Zee lagged behind, looking around the table, under it, moving chairs—I guess looking for something.

"Sorry to've kept you fellows waiting," Fortunata said. "A little artistic temperament."

He sat down, putting his script on the table, and turning to the woman with the hair problem, said, "Would you ask Hampton to bring me a juice? You folks?"

Us folks ordered another round of our same.

"So," said Fortunata, settling back.

"I don't believe we've been introduced," said Bradley once the lady got off the phone.

"Oh, sorry," said Fortunata. "Forgive me. This is my production assistant, girl Friday, Saturday, and Sunday, good right hand, in-dis-*pen*-sable aide de camp—"

"All right, already!"

"Barbara Aronson—to whom I most sincerely apologize, and who will also be my witness in case you write lies about me."

We said heh-heh and hi-yuh, Barbara, and she sat down with us at the table. During which she dropped, then recovered, the scripts, notebooks, and a purse big enough to hold half her worldly possessions. And all the while constantly pushing the hair out of her eyes, driving me crazy. I still hate Anouk Aimee.

"Now, to the book," said Fortunata. "How do we do this?"

"Generally I ask a bunch of questions," Bradley said. "We talk, get to know each other. I get a sense of my subject. You get a feeling about me. And then we more or less formulate a modus operandi that's comfortable for both of us."

Which he seemed comfortable with—since it included no method and every method—then turned to me. "And you?"

"Generally I do likewise on the M.O.," I said.

"Why do I get the feeling you're—Ah, now I remember," he said, snapping his fingers. "*Rayford Goodman: Fixer to the Stars!*—you're *that* Ray Goodman—who wrote that book."

"That's me."

"Us," corrected Bradley. Writers, writers . . .

"So," continued Claudio. "Are you working a case now?"

"Well, I was. You."

"Me? I'm no case."

"Not exactly a case—I was looking out for you."

"You were? How come? I never hired you."

I shrugged mysteriously.

"The studio?"

I smiled mysteriously.

"Yeah, the studio," he said.

"Could we?" said Bradley. "Our business now—together, god help us—is to collaborate on *your* book."

"And see I don't get killed?"

"At least till after we write it," Bradley added, keeping his priorities in order.

"Well, not really," I said, to set the record straight. "I'm off that other assignment. But just out of curiosity, any idea who might've wanted to pop you?"

"No one I can think of. Maybe a couple of Oscar runners-up, heh-heh. I just figured they really were after old Hamilton Cohen, poor guy."

I didn't think that for one minute.

"Maybe so," I said. "What do you think, Miss Aronson?" I asked the frowning girl Friday, Saturday, and so forth.

"I can't imagine anybody wanting to hurt Mr. Fortunata," she said, pushing her hair back.

"Beautiful reading," said Claudio. "Isn't that great?

Right down the middle, no idea what she really thinks. Your talents are wasted."

"What do you really think?" asked Bradley, sucked in.

"I think Mr. Fortunata was very . . . fortunate to have been off taking a *walk* at the critical moment."

"Speaking of taking a walk," said Fortunata, still smiling but I'd say with an edge, "why don't you go see what's keeping Hampton with our drinks?"

A person who knew when she was being dismissed, Barb split. Billy Zee, evidently giving up his search for whatever, joined us.

"Wasn't it a good thing you were taking a walk?" I repeated to Fortunata.

"What I was taking, as I mentioned at the time, was a little sexual exercise. Which, by the way in case you're interested, isn't easy bandaged from ear to ear."

"But if anybody could manage it, iss my man here," said Billy, I decided with a Teutonic touch.

"And as you said at the time, you're too much of a gentleman to tell us who the lucky lady was?" asked Bradley.

"I know it's a dated quality. But I've always believed a gentleman didn't tell."

"How about a gentleman who's gotten a huge advance on a book contract?" said Bradley.

"Well, can't we sort of . . . generalize?"

"Like?"

"How about *I* tell you?" said Billy. "OK, babe?"

Fortunata shrugged phony modestly.

"Well, to make a point about this dude's making the most with a handicap, like the head wrap, there wuss the time we were in Sidona making *Pony Rider* . . ."

I decided he definitely was German. Forget the fake hip attitude and the hairdo. What he most reminded me of was the S.S. man who asks the hard questions in old Nazi movies.

"Anyway," he was saying, "old Claude got thrown from his horse and broke a leg. You should have seen, he had this absolutely humongous cast on it—"

"I'd really rather hear it from the horse's mouth," interrupted Bradley.

Billy bowed, turned his palms up, and offered the stage back to Fortunata, who didn't seem all that shy about continuing.

"Well, there I had this cast on my leg, and I suddenly

realized I was about to lose the services of one of our actresses—"

"Totti Anderson?" said Bradley.

"Ah, see, we're going to have trouble. Without confirming or denying the lady in question—or the questionable lady—the point is, somehow I'd been slack about fully examining her character."

"Are we talking boffing here?" I asked.

"Uh, Ray, just let Claudio tell it in his own words," said Bradley. I thought I was supposed to help.

"At any rate," Fortunata went on, "this was your basic last-chance situation, so leg cast and all it was sort of now or never. Well, I had no idea she'd turn out to be so acrobatic—a virtual fucking Wallenda. She carried on so energetically, first thing you know I got tossed out of the bed, bounced on the floor, cracked the cast, threw out my back, and more's the pity, simultaneously prematurely ejaculated."

Billy laughed till he cried.

"Speaking of stories, especially these kinds," continued Bradley after a moment, checking some notes—I guess he was a little better prepared than I was, being I had no notes—"there's an underground rumor a person can tell by screening your pictures just when you took each of your leading ladies to bed."

"Well, of course that's a flattering exaggeration. But I will admit that kind of attention does bring out the best in them," said Fortunata. "And I know it brings out the best in me."

"Or the beast," said Billy, who was beginning to annoy me a lot.

"So, are we going to be able to tell from the dailies when you and Maurissa start the inevitable . . . ?" continued Bradley. Boy, he really got personal!

"I think the boat's already docked on that one," said Billy.

"Billy, will you . . . ?" said Fortunata, I got the feeling not really all that upset.

"Sorry."

Sticking to business, Bradley continued, "I somehow got the impression she and Terry—?"

"Well, yes, now . . ." said Fortunata.

"This isn't their first picture," added Billy with a nasty

laugh. Definitely S.S. "But you notice he thought enough about her work to cast her again."

I don't know. Struck me a little embarrassing, even for guy talk.

It was right about then Barbara returned with the drinks.

"Um, take five, chaps," said Fortunata. Which meant he didn't want to discuss girls in front of old Barb. Reasonable enough for a gentleman in general, but my instinct suggested wasn't just because he was too refined.

She put down the drinks. We thanked her.

We took a long sip. Bradley checked his notes.

"We were talking about leading ladies," he said. "Might as well stick with that for now," he continued, missing the signs.

"Tell you, Barb," said Fortunata. "I don't need you here for a bit, why don't you go catch up on the mail?"

Barbara nodded. She didn't miss the signs. Me, neither. Barbara and the boss. Maybe no more, but at least some time in the past. You wouldn't thought it likely, considering her plainness. But it was probably the old mountain thing. Came a day she was just—there. She left, heading off toward the far side of the house.

"Well, while we're on the subject," continued Fortunata, "I remember one time we had these twins on a picture, *Double Dilemma* . . . no, no, we can't use that, really. Forget I said anything."

"We're going to have to make some ground rules," said Bradley. "The idea of a tell-all book isn't to tease-all. But, for now OK, off the record."

So we got to listen to another half hour of how movies and actresses got made, which I, for one, didn't exactly consider big news being an old show business shamus. But Bradley seemed interested enough to take about a zillion notes.

When Fortunata finally stopped to take a breath, Billy quit leering long enough to ask if there was anything he needed from him. Fortunata said not at the moment, so Billy said he was going to run a few errands and left, heading around the same side Barbara had. Fortunata took a deep breath and was about to go on regaling us with more twat tales when Arthur Treacher Hampton shuffled back in ("walk this way") and ahemed Fortunata was wanted on the phone.

He reached for the one on the table.

"The private line," said the butler.

"Tell whoever—"

"It's . . . them," interrupted Treacher Jeeves Hampton.

"I'll take it in the study," said Fortunata, a line I'd sure heard in a picture or two.

"Be right back."

But instead it was the butler who came back after about ten minutes and the rest of my drink to tell us the master had been unavoidably detained and would be unable to continue the interview and would we be kind enough to re-*shed*ule tomorrow?

We would be kind enough.

"I think that's our cue to split," I said, rising.

"I'll show you gentlemen out," said Hampton.

I've always suspected when people got shown out it was because someone wanted to watch you didn't swipe the family silver. Which they figured you might if you were allowed to find your own way out.

The huge, funny-looking metal doors with all the pictures bas-reliefed had just shut quietly behind us and we were halfway in the car when the shots rang out. Four of them. Not really ringing, of course, more like popping.

I dashed back to the door and started pounding on it. Which the Irish wolfhounds took for play, jumping all over me. I was busy fighting them off, and had just about given up on the front door and decided to circle around back when with a quiet whoosh the door finally reopened and there was Hampton.

He took a short breath, whistled the dogs quiet, and announced evenly, "Mr. Fortunata appears to have been shot." With about the same emotion as dinner being served.

Bradley was right behind me as I kept stepping on the old butler's heels, trying to get him to move faster.

"Come on, man," I said impatiently, nudging and pushing. "Seconds count."

But he just couldn't go any faster, and as it turned out it didn't matter all that much. When we got to the study we could see right away neither seconds nor minutes, hours nor days, were ever going to count a whole lot again for Claudio Fortunata.

8

Mark Bradley

I don't *care* for this. This is not my bag. Not even my purse.
I am a writer, not a finder of deceased bodies. Well, co-
finder. Once you start collaborating with the likes of Goodman, it's apparently only a matter of time before you're
also keeping company with whole corps of corpses. But evidently I wasn't the only one who found this offensive, as the
erstwhile unflappable Hampton editorialized, "Oh, shit."

"Oh, shit"? "Deuced defecation," I might expect. Even
maybe a "merde" . . . And here I'm being flippant, when
what I really want to do is throw up. God, it's hard. How
do people stand this? People work around this kind of
thing—Jesus, I'll have nightmares forever. Don't, don't—
don't throw up. It won't make you feel better.

"OK, podner?" said Goodman.

"Shum." I nodded; even tried a little smile. The perspiration I couldn't do anything about.

"I have the rather appalling feeling," continued Hampton
in his understated way, "the curtain is about to ring down,
the play's no longer the thing, and the part's kaput."

I'm sure we all entertained various degrees of shock (me,
most) viewing the multiply shot, incredibly messy remains of
the hitherto always immaculate—and "well-liked"—Claudio
Fortunata, of whom my researcher Francine had absolutely
declared: "Loved by man, woman, child—and the occasional amorous animal." Apparently there was a sharp exception to the rule. Four bullets to the head tending to rule
out suicide.

The act and its aftermath had done rather fierce damage
to the surroundings, too, which were sort of Spanishy-
English. It was a study in the very traditional sense of
leather and books, though no hunt prints or English gentlemen on horse. The books for the most part looked actually
read, however. Though Claudio hadn't resisted the Holly-

wood imperative for everyone connected with a motion picture to have the script bound in the finest of Moroccan leathers and mounted in the most expensive way. A really silly affectation, since I sincerely doubted anyone ever read a movie after it'd been made. At any rate, there were literally dozens of these, attesting to a long and successful career, notwithstanding its termination *One Fell Swoop* short. Somebody cancel the bookbinder!

"So," said Goodman, addressing himself to Hampton's remarks, "you've been *acting* the part of butler?"

"No part too small, no actor too big. And the stinker did keep promising next picture, always the next picture—a real role. Meanwhile, I exercised my craft, in a manner of speaking, and managed to keep my medical vested."

"What I'm hearing, you weren't exactly on real good terms with Fortunata," said Goodman.

"I see where you're going, but believe me, there is no profit in that area of speculation. If I were to kill for every part I hadn't got in the last dozen years, the film industry would have ground to a halt. Though I did come close when they incredibly overlooked me as the new spokesman for the Smith-Barney commercials."

I could see it.

"On the other hand, you don't look exactly overwhelmed with grief," I suggested.

"Mr. Fortunata was a fine director, with many an idea on how to enhance one's performance. Alas, that is not an attribute one finds attractive when manual labor is involved."

With which he uprighted a chair.

"I wouldn't touch anything," said Goodman.

"Reflex. Of course you're right."

"Who else is in the house?" I asked.

"Barbara, a brace of gardeners, I should imagine, cook, perhaps the housekeeper, and whoever didn't leave from the meeting."

"All the cars're gone from out front," said Goodman. "Except a Karman Ghia—"

"Barbara's," said Hampton.

"Where're the cook's and the gardener's and the maid's? Yours, for that matter?"

"Staff's motorcars are parked around back." He indicated an area through the window in which I could see a gardener's truck, poolman's, a Honda sort of compact, and a very ancient hunter green Jaguar sedan.

"So in theory, then, everyone from the meeting's gone?"

"So it would appear," said Hampton. "Shouldn't we be giving the police a jingle?"

"Yeah," said Goodman dismissively. "How about security—what about the gate? I see high walls."

"True, but with all the traffic to and fro-ing," said Hampton, "security's questionable. A car departs, another could easily enter—the gate requiring something like twenty seconds to complete its cycle. I say, would anyone mind terribly if I sat down?"

And he suddenly looked like a very old actor, indeed.

"Fine," said Goodman, "but let's don't here. Crime scene?"

To say nothing of minimal sensibilities.

So we left and went next door to another office, similar to but much smaller. Perhaps Barbara's? She wasn't there.

"I wonder," said Goodman as we headed for chairs, "could we have a drink?"

"Considering the dubious state of my employment following this third act denouement," said Hampton, "in the American vernacular—help yourself." And he indicated a small bar tray atop a low file cabinet.

Goodman wasn't apparently offended by this withdrawal of service, as he crossed over and fixed himself an extravagant quadruple shot of vodka.

Hampton seemed suddenly quite deflated, his chin almost sunk on his chest, as if all the starch had gone out of his character with the curtain's unexpected fall. I joined Goodman at the bar.

"The police?" I said.

"A minute. Listen, we got two ways to go on this, and I like number two."

"Which is?"

"It's none of our business. We report it, walk away from it, and tell Penny the book's dead."

"You don't understand the publishing business. With Fortuna murdered, the book'll be hotter than ever. No way Penny would drop it. So forget the second way, what's the first?"

"We try like hell to cover our asses."

"And how do we do that?"

"You're not going to like it."

"I'm sure."

"You give me the keys to your car; I get out of here."

"And leave me to face Broward?"

He took a dramatic pause, or maybe just another large gulp, and set his drink down on top of Claudio's script on the desk.

"Look," he continued, "the truth is, we're both in the clear. We were outside when the shots were fired, and Eric Blore here can testify to that."

"So why can't you stay?"

"Because Broward will still haul me in, just on general lack of principles, and I've got better things to do with my life than pay lawyers and waste my days getting phony charges dropped."

I had to admit there was a certain logic to that.

"OK, deal," I said, handing him my keys.

"But meanwhile, you could still look around," he continued. "You might interview Barbara—and where is she, by the way? And the cook and the bottle washer and whoever."

"I'm no detective."

"Right," he agreed so quickly I found myself strangely annoyed. "But you do have some fairly good instincts every once in a while. And it's possible we may not be as home free as I think. Anyway, what could hurt?"

This would prove a prophetic question, but at the time it seemed all totally reasonable.

"OK, go for it," I found myself saying. "I'll give you a head start, then call the cops."

"We'll compare notes later," said Goodman. Then he added for Hampton's benefit, "I'll just let myself out." And left.

I took a breath, went to the window to see if maybe Barbara was out there. Nothing doing. No one anywhere in sight.

"I wonder," I heard the tired voice of Hampton, "would you be good enough to fix *me* a small libation?"

"Of course," I said. "What would you like?"

"In the cabinet beneath the tray, I believe you'll find a cache of really impressive Napoleon brandy. That would do nicely."

He made as good a guest as he had a butler.

* * *

The kitchen was of a size and with equipment suitable to servicing a small restaurant—not all that unusual among the more active party givers in tinselville. In addition to Wolf ranges, walk-in freezers, and a Thermador combination traditional convection and microwave oven in a smoky glass sleek design that looked as if it could fly, there appeared to be every electrical kitchen appliance I'd ever heard of, and several I hadn't. The kitchen had everything—except help.

A walk through the downstairs section of the house had produced no live bodies, either. I was back at the broken china breakfast room and about to double back when I saw there was a small outbuilding to the far side of the pool house. Turned out it was a little guest house and/or auxiliary office.

I found Barbara there.

She hadn't heard a thing.

I gave her the news.

She certainly reacted appropriately. I had to wait a good ten minutes till she stopped crying and hiccoughing.

It convinced me—more or less (remembering Claudio had said she was a consummate actress—hiccoughing would be a nice touch).

"I've called the police," I told her. "But I wondered if maybe before they come, you could answer a few questions for me."

"Why should I do that?"

"Why not?" And why suddenly hostile?

"You're still going to do the book?"

"I'm pretty sure. Though naturally, we could talk later if you really prefer. I just thought, I know it's an emotional time, but you might, you know, have some insight who might have done this."

"I'm not even *used* to this. Let me think . . . I don't know, how would I know?" And she succumbed to another paroxysm of sobbing. "It's such an awful shock."

I gave her another moment to compose herself. "I'm trying to put some things together in my mind, while it's still fresh. For example, right after, there didn't seem to be anyone in the house—or even leaving—that we could see."

"Well," she said, simmering down to a sniffle or two, "it's a very large house, an enormous house."

"True."

"A lot different than when Claudio bought it from Vernon."

"Vernon owned this house?" It seemed so sumptuous.

"Well, sort of. What he owned, I'm talking back in the fifties, was a lot different. The same land basically, but there are really only a few walls left of the original, which was sort of a fixer-upper."

"It's hard to imagine any Beverly Hills house, let alone a mansion, ever being a fixer-upper."

"You'd be surprised. A lot of them were very modest to begin with. And while he doesn't look like he'd be all that handy, they tell me he was quite a do-it-yourselfer, which was sort of in at the time."

I wondered were we talking motive here.

"I guess Vernon must feel awful having sold way back before the real estate market took off. It must have been less than a tenth."

"A twentieth," she corrected. "And I guess he was sorry; anybody was sorry who sold back then."

"Hm."

"On the other hand, he took that money and bought himself a ranch in the valley, and that appreciated at least as much."

I felt wind leaving the old sails. Another shot: "Would you have any idea who might benefit from Claudio's death?"

"Yes, of course. I've read his will, for one thing."

"And?"

"Well, lots of people benefit—me, for example; the servants—me a lot more than the servants, of course—his ex-wives. Billy. Even Claire."

"You had an affair."

"I don't think this is a good time for this," she said.

"We don't have to go into that right now."

"No, forget it," she said, clearly ending the interview. That was all I was going to get. And not much. I couldn't help feeling I'd blown something here.

"OK, right," I said lamely, adding a hopeful "We'll get together another time. When you're feeling better. Doesn't have to be all that personal if you don't want." But she'd already started out of the room. I was about to ask if she knew where the servants were, but that got itself answered in a hurry as a station wagon pulled up around back and out came what I learned were the cook and the housekeeper. They'd been shopping for groceries. The maid was off.

There were some peripheral people. A poolman—Korean. Didn't see, didn't hear, didn't speak the language. Two gardeners—Mexican. Didn't see, didn't hear, didn't speak the language. I considered all of them too remote to be likely suspects. It was, of course, entirely likely someone did see or hear something, but it was beyond my capability to find out. Leave it to the police—who seemed to be taking their time.

Then it occurred to me, there was one question I'd like answered before they came, and Hampton was the one who'd know. Who had phoned with a message that was either so urgent or so unnerving that Claudio had to cancel the rest of the interview?

I hurried back into the main house, and to the small outer office next to the study. Hampton wasn't there. Hampton wasn't anywhere. Frustrating. And strange.

I was starting to wonder why I had to stay and confront the police virtually alone, and leaning toward just plain getting the hell out of there, when I figured first a little look around couldn't hurt. More famous last words.

I stuck my head back inside the study. Fortunata lay as before. No big surprise. I doubted a whole lot of bodies got snatched the way they did in movies without leaving a trace and the place totally cleaned up, making you look like a mental case when you claimed, "Officer, I'm telling you there was a dead man here just a moment ago." I guess I'd hoped it was all some sort of hallucination. It wasn't. I wanted to go take a look through his desk drawers, but the body was right there, and I was neither that adventurous nor yet that staunch of stomach. In addition, I managed to convince myself I was also inhibited by my great respect for the laws against evidence tampering. Everything seemed the same, anyway.

I stuck my head back into the smaller office. Everything the same there, too. Or was it? Something. What now, what the hell was different?

I snapped my fingers. (No one's chic all the time.) The script! Claudio's script had been on the desk out here. I remembered it clearly. Goodman had put his drink down on top of it.

But before I could figure out what this absence signified, there was the sound of approaching sirens and I knew I'd exhausted my options after all. I wasn't going to be dodging the police.

Another way I knew was I got coshed on the back of the head and everything went—sorry—black.

9

Rayford Goodman

They were keeping Bradley at St. John's a day or two for observation. When I talked to him over the phone, he said he was trying to get put in the Elizabeth Taylor suite. Which, he said he had on the highest authority (the *Enquirer*?), consisted of two bedrooms, a living room, a kitchen, and an anteroom for security forces. But so far Blue Cross wasn't going for it. The only celebrity fringe he had latched on to was a uniform outside his door, courtesy Santa Monica P.D., accommodating Chief Broward of Bev Hills P.D. He didn't sound too badly hurt.

"More sort of a mood-altering incident," he'd said.

Actually, he seemed in pretty good spirits. Or on pretty good dope, Francie had suggested. Whatever, it was a comfort, because I was feeling more than a little guilty leaving him there alone, it turns out with the likely perp still on the premises. I appreciated him having a good attitude. Though he did also say, "I hope whoever did this gets cluster headaches every day of his life, a thousand boils, patchy baldness, psoriasis, herpes, hemorrhoids—and bad luck." Which I guess showed a little resentment.

I'd been trying to decide whether not sending flowers was because *I* wouldn't've wanted any or just frugal. Maybe a tasteful plant if he stayed on. Else it would be just something to have to carry.

Then he'd filled me in what he'd been up to. He told me about his meeting with Barbara, what she said and what he felt she didn't, which could or could not mean something. He apologized for letting her clam up. But the truth was even without being Fortunata's ex-girlfriend, having your boss murdered was a smidge unnerving. And he told me about the missing script, which I guess must have had something incriminating about it.

He also told me about interviewing—or trying to—the

Mexican gardeners and the Korean poolman. And figuring it not too likely any of them was involved, which I agreed. Also even they saw something, being probably half illegal, they'd tend to keep a low profile not to bring attention on themselves. Not much chance getting something in that area.

Again, the housekeeper and the cook seemed to alibi each other being out during the time of the murder. But since they both evidently got something in Claudio's will, I'd have to check them out. Along about then Bradley said a very Nordic male nurse had come into the room to conduct some procedures on him which I certainly didn't want to hear about, so I'd hung up and promised to check back and if they kept him another day pop over for a visit.

Just to cover the bases with the housekeeper and cook, I later dropped by Jurgensen's—grocer to the stars (flip of the coin whether Jurgensen's or Gelsen's)—and lucked out. They'd been there, even signed chits for the purchases. Unbelievable prices.

That left as potentials Barbara, the missing Hampton—and why?—who I'd take a shot at finding through the Screen Actors Guild later today; Billy Zee, everyone at the meeting—especially Heather Hansen—and whoever else happened to be in the western hemisphere yesterday.

I was bringing Francine up to date during the early morning hours after I'd brought her up to date in other things during the late night hours. We were cozily waking up in the bedroom of my sumptuous estate high atop one of the bird streets at the westernmost end of the Hollywood Hills. Actually, it was the same not so sumptuous estate I'd had ever since I started doing okay back in the good old days when studios still made movies instead of Japanese takeover targets. But with the sudden—since the book—influx of bucks, I'd fixed things up. Like, actual clear water came out the faucets now.

The main attraction about the place, though, it was higher than the Empire State Building—which I don't care what they build, as far as I'm concerned will always be the Tallest Building in the World.

Helicopters flew under it—and there was a view took your breath away. Or maybe that was the smog. But mainly I loved it because it was just about the only thing I'd salvaged when my ax-wife departed for younger pastures and took everything else, including the family jewels.

For longer than I like to remember, I thought my batting slump in the sexual department—as a shrink I was crazy enough to go to once said—was due to my lowered self-esteem. Something was lowered. But it turned out there were other factors, too. Business being bad, health being bad, and your old lady taking off all did tend to take away your basic joy of life. But besides that, after the heart attack my probably sexless himself dopey doctor hadn't bothered to inform me taking beta-blockers and diuretics for the blood-pressure thing could result in your not being able to play in the major leagues anymore.

But things change (besides, for sure, medication). At the moment, there was my delightful dalliance with Francine, a cure in itself. Then, I was looking at a bunch of money, which wasn't something happened in an awful long time, either. And starting to get actual jobs again. More of that and it'd be hard to stay cranky. So, where the place'd been rundown and racked with ruin, now it was up to date and peachy keen. Where it'd been sloppy, now it was neat. And most important of all, where the master bed'd been empty, now it was full—of fancy Francie.

Which reminded me.

I reached over, burrowing into her neck. That always got her.

"No," she said.

Always got her *before*.

No? What'd she mean, no?

"No, like in the biblical sense."

No?

"No, like no carnal knowledge."

No!? Like, no fooling?

"Rayford, I said no!"

Ah-hah. Then I knew it was really no. When someone calls me Rayford we're talking trouble. Ray is a pal. Ray is someone you have fun with. A Rayford is someone about to get bawled out. ("Rayford, you get in the house this instant!") OK, so why's she saying no after a herniated disc's worth of yes?

"Because if we do do that voodoo that you do so well, we both know you won't do your walk," she said.

We talking cute, or what?

"And the doctor says you have to keep up your exercise," she continued.

"Keep up what?" I said. I really believe exercise is exercise, and a push-up's a push-up.

We were spared a whole lot of pleasure by a pounding on the door clearly wasn't going to go away by itself.

I got out of bed, slipped on the kimono Luana'd swiped from a hotel in Kuala Lumpur while on a celebrity tennis freebee and given me instead of a gift, and went to the door.

It was a couple Mr. Cifelli's associates. One original— Vincent; one Angelo's replacement—whoever.

"Didn't you guys ever hear of the phone? Didn't you ever hear of office hours?"

"Didn't you ever hear shut your face?" said the sub, I thought with something less than good humor.

"Mr. C. requests the pleasure of your company," said Vinnie, already into the new literate hoodlum rap. Definite executive material.

"I'll dress."

"No need," he said, pushing the door open wider and allowing me a glimpse at the familiar Mercedes limo. With Armand (The Dancer) Cifelli waiting inside.

On my way out the thought occurred to me if other mobsters had nicknames like the Italians—Jimmy (The Weasel) Fratiano—we could have stuff like Seamus (The Heavy Drinker) Finnegan, Sidney (The Chiropodist) Feinstein, and Leroy (The Motherfucker) Washington. I think I was getting hysterical.

The sun was just coming up, and it was a real keeper, a clear, bright morning with no fog-mist-haze whatever having to burn off. It was one of those days you could see Kansas City on the left all the way to Hawaii on the right. Los Angeles may not be much to visit, but it's sure a nice place to live. Minus the complications.

The smoky rear window in the Mercedes hummed the rest of its spooky way down, and a smiling Cifelli stabbed me with a pair of icy eyes, cracked the door, and asked me in. I figured I'd accept.

"I hope I'm not disturbing you," he began in his usual way.

"It is a little early . . ."

"Truly sorry."

"But this way I can get a good jump on my day."

"I appreciate it. The problem is, things have become somewhat . . . troublesome of late."

"Angelo."

"Him, too, of course."

That wasn't my fault, clearly. Was he thinking of Claudio? "Sorry about Fortunata," I said. "Although I didn't really know was I still on the case or not."

He sighed. "Yes, yes. I could have been more specific."

"I mean, I thought it was so long as he was at the Ermitage."

"I definitely miscalculated. Don't hold you responsible."

You know how to spell relief? So, then?

"What I wanted to do was . . . enlist your support in what appears to be an ongoing hassle with Barry Nash."

Oh, boy.

"Rayford, we've known each other quite a while now. And I think we've earned each other's trust."

"Right." I trust you're not going to get mad at me.

"I think it might be a little easier for you to operate if you knew what's been going on."

I don't want to know; I really don't want to know. And I definitely don't want to operate.

"Originally, I obtained a financial interest in Fortunata's picture, *One Fell Swoop*. You think that's a good title for a movie, *One Fell Swoop*?"

Is that a trick question? That couldn't be what this was about.

"Well, titles are funny," I said. "A lot don't really make sense, once you think about 'em."

"You don't like it?"

"Yeah, I like it, it sounds good. So does, like, *The Sun Also Rises*. But what does it mean, it sets and it also rises? When I get up from bed I also rise—you know? They sound good, till you think about it. *Across the River and into the Trees*—what, across the river and into the parking lot? So, I guess, *One Fell Swoop*'s OK." What the hell was I so nervous about? He said I was all right.

"Maybe they'll change it. Anyway, along comes Nash. He knows I'm in the deal, he ought to respect that, but . . ." Here he gave an Italian shrug—some people never learn. "Meanwhile, he's got some money he wants to wash. So the sequence is, part he wants to do that. Part he wants to 'buy' a lot with a little . . . intimidation. And no small aspect, part he just plain wants to piss me off."

"Uh-hm."

"Ordinarily, any other time he tried something like that, I'd have to go to the mats. But I'm occupied with other things right now. I also got to thinking, maybe *One Fell Swoop*'s another *Cotton Club*, which they go around murdering each other over stealing the profits and the dumb picture winds up a dog grosses eighteen dollars."

"Hm."

"Plus which, he must be making some big threats to get in. With me, they were dealing with an established firm, and reasonable. For various considerations they'd have gotten service, no union troubles, and no hidden costs. With him, god knows. And, of course, at the time these people're under my protection. So when Nash gets specific and makes the threat against Fortunata, I'm obligated to save face, to take some counter action. Which is when I get you."

"Telling me Fortunata's Mr. Deeds."

"Need to know," said Cifelli.

"But why would Nash do that? I mean, say he wants in, all right. You're in the way, so he bumps Angelo. That was him?"

"My reading."

"Then why not wait and see what you'd do? Maybe you'd decide, like you did, the hell with it. Why hit Fortunata— or, turned out a guy named Cohen."

"I can't figure it, either."

"Then he's in, he's the new executive producer. So it's clear he made his deal; why *then* hit Fortunata? I mean, Fortunata's an asset, he's part of why the deal looks good. There's no logical reason for Nash to order that hit."

"Except he still didn't know for sure whether I'd back off."

"Even so. He wants to do the picture, Fortunata's a main part of it. One more time, why order the hit?"

"How about because the man's a sociopath. I think it has something to do with his size. He's practically a midget, you know."

Not good enough.

"OK, if you say."

All I was going to get.

"Maybe it's an insurance scam. The point is, Ray, I'd still

like to be kept informed about what's going on. I still have an interest. Call it curiosity."

"But I don't even know if I'll still be that much around," I said, looking for escape routes. "Now Fortunata's out of it."

"Sure you will," he assured me. "As co-writer, you'll be interviewing people, people he worked with, lived with—that'll keep you in contact."

"Yeah, I suppose," I had to admit.

"Plus I did want you to know I have no beef with you."

That was nice to know. Very nice to know. With which he reached across me and opened the door.

"Well, thanks, Mr. C. I'll keep in touch, then," I said, getting out of the car. And starting to breathe again.

"Beautiful view you've got up here."

"Thank you," I said. I always said thank you—like it was my doing the view was beautiful. And turned to start back toward the house.

So the upshot was, Cifelli was no threat to me. I did get the sudden thought *he* might have ordered the kill on Fortunata, to get back at Nash for stealing the deal from him. But then, Claudio'd been done so sloppy, it really didn't seem professional—which, come to think of it, would tend to rule out Heather Hansen, too. The really important thing was Cifelli was no threat to me.

Unless he was lying.

Then he threw a monkey wrench in the whole thing. He called me back, and as I leaned in, said, "I don't know if I've made myself totally clear. I want you to stay on the case."

"What exactly you mean, 'stay on the case'?"

"Solve the murder."

"That's not my job."

"It is if I hire you. I'm hiring you."

"To solve the murder?"

"Right—prove Nash did it."

Ah-hah, this is the way hit back for Angelo.

"Suppose he didn't?" I asked.

"He did."

"But suppose?"

He took a minute, like he was seriously thinking it over, then answered. "Work it out."

*   *   *

Francine was up and in the kitchen, making breakfast on the off chance I'd survive my meeting with The Dancer. It's nice living with an optimist.

She asked me what was that all about. Being she was involved with the book—as researcher; and involved with me—as lady in mating—I figured she deserved an update. So I more or less told her my conversation with Armand. She was smart and maybe it would make some sense to her it didn't to me.

"But why would Nash, once he was in on the picture, want to kill Fortunata, an integral part of it?"

"My question exactly," I said. Maybe she wasn't so smart.

"And while we're at it," I continued, "when his hit girl did in poor Ham Cohen by mistake at the Ermitage, why the X's burned in his cheeks, what's that supposed to mean?"

"You mean besides symbolizing a double cross?" Maybe she was smart.

"Ah-hah, but who what?"

"I don't know, but you'll have to excuse me," she said. With which she rose from the kitchen table and ran to the stainless steel sink—where she quickly turned on the water and lost her breakfast.

"I'm so sorry," she said, looking really embarrassed.

"That's all right, it's stainless," I said. Though I've noticed stainless gets more stained than enamel by far. I can't figure whatever made them create an easily stained material and decide to call it stainless.

"I mean I'm sorry about this," she said.

"That's OK, no big deal. We all get upset stomachs now and then."

"It's not exactly an upset stomach."

"Could of fooled me."

"It's more sort of morning sickness."

Dum de dum dum.

10

Mark Bradley

At St. John's I slept a lot, had four thousand dollars worth of tests and procedures, a visit from Brian, visit from Francine, visit from Goodman—and a call from Penny's secretary. Her boss wanted to know if my "vacation" would put the book behind schedule.

Plus the other visits.

Actually, the time sequence got very mixed in my mind. I remember being in the hospital already, and it seemed then that I was staring up at the ceiling and being shook by Chief Broward, whose first question had been where was Goodman, and whose second was to ask why had he done this thing to me, whatever the thing was. Then I remembered the thing, being hit over the head (actually, *on* the head) while in Fortunata's office. I started to share Goodman's assessment of Broward. There followed a pair of paramedics whose primary ministration seemed to be the suggestion I get to the hospital for X rays and brain scans. Evidently they weren't inclined to take me. I resisted the notion, anyhow. I didn't want to go to the hospital. I'd been to too many hospitals, too many times, and left too many friends in them.

No, I could handle this myself. Maybe a trip to the doctor, maybe just a cold compress—maybe no argument, since I fainted.

Now it was the second (third?) day, definitely not still the first, because the first I just talked to Goodman, and now I remembered Goodman had been here since (this might have something to do with drugs, it occurred to me—or, more accurately, to Francine, who suggested I palm the next offering and slip it to her, based on the somewhat communist rationalization that her need was greater—and the erroneous assumption I was such an amateur I was getting it in pill form). At least I was pretty sure Goodman had been there. Something about a prickly cactus. Yeah, there it was. Right, right, sandwiched between calls from the *Enquirer*, the *Star* and something called *Dirty Doings*—all offering me money to say something awful about the late Claudio Fortunata and/or preview the contents of my forthcoming (to be forthwritten) book about same. A tribute to my character, I was hardly tempted—even by the *Dirty Doings* inclusion of a bonus credit at a notorious escort service.

I remember between comatose hazes slightly less vague hazes, and somehow up and wandering in the hall and, I don't know, a dream?—back in the room and there was whatsisname, the line producer, Vernon something. Charles. Who seemed to be straightening out my closet.

"Oh, there you are," he'd said. And there I was, not a little surprised he'd come visit me, whom he'd scarcely met. "How ya doing?" Why would he be in my closet? Bathroom?

"Doin'? Oh, yeah," I'd said, something to that effect.

"Sorry this happened on our picture," he went on, sighing and massaging the bridge of his nose. "Though technically not exactly on our picture, in terms of responsibility and that sort of thing."

Ah, the legal eagles must've sent him.

"I wasn't immediately thinking of a lawsuit," I said, then remembered my condition, that I might not be exactly fine-edged, and cannily kept the door ajar, "though this doesn't constitute waiver of my rights, should subsequent reevaluation prompt comparable reconsiderations of corporate and/or personal liability. Care to sit down?"

"No, no, I just . . . wanted to say hello, see how you were getting on."

"Well, apparently OK," I said craftily. "Nice of you to drop by. I think I'll go lie down now."

And I did, I think sleeping for quite a long time. In fact, it seems, till—right, Goodman.

"Really sorry about this," he was saying, first I remember. "If I'd thought there was the slightest danger, I'd never've left you alone."

"Hey, those're the cookie crumbles," I'd said, somewhat wrongly I realized, but didn't feel inclined to correct.

"You up to talking about the case?" he'd asked.

"Urrn," I'd answered.

That seemed to satisfy him.

"I imagine you're going to have Broward over here again any time now. I think with him you're better off not saying too much."

"There's not mush to say," I said mushily. "I don't remember anythin' 'cept looking for Hampton—ask what was the call Claudio got. But no Hampton."

"And still no Hampton," said Goodman. "I haven't been able to turn him up anywhere. Not in the phone book. Screen Actors Guild wouldn't give me his address, either. I could've gone to sources at the phone company—a lot easier when there was just one phone company—wasn't that an improvement! But I didn't have to because instead Francie hacked into the INS Green Card file. But he hasn't been home since Fortunata bought the farm."

Did he actually say that? Maybe it's the Dilaudid, which, by the way, some kind of national treasure, should be about time again—I feel a song coming on. Oh, god, I'm turning into Francine. Whose name I must have mentioned.

"She's been very cold to me lately," he confided. Well, there was a lot of *that* going around.

Then, after a silence? Goodman let out one of those older folks' sighs (why'd they do that, some sort of erosion of the respiratory tract?).

"Nothing, you don't remember anything else?" he was saying.

"Just I told you, I told you, right? I was in Claudio's office, I noticed the script gone, and I got beaned where's my shot?"

Shazzam, which is when the handsome assistant nurse entered the room with a towel-covered tray and a sly smile. I smiled sly back. With which he unveiled the implements.

"Won't be a minute, just need to take a little blood," he intoned, intuned? to my bitter disappointment and his evidently sadistic amusement.

"Jesus," I said, "you've taken enough blood to cater a Transylvanian Oktoberfest. Why don't they use the last blood?"

"Not my department," he said. "I'm the taker, not the user." And he set about his nasty business, first donning latex gloves.

"Sure you don't need a spacesuit?" I said testily.

He didn't seem to mind. "Standard procedure these days, love—with everybody."

"I guess while they're at it, they give you the AIDS thing, too—right?" said Goodman.

"Wrong," said both the orderly and me. He was evidently well briefed by the hospital's legal department. I was simply pissed off by the implication.

"We're going to get into that now?" I asked.

"Hey," said Goodman, "I was tested myself when I went in, in case they had to operate. Negative," he added reassuringly.

I decided, both because I was so weary—it was definitely time for my shot—and because it was Goodman, to just let it drop. No such luck.

"I have a theory about it, you know," he continued brightly. "I read once where the number of cases doubles each year. If you halve the cases each year and keep going back till you get to case one, you know when that is?"

I didn't.

"It's 1969."

"OK."

"And you know what happened in 1969?"

I didn't.

"We went to the moon."

All right.

"And we brought back stuff. Moon rocks. This is a disease never been on earth. There's your virus, from outer space."

It was a thought.

"We shoulda stopped with Teflon, or at least pre-screened whatever guy handled the rocks," Goodman editorialized. Being irritated by the man's continuing homophobia, and maybe just a teense suffering baby withdrawal, I turned my back and indicated a desire for solitude by declaring, "I think I'll get on with my recovery now."

"OK," said Goodman. "I got things I should be doing, anyway. Researching the book, and like that. You just relax and take care." And to show there were no hard feelings, he punched me in the bicep, which solidified our male bonding and paralyzed my entire arm. My partner. I think then he left, and—accounts will vary—exactly how long after that I can't actually say, awhile—the orderly finally returned with another tray. This time when he lifted the towel he held aloft a hypodermic.

"Good-time Charley has arrived," he trilled, arming it with the goods.

As I coyly rolled down the edge of a pajama bottom, it suddenly occurred to me he seemed almost too happy. Maybe I was being a bit overly sanguine about all this. Maybe he wasn't really an orderly at all. Maybe I was actually in mortal danger! It also occurred to me maybe I was just reading too many Robin Cook novels.

When I awoke, I figured I was OK. I mean, I awoke. Close call? Hard to tell. "Nah," suggested Francine, who seemed to've shown up, "just doper's paranoia."

Then I noted she was no longer in the room. Had she ever been? Could she have shown up just for one line? Perhaps some time had elapsed.

I spent the day/days like that. I guess. Unless somebody tells me different.

I know Brian visited, and I have a feeling it wasn't entirely satisfactory, as I've totally wiped the memory from my mind. Ah, Brian, what happened? Why is it all turning to asses? But no, I wasn't going to cry anymore. Francine was probably right, it was more than likely just a result of the drugs (though I seemed to recall the reason I liked it was it made me happy). The well-known Paradox Reaction (Paregoric?), that must be it.

I—have—made—a—decision! I will take no more shots. Period. Over. That's it. They'll never take me alive. Just say nyah-nyah.

I felt good about my decision.

I felt bad about my renewal of pain. (Right, there was another reason for medication.)

And more time passed, and I did feel a bit better. Food had started to seem like a good idea—till you actually tasted it. But whether that was a result of my condition or the institutional quality of the offerings, I couldn't say.

And finally, I had one last visitor.

She was very tall, with lots of length between the bust and the hips, the kind of body which hadn't existed a generation ago (Susan Haywood, Lana Turner, Betty Grable? Kidding?): that long-waisted, flat-tummied, ante-junior high fashion look, with everything wonderfully sculpted and sensationally firm, femininity defined by strength instead of softness. Unsurprisingly, she seemed very sure of herself, with an intelligent look to her eyes and a ready smile showing perfectly matched teeth. I'd never seen her before.

"So, how are you?" she said.

"I are fine. How are you?"

"Fine."

"*Who* are you?"

"Oh, I'm sorry. My name is Jennifer Charles."

Well, if it wasn't Kimberly, I guess it had to be Jennifer.

"And you're in the right room?"

"Yes, of course. We haven't met. I'm Vernon Charles' wife."

"Vernon Charles."

"The producer?"

"Oh, that Vernon Charles. Right, he was here earlier."

"He was?" That seemed to surprise her. "You're sure? Here?"

"Not exactly here—over there. Yes, I'd say he was here. I think the legal department sent him."

"Oh, I doubt that."

"They send you, too?"

"Not at all, no, no. I came on my own. I guess that may seem a bit strange, since we haven't actually met. But I know your work."

"Really?"

"I read everything about Hollywood," she said, which qualified the compliment a bit. "Show business is my life," she added with that dazzling smile—plainly kidding. Not plainly, gorgeously kidding. How had that drab Vernon Charles ever snagged a winner like this? Do de word *producer* strike a familiar note?

"Actually, it's a combination," she went on. "I love everything about Hollywood, and I love mysteries. So your book about that clever Rayford Goodman"—(*clever* Rayford Goodman?)—"I found really intriguing. Especially when you're working on my husband's picture and his director got murdered . . ." (Her husband's picture? His director? Of course, at her house I suppose he might seem more important than to the rest of us. He was only a line producer. Which these days is not like a Sam Goldwyn or a David Selznick—totally in charge. More like a technician, someone who would have been an associate producer in the old Louie B. days (bidets?). Before pictures had almost as many producers as television shows. A sort of foreman, really, seeing that the plant operates efficiently—or what passes for efficient in Hollywood, a business only slightly more cost-effective than war. Anyway . . .)

"So I thought I'd drop in and see how you were doing, with all this excitement."

"Kimberly, it doesn't bother you—"

"Jennifer."

"Jennifer, it ~~doesn't~~ bother you your husband's director . . . ?"

"Well, of course," she replied, bursting into tears.

A simple yes would have done.

"I'm sorry, I didn't mean to set you off."

". . . killed him . . . he just . . . dead. Poor Claudio, oh god . . ."

And she cried as if her heart would break.

Or so it seemed.

I even seem to think I joined her for a bit. But I was very emotional at the time. Also a bit delusional. Not total perfect recall.

"It's so awful," she was saying, getting hold somewhat. Or totally. Was she maybe an actress? "The man had family."

"Several, from what I hear," I replied.

She seemed to pull herself completely together then—and wonderfully together, too, I could appreciate objectively— or obliquely.

"You didn't by any chance see who hit you?" she asked out of left field.

"Nope."

"Anyway, I happened to be in the hospital . . ."

"Um."

"I thought I might as well drop by and say hello."

"Thank you. Since you were in the hospital?"

"Actually," she confided conspiratorially, "I pop in from time to time to check there's no animal experimentation going on."

"Ah-hah."

"I hate that."

"Right."

"So. I guess you're pretty nearly recovered."

"Pretty nearly."

"Well . . . nice to meet you."

And she leaned over and kissed me. Whatsername— Jennifer. Whatsisname—Vernon's—wife.

What was that all about?

11

Rayford Goodman

Since it was my writing partner got coshed, I couldn't help take it somewhat personal. It was your basic professional embarrassment. Add the other forces—Cifelli and Nash, both pulling and shoving—and it was clearly about time I got back to the detecting business and detected what was going down. Lest it wind up being me. I couldn't much afford to leave finding out who killed Fortunata to Chief Broward. He was good at who made the counterfeit Guccis, got light-fingered in Hermes, or worked the switch at Fred's. (What a name for a chic Beverly Hills jeweler—Fred.) Murder was a little too down-scale for old Ed to deal with.

So, since I had to start somewhere, I chose alphabetically. And called Billy Zee, Claudio's German gofer. He was still living at the Casa Muy Grande, and apparently able to clear his calendar. "No problem" (the first two words all foreigners seem to learn), he said, right away agreeing to let me buy lunch. I suggested Mirabelle's. He thought Le Dome sounded like a better idea. For at least fifty bucks more it oughta sound like Stardust. I didn't doubt he was an old hand having people buy his lunch. I also figured he was used to singing for his supper, too. So maybe springing for the costly viands could produce some results. But oh how I missed the good-but-only-medium-priced restaurants, evolutioned out by the high-flying, opulent eighties, along with what used to be the Middle Class. The Frascati restaurants—a whole wonderful chain, gone—and now, unbelievably, some new owner had driven Scandia into the ground. Not that Le Dome was overpriced—by today's L.A. standards. Only sort of by my yesterday's standards. At least good value, I admit—if you were on an expense account, or made toy rock 'n' roll money.

Speaking of which, or the opposite thereof, I had a Benny

Goodman tape on the car box—what Francie says in a sixty-four Eldorado convertible gets scary close to time travel—and was turning into the parking lot, just as Peggy Lee said to get out of there and get some money, too. To God's ear.

It was a dumb setup. You had to balance your car on the smallest bit of near-level ground and get out, leaving the motor running and the vehicle perched at the top of a very steep hill, hoping some irresponsible, dope-crazed parking valet would get to it quick. Before that happened, more than one person had seen their car take off down the slope, heading for serious damage to itself and probably the even more expensive car it was going to hit.

Billy Zee was already at the bar on what would turn out to be his third Bloody Mary when I got the check. He made up for promptness with naked greed.

"I finished up my appointment early over at Coralco, they're interested in a property I'm developing"—him and Suzanne Pleshette's gardener—"plus I wanted to get an early jump on my freeloading," he added with a kind of Heinrich Himmler charm. He still had just a touch of accent, despite having become as Hollywood as a blue-sky three-picture deal, with serious gross points and merchandising rights in southeast Asia.

Actually, though, it was just as well he was out front about it (the freeloading, not the gonna-make-a-movie bull-shit). He knew he didn't have to put on any real show for me. Billy Zee would know he couldn't. Because if there was one thing the ex–Wilhelm Zweig surely had, it was strasse smarts. My guess is the main reason he agreed to come in the first place was the off chance I could steer him to a new connection. Now that his erstwhile golden goose went and got himself fricasseed.

He didn't seem to be having a whole lot of trouble managing his grief as he lounged familiarly on the bar stool sucking celery. On the other hand, cruddy as he was, I wouldn't bet ten cents on him being the killer. Besides the anti-motive of losing his meal ticket, he didn't strike me the kind got physical. Certainly not that kind of physical. (Maybe poison, or a *thin* knife . . .) No, his riff was more to be a latcher-oner, a small part of somebody else's scheme, pseudo-development deals at Coralco notwithstanding. Mine was to hurry up and try to get even in the booze department and then see if my hunch he had enough inside info to be worth taking a show biz power lunch with was on the rhinoplasty. But before I could make much headway on the plan, Eddie came over and said, "I can seat you now, Mr. Goodman," which was impressive inasmuch as I was a very seldom customer. I did notice he sort of addressed it between the two of us, leaving it a fielder's choice.

"Thank you, Eddie," I said, settling it for him, and pointing for Billy to follow him. We were taken to my favorite room, the long, narrow one to the left of the bar. You can guess we weren't taken there because it was my favorite, but because it had the only two-seater tables in the place. I think he caught on right away I wasn't going to outspend any of the regulars connected with the top forty.

"So—how did you hook up with Fortunata?" I asked Billy once we'd settled into our seats, checked out the blonde and beautifuls, and ordered fresh drinks.

"He was in Berlin, shooting *Through a Crack in the Wall*—before the wall cracked all the way, natch—and he needed someone local to smooth out the bumps—"

"Let me guess, and you needed a ticket out of there."

"That's it, amigo." Which was a little bit funny, coming from that pinched Euroface.

"And after the picture he, what, adopted you?"

"Not exactly. I just sort of made myself . . . invaluable." He would. But it had to say something about Fortunata's character that he could be taken in by this blatant in-your-face hustler. Was it see-no-evil sainthood? Or birds of a feather?

"So you've been out here for . . . ?"

"Two pictures already. Or, I guess, altogether."

There was a moment of almost sadness, it seemed.

"I know you don't believe this, but I'm gonna miss him," he said.

"Oh, I believe you," I said. I believed what he'd really miss were the high old times that came with hitching your Volkswagen to a star. "Let me ask you, you have any idea who killed him?"

"Let me ask *you*—what's the in-thing here for lunch?"

A touch evasive, I thought. So we talked instead of hot duck salad, and mushrooms ounce for ounce like gold, and lettuce from the far-flung corners of the world. All those things erstwhile gutter rats are so conversant with. He was beginning to annoy me.

"Talk to me," I said. I wanted to get something for my money. "What about Barbara? Her and Fortunata . . . ?"

"Sure, but before my time."

"Still hot to trot?"

"I think. But hard to say, y'know? Claudio had a way of keeping all his women happy, even when he stopped keeping them real happy. Everyone stayed friends with Claudio."

"Not everyone."

"I guess not. What're you having for a main course?"

"The duck salad *is* a main course."

"No, it's not, it's an appetizer."

"*I'm* having it as a main course."

"Maybe some kind of veal. Is this the A room?"

I started to get the feeling I was going about this the wrong way. This was not a guy to bribe—there'd be no end to it. This was more maybe a guy to rough up a little. Or was that just wishful thinking?

I ordered my appetizer–main course, he ordered half the things on the menu, reading from the right, and I started to get really hacked.

"Willy, did it ever occur to you maybe it's not a snatch-and-grab world, that it's not all take?"

He delivered himself of a small smile, sort of a slit in his bony face. "I'm so sorry, I thought it was freely given. You could cancel the pommes soufflé."

"Fuck the pommes soufflé, that's not the point." What the hell was I doing, I'm going to teach him manners? "Forget it, forget it," I continued instead. "Let's get back to Barbara. You say she was still friends even after Fortunata dumped her. Isn't it possible she wasn't really all that friendly?"

"It's possible. So, what—you want me to keep the potatoes?"

"Keep the potatoes! Barbara . . ."

"Barbara, Barbara, well—Barbara . . ."

Something there. Something a little reluctant to say?

"Talk to me, Billy, what about Barbara?"

"Nothing, really. Only, hard to say what she really thinks. She's Jewish, you know."

"What's that got to do with anything."

"Oh, I'm sorry. You're Jewish, too?"

"No, I'm not Jewish."

"There's so many out here. I should be more careful, right?"

"We're talking about Barbara."

"Hey, not that I've got anything against the Jews."

"You hardly left enough to have anything against."

"You are, aren't you? I offended you. Please, I was just trying to answer your question."

Now what is this? What am I supposed to make of this? Any bearing on anything important to a *shaygitz* like me? Or indirectly? How about, for one thing, remembering the first victim, Hamilton Cohen, was a Jew? True, whoever killed him thought he was Claudio Fortunata. Or did he? Could it be possible Cohen was killed on purpose? Because he was a Cohen? Our little neo-Nazi was going to bear some closer watching.

The duck salad was served. The gutter gourmet found it a little dry.

"Listen, uh," I said, figuring if I pushed it in his face I'd not only lose the purpose of the meeting, but my lunch as well, "what do you know about Fortunata's script?"

"What do you mean? I don't understand the question."

(I only follow orders.)

"When my partner and I were in Fortunata's outer office, just after he'd been killed, there was a script on the desk. His copy of *One Fell Swoop*."

"Ja, yeah . . . It's underdone, too—see the pink?"

"It's fine, the duck's fine; they make it terrific. Don't change the subject."

"What's the subject?" He assayed another taste, then another, the while shaking his head, the while polishing off everything but the finish on the plate.

"The subject," I continued during the above, "is Fortunata's script."

"Uhrm," he said, chewing thoroughly.

"When my partner went back in the office there, he noticed the script was missing."

"Argm."

"So I was wondering, have you any idea why anybody would steal his script? Isn't it the same as anybody else's?"

"Well," said Billy, wiping the corners of his mouth, the

plate dog-empty, "for one thing, it's got his directing notes in it."

"Why would that interest anybody?"

"I don't think it would. Except maybe another director, or a cinematographer—for whatever reason."

That stopped me a minute. Laszlo?

"Laszlo?" I said.

"Well, maybe in some way, but he'd have the same notes in his own script anyway."

So much for intuitive leaps. But there had to be some reason why someone took the script. It didn't just walk away.

"All right," I went on. "Forget the who. Why would anybody steal his script?"

"Oh, that's a different story. It could be for a lot of reasons. Claudio used his scripts to keep his records in."

The waiter served the veal. Billy picked up his knife and fork like someone going into battle. I closed my hand around his wrist—not about to wait while he ran down the food before stuffing it down.

" 'A lot of reasons.' Give me one or two."

"He kept track of his finances, used it as a diary, kept his phone numbers in it—whatever came up." He wrenched his hand free, cut himself a bite. "Since it would be the one thing he'd have with him all day every day for months to come, he used it to write down everything that happened or needed writing down, to keep track of." He bit off a hunk, chewed it thoughtfully while I waited. Swallowed. Continued. "*Some*body probably didn't want *some*one to read *some*thing Claudio'd written there."

Why'd he make me feel like it was a challenge?

"Now, the veal is really good," he added.

"Which narrows it down to practically anybody," *I* added.

"That's about it," he said. Then, mouth full, chewing, looked to have something to add.

"What?" I prompted.

He waved a fork at me, finally finished swallowing. I leaned in. He said, "What's everybody eat for dessert?"

The valet parking sign outside informed the world that the fee for what for decades had been free parking was two dollars and fifty cents. I'd just love to see how fast they'd come up with half a buck if anybody ever gave them three bucks and waited for change. They didn't even pretend to make a move in that direction. While I waited for the Eldorado, and at least two guys who came after me got theirs first, Billy had pushed himself into a group of guys I recognized as executives from Universal.

The guy brought my car, balanced it at the crest of the hill. I turned back to Billy, to tell him the car was here and let's get moving, heard him say, ". . . properties Claudio had optioned . . . full authorization to deal . . ." and, ". . . Thursday's good, one o'clock, La Serre. Give my regards to Lew." Which meant, I think, he'd managed to latch on to the rights to some potential movies, which further meant, I think, a chance to promote some big bucks, which even further meant, I think, he had a very strong motive for murder.

Which is when I turned back, just in time to see my car ever so slowly start to slip back down the hill. I felt like I'd been punched in the chest, and the fist left there, as we all just stood there Krazy-glued to the spot. And watched as it went faster and faster by the second, and finally crashed into a Ferrari Testarossa. Which I think is the most expensive car in the world. Certainly up there among the top one or two.

12

Mark Bradley

I couldn't remember ever having a headache that bad when I hadn't at least earned it by some kind of terrific carryings-on the night before. I hadn't an inkling (which is not a baby pen) there could be so much pain connected with such a little curiosity. If I had, whoever bonked me could've easily negotiated a much less traumatic way for my retreat from the enterprise. But now, three days later, I was feeling almost human, which is to say I was furious and aching to get even.

Goodman called for me bright and early at U.C.L.A. Medical (he bright and early, me merely early), since I was scheduled for release at eight-thirty. But the doctor evidently either overslept, forgot, or was called away on an emergency. What a wonderful built-in cop-out doctors always had. The upshot of it was by ten o'clock there was neither doctor nor anyone in authority or otherwise either permitted or willing to make the final determination I could leave.

Correction: one was—Goodman.

"Come on, let's go," he said.

"I'm sorry, sir," replied Nurse Cratchit. "No patient can leave without being signed out by the doctor."

"Wanna bet?" said Goodman, taking hold of my tote bag with one hand and my arm with the other.

"And under no circumstances without a wheelchair," screeched Cratchit.

"OK, get a wheelchair," said Goodman.

"When doctor gives permission," replied the recording.

"We are supposed to wait," I offered lamely.

"You didn't break your word; you're here," he said. "I'm here. Nurse is here. Doctor's not. Fuck doctor."

He was right. We defer too much to physicians pretending medicine is still some kind of high calling instead of merely the viable intensive revenue-generating alternative to law-yering it's become.

"We're out of here," said Goodman. And so we were, nurse following and snapping at our heels, with dire empty threats about what would happen if everybody broke the rules.

Outside in the parking lot, we wandered for a good ten minutes in search of Goodman's car, the exact level and location he had failed to mark. ("Because they don't put up adequate signs!" And because it turned out it wasn't exactly his car but a loaner, which was a long story I was spared hearing.) Meanwhile, what I did hear was a report on his luncheon with Billy. The incidental intelligence gleaned that Billy had some double-dealings going didn't come as an enormous surprise to either one of us, though it was an interesting development.

We finally did locate the loaner (which unsurprisingly turned out to be a foreign clunker considerably less spiffy than his own) and headed for my place so I could change clothes for Claudio's funeral, scheduled in about an hour and a quarter. They'd pushed through an accelerated VIP autopsy which, according to Goodman's sources at the morgue, had revealed no big surprises. Death by bullets ("multiple .22-caliber gunshot wounds"), traces of booze, no measurable drugs, possible unspecified venereal disease. Motive there?

Then he told me about his earlier meeting with Cifelli, and to my surprise, seemed reassured by the conference. I had a different reaction. Maybe it had something to do with being a total stranger to sit-downs with capos, but it left me with a decidedly unsettled feeling, which I shared with my—god help me—partner. My reservations went as follows: why did Cifelli want to meet Goodman in the first place? What did he care what Goodman thought? Why did he want him to keep an eye on Nash if, as he said, he was out of the deal on *One Fell Swoop*? If it was for his "retained interest," wouldn't that come later, when it was released? And wouldn't the picture be dead anyway? What would be the ongoing hassle with Nash in that event?

Further: maybe we were being thrown off the track by the fact Goodman saw Heather Hansen at the Ermitage at the time of Cohen's (mistaken) killing and again with Nash at Fortunata's. That called for an automatic assumption

Hansen was both working for Nash and was the killer. There was at least a remote possibility she was working—that time—for Cifelli. He seemed to have more motive for wanting Fortunata dead than Nash did—as revenge on Nash, for one thing. And further . . .

Further—Goodman didn't seem to welcome these speculations.

"I don't know what happened to you when you got hit on the head, but you're really speeding a little too much for my taste."

"What's your problem?"

"My problem is I like when I decide something for it to stay decided. What you've done is just send me back to square one. Less than square one. That's an awful lot of theories."

"Well . . ."

"But a lot of what you say makes sense. I hate it, but it makes sense."

I let it rest for a while. He was thinking about it, though. I could tell, because he almost ran into a cute little Miata.

"Goddamn toy car. Can't hardly see them. Get on the sidewalk where you belong, why don't you?" he yelled helpfully.

We drove in silence for a bit. There were things to work out, problems that affected me, too. I finally decided to take another shot.

"But the bottom line is you're still sort of on the case for Cifelli, too," I said. "Right?"

"As long as the book's still a go, why not? Especially since saying no to Cifelli's one of the things the surgeon general warns you about."

By which time we were at my condo. I had previously told Goodman the sequence of numbers that opened the gate to the garage, which he now punched in, and after the grill swung back he eased the borrowed heap up the ramp and in. My car was in its slot, where Goodman'd returned it the other day, and the spot next to it—Brian's—was empty. So Goodman pulled in there.

We got out and crossed to the elevator, for which we had to wait, as it was on the top floor.

"J'ever notice," he said in a cranky imitation of Andy Rooney, "you can always tell how your day's going to go by things like when you're in the basement, the elevator's up at the penthouse? And when you finally get it, how it gets stopped at every floor, and—"

I raised a hand, stopping him before he could give a completely depressing review of all the things that could ruin your day and now probably would. "Yes, I've noticed, and I don't want to hear about them," I said.

"You know, in the morning when you go out and your newspaper's all soaked from the sprinklers—"

"I don't want to hear it! I don't want to hear about the sprinklers, the elevator, the car, or the state of your bowels."

"I guess you're a little out of sorts from the hospital stay and all," he concluded. Hopefully.

The elevator did come. Eventually. And when it got only as far as the lobby before it was stopped for additional passengers, who then punched in stops at each floor along the way, for some reason or other Goodman made me feel guilty about it. And I was going to write another entire book with the man?

We did, in the fullness of time, arrive at my floor, and then my door, and eventually even my apartment, on the welcome mat of which someone had spilled a pizza.

"See what I mean?" he offered. "Not going to be a good day."

We entered the apartment. He was right.

It was a mess. Cigarette butts overflowed the ashtrays (neither I nor Brian smoked), a dozen sticky glasses were sticking here and there (neither I nor Brian used a dozen glasses), dirty plates, crumpled napkins, chicken bones . . .

"You sure run a tight ship," observed Goodman wryly.

"It surprises me," I replied.

"I thought you had a maid."

"Cleaning woman, housekeeper. I do. Bernadine."

"I hope she hasn't been here already."

"Well, she misses work a lot. Gets sick. Dirty apartments especially make her sick. And then there're all the holidays."

"Holidays."

"Martin Luther King's birthday, Yom Kippur, Tet . . ."

"Gotcha."

But what I wasn't saying and what I wasn't liking most of all was the indication that with me in the hospital, virtually at death's door—or anteroom, anyhow—here Brian was living it up having a party!

"I think you better get going, buddy, or we're going to be late for the funeral thing," said Goodman.

"Right," I said. "Just give me a minute." And I went into our bedroom and tried very hard not to see or find anything that would tend to incriminate Brian and/or force me to deal with anything I didn't want to deal with at this particular juncture in my life.

I settled on a Turnbull and Asser white striped blue shirt, a forties Sulka antique blue and red deco tie, an Armani navy blazer, and generic light gray slacks. With a pair of matte black Ferragamo loafers completing the look, I was certainly properly togged for your basic Hollywood celebrity memorial "celebration of life." We tiptoed through the trash and hied us away hence.

The services, originally scheduled for a major Catholic church, had been hastily rerouted to Forest Lawn instead. The brief public relations contretemps had been quietly and speedily resolved. After all, Claudio had not only been married at least four times, there'd also been—among other fairly public transgressions—that business down in Baja with the fourteen-year-old girl from Tustin. Given his zest for life and his cavalier attitude toward rules and regulations, it was hardly surprising that the final determination of his religious status would fall somewhere between lapsed and eternally damned. Definitely not a candidate for consecrated ground.

At any rate, now that the ceremony had been transferred to a sizable and creatively nonsectarian chapel at Forest Lawn we heard various of his associates and friends eulogize the man and laud his contribution to "the industry." In the absence of a priest, a high-ranking representative of the Director's Guild read a list of his credits and their grosses. There was a scattering of self-conscious applause. ("I'd like to thank my cast, the producers, my embalmer . . .")

Since in movie-making your most recent co-workers were your closest and dearest friends, the greatest grief was manifested by those whose lamentations were heavily motivated by the loss of employment on the now presumably demised production of *One Fell Swoop*.

Following an expression of regret from the studio that

was to house the production ("We are all the poorer for the many motion pictures he will now never get to make"), Maurissa rose to pay her respects.

"To miss the chance to like make one more picture," she said, "with this like giant among giants . . ." (I couldn't help wondering if there weren't some anatomical allusions here) ". . . is itself a great loss—like personally. But for the world to have like one less Fortunata picture is truly tragic. We shall not like see his like again," she concluded movingly.

Terry Coyne said he would be brief. What Maurissa said went double for him.

Harvey the writer—I never did get his last name, maybe it was The Writer—delivered a lengthy and impassioned eulogy along the lines of "Friends, Romans and countrymen"—bemoaning the loss of one who had so enlightened our course and illuminated our way, despite the insignificant differences they may have had en route, like being humiliatingly and publicly fired.

Laszlo Nagy unfolded several pages of notes, then began to weep so profusely he was unable to read a word and had to be helped back to his seat. Well he might cry. According to my understanding he'd never worked for anyone but Fortunata, and the future could hardly look bright for an aging cinematographer whose meal ticket had just been cashed in.

Billy Zee, the Resident Friend, contained his grief more stoically. Yet there was little doubt his loss was enormous—at once that of friend, confidant, spiritual brother, and him from whom all goodness flowed. The sunshine had gone out of his life—to say nothing of free lodgings and decorator booze.

I leaned over to Goodman and whispered I'd be willing to bet there'd been something between Billy and Claudio.

"You mean what I think you mean?" he asked.

"I mean yes, Claudio could've been gay."

"You think everybody's gay. The guy married four times!"

"A little overcompensating, wouldn't you say?" I suggested.

He rolled his eyes and turned his attention back to the next eulogy. Claire Miller, the tall, rangy agent, said (in her Texas/Alabama way) she spoke for "evuhbody" at Creative

Assassins when she said "Clawdo will be soahly missed." A client like Fortunata didn't come along every day. But you got the feeling when one did, guess which agency was going to get him. "Clawdo had hoart"—there were big bucks in "hoart." For her, the ultimate accolade. Next Freddie Forbes, the set designer with the Hoover collars, revealed he had never worked with anyone who was so inherently wise to the subtleties and nuances of set design; the composer who had never before experienced such rapport with a director—although they hadn't yet discussed the score, or actually met; the editor with whom Claudio was so much in sync—I was beginning to think maybe sainthood wasn't out of the question—on to I think even the guy who held the clipboard at the gate.

I noticed Barry Nash was nowhere in attendance, or any of his contingent—Heather for example. I didn't quite know what to make of that. Perhaps nothing. Yet gangsters were usually big on funerals.

There was, however, sizable representation from the four families he had fathered—a tearful testament to his potency. Ginny Warren, one of his wives, I recognized from a TV series. That all four ex-wives were also there spoke as well to his ongoing charm, and gave further credence to Francine's earlier assertion that Claudio had been a man extremely well liked.

Vernon Charles, line producing the funeral, rose to conclude the eulogies. But first he had just a few announcements he wanted to make, in what seemed a very camp counselor-y way. One, he hoped as many as possible would join him and the company following the cremation in the special buses being provided (with, incidentally, snacks and complimentary beverages of choice included en route) to transport them all to Long Beach. There they would all board a ship belonging to the Neptune Society from which would be scattered Claudio's ashes somewhere between the point of departure and Catalina Island—and presumably between hors d'oeuvres and lunch.

I didn't expect there'd be an overflow crowd for this even among such major league freeloaders, judging from the remarks I could hear. ("How can they expect you to dress for both a funeral and a boat ride?" was one.)

It seemed it would be, in general, passes on the ashes.

Till old Vern made his second announcement. "It's

maybe not the most appropriate time, but I think Claudio would have liked me to say right off, the studio's decided *not* to cancel *One Fell Swoop*. Instead we're going ahead and make the picture with Laszlo Nagy directing."

That provoked a spontaneous smattering of applause which quickly subsided to a more appropriate hubbub of whispered yet delighted surprise, and an almost unanimous changing of minds about the strewing trip.

"Now, as to the man himself," droned Vernon. "Who among us has not been enriched by merely knowing him?"

"Someone," whispered Goodman, "definitely didn't feel enriched. Or maybe they're more enriched now. Certainly, it turns out, Laszlo. And by the way, have you noticed Barbara Aronson among the missing?"

"Artist, showman, performer—all these and more," continued Vernon in a maddening monotone, giving every indication there would be an excruciatingly lengthy description of the "more."

When we left the chapel—getting that full sun in the face a surprise feeling like coming out of a movie matinee—it took me a moment for my eyes to adjust, and another before I spotted Chief Broward of the Beverly Hills Police off a short distance, clocking the comings and goings.

What took me even longer to notice was the elderly worker (grave digger?) nearby, mustachioed and mutton-chopped, wearing earth-colored corduroy knickers and an old sweater, edging his way toward us. There was something familiar about the man as he shambled closer—a thatch of white hair leaking out the sides of his cap.

"Look who's here," said Goodman suddenly, crossing to the old gentleman's side.

"Please don't look at me, Mr. Goodman," came the at-once familiar voice of Hampton, heavily made up and on second look too theatrically disguised. Slipping him a card, he whispered, "Just meet me at this place at half after seven tonight."

"Why's that?" said Goodman, out of the side of his mouth.

"Because I need your help and I think we'll be safe there."

"You've got something you're going to tell us?"

"Exactly. I know who killed Mr. Fortunata."

With which he shambled on past (shambling was his thing).

"You wouldn't care to give us a hint, now?" I offered sotto voce, mindful Broward was eyeing us suspiciously.

But he done shambled off.

"Sir?" I called after him with quiet urgency.

Nothing doing.

"I guess we'll just have to wait till 'half after seven,' " said Goodman. "You don't suppose he meant thirty seconds after seven?"

"I don't like it," I said, ignoring him.

"Why?"

"You know what happens. Whenever anybody's going to give you the name of the killer only later . . ."

"Yeah?"

"They turn up murdered."

"In fiction. In real life they turn up alive only with a totally dumb idea has no bearing on reality."

"Where's the meeting?"

Goodman looked at the card. "It says, 'Nigel Hampton—acting neatly done.' "

"Other side."

He turned it over, hesitated.

"Well?"

"Whip and furry?" he said.

"Those English are so kinky. Let me see."

I took the card. "It's the Whip and Surrey—probably a pub."

"Then why don't they call it the Balls of the Cock, like they usually do?"

"That one was probably taken," I said.

"Or the Tail of the Twat . . . or the Crab and Lice . . ." and Goodman was off on one of his celebrated tangents.

13

Rayford Goodman

I decided we ought to cover the sea voyage hauling Claudio's ashes, in case anything rocked the boat. I also decided Bradley ought to do that alone rather than waste both our time when I could be doing something else. The something else I could be doing was not throwing up. I didn't think it would do much for my image to let on I was so apt to get motion sickness I had to practically take a Dramamine to drive over Laurel Canyon.

"So why don't you just hop on the bus, latch on to a couple those beverages of choice, and enjoy yourself a boat ride?" I said.

"I had every intention to," said Bradley. "Scattering Fortunata's ashes to the winds strikes me as a great way to start the book."

"Right, so we'll get that done."

"Won't we?" he said, I thought with maybe a touch sarcasm.

Then, in case he had the idea I intended goofing off instead of working on this great bus ride with the free drinks, I added, "The reason I'm not going, I figured the time'd be better spent we divided our efforts."

"Whatever you say. I know I'm going to be writing this book myself anyway," said Bradley.

"That's not so, I'll be right in there with you. It'll be just like last time. The whatever title we come up with, by Ray—I like Ray better than Rayford—Goodman, as told to Mark Bradley."

He looked a little sick. Maybe he wasn't up for the boat ride, either.

Turned out that wasn't quite it. "You have to be out of your fucking mind," said Bradley, not too friendly, it struck me. "The reason you had that billing last time was it was about you, and it's customary to pretend to autobiography.

This is not about you. What I had in mind was—whatever title, maybe 'And . . . Action: The Life and Times of Claudio Fortunata . . .' "

"Too long."

"Or just plain 'And . . . Action' by Mark Bradley, in large type, with, farther down, in smaller type, 'with Rayford Goodman.' "

I think he just wanted to annoy me.

"Don't be silly, you know how this town is. Once you cut your billing—"

I was a little afraid he might hurt his teeth biting down that way, not to say being a little surprised he could talk through that kind of clenching.

"I'm the writer, you're the detective. Let me write, you go detec."

"Exactly my plan. You for the boat, and I'll be off to see I can't do a little better with Barbara Aronson—which I'm not criticizing you. At least find out why she didn't manage to be here when they faded out on old Claude." Which is more or less what we wound up doing.

So he was off to Long Beach and the Neptune Society, and I was going to go back to Beverly Hills and look up Barbara. But first, I figured I better take Francie to lunch, what with "the great news" and everything. I must say I did think I could stop worrying about girlfriends getting pregnant and all that a long time ago. Of course, in those days it was real trouble, like where am I going to get five hundred bucks and find someone won't kill her in the bargain. I really couldn't believe there were people not only willing but campaigning to get back that arrangement. Another thing I never understood was why the right-wingers were the ones so anxious to make the poor people stay pregnant when they were going to have to support all those unwanted kids on welfare. I suppose it had to do with Not Interfering with God's Will ("He Braketh for Nobody"). It was getting very hard to be a reactionary with the kind of people on your side.

Then, too, of course, with modern women opting for all sorts of things, there was the chance Francie might just want to have the baby. The old biological clock bit. Given that, there was also the chance she might think the kid oughta have a resident mom *and* pop. There was a lot to think

about—or at least clear the air about—before we got around
to dealing with God's Will.

Francie, nevertheless one of His hotter creations, was
waiting for me at The Ivy, a semi-trendy mostly lunch spot
on Robertson Boulevard. The Ivy was really an old house
they'd encouraged the vegetation to cover up, behind a
picket fence and a couple valet parkers. I was a little sorry
she'd got there first, as she'd already settled into an outdoor
table (The Ivy was also semi-sidewalky—they'd paved the
lawn), which I never much cared for. The idea of eating
exhaust fumes and listening to traffic while fighting off bugs
and flying dirt in the noonday heat struck me something
less than a treat.

Anyway, al fresco it was, and I could see the way the
umbrella was situated I was also going to have the sun beating down my back. I loved it already.

Francie was sucking on some fancy pink drink through a
straw which had the effect of enhancing her dimples, which
had the further effect of mellowing me out a whole lot.

"Hello, Francie," I said, sitting down on a sunned-on
metal chair hot enough to fry folks, which got me back on
course. "Waiting long?" (J'ever notice the second person
to arrive always says that?)

"Hi there, big guy," she replied. "Not long. What's
today, Thursday?" I'd been a little late—couldn't find a
parking spot, and after circling twice had to surrender the
loaner Toyota to the bandits at the toll booth out front.
How much you wanna bet I get the car back with the radio
on a goddamned country-western station?

I sort of bounced a few times, trying to get my rear end
used to the heat, and turned my attention in the general
direction of being sociable. "What're you drinking?" I said.
"On second thought, I don't want to know. Pink? Nothing's
pink."

"Actually it's a vodka Bismol, concocted especially for us
expectant mothers." With which she withdrew a pillbox the
size of a change maker and selected a bottle with a prominent "NO ALCOHOL" warning on it. She flicked out a pill,
popped it in her mouth, and washed it down with the pink
stuff.

"There's a reason, I bet, why they put those warnings on
drugs about drinking."

"Oh, I know that," she said. "They don't want you to have any of the awful side effects—like euphoria."

"Anyway, I thought you weren't—"

"This is medicine."

"Because I mean, besides your word—your health and . . . everything."

"Right."

The waiter came over and I ordered a Denaka on the rocks, with a small bottle of Pellegrino. I knew this was going to cost a good six to eight dollars because they considered it two drinks. But it was the only way I knew to get vodka and soda without the soda being that gunk came out of a hose at the bar.

"And I'll have another of this devil's brew," said Francie, lighting up a cigarette.

"Should you be smoking, too?"

"Should you be pissing me off?"

"Sorry," I said.

"So how was the funeral?" she asked, changing the subject.

"It was more fun than television—less than the movies. Don't we have to talk? Aren't there things we should be discussing?"

"We're talking."

"But not discussing."

"One out of two."

So, OK, nothing'd been decided, looked like. I could get back of that. It's an important decision.

"You get any feeling, any suspects?" she asked. I suspected me. She meant the murder, of course. "What was the funeral like?"

"No one suspect, a batch of could-bes. What was it like? A whole lot of 'respecting' and 'beloveding' and 'going to be sorely missed.' I guess the guy was really well liked."

"It only takes one."

Right. Same for you. She didn't seem to want to talk about it. I guessed I wasn't supposed to say anything. Her body and her choice. Still, she had to know if I'd wanted a kid I'd've had one by now. Why was it I didn't think what I wanted was going to count a whole lot here? Funny feelings.

The waiter returned with the vodka Bismol for her, and for me a glass of vodka on the rocks and another glass of ice and a liter of something with the label smeared. God, they couldn't be bringing me bottled Mexican water?

"No Pellegrino," I said.

"Jais," he said, handing us each menus and departing. The cuisine was sort of Italian-Louisiana-Hollywood, with side trips to Mexico and India. To which they added a lot of the word *light*. Called "having it all." When you put that with, say, the words Cajun, or Maui onion, or black pepper, I tend to pass. I never could understand pleasure in eating a lot of heat and burning the candle at both ends, so to speak. Then again, I'm no gourmet—though I can, blind-fold, identify the three major brands of ketchup.

Francie gave the menu a quick look and tossed it aside. She picked up her bag and pushed her chair back.

"Excuse me, ladies' room."

I did one of those shift-your-weight things that covers looking like you're going to get up.

"Want me to order meanwhile?"

"No, I won't be hungry," she said, answering more than I asked, or wanted to know. And left for the privacy of the ladies' john.

She promised! We had a deal! Boy, I didn't care for that. I knew it was a bad time, but damn it! It was getting where we had to have a serious talk. I really didn't like this.

But speaking of things I didn't like, I got to interrupt that particular trend of thought when a whole lot of noise and action got my, and the immediate world's, attention. Here came the maître d' and about half the restaurant's employ-ees escorting Barry Nash, Heather Hansen, and Barbara Aronson to a table inside.

They settled down with no more fuss than a Concorde landing—busboys and waiters and flunkies in constant mo-tion. Fear'll do that. Plus, in fairness, he was probably a big tipper, too. Gangsters seem to want to believe they're well liked for themselves. Sort of like girls with big tits.

Barbara with Barry, now what do I make of that? Heather, I was beginning to think, was like a sly way of having a bodyguard without featuring it. And one of these days I was going to have to deal with her knowing I knew she did Cohen at the Ermitage—thinking it was Fortunata—which certainly made her an A number one suspect for *actu-ally* doing Fortunata. And an actual threat to me. Heather definitely needed watching. I could understand what she was doing with Nash. But Barbara? All right, for his part, a friend at court, a little inside info, maybe. But with her, such a primary allegiance she's here with him having lunch instead of burying—scattering—her ex-boss, ex-lover?

As if responding to my interest, Nash looked up. At his height, he always looked up. And caught my eye. I gave a little finger wave. He smiled. I think it was a smile. There was this slit through his mouth. Then he managed a small nod, indicating I drop over. It fell under the category of command appearance. I got up, squeezed between the tables, which were about as far apart as an NFL guard and tackle at the goal line, and made my way to his side. He didn't get up.

"Raymond," he said. "Pull up a chair, join us."

"Thanks," I said, not correcting him. "I'm with someone."

"A minute."

I felt a chair contact the back of my legs, nudging me to sit. Nash got good service. (They liked him.)

"Ladies, whyn'tchu go powder your noses?" he continued. Equally quick, their chairs were pulled gently back by willing hands, and Heather and Barbara departed.

"Uh," he continued when we again had privacy, "I was surprised to see you the other day to Fortunata's."

"Why's that, Bar?"

"I thought we had an understanding."

"Gee, I guess not."

"I'm going to have to talk to my help, they don't send good messages anymore."

"Oh, that. Yes, I understood that. You didn't want me representing Armand Cifelli's interests."

"And . . . ?"

"And, I don't," I lied. "I represent my own." True enough, self-preservation being one of them. "I'm co-writing a book on Fortunata's life."

"Get outa here."

"Really. I'm a book writer now."

"Well, that won't go on now he's dead, right?"

"No, you're wrong, it's a hotter project than ever."

"Which means?"

"I'll be around a bit, poking my nose here and there."

"I don't care for that, Raymond."

"It's business, Barry. I gotta make a living."

"Hey, a living's only good if you're living."

"Whew, more messages. You're beginning to annoy me." This was a calculated risk. There're just so many people you can let bully you before it begins to tarnish your reputation. I figured it was enough Cifelli had my number. Besides, Cifelli threatened but paid, which gave him some latitude.

"Don't be a hero, shamus." Shamus! He called me shamus!

Still, I'm not in the kind of shape to be a total hero.

"Look, I'm not interested in anything more than writing the book," I lied again.

"Then, tell you what. Get yourself an office, a typewriter, sexy secretary, and stay there and write."

Didn't sound half bad.

"I wonder you'd answer me one question—as this writer—before I go investing in offices and secretaries. Did you know Barbara Aronson from before? Or is this a new association?"

"Go back to your table; this conversation is over," he replied. I don't think it was much of an answer. Or maybe it was.

"I don't suppose you'd like to talk about sending Heather Hansen to the Ermitage?" For what reason I can't imagine, I took a shot.

He turned eggplant on me, which I think would go very nice with a couple the pastas they had on the menu.

"On my way," I said, and rose. Looking down the top of his head, I saw there was a lot of lost hair there. Made me feel good somehow. Then I broken-fielded my way back to my table, just as Francie returned from the ladies'.

I held her chair, then eased down on my sunbaked one. "So, you wanna order?" I asked.

"Just, maybe a salad," she answered, taking out a pocket mirror and checking her nostrils in the light for any lingering traces of Peruvian marching powder. "I'm not hungry."

"I guess not," I said. She couldn't not know about drugs and pregnancy. This wasn't going to be easy.

The waiter came and I ordered her a salad and me some lime-grilled chicken. I wasn't feeling that adventurous.

I watched as Heather and Barbara came back to Nash's table.

"Did you and the girls exchange any gossip?" I asked

Francie. She just shook her head. Euphoria seemed to have escaped her this time, as she looked more pinch-mouthed and depressed. It didn't seem the time to have any significant conversations.

I nodded at the waiter, circling my drink.

"Momento," he said. But after a couple momentos, instead of a refill brought over a bottle of wine.

"Compliments of *señor*," he said, indicating Nash—who gave me another slit-smile—then whipped the bottle into a presentation mode, showing me the label. It read "BACIO DI MORTE."

"Do you happen to know what that means?" I asked, figuring the Spanish was probably close to Italian. But he merely gave me a blank stare, which was the Mexican equivalent of an Italian shrug, or an American actual answer.

"You don't know," I interpreted that to mean.

"I do," said Francie, whose last name, after all, was Rizetti. "It's 'Kiss of Death.' "

What a swell name for a wine.

14

Mark Bradley

We whoopee-bused to Long Beach, thence by boat midway to Catalina Island, during the former of which I got nicely pebbled (it wasn't long enough to get stoned), and during the latter picked up a nasty burn (plenty of life preservers; not one little tube of sunblock). Somewhere along the line, the ashes of Claudio Fortunata got scattered to the four winds, at least one of which was blowing back in our faces. Not my most pleasant moment.

Properly somber out, the mood changed abruptly once the celebrated director had been consigned to the deep— or, in this case, the shallow, since ashes at first float. After imbibing in several toasts to "the irrepressible Claudio" (who, it seemed to me had been pretty efficiently *re*pressed) there had followed some agitation to continue on to Catalina and make a day of it. "In tribute to his spirit," as one of the ex-wives, Ginny, put it. But Vernon Charles had scotched that idea since there was lots of re-pre-production work yet to be done on *One Fell Swoop*, and just so much time you could in all fairness to the company that employed you devote to paying your respects to someone no longer pulling his corporate weight. Several of the late director's progeny found this an inadequate reason for cutting short the festivities, and manifested their objection by attempting to set fire to the boat. It would seem they were no more adept at self-restraint than their father had been. The captain, apparently well versed in juvenile high jinks, damped both the fire and the kids with a short burst of extinguisher foam, and proceeded to head the boat back to shore with all the limited knots at his disposal.

I hadn't really learned a whole lot (except that one should more fully test the wind before scattering, etc.), and my nose was a cherry red from exposure. It was, theoretically, a good place to start the book. But in practice Claudio

hadn't been much the focus, barring the few moments he was
actually being dispatched. The ladies (his exes) appeared on
friendly enough terms with one another. Though bereft of
Fortunata, they seemed to find common solace in the fact
they'd be partially compensated by a future of enhanced financial security. Based on identical promises made to each, I'd
managed to learn. All seemed able to take their loss brave-
spiritedly—increasingly as the afternoon and the toasts wore
on. Similarly the others not related by blood or divorce.

Then I noticed Maurissa in whispered conference with
Terry, and assumed it involved an assignation ("Ever hear
of the sea-level club?") except that instead of reaching for
her body parts, he slipped her a package. Somehow (guilt?)
my presence announced itself, both suddenly noticing I was
witness to this transaction. They exchanged a few terse words,
after which Maurissa headed off in the other direction and
Terry crossed to my side, offering an Isuzu of a smile by way
of establishing a sudden newfound desire for friendship.

"Hi, there, what's doing, Marvin?" he said.

"Mark," I explained, looking over his shoulder at the
departing Maurissa.

"Say, listen, you write books. It must be great."

"Great."

"You make them up."

"Right."

"It just comes to you, Marvin?"

"Mark." He was so transparent, my interest was now
more fully engaged than ever. I'd been stalled enough.

"You'll excuse me, Jerry—"

"Terry."

"But I don't feel so good, and I don't want to barf on
your shoes."

It seemed pretty clear he didn't want me to barf on his
shoes, either.

"Italian, right, Jerry?"

"Right," he allowed, quickly stepping back. "It's Terry."

"Catch you later," I mumbled in apparent distress, heading
for the rail, and given a wide berth by Terry. It was, of course,
a feint. I then quickly hurried to the other side of the ship,
where behind a lifeboat Maurissa was emptying a brown paper
bag over the side. I'd gotten there just in time to observe how
beautifully the afternoon sun glinted off the barrel of the nickel-
plated gun she was dropping into the sea.

* * *

"Which is about the last anybody's going to see of the murder weapon," Goodman said in response to my recounting of the day's activities. He was driving the loaner Toyota, with Francine beside him, after picking me up on my return from the strewing. With my nose burning and my legs all cramped from over an hour in a backseat clearly designed for short, bow legs, I was not in the best of humors. Add to that we'd been circling the parking lot of Hughes market in Beverly Hills for going on ten minutes, and you get the picture.

The reason we were circling all this while was (the gospel, according to Goodman) the architects, in their wisdom, had failed to plan for anything approaching adequate parking when designing the facility. Well, actually, there had been talk of a two-story lot, but some technical impediment— like inadequate bribery—had somehow precluded this. The result was an extremely popular store with totally inadequate parking.

"So," repeated Goodman, "Maurissa dumped what's most probably the murder weapon."

"One would have to suppose it was more than an indifference to pollution," I agreed.

"Plus, with Terry trying to stop you seeing Maurissa deep-sixing the gun, you've got several interesting options. Either Terry knew Maurissa did the murder and was helping her—"

"Or Maurissa did it and convinced Terry she hadn't but there was another reason for dumping the gun."

"Or," continued Goodman, still circling, "Terry did it and she's helping him cover up."

We mulled that for a bit as Goodman continued looking for a parking spot. "One coming up," he said, establishing a road block—and incidentally holding up a long line of other cars also circling—behind a woman loading her car with several bags of stuff. "You go on ahead. This'll take awhile."

"We can wait with you," I said. "Shouldn't be long."

"You kidding? She's gonna first take a month and a half to load, then get in, belt up, put on a whole new batch of makeup, light a cigarette, and choose from a collection of tapes to play. *Then* she's going to decide to start the car and find she doesn't have the keys. So she'll have to unbuckle her seat belt, open the door, get out, look around and on top and under, and eventually go back to the trunk, where she'll have left them in the lock."

"Boy, you're really cynical," I said.

"Besides, I hate supermarkets, with the goddamn carts always going around in circles. Why can't they for chrissakes make carts with front wheels stay in alignment? Then you do your shopping and get in line back of a woman's only got about four items and turns out she's also got eight thousand coupons, a three-party check, and a damaged can from last time she wants credit for the manager's going to have to okay—"

"Hey, we're out of here," said Francine as we both popped out quickly, trying not to acknowledge our association with the man in the Toyota, now the brunt of angry horn honking and finger flicking as the people in the other cars somehow held Goodman co-culpable for the hangup. I sneaked a look back, and son of a gun the woman *was* getting out of her car and looking for keys which *were* in the trunk. Justifiable homicide.

Ever the soul of equanimity, Francine had meanwhile managed to roll a joint the size of Managua and taken a few giant sized tokes.

I looked back to see if Goodman had observed this breach of the Agreed Rules of Conduct. But he hadn't noticed, being too busy finally working his way into the slot at long last vacated by the winner of the West Coast Leona Helmsley Sensitivity Award. "I thought you weren't going to do this anymore."

"True, but I've been under a lot of stress lately, and after a lot of soul-searching and stash remembering, I decided keeping my word was a teense less important than my sanity."

"Uh-huh," I allowed. "However, I was under the further impression that there were medical considerations involved, like a blessed event being somehow different from a blissed-out event," I continued as we approached the entrance.

Hughes, while advertising itself as one of the price-busting, money-saving supermarkets, had almost as a challenge to conspicuous consumption established itself in Beverly Hills (opposite Chasen's yet), a very viable alternative to the more costly Chalet Gourmet, Gelsen's, or Jurgensen's. Hughes was both cheap and chic, and you can't hardly get that combo no more, which is another reason why you also could hardly ever find parking space.

Just outside the door, a carefully coiffed blond but painfully overweight woman sat overflowing a folding chair in front of a bridge table, on which rested whatever of her weight the chair couldn't accommodate and a box of some sort. Francine immediately headed over.

"Where're you going?" I asked her.

"To sign the petition."

"How do you know what it's for?"

"Whatever it's for, I'm on their side. You don't see a bunch of reactionaries hanging around collecting signatures to get the capital gains tax reduced. It's a worthy cause, take my word."

"Automatically?"

"Automatically."

We walked over. Francine looked for the petition, but there was no paper in evidence.

"What's it for, what're you doing?" she asked.

"It's to find homes."

"Ah, for the homeless."

"For these kittens," the woman replied, indicating the box atop the table in which a litter of mewing baby cats to no great surprise presented an endearing sight.

"Ah, cats," said Francine. "I thought it was a charity thing."

"It's cats," said the woman. "Free." Naturally free. The only ones who ever paid for kittens were divorced fathers in mall pet shops during their weekends of tot custody and guilt-alleviation.

"Well, good luck," said Francine as we passed the woman and entered the store, at the door of which she turned for one last look. "You don't suppose that's Doris Day?"

"Not likely," I replied. "I think Doris Day's the one who kept her looks."

We went through the turnstile and over to a stack of carts jammed together so tightly it took our combined efforts to extricate one. I tested it—wheels pulled to the right—tried another, same difference. (Did they actually manufacture them that way? Or was it just material for frustration on behalf of the Rayford Goodman in us all? God, was the guy right—about life, about the awfulness of it all? You did have to wonder why a country that could put men on the moon . . .) The good news was he hadn't caught up with us yet, and we didn't have to listen to his tirade about it.

I told Francine about how crappy it was going with Brian. She told me it was mostly okay with Goodman, but the pregnancy wasn't a complication she was too thrilled with. And she hadn't a clue what he thought about it. I suggested she ask him. She suggested I go do unto myself.

Meanwhile I kept piling stuff into the cart, fighting the pull to the right (always the right), and she kept dumping stuff in as well.

"Just a passing thought," I said, trying to remember which was hers and which was mine. "How're we going to know whose is whose and how much is what?"

"To each according to his need, from each according to his ability to pay. You take what you need, I'll take what I need, and we'll charge the whole shmear to the book."

She spent another few moments sort of examining Pampers and talcum powders and baby oils. (In a more perfect world, these would be displayed next to diaphragms and condoms, *I* would think.) I decided not to comment. Apparently the nesting instinct in action. Though Francine as mother earth constituted rather offbeat casting, to my view. It was about then the object of this speculation gave a head-canting pantomime indication I was to look down the next aisle, where lo and whatever were to be seen dowdy amanuensis Barbara Aronson apparently co-shopping with Amazonian agent Claire Miller.

"Now, that's a pair of strange bedfellows," I allowed.

"*You*'re talking?"

"Well, actually on second thought, I certainly figured Claire to be a dyke."

"But Barbara? I thought she was supposed to be one of Claudio's exes."

"It's not mutually exclusive," I replied. Which was when something struck their mutual fancy and they burst out laughing, followed by the gargantuan Claire engulfing Babs in an obviously significant hug.

Observing the same, Francine remarked, "Maybe she's what they mean by bi and large."

I gave that the silence it deserved. "At least they don't seem to be suffering inordinately over the loss of Claudio. Should we say hello, do you think?"

"I'm not feeling all that social," she replied. "Let's get this over and get out of here." So we finished loading the cart, made the Goodman-predicted disastrous choice of checkout counter—the one with only two customers before us, the second of which it developed did have eight thousand coupons, a two-party check, and wanted credit for the return of a dented can of hearts of palm. Probably wouldn't take more than half an hour.

I was more or less congratulating myself for my patience, enduring all this with a semblance of good humor, plus being enormously grateful Goodman had evidently elected to stay in the car, when Francine took out a pill, popped open a can of Classic Coca-Cola to wash it down, reached into her stash, pulled out a joint, and lit up.

With her customary good luck, none of this activity drew the notice of anyone in authority (in a place where you couldn't even smoke cigarettes!). Legal jeopardy aside, however, I couldn't help asking, "Why, oh why, when you know what's going on, when you've read the literature and can't help but be aware how dangerous this sort of thing is to a fetus, do you persist in this outrageous and totally irresponsible behavior?"

She rummaged through her bag, found yet another pill to engage her interest, popped it, washed it down, and in a cold, steely voice replied, "Because, you stupid asshole, given my age and history with drugs, you can't for a minute seriously think I'm going to risk bringing a baby into this world with that kind of chance of paying for my dissipations!"

"Oh," I said, since from her anger alone I knew this decision hadn't come without a considerable measure of regret. "Oh. Right. Oh."

"I just went to too many parties where I was the only guest," she added quietly.

And finally the woman in front of us finished cashing in all her coupons, and got her credit, and located her checkbook, and borrowed a pen, and was informed of the date, and wrote the check, and got her ID verified, and actually concluded her transaction. Which made it our turn.

"Plastic or paper?" asked the bagboy.

"Plastic," I said, trying not to think about the non-biodegradable world we were passing on to future generations.

And he packed all the stuff, and I paid the bill, and we went outside—and Francine took a kitten from the fat lady.

"Rosemary Clooney," she said. "That's who I was thinking of."

15

Rayford Goodman

Bradley and I were standing in the parking lot of Hughes market, me with a small cat in my hands—with very sharp claws for such a tiny person. The reason we were standing, we couldn't sit in the car. Because when you sat in your car the people who were circling around looking for a place to park figured you were just about to pull out. And got really pissed when you didn't. The reason we were hanging around altogether, Francie had to go back in the store to get kitty litter and a turkey fry pan to put the litter in and a bunch of cat food. I judged from all the squirming and complaining this was a cat seriously hungry. Given the time it took to get through the checkout line at Hughes, I figured the little guy faced a life-threatening situation. For my part I certainly wasn't thrilled holding a howling banshee in the hot summer sun in a baking parking lot. Not exactly my decision, though I'd no doubt have to live with the consequences. That tended to happen when you were involved with someone, I was being reminded.

"So what do you do now?" said Bradley, pulling me back from Philosophy I.

I knew he wasn't talking about the pussycat.

"Well, I've got your basic dilemma," I answered. "Looks like Maurissa and/or Terry, for whatever reason, killed Claudio."

"Which, if you could prove it, would be good for the book."

"But which, if I could prove it, might not be good for me, since it'd tend to irritate Cifelli, who wants, hired, and threatened me to find Nash did it."

"Still and all, we're dealing with a biography whose subject was murdered. Solving the murder can't help but make it more successful."

"Yeah, and if one or both the co-authors gets murdered, too, wouldn't that sell a lot more books?"

"You mean if it turns out Maurissa and/or Terry did it, and we said so, Cifelli would really . . . do something drastic?"

"You don't begin to know drastic till you cross one of those guys. You forget already he kidnapped you once just to annoy me? Believe me, not a good move."

"I do think we should first make sure it was Maurissa or Terry. After all, it could still be Nash somehow. It was Nash's hit-girl Heather Hansen who killed Cohen at the Ermitage."

He was right, of course. Not that I was all that thrilled at the prospect gaining Nash for a lifelong enemy, either. He was another one of those guys "lifelong" had a way being less than nature intended. But the fact was, either/or, Bradley was right—I'd have to find out. After would be time enough to decide what to do about it.

As we waited for Francine, and the kitty cat tested just how deep it could drive its nails in my hand, to my surprise, Claire Miller and Barbara Aronson came out together. Bradley clued me how they'd spotted the girls being clubby and figured they had a thing going. I had my doubts. Like most gay people, I found, he liked to believe the whole world was gay. Even if they didn't know it. Even if they spent all their waking hours making out with someone of the opposite sex. Especially.

On the other hand, Claire *was* wearing a very large wristwatch. Each carrying a couple bags of groceries, they headed for a Corniche parked in a corner by the Goodwill bins. Didn't seem likely anybody'd mistake the Rolls for a donation.

"Look at that," said Bradley, pointing his chin at the license plate.

I saw it read "FILMER." "Most probably Fortunata's, right?"

"I gather they're not letting sentimentality stand in the way of utilizing his things," Bradley noted as we watched them get in, Claire behind the wheel. The car belonging to Barbara's ex-boss, you'd expect she'd be driving. Unless, of course, Claire was the mister of the combination.

They drove off without spotting us. Then Francie came back out, carrying the load of cat stuff, and she and Bradley piled into the Toyota. I peeled the cat off my flesh, handed it to Francie, and got in myself (driver's side, being the mister).

"Tell you what," I said. "It's a little after four. I'd like to have another go at Barbara before we connect up with Hampton at the Lance and Mace—"

"Whip and Surrey," corrected Bradley. I knew that.

"Where do you want me to drop you guys?"

"Are you saying you want me to take the cat to *my* apartment?" said Francie.

"Did I say that? I didn't say that. Why do women read in meanings?"

"Well, isn't the first thing to get the cat settled in?"

"Yeah, I guess that's the first thing."

"So, do you want me to take it to my place or yours?"

"Hey, my place, naturally. After all these years waiting for just the right cat, you kidding?"

Heavy looks. Tippy-toe, buddy—booby traps out there. I eased on the ignition.

"Mark, you don't mind if we stop there first before he drops you off?" said Francie.

"Not at all," said Bradley, the two of them talking to each other but talking to me. "Or I could go along to interview Barbara," he added to her to me.

"Let me take a shot alone. You already tried," I reminded him. "Besides, I'm only assuming they'll wind up back at Fortunata's. Might not."

"More likely they'll be in the Blue Moon Motel locked in a libidinous embrace," said Bradley with a touch of enthusiasm.

I didn't answer. Just let it lay—so to speak. I backed out of the space and headed off, real slow. Getting out of Hughes market was almost as hard as getting in. You had to get in line with the people trying to get in in order to get to the place where they were trying to get out. Maybe it was time to check out the Irvine Ranch market. I eventually got to the in-and-out driveway to Doheny, took an out, hung a right, and drove on up to my house in the hills. I helped them unload the stuff and carry it into the house. Bradley said he'd hang around with Francie and work on the book at the house, which I could see meant play with the kitty cat.

So what I did then, I got out the phone book and looked

up the address of the Whip and Surrey—under cutesy. I didn't want any surprises. So Bradley and I made up to meet in what I teased him was the Moat and Portcullis parking lot ten minutes before our appointment with Hampton. Then I went back outside, got back in the awful Toyota, and headed off toward Beverly Hills.

I did think she could of asked did I want a cat.

My plan was to question Barbara, who, next to Maurissa and Terry, was certainly one of the hottest suspects. First being demoted to Fortunata's ex-girlfriend (the woman scorned); second being named in his will (the woman profiting); and third, with all that at stake, passing on both the funeral and the ash strewing (the woman showing a lot of hard feelings). Whether being "that way" with Claire added or took away from the above was another thing I'd have to sound her out on. All the same, just as I was about a block and a half shy of Benedict Canyon, I couldn't help feeling the timing was wrong. Either she wouldn't be there yet, or be there with Claire, which'd make getting anything out of her either impossible or at least a whole lot less likely. So instead I made a quick turn up the driveway to the Beverly Hills Hotel. It was a potential embarrassment being seen in the Toyota. On the other hand, in this part of town it lent you a kind of invisibility. Besides, I wouldn't be expected to tip all that much, either. Every cloud and all that.

So now I had something like two and a half plus hours to kill before meeting Bradley in the parking lot of the Crossbow and Dildo. In order to make sure I didn't waste my time, I went to the bar in the Polo Lounge. A bartender with a hi-tech manicure laid a cocktail napkin before me and raised an eyebrow. I guess he didn't figure he had any speaking lines. To my surprise I found myself telling him I'd have a Tanqueray Sterling in a tall glass and a small bottle of Schweppes club soda. (With Perrier a suicide, I hadn't yet settled on a chic seltzer.)

It was time to stop lurching around and start organizing. I did have to solve this thing, so I better have some kind of plan. First I took a fortifying sip of the Sterling. I hadn't poured the Schweppes in yet because I wanted to be sure it was Sterling—life had really gotten complicated when they started making vodkas with flavor. Then I took out a little pad and Cross pen Luana'd once given me. After another taste (maybe you didn't really need the Schweppes, after all) I made a list of everybody I knew connected with Fortunata some way or other. The list looked like this:

Barbara Aronson, right-hand "man"—or whatever
Claire Miller, the agent, and/or
Terry Coyne and Maurissa Burroughs, the stars
Armand Cifelli and Barry Nash—the gangster guys
Heather Hansen, Nash's rod-Friday
Nigel Hampton, Fortunata's actor/butler
Vernon Charles, the producer
Harvey Pitkin, the writer
Freddie Forbes, the set designer
Laszlo Nagy, Fortunata's cameraman
Billy Zee, the resident gofer
A couple ex-wives
And the late Hamilton Cohen, Fortunata's
stand-in for murder.
(There has to be a book with *that* title.)

It seemed to me likely one of the above was the guilty party. At least the list was a reasonable place to start.

If it was only the first murder, Cohen, I'd be pretty much inclined to suspect the professionals: Cifelli, Nash, or Hansen. That'd been fairly clean, bullets to the head, .22's, and barring that they got the wrong guy, a pretty workmanlike job. But it hadn't stopped at that. There'd been the second, and successful, job on Fortunata. Only this one sloppy. So unless you go a lot of weight to the idea of two separate killers (which I definitely didn't want to deal with) you had to figure instead that the killer ran into some problem with number two he/she wasn't equipped to handle. Or the circumstances were different.

It was too much of a coincidence for it to be anything but done by the same person, with clearly Fortunata the target both times. At L'Ermitage when they got Cohen, what was he—a post-operation guy, mostly covered by bandages, no doubt weak. Maybe full of painkillers. Not likely to put up much of a fight. Especially he didn't know what was coming. But Fortunata, by the time the killer got to him, was much further into recovery. He had the bandages off, was out of the facility, and already back on the job. More or less recovered. So you go take him, he's going to fight back—hard. Plus, being .22's, according to the autopsy, it could easy take more than one to stop him. Given same caliber, too, in both cases, made it another reason to figure two murders, one killer. Plus make a note, check was it the same gun?

But who?

So now, having made a list of everyone with a possible motive to kill Fortunata, I decided to visit one who wasn't on it and likely didn't.

I told the bartender to set 'em up again, minus the Schweppes, and to mind my seat while I went to make a call. I walked out to the hallway and around to the phones. I got the book and took a shot.

The Beverly Hills phone directory didn't list Hamilton Cohen. The Beverly Hills phone directory hardly listed the phone company. Most people never even tried the phone directory. Who'd want to talk to anybody *listed*? Long shot.

Not that finding Cohen's home address was going to be tough. I could get it, from for example, the B.H.P.D. report on his murder (which would require a favor from a place where I'm not a favorite). Or there'd be a record at L'Ermitage. Also take a little doing. Though I'd hardly mind a face-to-face with that gorgeous Tiffany person ran the place, even it wasn't too likely she'd violate celebrity confidentiality. There was also the DMV (which always sounded like a Russian secret police) but chances were anybody rich enough to be face-lifted to L'Ermitage would be mindful of security and have a business address on his license. So that left me with two other easy choices to find it. Likely he'd been buried out of a Jewish mortuary. Find the right one and I could no doubt promote the info. The yellow pages helped with Star of David logos, plus on the nose names like Mount Sinai and Malinow-Silverman. But I got a feeling asking the ethnic question would be a little embarrassing. Anyway, is a Jewish mortuary one owned by a Jew, or one who buries Jews, and/or either? By the time I had that many second thoughts, it was pass on that method.

I went back in to make sure my drink hadn't disappeared, got a handful of change, took another swig, and headed back out again. Time to put my alternate plan into action. Lord knows there were a lot of expensive florists in the neighborhood. But it only took a couple tries to establish David Jones somewhere around top of the list. They were the only ones totally disinterested in quoting a price over the phone. So I figured they were a good bet.

I finished off the drink, left a sizable tip. That may surprise you, but I figured I'd used up the guy's space and he was entitled to it. Besides, the difference between usual and sizable was only a buck. Not that he thanked me. Maybe he was a mute. And left.

Outside I left a usual tip (what I figured for a Toyota) and *got* a thanks. Go figure. Then I went to David Jones. At the shop I selected a tasteful arrangement of broken twigs, two pebbles, and half a bird's nest. I plopped down the hundred and ten and told them to deliver it to the Hamilton Cohen house, and quickly split. No one chased me to get the address, so I knew I'd struck pay dirt. It only took half an hour before they'd booked enough orders to make a run.

I followed their truck make two false starts (a bouquet with "HAPPY BIRTHDAY, MELINDA" on a Mylar balloon hanging over it, and one perfect rose to the apartment of a Hortense Marsh, odds on from a guy who'd got lucky last night). The third delivery was to a substantial house on Dalehurst in Westwood, just this side of UCLA, with what seemed more than an average number of cars parked out front. (Not all Beverly Hills people live in Beverly Hills.) After I found a spot far enough away to hide the Toyota and headed back, I saw the florist's van driving off. So this was either it, or I was out a hundred ten bucks without passing Go.

I could hear a lot of activity inside, so when nobody answered the bell, I tried the door, found it open, and invited myself in.

There was a large entry hall featuring a grand staircase, on which lots of people sat, bleacher-style, eating, drinking, and socializing. To one side of the stairs was a table, on which were several arrangements of flowers, at the end of which had been jammed a familiar set of twigs, pebbles, and bird's nest parts. To the left was the living room—tended bar in the corner, I noted—and to the right, an entry into I guess a family room. I made a courtesy stop at the bar. In order to gain the confidence of the bartender, I forced myself to have two drinks before asking him to identify the widow for me. He said he didn't see her at the moment. I had another drink so he wouldn't get suspicious—letting him figure me for a freeloader instead of a terrorist. The sacrifices you have to make in this business. I noticed, to my surprise, in a far corner, the ex-writer on Fortunata's picture, Harvey Pitkin, dressed in about fifteen dollars worth of used clothes, unsuccessfully trying to convince a starlet type he really was a successful writer. Evidently she hadn't been in town long enough to know they all looked like that. I wandered into the family room, where a whole lot more eating and drinking was going on—and got a second shock when I saw the set designer, Freddie Forbes, looking to be comparing Retin A results with another of his ilk. What gives? Picture people weren't the sort who'd be paying their respects to a casual civilian stepped in front of a bullet. Weird. But no one seemed to be featured here, so I continued reconnoitering, looking for the widow Cohen. I followed several more people crowding into a dining room. No special candidate seemed to stand out there, either. What I couldn't help noticing, it wasn't a particularly grim gathering. Lots of chatter, no subdued voices—more than occasional laughter. (How quickly they forget.) Everything was seriously lavish and expensive. An incredible amount of fresh flowers and smoked fish. From the looks of the buffet table there were going to be a lot of new mink coats in Nova Scotia this year.

There were a surprising lot of people. Especially inasmuch as old Ham had been buried going on five days ago and this wasn't a memorial service, per se. I learned in casual conversation with a rather attractive prematurely blond matron it was an ongoing "shiva" being sat. She also informed me that not being a member of the family her grief didn't extend to giving up dating. I took her number. I find taking numbers is a lot easier than explaining you aren't interested. She made me promise I'd call. I don't know why she thought a person who didn't want to call would just because he was bullied into promising. Especially since there were some other very attractive women there— many without cream cheese on their upper lips, too. Given the chic and well-attended turnout, it was beginning to look like the late Hamilton Cohen wasn't just some shnooky C.P.A. with terrible luck.

In a corner, another really great-looking woman I'd seen at Fortunata's funeral was talking to a small group. I edged over where I could listen, and get an unobstructed view of her breasts.

"But, Jennifer," another winner was saying to her, "which one do you choose? There're so many."

"All the animal-protection groups are good. But I like PETA best—they identify which companies are testing on animals, and they're into lobbying for more humane animal farming."

I decided I wouldn't mind farming at least one or two of these young animals—humanely, of course.

Jennifer. I remembered, that was Vernon's wife. Surprise, surprise.

"I really respect all the time and effort you spend on the animals," said her great-looking friend.

"Well, you know when Fluffy was murdered . . ." I could see her eyes fill with tears. "It's still so hard, after all this time."

"Anybody would do that sort of thing to a cat . . ." said the friend.

"I just vowed," continued Jennifer bravely, "to make something positive out of it. And, well—there you are."

There we were. So, moving right along . . .

Beyond the dining room, the kitchen was full of people, too. There were lots of guests in the way of some very busy catering folks, who were evidently used to it. And finally, in the center of all this action, another dynamite-looking woman in a very tight black dress that looked to set a new trend in mourning Lambada-wear, was what had to be the elusive Mrs. Cohen. She was a hot-face little number, clearly dealing well with her grief. I had a flash remembering the note in Cohen's room at the Ermitage and decided to cast my vote for Sherry over Shirley. When I finally managed to tear my eyes away from Sherry/Shirley I found to my surprise that the other person she was noshing nicely with was, of all people, Laszlo Nagy.

This hundred and ten dollar hunch seemed to be paying off.

16

Mark Bradley

I really intended to work on the book. But even after the usual work-avoidance stuff—playing with the kitten, reorganizing my address book, cutting my fingernails, updating and revising my list of "must do—urgent" matters to "quite urgent," "tremendously urgent," "not a minute to spare," and "too late"—I still wasn't ready to work. Mostly, I hadn't a sense of structure. It was one thing to do a biography of a living subject, and another of a deceased, and still quite another of a deceased murder victim, the latter subcategorized further into murder/solved and murder/unsolved. I just simply didn't know enough to determine how to proceed.

Alternatively, I didn't want to go home, because Brian would probably be there and we were fast approaching a time when we'd have to have a talk. Given that at no time in the past had a talk yielded any results whatsoever, other than to intensify my feelings of frustration and alienation, this was not a prospect, either, to which I looked forward with any degree of equanimity. Yet I couldn't just let him proceed with a life that was destructive of my own without at least registering a protest. But in my heart of hearts I dreaded it. The last thing I wanted was a severance of our relationship.

The next-to-last thing was to continue kidding myself.

But I didn't want to stay where I was because Francine's company was about as much fun as a root canal. Oh, I'd be willing to suffer it, were I doing her any good. But it was all touchy ground. And of course, except in the way all human experience is communal, unfamiliar.

So I wasn't exactly distressed when Goodman phoned, offering diversion.

"Guess where I am," he said archly.

I'd be willing to lay odds against a gay bathhouse.

"At Hamilton Cohen's house."

That surprised me.

"Together with, get this, Harvey Pitkin, Freddie Forbes, Jennifer Charles, Laszlo Nagy, and a cast of thousands."

That surprised me even more.

"So you have to ask yourself, why are all these people, only a couple hours back from the funeral of their ex-boss, here sitting *shiva* with the widow of a guy we thought of as just someone happened to be the wrong place at the wrong time."

You had to, indeed. *Shiva*?

"And what it turned out, best I could find out eavesdropping and snooping, the late Hamilton Cohen seems to've had an interest in an enterprise called Fortaco."

"The Fortunata Company? How big an interest?"

"Well, start with the *co* in Fortaco wasn't 'company'—it was *co* like in Cohen."

That big an interest.

"And watching these big-time celebrity folks falling all over each other to kiss up to the widow Cohen, I can't help feeling it's an ongoing interest."

Fascinating.

"So what I want, before you meet me at the Beef and Barf, is to get Francie doing her computer thing. I want to know exactly how involved they were—talking Fortunata and Cohen. And whatever else she can come up with about Fortaco. Chances are it's a California corporation—"

"In which case, I'm sure Francine will be able to tap in."

There was, you should pardon the expression, a pregnant pause. Whether prompted by Francine's name, I couldn't say.

Then Goodman continued, "The main thing is, I'm sure you catch on—we all just assumed Cohen was some kind of outsider. Killed by mistake—"

"And now we find out he's an insider, very possibly killed on purpose!"

"That's what *we* found out," he reminded me, defensively proprietary.

"I'll have to remember that—when *we* write the book," I responded, an unworthy riposte, pettily petulant. Except considering how much he continually pissed me off.

*   *   *

Francine managed to tear herself away from the kitten—a feisty little reddish-blond heartbreaker she'd named Sven—and promptly went to work on her powerful Compaq laptop. I took the opportunity to scout Goodman's bathroom for something to soothe my seriously sunburned nose.

There were two bottles of never used cologne (probably gifts), a can of assorted Band-Aids (clear—a no doubt masterful solution to the old flesh-colored dilemma now that enough blacks had money to bleed), Listerine, Bromo-Seltzer, aspirin, razor, shaving cream, styptic pencil (I didn't know they still made them), and toothpaste and brush. It was somehow touchingly spare. And of course nothing for a sunburned nose.

By the time I sauntered back to the patio, Francine had already done a bit of rabbit pulling. Judging from the smile on her face, which had been sorely missed lo, these many . . .

"And what have the eleven magic fingers of computerville come up with?" I asked.

"California corporation. Fortaco the parent company."

"Aha, which begat?"

"Several entities, most of which I recognize as titles of former Claudio pictures. The one I think you'd be most interested in right now is called 'Fellswoopy.' They're often cute. This is a corporation organized for the purpose, quel surprise, of producing a motion picture entitled *One Fell Swoop*. It is vague about financial origins, but structured very specifically about the distribution of profits."

"How do you find out all this stuff?"

"It's public record, this part's not even sneaky."

She constantly amazed me. I was certainly a child of the computer generation—I'd never even *used* a typewriter—but her knowledge of where to go and how to go verged on the miraculous, it seemed to me. But then again, maybe that's why she was a professional researcher.

"You wanna hear?"

"I wanna hear."

"Fifty percent of the company is owned by Claudio and Cohen, sixty-forty. Of the other fifty percent, ten goes to Terry, starring; ten to Maurissa, co-starring, two point five to Vernon Charles, producing; two point five to Laszlo Nagy, cinematographing—"

"That's interesting. I wouldn't think the cameraman would rate points."

". . . and the final twenty-five percent to Sorrento Ventures."

Sorrento, Sorrento—where'd I heard that? That sounded familiar. Hm.

"The money for Terry, Maurissa, Vernon, and Laszlo is contingent on credit," she continued.

"Meaning there has to be public agreement they performed the duties for which they were hired."

"Right."

"And of course, weren't fired or quit meantime."

"Or got murdered."

"Or got murdered. You said Terry, Maurissa, Vernon, and Laszlo."

"The above-the-line folks. Talent."

Twenty-five percent for talent. Not excessive.

"And what happens," I wondered, "if someone doesn't get on-screen credit?"

"His or her share stays in the pool, either to be assigned to a replacement or if they get a replacement they don't have to share it with, then it's divvied up pro rata."

"What about Cohen, he doesn't get credit."

"The split between Cohen and Claudio isn't part of that. I think theirs is theirs, no matter."

"There must be some provision for death."

"That's a good title—Provision for Death. Yeah, there is," said Francine. "Survivors pro rata."

The Whip and Surrey didn't offer a whole lot of surprises. It was more pub than club, but a little of each, and seemed to be fashioned almost entirely of leather and brass. It all but shouted, "We're Bullish on John." In addition to prints of English gentlemen at sport, and English gentlemen roguishly engaging the attention of sundry over-endowed wenches, there were signed photographs of the likes of Basil Rathbone, David Niven, Alan Mowbray, and Cedric Hardwicke (what a name!), attesting to its popularity during the Great English Actors Invasion of the thirties and forties.

As planned, I'd met Goodman in the parking lot. Actually, I'd had to wait, as he'd parked elsewhere—some blocks elsewhere—being morally committed to not paying for parking if he could help it. There was something there in the parking lot that disconcerted me. But I just couldn't put my finger on it. What? What? But before I could figure out what it was, a breathless Goodman had labored up, ranting and raving over a sell-out government that gave bums and idlers all sorts of money or parole, enabling them to buy or steal all the cars taking up the space he needed to park in. I managed, finally, to turn our attention to a topic of possible mutual interest, namely what strategy we ought to pursue in our forthcoming interview with Nigel Hampton. He'd evidently given thought to that, as he had an answer prepared. To wit: "Just let me do the talkin'." If I was going to do the writing, I was going to do at least some of the talking, but I reasoned there was no great point in belaboring that prematurely.

We'd settled down at the bar, facing a mirror through which we could see various middle-aged types with clearly ruinous blood pressures evident on Englishly rosy cheeks partaking of tankards of, presumably, beer or ale (though given the surroundings, mead was not totally out of the question).

The raucous crowd was apparently still in the throes of Jolly Hour, and Hampton was twenty minutes late.

Goodman ordered us a drink and brought me further up to date on all that had transpired at Chez Cohen. For my part, I told him what Francine had discovered vis-à-vis the Fortaco and Fellswoopy Corps. Before I'd left she'd gotten a printout on the amended articles of incorporation which substitued Atlas Enterprises for Sorrento Ventures as the third major shareholder. Nash for Cifelli, Goodman surmised.

That took us through a second vodka soda and another ten minutes. And still no Hampton.

"He ought to be here," said Goodman, checking his watch. "It's half after plus thirty—or sixty after."

"Not coming," I said.

"Sure he is. He's the one wanted the meeting."

"I told you. Anybody who says, 'The name of the murderer is . . .'—in Hollywood—is not going to make it to the closing credits."

"He'll be here," insisted Goodman as another round of drinks appeared magically before us which I hadn't seen him order. Raised his eyebrow or something. Make a hell of a silent bidder at Sotheby's.

"The, uh," he continued, ". . . survivor situation."

"Between Claudio and Cohen."

"Yeah."

"Don't know. Francine's looking, but doesn't seem to be on whatever it is she's reading."

"Barbara," said Goodman. "She'd know. Or Claire Miller, the agent."

"Ah?" I suddenly thought—does that make them strange bedfellows besides being strange bedfellows? Maybe.

"We'll have to look into that."

We retired to mutual corners to mull those probabilities, and finished our drinks, waiting a total of an hour and fifteen minutes—long after I knew it was no-show.

Finally Goodman relented. "OK, he's not coming," he admitted, handing me the check.

"What's this?"

"Isn't it charge account? On the book? Research."

"Three drinks each, research?"

"Sounds about right."

"You've got a lot to learn about your publisher."

In the end we divvied it up, got up, headed toward the parking lot. I cracked the door, held it open for Goodman.

"Thanks," he said, and stepped out into the lot. He turned to say something to me when I heard a pop, pop, pop—and maybe one more pop—after the first of which Goodman had already grabbed me and pulled me to the pavement, falling on top. Jesus Christ, were those bullets?

We waited a moment or two. I could hear his labored breathing above me—even over my own, supporting his two hundred pounds of beefy P.I. I was reasonably sure it wasn't motivated by passion. Jesus H. Christ—getting shot at! Ridiculous—I'm not that bad a writer. Actually getting shot at! Unbelievable! I looked around cautiously. It seemed to be over.

"Do you see anything?" I asked.

He shook his head, gasping for breath. Heavily.

"Hey, you all right?" I asked, gently rolling him off and kneeling beside him. "You're not shot?"

"No, I'm . . . not . . . shot. Just give me a second get my breath." He got to his knees, massaging his chest. But I didn't see any blood. "OK," he said. I got cautiously up. He followed, laboring upright. "You see anything?" he said, wheezing.

"Not a thing," I answered.

Evidently nobody'd heard anything, either. Certainly nobody was paying any attention. Passersby were passing by.

"Let's check it out," he said.

We commenced a halting tour around the lot. Whoever'd done the shooting was clearly gone. But who'd want to shoot us? Either or both?

About then I found the answer to my early feeling that something in the lot had reminded me of something. It was a certain aged green Jaguar I'd first seen in the employees' lot at Claudio's house. Not as if there was any great doubt, but we looked inside, and sure enough, there behind the wheel, in an attitude of quiet contemplation was the familiar rotund body of Nigel Hampton—a small round hole in his left temple.

17

Rayford Goodman

I put it as simply as I could. "I don't want to hear any 'I told you so' crap."

Bradley just shrugged, which I appreciated. I also appreciated he didn't throw up or go ape-shit, either. Maybe he was turning into a pro. Of course, it made it a lot easier this was another neat killing. Another twenty-two, looked like. Ooh, that damn chest pain again. Whew, boy—god, it was awful. I was breaking major sweat. Like, pouring. Hard to be casual.

"You sure you weren't hit?" said Bradley.

"I think I'd of noticed," I gasped out, trying to smile. "Just a little out of breath." Now, how do I slip a nitroglycerin tab under my tongue without him noticing and making a big deal about it?

"Reach in and see what's in his jacket pockets, can you?"

"Isn't that against the law?"

"Yeah," I said, turning away and groping for the pill I kept handy in my side pocket. "Go on, do it. I'll play chickie for you."

"Is that a sexual overture?" said Bradley. "Jesus," he went on, as another shock wave roared through. "We were shot at!"

"Uhm," I said.

"You think, what, Heather?"

"I don't know. Didn't see. Might have been just to keep us *from* seeing." And now I had the nausea under the jaw. "Go on, look in his pockets."

He reached in through the open window and started gingerly sticking a finger in the least likely, but least repulsive one, the outside breast pocket. But it was enough to cover my popping the pill in my mouth and quickly sucking it before he came up empty and pulled his head back out.

"Shouldn't we be calling the police or something?"

"More like 'or something.' Keep looking."

He went back to it, this time first taking a deep breath and holding it as he reached inside the jacket.

The pill dissolved. The good news was in seconds the pain started going away. The bad news was that made it definitely angina and not indigestion, stress, or hiatal hernia. So what else was new?

"Find anything?" I asked.

"Just this," he said, backing out and sucking air on a new breath. He handed me a folded sheet of eight-and-a-half by eleven, which I crammed in my pocket. Time to check it out later. "Come on, let's make tracks," I said, starting for his car. But he just hung there. "Come on, let's go!"

"You're not gonna, we're not gonna?"

"Same story, part two—I don't need Chief Broward up my ass. No offense. We've got work to do."

He still showed he wanted to hang back. But since it was clear I wasn't going to stay, plus he'd already once waltzed around with Broward, I could see the wheels turning. Ever have the feeling that ya wanted to go? And yet have the feeling that ya wanted to stay?

"Hey," I said. "Considering how often I'm around when this shit goes down, no way I'm not going to get hauled in, even somebody impartial."

"But I could be your alibi," the solid citizen replied.

"You could be more than that—you could be a co-conspirator," I said, finished arguing and heading off.

"I guess," he said, catching up with me. We reached his BMW and piled in. I told him where I'd parked, and he started out. En route, I took out the piece of paper, which was folded in thirds, and carefully opened it.

"Well, what have we got?" asked Bradley.

It turned out to be part of the script of *One Fell Swoop*.

"Just a page of dialogue," I said. "Page 107." Nothing special there I could see. Then I turned it over. The reverse side was a lot more interesting. It was covered with notes, a lot of which I could only guess at. There looked to be references to camera angles, stuff about wardrobe, a reminder to tell Terry not to externalize a character flaw (probably an acting-directing thing—or Terry's character flaw?). Then there was a rough sketch of a set—I'd guess the one this shot would be made in—and some other technical stuff I repeated to Bradley. I almost quit on it before I saw another tiny note in the corner saying 'gave X $153,846.'

"And what the hell that means, I can't imagine," I concluded to Bradley.

"Well, it seems to me a payment of some kind."

"Yeah, but $153,846? You don't find that an odd amount?"

"Yes, I suppose."

"Like, what does $153,846 buy? A house? It'd surely be one fifty-five, or at worst one forty-five fifty. And not enough. Even as a payment, it doesn't divide. A boat, what? Nothing's one fifty-three eight forty-six."

"All right."

"But it's something. And it's at least part of what Hampton wanted to tell us. Maybe the whole thing. He wasn't carrying it instead of Kleenex."

"OK," said Bradley, pulling up beside my car. I handed him the paper, which he studied, reading it over at least twice.

"Notice anything else?"

"On the paper? No."

"Or at the scene."

"At the scene." He thought for a moment. "The wound? One of those twenty-two numbers?"

"Right on! Another killing, another twenty-two. What's different about this one?"

"Is this for my thesis or what?"

"Just trying to give you an education. Same as, I certainly expect, you're going to give me some more tips about writing."

"I'll give you a tip: stay out of the business. I'm kidding; tell me."

"All right," I continued. "If, as it looks like, Hampton got it with a twenty-two. And if, as seems likely, it was done by the same person. And if, as seems likely, that same person used the same gun—"

"I get it," said Bradley, excited. "It couldn't have been Terry or Maurissa, since that gun's at the bottom of the Pacific Ocean off Catalina!"

"Bingereeny."

But before I could take any bows, Bradley had to go and add, "Of course, they still could have done it, either or both, just not with that gun. Or, not Hampton, anyway."

Which I had to agree. It was hard to make progress when

every step forward wasn't necessarily *forward* forward. "Another thing," I added, getting back to teaching this beginner, "here we have Hampton killed *neatly* again."

"Meaning he didn't fear his killer, I know that one."

"Yet obviously the killer feared him. Enough to kill him. So what does that suggest?"

"Not another mistake? We already had one mistake—with Cohen—or so we thought, though maybe not. Could be we were mistaken about the mistake. Can't we keep it simpler?"

Didn't I wish. "All right, pass on that a moment. Let's back up. What we have now, Hampton sometime or other got a peek at Fortunata's script—maybe even as he was making his notes. Could have done that easily, putting down a drink, puttering around. So, Fortunata's making a note, the way he kept doing the day we were there. After the murder Hampton—we were all in the room together, remember—got to thinking of the info in there, went back, and tore out this page. Could have been for some purpose of his own, could have been for his own protection—if he knew what it meant. At any rate, whoever the note in the script nails realized that, and went back to the house and stole it after the murder."

"But there wasn't time for that, we were on the scene."

"Which means," I realized with a kind of groiny thrill, "whoever did it was still there while we were."

"And maybe even after the police came!" added Bradley.

Which got pretty weird. I'd given the place a casual going-over before I split, Bradley'd gone room to room, and the cops'd certainly searched, although there was time between Bradley getting bopped and the cops actually arriving. But it sure looked like somebody'd given us the slip. Or made us think so. That's it, made us think so!

"You know, an illusion. Now you see it, now you don't."

"Now I see what?"

"Whoever swiped the script."

"But I didn't."

"That's what makes it 'now you don't.' Let me put it another way: the hand is quicker than the eye."

"That's true," agreed Bradley. "The hand is quicker than the eye."

I stepped right into it, nodding like an idiot.

"But the tongue is quicker than the hand," he said.

Ugh. Cool it, I told myself. He can't help it. It's in his jeans. (I have a sense of humor, too.)

I got out of his yuppie BMW and into my loaner Toyota.

"What happens now?" asked Bradley, leaning out the window.

"Life goes on," I answered evasively. "What happens with you?"

"I guess I'll start writing."

"OK, and I'll keep detecting." With which he started off. I'd barely got my ignition key out when I heard a screeching of brakes and he backed up beside me again.

"Just had a thought," he said. "We're splitting the money on the book . . ."

"Right."

"How come we're not splitting the money on the detecting?"

I didn't have a total answer, so I just gave him the kind of laugh like I knew he was kidding, raced the motor, ground the gears, and drove away.

Normally, I had repair work to do on the Caddy, I'd've gone to a place I knew on Pico near Hauser that didn't feel they had to make enough each job for a two-week vacation in Biarritz. But the Le Dome restaurant and parking hazard had assured me they'd be picking up the tab for the damages—clearly not the first time this'd happened to them, with that dopey hilltop exchange they had. So I'd decided instead to go first-class. Which is why I'd taken the car to Executive Motors Cadillac in Beverly Hills. Big mistake.

First place, they must have been on the take from the insurance company; they wouldn't jack up the bill to cover the deductible. I mean, everybody did that. Or else what, were they making a statement? And add on they wouldn't replace the convertible top as part of the deal, saying a fender crunch had nothing to do with a tattered top and fogged-up rear yellow plastic window. Was I asking their forensic advice?

They wouldn't even take a shot.

When I told them such a lack of customer cooperation could only result in their losing my business, they seemed to manage their disappointment pretty good. You might say, took it right in stride. But I had left the car, and I *had* told them to go ahead with the top, too. I'd just gotten a new paint job as a part of my fee for a recent job entrapping a sneak in another garage. Being I was so close to making the '64 old heap into a classic, I'd decided to finish the job by getting a new ragtop, anyway. Admittedly, first under the impression it'd be a little gift from the Le Dome folks. (What about mental suffering, wasn't that worth something?)

Anyway, add to mental suffering, status embarrassment having to drive the Toyota, and I still got the feeling there had to be some grounds for legal redress. But that would come later. The important thing now, they said the car was ready.

Executive Motors Cadillac stayed open till nine—I guess figuring most executives worked late. I just got in under the wire. I had been working, too. Getting shot at and finding corpses wasn't exactly recreation. At any rate, I pulled the squawking Toyota into the garage, eased the creaking door open, and pulled myself out, hopefully for the last time. And there, lo and behold, was my beautifully restored old road hog. Looking like Luana after two weeks at the Golden Door. Whatever the aggravation, at the moment I had to admit it seemed worth it. I almost didn't mind they'd stiffed me for the deductible. Almost. I did love that car. It was even worth putting up with Francine's constant zingers. About the ecological damage driving a vehicle got seven miles to the gallon did to "this fragile planet we all have to share."

Now, five or ten minutes later, I was just settling up with the cashier, who had some strange reluctance to take my personal check, when I noticed a salesman on the floor proudly pointing out the features on a brand-new Seville.

The customer with him kept nodding his head. And then it looked like they must have struck a deal, because the salesman broke out in a big smile and gave the other guy a great big hearty old handshake. The other guy shook back, and then he turned, which was the first time I saw the other guy was none other than little old Wilhelm Zweig, a.k.a. Billy Zee—Fortunata's Frankfurt-born professional best friend and ex-gofer.

That's when I started to smile, 'cause I got a flash. $153,846 might be a very odd amount in dollars. But it might, on the other hand, turn out to be a very round number in some foreign currency. Like deutsch marks, for example.

18

Mark Bradley

I'd put on a pretty good show for Goodman (another body—what a bore), assuming he interpreted dumb shock for suave indifference. But the truth was I found it a touch wearing on the nerves. So pulling the car into my empty assigned parking slot in the condo garage felt more than a little like berthing at ye olde safe harbor. But if I were still in the market for further, albeit different, distractions, I hadn't far to seek. Assigned spot number two was also empty, from which it was not hard to deduce that one's friend, cohabiter, roommate, buddy boy, and trusted lover was apparently elsewhere than one would desire. Which was a roundabout way of suggesting this had all the earmarks of a long, lonely evening.

Upstairs, the apartment looked fairly neat (at least no on-site parties), and semi-cleaned. The kitchen was spotless, indicating part-time housekeeper Bernadine had been there, and part-time paramours had not. Of the former, further evidence of her recent presence was to be found in the vacuum cleaner abandoned in the middle of the living room—together with a pail of some sort of cleanser, draped over which was a damp cloth.

This often happened with Bernadine. Though she was scrupulous in matters of attendance (she always called before her dozens of emergency days off) her continued efforts on any given day were always a matter for conjecture, given my absence. She often seemed arbitrarily to abandon her labors (with implements scattered willy-nilly, hither and yon) either on random impulse or in support of some sort of subliminal racial rebellion. Or perhaps to ensure I knew she'd been there. Which was more than I could say for T.S.P. (That Sertain Party).

I put away my things, rinsed my hands and face, toweled off, and accepted as casually as I could that there was no note. I didn't really feel like checking the messages on my answer phone, but it was always possible I was getting worked up over nothing. Possible, but hardly likely.

1. "This is Hi-Tech/Home-Tech. We tried to repair your washing machine, but no one was home for the appointment. A traveling charge will be imposed. If you still wish the washing machine repaired, please call and reschedule. Thank you for calling Hi-Tech/Home-Tech." And thank you, Brian, for a still broken washing machine, and a charge of forty bucks or so for the privilege.

2. "Hi, tikimonumnits? Hewow? Tikimon? Wiffummob. Hello?" I hope whoever that was, it wasn't important to whoever it was they thought they'd called in whatever language.

3. "Mark Bradley, this is the office of Chief Broward at the Beverly Hills Police Department, Sergeant Kleindeist speaking," a breathy female voice informed me. "The chief would appreciate you calling to schedule an appearance in his office at your very earliest convenience. First thing in the morning. I thank you and hope you have a nice day." She did make it sound like a social invitation. But it was beginning to look like lying low and copping out weren't totally working. Or unlisted phones.

4. "Mark, this is Jeffrey Sash? We met at Bruce Woodcock's party for Misha Poppiani in June, celebrating gay pride? I came as Raggedy Ann? Anyway, I'm allowed one phone call. There's been a little misunderstanding, and I'm here at the West Hollywood sheriff's station, where they tell me I need five hundred dollars for bail. I know we're not real good friends—" I fast-forwarded.

5. "Hi, my name is Jim. I'm with the *Los Angeles Times* home deliv—" I fast-forwarded. The robot told me I had no more messages. It would erase my messages. If it told me to have a nice day I'd've punched its little integrated circuits out.

I was cranky.

While it was true I never hankered for a chubby cherub gummy-handedly hugging my neck, and/or also never wanted a little woman to share the burdens of a day at home made nigh impossible by my absence, I wasn't getting what I did want, either—which was a loving, caring, committed partner.

Maybe turkey Dijon tonight. (At least I didn't have to worry if the microwave was making me sterile.)

And there went the phone.

I let it ring. My prerecorded message clicked on: "Go at the beep" (long gone the cutsey ones to the effect I might or might not be home but the killer guard dogs were barricaded behind the electrified door, etc.—nowadays quick out and hope they hang on), after which I heard, "Hello, Mark? This is your mother. Are you there, Mark? I'll wait. Answer the phone, Mark. This is your mother. I know you use this machine just so you don't have to talk to me. Which is a fine thanks to get after all my effort and sacrifice, and loving care—I don't even mention the pain of childbirth—to be deliberately ignored like I was just nobody. Some stranger calling up. A stranger who gave you life. There are times I think you ought to be ashamed of yourself, Mark. This is your mother. I know you're there." Click. How do they know?

I got up early, careful not to wake Brian. Not that I was being considerate of him. I was being considerate of me—not relishing a confrontation first thing in the morning.

He'd come home well after two, and I'd chosen to pretend sleep rather than have it out when at least one of us wasn't at his best or most rational. I think. Cowardice might have played a part, too.

At any rate, I eased out of bed, got myself together, decided I would eat out—and was just about to get out when Brian shambled into the hallway, looking cute as a baby goose, in rumpled jammies, a lopsided grin on his face, and said, "Hi, yuh. How's it goin'?"

"Uh, goin' good." Nobody likes a complainer. "Gotta run, but tell you, let's plan on dinner tonight."

"Well . . ."

"I'll make reservations someplace nice."

"Well . . ."

"Eureka," I added, referring to Wolfgang Puck's newest mother lode, immediately sweetening the offer. Brian loved going out, especially expensively.

"Well . . ."

Don't press for a limo, I'm only prepared to go so far.

"We'll get dressed, it'll be nice."

He mulled it over. Serious issues to be considered. "What're you gonna wear?"

Breathing time. Breathing room.

"Talk about it later. Gotta go. Busy, busy." I kissed the air somewhere a foot short of his face, got into my busy, busy stride—and the hell out of there.

Breakfast, breakfast. I got in the car, headed north—toward the outer limits of my bailiwick—moving both geographically and emotionally from the personal to the work areas. Where shall I eat?

While deciding, I picked up the phone, checked in with Goodman. (Did everyone who had a car phone make most of his calls from it?)

I caught him at the door, just about to leave for his morning walk.

What was new?

"I decided to give up smoking."

That would be nice.

"The reason I'm announcing it, you catch me doing it, I gotta pay a fine."

And if I knew Goodman, a good choice of motivational stimulus. I suggested a thousand dollars might be an appropriate amount.

"Hundred," he negotiated, evidently not all that committed.

I acceded. What else was on the agenda? "Or will not smoking be taking up all your time?"

"Very funny. I'm gonna go out to the shoot."

"Which is what, where?"

"The *One Fell Swoop* folks're back in production. Shooting interiors at Twentieth."

"How do you learn that kind of stuff?"

"I have my sources."

"The woid on da street?"

"Plus you call up and ask. Anyhow, I figured it wouldn't hurt to mix and mingle a little. Maybe I can find out where everybody was around eight-thirty last night."

"I think somebody knows where *we* were. There was a message on my answering machine to check in with Chief Broward for a little tête-à-tête."

He made a comment of the fecal variety.

"I guess you gotta go," he added.

"I can't see how not."

"Just don't volunteer anything."

"You mean out of my vast store of knowledge about this case?"

"Right." I guess irony wasn't his strong point. "After you do that, or before—there was a notice in *Variety* this morning Fortunata's will was admitted to probate."

"Yes?"

"Send Francie down to the county clerk's office at the Superior Court—that's 111 North Hill Street—and get a Xerox of the will."

"Can just anybody do that?"

"Yeah, it's a public document. Shouldn't be, it's really nobody's business. But all you gotta do is ask, and they give it to you for a few cents for the Xerox. Might be something there could prove interesting. Worth a shot."

"Francine's not with you, I take it."

"You take it right. I got custody of the cat so far." After which there was what seemed a long moment of not discussing it. For some bizarre reason I found myself hoping they hadn't really broken up.

"I guess she's at the office," I offered, as if it were the only possible reason not to be with him.

"I wouldn't know," he replied after a beat.

More and more beginning to sound like a long, long time from May to December.

"All right, got you. Anything else?"

"Not that I can—oh, yeah. Have her check the going rate of exchange for deutsch marks, too."

"OK." Whatever that means. "That's one will, one cat, one deutsch mark, sure this isn't some new TV game show? 'What Doesn't Go With What'?"

"I'll be in touch later," he replied, ending the connection—clearly not having a good day, either. I'd get to Francine shortly, but at the moment I was on Santa Monica, heading west, still on the fringe of my "area." On impulse I decided to breakfast at Hugo's, which was nicely down the middle. Where straight meets straight, gay meets gay, and boy can meet eggs over easy.

I didn't see Francine's car in the lot. Which was reasonable enough since Francine wasn't at the office. Publisher Penny's car was, and publisher Penny was.

"Well, nice to see you, Mark," he opened, jack high.

"Dick," I replied. Or opined, really. He'd caught me in the hall, a place of vantage in which he traditionally lurked.

"How's it going?" he demanded.

"Slow but sure," I fended.

"Yeah, I noticed the slow part. I don't seem to be seeing a lot of pages turned out."

"Plotting, planning. Avoiding the pitfalls."

"Loafing, procrastinating. Trying my patience."

Sigh, two, three, four. "Come on, Dickie, we've been through all this. I think it was Ben Hecht who said, 'Do you want it fast, or do you want it good?' "

"And I think it was Jack Warner who said, 'You're fired, Ben.' I want it good and fast." Which really taxed his capacity for repartee, so he limited his parting shots to direct attack. "Plus don't think I haven't noticed the absence of your little doper friend lo these several days."

"You can't, in these times of newly defined broader limits on slander, be referring to my research associate? Who maybe once in her foolish youth, in the interest of intellectual experimentation, tried a controlled substance, even as Aldous Huxley or Betty Ford—"

"All right, all right, all right. But meantime it _would_ be nice if she dropped by the office once in a while, other than to pick up her check."

"Mr. Penny, a research associate who isn't out in the field probing for information is hardly operating at optimum efficiency."

"Stop it, Mark, before we're up to our gonads in guano." For Penny this was such an unexpected flight of verbal imagery that he seemed to surprise even himself. At least confident he wasn't apt to top that, he assayed a self-satisfied smile, mimed typing at me, and departed.

I reached Francine at her apartment, not exactly awash in the river of goodwill to men. She instructed me how any fool with half a brain could get the day's quotes on deutsch marks, and how once in possession I could take that and join it with the copy of Claudio's will I would be getting myself and secrete both in a place unblessed by old Sol.

"Other than that, how's it going?" I asked to the already dead phone. Female Troubles obviously didn't do a whole lot for one's disposition.

* * *

Broward's office was in a temporary wing of the Beverly Hills City Hall, while the burgeoning Beverly Hills Civic Center was in the monumental throes of construction. (The new complex so dwarfed the old, it was hard to imagine the same city was to be serviced. And, indeed, by the time the city finished paying for the new center, already doubled, tripled, and quadrupled its original estimates, it might have to take in administration day work from other cities just to cover its finance charges. And do windows and laundry, too.)

His secretary, or aide-de-camp, the Sergeant Kleindeist with the dial 1-900 voice, turned out to look considerably at odds with her phone personality. She was a very solid, many would say attractive, blond officer who wore an extremely prominent set of militant breasts as if they were medals of commendation. She was, one noted, once you got past those first impressions, smartly attired in a finely tailored uniform, carried a very impressive, probably high-calibered sidearm, supported by a gleaming Sam Browne belt that seemed somehow to combine military conservatism with sado-masochism. She informed me in her in-person curt voice that the chief was in conference and would get to me when he could. Inasmuch as his temporary quarters were behind a glass partition, through which I could see clearly that he was alone and not particularly busy, I couldn't but feel the ploy was intended to be transparent, as it were.

I checked my watch and gave him exactly five minutes.

"Excuse me, Sergeant," I said to the *madchen* in uniform after the designated time had elapsed. "Would you remind the chief I'm waiting?"

"He knows you're here," she replied sulkily, without looking up, making some sort of note on a pad, hidden beneath her chest works. I wondered how she managed to be both good cop/bad cop in one package.

I sat down, gave him another five minutes, got up.

"When is it that you think the chief will be finishing his conference?"

"Hard to say with these things," she replied. I imagined it'd be hard to do a lot of stuff with those things—like maintain her balance.

"Well, I'll tell you what. To simplify matters, tell the chief one of his *employers* dropped by at his invitation, but inasmuch as he's so totally tied up, we'll just have to do it another time. Once he's gotten a judge to put it in writing." I could see out of the corner of my eye that he was peeking out at us. "Till then," I continued, "I'll be hieing myself the fuck out of here." With which I turned to leave.

For a big man he sure moved fast. I'd taken only a step or two when I could feel the hot wind of his bullying voice.

"OK, inside, fella."

"Look, I'm not a fella, I'm Mr. Bradley. And I don't care one whit for this whole road company theater of intimidation you've got going. I'm here as a cooperating citizen—"

"You're here because I said be here. So stop this A.C.L.U. crap, and get your ass in my office before I show you some real civil liberties violations."

I did want to hear what he had to say.

"Plus, for the record, you're not my employer," he continued, following me in. "You're on the other side of Doheny."

"Which also for the record means I'm on the other side of your jurisdiction."

"Wrong about that, but tell you what—you don't play games and I won't play games."

"Suits me, what can I do for you?"

"That's better. Actually, it's more what I can do for you." I bet. My good friend here. I waited.

"Lot of murders. Lot of lot of murders. Not our thing, in this community. Adds up, a lot of pressure. Naturally, I do my best, one way or the other. It's just pressure don't help."

I waited some more.

"Now I know you're not exactly the best friend I ever had . . ." continued Broward.

I could see how he would feel that way, considering our last book and the way we'd dredged up his failure to solve the Rita Rose murder. (Of course, we hadn't exactly let on that Goodman's solution was faulty, either. Another opening, another show.)

". . . but I like to think I'm big enough I won't hold past associations against you."

I still didn't say anything.

"I personally would not like to see you go to jail."

"Jail? What the hell're you talking about?"

"Well, start obstruction of justice. It's just, hey, let's not get ahead of ourselves. Maybe you'll see the light. Maybe you won't obstruct, you'll actually help."

"Help what? What do you want from me?"

"Basically, I see you as a victim of evil companions. I mean, if you hadn't teamed up with Goodman, you probably could've gone your whole life without committing any crime that wasn't what we've come to call victimless."

I had to deal with this, now. "I'm here to discuss the liberalization of the consenting-adults laws?"

"You're here because I'd like your cooperation about Goodman. Which I don't exactly need, mind you. Just it would make my life easier. Let's start with a little diary, what you know about Goodman's movements starting . . ." and here he flipped open a little notebook, uncapped a pen.

"Wait, wait, wait. I don't know what you're trying to do. Or what you have in mind. I do want you to know you can't intimidate me."

"I can't?"

"No, you can't. I'm no Goodman—who I don't notice you doing such a good job intimidating, either, by the way—with a license to maintain, which is somewhat dependent on good terms with the police. There's nothing you can do to me."

"You're sure about that."

I think I was sure. "Sure. In fact, I don't care for the whole direction of this interview. I'm going to leave here. I know my rights. There's not a thing you can do to stop me." With which I rose from my chair.

"Well, there is, sort of," he replied.

I waited. This ought to be good.

"I can put you under arrest."

"Yeah, right," I said, and started for the door.

"Which I'm doing. Sergeant!"

The sergeant stuck her bosoms into the room.

"Arrest this man!"

And he really thought this kind of childish move was going to work on me?

"OK, I'll play along. You're going to arrest me. For what, again?"

"For complicity in the murders of Hamilton Cohen, Claudio Fortunata, Nigel Hampton, and Angelo Mordente."

"Angelo Mordente? I never even heard of Angelo Mordente."

"You will. Just so you can tell your lawyer, Mordente was the driver for a man named Armand Cifelli your collaborator works for."

"You've got to be kidding," I said, not too originally. Absurd as it was, I have to admit I wasn't without the slightest tinge of fear. And in fact, I *had* met this Angelo Mordente. He'd driven me once upon a time when Goodman and Cifelli'd crossed swords and Cifelli'd taken it out on me to make the point with Goodman. So there was a remote connection. Not, of course, that I was guilty of anything. Provable.

"You're not really going to put me in jail."

"I really am. With real bars. And real other felons. You'll hate it."

I was sure I would.

"Read him his rights and get him out of here," said Broward.

And as she did and I was being cuffed, the thought crossed my mind there might be a silver lining in all this. I'd probably miss dinner with Brian and put off the shoot-out at the not so hot corral.

19

Rayford Goodman

I came home from my walk wondering why it was exercise seemed to energize all the young people and tire out all the old. Tiring out wasn't that big a help. I suppose really I was feeling a little on the down side because one of the two old guys I always saw walking together wasn't there today. And from the moping along, I got a feeling the remaining old guy was the *surviving* old guy—and his buddy wasn't just taking a week off surfing in Maui. The days dwindle down.

And while I certainly didn't fit in that category, excepting hearts and maybe livers, I was getting up there. I'd been starting—before I met Francie—to be that extra man at the party to even out the numbers of the next of kin. Sort of somewhere between the ages where the young, luscious ones call you sir a lot more than necessary and the widows have you over for kreplach and mature fornication.

Well, they were wrong, I was still in the game. I will give them this much—I was at an age where I had to start using conditioner on my eyebrows. Maybe the guy wasn't dead. Maybe he was so busy living the good life he didn't have time for walking.

I really didn't want to lose Francie. I mean, basically, things were really going good. I had a few bucks, a look at some more, the house was getting back in shape, things were happening. And I almost sort of really, you could say, was halfway falling for her.

About then I felt a tiny furry rubbing against my ankle as Sven tried to con me that hunger was the same as love. You didn't have to care a whole lot for animals to find kittens cute. I picked him up. The whole cat felt like it weighed about two ounces. He had the warmest, softest stomach. They are cute. I carried him into the kitchen, put a little of the cat food gunk in a plate, and set him down

beside it. That little pink tongue got working on it right off.
They are damn cute. Not something I'd always planned on.
But I could see how you could get attached to them. If that
was what you wanted. I mean, for some people. I gave him
a little milk, too, which I guess he liked a lot. That really
looked cute, the little tongue slurping it up, getting little
drops on his little whiskers. A lot of people really go nuts
over animals. I never could understand that.

But I had more important things to do. I popped in for
a very fast shower (L.A. in its fourth year of drought).
After, I opened the closet and had to decide what to wear.
Easy in the old days. All I'd had was a pair of gray slacks
and a blazer. Now that things were going a bit better, I had
to make choices. Between three pairs of gray slacks and
three blazers.

I'd talked earlier to Bradley. He was going to contact
Francie to follow up my hunch about Billy Zee—whether
deutsch marks didn't divide even into that $153,846 Fortu-
nata'd written in his script—plus get a copy of the will. So
that was working. For myself, I was going to go get a good
breakfast and then make it over to Fortunata's and finally
catch up with Barbara Aronson, which I'd been meaning
and somehow not getting around to doing for days.

Before leaving I made sure all the doors and windows
were closed. Not only to keep Sven in but to keep the
coyotes out. Being they liked a little pussy now and then.

In the garage, the great old gas gulper was looking beautiful. I got in, revved her up, and drove her out, top down—
I dare you, skin cancer.

The radio was tuned to some AM country and western
station. I guess whoever worked on the car didn't exactly
share my tastes. I love the way it became country and western. When I was a kid back East we just called it corny
music. I slipped in a tape of the Ella Fitzgerald/Duke Elling-
ton 1966 Sweden Concert, and the world started to look
(and definitely sound) a lot better. Was she ever on that
night!

I hung a right on Sunset, drove a mile and a quarter.
Then I turned south on Beverly Drive and through the maze
back of Will Rogers Park across from the Beverly Hills
Hotel, where some city planner on speed thought it'd be
pretty funny to have Crescent, Canon, Beverly Drive, and
Lomitas all intersect in a kind of star pattern. Since nobody

could figure out how to stoplight that complicated a design, it worked itself out in a very Beverly Hillsy style. Rolls-Royces had the right of way, then limos, top of the line Mercedes, Jaguars, and on through Cadillacs, Lincolns, and so forth. And believe it or not, on a five-way intersection I'd never seen even so much as a single fender bender.

I did yield to a tiny white-haired old lady whose head was lower than the wheel driving a huge Continental she hadn't thought to trade after her husband died. She just went straight on ahead. Chances were she either couldn't see over the hood or figured at her age she had least to lose. Once past the fun corner I continued on down Beverly Drive, stopped, and parked a long block short of Santa Monica Boulevard. For a while anyway, I'd want to protect the finish on the Eldorado and not be risking any more parking lots than I had to.

From there I walked on down to Nate 'n Al's. Nate 'n Al's had been *the* delicatessen in B.H. till somehow or other they didn't fulfill Marvin Davis' expectations—or belly—enough, and he became the driving force behind getting a branch of New York's Carnegie Deli here. As with a lot of things for so many reasons—not the least of which I always got a seat there—I liked the original better than the new.

I looked at the old menu—we're talking really old, they still had a Bobby Breen sandwich—just as if I didn't know I was going to have eggs and a lox and cream cheese on bagel. I was giving up smoking, what more did they want from me?

A waitress who looked like a Jewish Melina Mercouri (Never on Shabbas?) plopped down a dish of pickles, and managed to find a pad and pencil stashed in the folds of her waist.

"Yeah?" she said by way of challenging me to order.

"Just bring me a cup of coffee, I haven't decided yet," I said, damned I was going to be pushed around by the help.

She was back in a sulky minute with the coffee. Even between in the cup and the saucer. Half the world tells you to have a nice day and the other half makes sure you don't.

I had more important things on my mind. I still needed a plan, some way to start making things happen.

I pulled out my list of suspects again. There was a little progress. I could cross off one name—Nigel Hampton. He'd got himself killed. Good going, Goodman. Well, we'd see what old Barbara could add to the picture.

But first things first. Because first things turned out to be the beefy body of good old buddy Chief Eddie Broward. And when he saw me and *smiled*, I knew which half of the world had dibs on my day. He waddled over and plumped himself down. My appetite got up and sailed out the window.

He sincerely hoped I'd enjoy my breakfast. He also hoped I'd take pleasure in what remained of my liberty. Because, he was real happy to tell me, he'd just come from the D.A.'s office and been authorized to offer Mark Bradley—who he'd arrested, by the way—total immunity in exchange for his testimony against me. Well, there wasn't anything he could really testify to. But Bradley wasn't used to the kind of pressure the Browards of this world could bring to bear. I couldn't be sure just how stand-up he'd be when the threats started coming hot and heavy. And there *was* withholding, and tampering. Minimum it was going to be a big nuisance.

"You're not going to say anything?" asked Broward.

"It sure amazes the shit out of me you've been able to keep that job of yours all these years being so incredibly fucking bad at it."

"Well, now, Goodman. That sounds suspiciously like verbal abuse of an officer in the performance of his duties."

"Your duties being? To cadge a free breakfast while intimidating a citizen?"

He chuckled at that. I sometimes thought hating me was the main thing kept him going.

"Besides, I figured you'd be retiring by now, what with the money you stole from last time," I chanced, referring to some jewels that got suspiciously disappeared under his very nose while he was misdirecting everybody else's efforts toward framing me again.

"You're lucky I have a sense of humor," he said at last, when he couldn't come up with anything funny. "We'll be talking real soon," he added, pulling himself up in fat chunks. He looked for a minute at an empty booth, then decided to get his freebie breakfast somewhere else. And left.

Pitiful. I got up wearily and crossed over to the phone.

I called the office, asked for Francie. She wasn't there. I called her apartment. She was.

"What?" she answered angrily. In general angrily, before she even knew it was me.

"Broward arrested Bradley. I thought you'd want to know."

"I needed that."

"Well, it didn't exactly happen to you."

"Anyway, so?"

"So I thought you'd want to do something about it."

"You do something about it. I've got an appointment."

"And that's more important than getting your friend out of jail?"

"Thank you for calling," she said. And hung up. She'd been doing a good bit of that lately.

It didn't sound too much like she was going to take care of it. So I called Penny at the office and told him. He said it was great. I said he misunderstood, Bradley was in the pokey. He said he understood perfectly—he just wasn't sure what to do first.

"How about call your lawyer?"

"Yeah, of course. But maybe before that our public relations folks. This is really great. It's even better than you getting locked up. I mean, both of you, that's fantastic."

"I knew you'd be all upset. Will you fucking take care of it?"

"Of course I will. Do you think I intend to let my authors suffer this prior restraint, this censorship before the fact? We live in America. And any Beverly Hills fascist polizei who thinks he can pull this stuff doesn't know what a formidable opponent he's aroused in Pendragon Press! Before I'm done, he'll wish he'd let sleeping pendragons lie. Well, something like that, the p.r. guy'll clean it up."

"I leave it to you," I said, hanging up and returning to my table.

Actually, it wasn't really so much worry over Bradley that was getting to me. I knew Penny'd get him out. It was Francie. And her appointment.

I was checking my time schedule and deciding to rearrange my plans when Melina Mercouri came back and wanted to know was I ever going to order or was it I just wanted to keep her from making a living out of this particular booth.

*   *   *

Not interviewing Barbara was getting to be a habit. But I knew where I had to be now was more important.

I was parked across the street, half a block back of the entrance to Francie's apartment's garage. I'd been there quite awhile. I didn't know what I was going to do. I just knew it was where I belonged. And then she came out, driving her great old green Mustang.

She drove slow, in no great hurry for the appointment. I was able to stay almost a full block behind and maintain contact without her noticing. She probably wasn't looking, anyway. We were heading east on Fountain. At Fairfax, she turned south. I followed. Between Olympic and Pico was an ordinary looking one-story building, no different from the ones on either side. You wouldn't really have noticed it at all if it weren't for the twenty or thirty pickets out front being kept more or less orderly by four police officers. And the TV news truck parked outside. Francie honked her horn at several protesters blocking the way into the parking lot. A fat cameraman followed a cute reporter lady chasing after Francie. A policeman cleared a lane for her to go through. I saw a spot open up diagonally across the street and made a quick U-turn to grab it. Evidently, the cops weren't going to lose sight of their assignment, or miss a chance to get on camera, because no one stopped or cited me.

From there I could see Francie come around from in back and make her way toward the front, where there was a sign reading, "FAIRFAX WOMEN'S FAMILY PLANNING CENTER." I guess this was it.

I would have been glad to be with her. But she hadn't asked me. Or made it seem like a good idea to ask her. I wondered if she'd asked Bradley and decided when he got locked up to just go through with it anyway. I didn't know why it made any difference to me if she had—except maybe not understanding I was, at least, her friend.

She didn't look right or left, just headed for the door, but I could hear the pickets offering encouragement. "Baby killer!" was one. "Christ died for your sins!" was another. I knew if Francie was more top of her form she'd have answered that one, something along the order of, "Not my sins; most of 'em hadn't been invented yet." But she wasn't doing any answering, she just kept her head down and marched straight toward the door.

"Pardon me, miss," said the reporter lady. "Could we have a word?"

Francie didn't stop. The lady was lucky, she wouldn't have liked Francie's word. The pickets promised her God's wrath, which was a very constructive argument. But the cops kept order. The group was playing to the TV. Which was a plus for me. I don't think it would have helped things much me barging out the door of my car and punching faces in the name of free choice if it'd become necessary.

She was in there a long time. The afternoon wore on. The TV reporter lady and the fat cameraman left. Then the pickets left, too. I wondered whether there was any real news left in this world or whether things just got acted out for the six o'clock. It was still hot. I turned on the motor to get a little air in the car, ran it awhile. The Ella tape ended. I put in a Ray Charles. I was afraid the battery would get run down. I turned it off.

The time went on. Didn't take more than two or three years. I lost ground on my bet; dug a butt out of the ashtray in the dashboard and lit up. Theoretically owing Bradley a hundred. Tasted awful. I didn't feel I needed any further punishment.

It got later.

The door opened. A lady from the clinic stuck her head out, checking the scene, held the door. Francie came out, slowly, helped by the lady from the clinic. They took tiny steps, walking toward the parking lot where she'd left the Mustang. It took four or five months to get there. They went around the building and into the lot, out of sight.

I turned on the ignition. The tape was still on. Ray Charles was singing "Georgia." I found myself crying.

That song always did get me.

20

Mark Bradley

"Hey, we could use a little more space around here," someone said one day at Beverly Hills City Hall. "Maybe we should build on." From whence sprungeth the unfinished Civic Center City at cost overruns that would have embarrassed Shah Jehan ("Hey, let's do a little something for mommy Mumtaz—we'll call it the Taj something or other").

Which is an admittedly roundabout way of recording that I was in a temporary holding tank awaiting transfer to the L.A. bastille because Beverly Hills hadn't decided on the tiles for its new jail yet.

Which gets us to—so far it wasn't all that awful. Though there was a fair representation of the accepted stereotypes—the burly black fellow pursing his lips suggestively and making sucking sounds (possibly just trying to rid himself of a corn on the cob residue); the slimy Middle Easterner who could arrange smuggled contraband for a price (chili from Chasen's?); the spiffily dressed South American cocaine entrepreneur (alleged) continually sprinkling cologne from a Bijan spritzer to neutralize whatever odors his no-doubt sensitive nose found offensive (guilty as charged); an irate Iranian who insisted that not paying his dinner check at Bice was merely a belated expression of disapproval for having been kept waiting and quite common in his culture (I told him being kept waiting at an in spot in Beverly Hills was common in ours); and a real nice, clean-cut sort of guy who was there on a misunderstanding—he thought he had funds in his checking account. He told me his name was Dennis, or Denny if I preferred, O'Donnell, and with a great deal of charm owned up that he was "a blackguard, a cad, and a bounder over third base." Translation: an admitted bad-check passer and guilty as sin.

"Though in this day and age, I consider it more like a

minor failing. After all, isn't it the duty of the straight and narrow to be doing something about the homeless?"

"You were homeless?"

"I would have been if I hadn't taken a suite at the Beverly Hilton."

He had a point.

"And shouldn't we be rewarding initiative rather than penalizing them what shows a bit of it?"

He went on in this ingratiating fashion for some time, the while it struck me there was something remotely familiar about the man. But since he clearly traveled in civilized circles, maybe our paths had crossed somewhere under more conventional circumstances.

"And you? What manner of socially reprehensible behavior did you manifest for them to be after incarcerating your ass?" he inquired.

"Well, it's a little involved . . ."

"We've nothing if not a bit of time on our hands." (I was starting to wonder if his mother hadn't some carnal doings with the likes of the late Barry Fitzgerald.)

"Sort of, I don't know, accessory to murder?"

"Murder? Now, aren't you full of surprises. You're suspected of a murder?"

"Four."

"Saints preserve us." (He really said that?) "I'm sure you have an excuse."

"How about not guilty?"

"Well, yes, and don't we all swear on our mothers about that. Murder? I had it on the tip of me tongue to say you don't look like a murderer, but then don't I like to think I don't look like a bad-check passer, neither."

"I don't look like a murderer because I'm not a murderer."

" 'Twas more along the lines just you were there? The wrong place at the wrong time?"

"I wasn't even always there."

"But the other times you were. Which time weren't you there?"

"Look, I don't imagine I should be talking about this. The whole thing's ridiculous, but even so."

"Now, now," (me boyo?) "I don't want you to go to thinking I'm any judgmental sort of a person. If you had a hand in murdering someone, or someones, I'm sure in me mind you had your reasons."

"I didn't murder anyone."

"Or were with someone who . . ."

Which is about when I remembered where I'd seen old Dennis or Denny if I preferred. Not in an Irish pub, quaffing a tankard of ale whilst pulling on a meerschaum pipe. I'd seen this joker in a police uniform, getting out of a squad car in front of the temporary trailers in front of City Hall when I came to spring Goodman.

"You're a plant!"

At which point the burly black gentlemen said, "Oh, you're playing that game? If I were a plant, I'd be a ficus."

"I can't believe Broward really thinks I've got anything to confess and would put a plant in with me to 'overhear' me being guilty. Though I suppose anybody stupid enough to go along with that brogue has to be considered a pretty good prospect for entrapment. And wasn't I after almost fallin' for that shit?"

"Hey," said Dennis/Denny, "worth a shot." With which he went to the front, rattled the cage, and when the guard responded, said the secret words: "It's a wash."

"If I were a wash," said the black guy, "I'd be Tide."

I'd gambled my one phone call on Brian. The theory was either I believed in him and trusted him and wanted a life with him or what was the use anyway. And by the by, isn't that really an awful rule, one call? Especially these days when you're so likely to have happen exactly what I was afraid of, getting his answering machine? Which counted as the call! What a rotten rule! One call should at least be that you talked to a *person*. ("Sorry about the governor's being unable to commute your death sentence; his call-waiting kicked in before we could ask.") I left the message, and my hopes for a future life, in the figurative hands of Brian's machine.

But there was talk now we were all going to be moved to either Los Angeles city or the county jail, neither of which did I figure to be in the area of improvement. To my way of thinking, Bel Air or Malibu would be much more reasonable alternatives. But somehow I didn't think reason had a very large chance to prevail. It was also rapidly becoming less an amusing story to dine out on than a source of extreme discomfort, annoyance, and abject terror. Since, too, my arrest, in the first place, was an act of harassment, I'd little doubt if I were moved Broward and company wouldn't be too forthcoming about where to, if and when Brian recovered the message about my ship heading into dire straits and made his move. The big hope of late had become (how we lessen our expectations!) that we'd get fed first, before the move. Since assuredly the Beverly Hills swill would be better than the county swill.

There was only a moderate din in the holding cell, not being the sort of pokey with a lot of screaming, carrying on, and playing of "Nobody knows de trouble ab seen" on the harmonica. I did get the impression, now that I thought of it, that the buzzing undertone which had been threatening a migraine was in fact a muted program of light classics being foisted via the Muzak. Potentially actionable, a possible cruel and inhumane. So when there was manifest a noticeable commotion down the hall, we figured it was either chow or time for the dreaded transfer.

We were wrong on both counts. The hullabaloo signaled the arrival of a very vocal, very pissed off, very apparently inebriated celebrity, and one of the principals in our little immorality play—Terry Coyne!

Before, during, and after vowing vengeance, wrath, and professional obliteration to one and all (though "You'll never work in this town again" didn't sound like something you threatened a policeman with), he was admitted kicking, screaming, moaning, and bitching to our inner sanctum.

"Dirty motherfucking no-talent sons of bitches," he shouted at the officer closing the gate.

"Listen," said the cop sternly. "I don't care who you are. I don't care how much fucking money you make, what kind of big shot, who you know, how much influence. You just shut your big ugly face and stop this shit, or you'll regret it to your dying day, which might not be that far away."

That seemed to get Terry's attention. Or perhaps he was wondering what picture it was from. At any rate, he quieted, managing only a greatly modified "Oh yeah?"

"Yeah," said the guard. "And another thing."

"What other thing, turnkey?"

"Who you calling turkey?"

"Turnkey."

"Oh. All right. Sign here."

"I already signed in, fuckhead."

He looked like he was wondering what kind of play on words that was, toughened up again. "I didn't ask whether you signed in," he said. "I just said sign." With which he handed Coyne a clipboard with a sheet of note paper on top.

Terry took it gingerly. "Where?" he said.

"Anywhere. Just write 'To my old buddy, Jeff' and sign your name. It's for my nephew."

"Right," said Terry, signing, on familiar ground. "To my old buddy, Jeff—tops in cops." And handed it over.

"Thanks," said the officer with the same name as his nephew, examining the autograph and leaving us.

It was then Terry finally looked around and examined his new accommodations. I half expected a Bette Davis "What a dump" line, but instead he said, "I know you. Don't I know you? You're the guy from the boat, and Claudio's house."

"Mark Bradley. I'm doing the book on him."

"That's right, that's right. So what're you doing here?"

"Gathering material, I hope. Something about complicity in the murder. Nothing real. You?"

"F.U.I."

I raised an eyebrow.

"Fucking Under the Influence. A holdup thing. Chick says I forced myself on her. Me. Like I gotta force myself on anybody."

"They're really going to make a case? Like attempted rape?"

"Nah. They'll just get their name in the papers, the studio'll give her some money. But meantime this shit."

"I'm sorry."

"I needed this. We're supposed to do eight pages tomorrow."

"Oh, yeah, I heard they'd started up production again. *One Fell Swoop*, right?"

"And I'm in every shot, wouldn't you know."

"The cost of stardom."

"And a little luck."

"Oh?"

"Between you and me and the lamppost, I get along a lot better with Laszlo than old Claude."

"But is he as good a director?"

"Truth? He was the director *before*. Laz did every setup, planned the whole thing. Always had. Claudio more like acted the part of director, with a lot of artsy put-downs."

"And took the credit?"

"And the money."

Pretty good motive for Laszlo to kill Claudio, one couldn't help thinking. Peripherally, if Terry so preferred being directed by Laszlo, a motive for him as well. But marginal, I had to admit. Whew! And we were under the impression Fortunata'd been one of Hollywood's best-loved. Maybe that *is* best-loved, for Hollywood. Getting locked up could turn out to be a break. Of course, staying locked up was something else again.

"Damn it!" said Terry, unprivy to these musings, and anyway, not very likely to let considerations of others interfere with his monomania. "That damned twat."

"Who blew the whistle, you mean?" Trying to keep track.

"Who blew more than that."

"Maurissa did this? *She* called the cops?"

"Don't be an asshole. Maurissa? Maurissa's my girlfriend."

"Ah. Somebody else. Somebody new."

"Not so new. And not the first time we made it, either." Then louder, to the cell and the office in general, "All right, which one of you finks is the *Enquirer* connection? Which one of you's gonna break the story Terry Coyne Arrested for Sexual Debauchery?" (I think he was making up his own headline.)

Nobody volunteered to identify himself. Though it was undoubtedly true—the story *would* break in the scandal press, the *Enquirer* would turn out to have someone on the payroll. (The *Star* was smarter, they merely had someone on the *Enquirer*'s payroll.)

"This town," Terry ran on. "Every time you slip the old pork to someone you gotta pay the piper."

"Wouldn't that be the butcher you paid? The pork?"

"Wha'?"

I shook my head; no answer was really required. I could hear footsteps coming down the hall. God, I hoped they weren't going to transfer us. That would certainly add hours to whenever it was I was finally going to get out.

"Really pisses me off," Terry ran on. "She's got some nerve. I mean, does anybody seriously think I have to push myself on any chick? Especially this one. Talk about your lipsuction. You know, you've seen her."

"I have? Who're we talking about?"

"That Tiffany dame. From the Ermitage. Tiffany Kestner."

"She's the one who filed charges against you?"

"Ain't that a kick in the cock?"

It was certainly something along those lines. Surprise, anyway. Not a twosome I could imagine. Although I guess they would have met. I found myself looking for surgical scars back of Terry's ears. Awfully young.

Which is when the footsteps reached the holding cell.

"Mark Bradley?" said the policeman.

"Present," I said. And accounted for, I thought to myself. "Out."

Damn it, looking bad. They weren't even moving all of us to county—just me. Broward's really getting out of line.

I stood resignedly by the gate as he unlocked it, then stepped out. It made a difference. Just not being behind mesh, let alone bars, made a difference.

"Follow me," said the officer. I noticed he didn't cuff me, or even grab me by the arm. Grateful for small favors.

Then I found out why I hadn't been cuffed. I wasn't being transferred, I was being sprung!

"Well," said Brian, standing at the last desk between me and freedom, and looking precisely the correct shade of White Knight. "Are you going to just gawk, or are we going to get going in time to keep our reservation at Eureka?"

21

Rayford Goodman

The face-lifted Eldorado barely made it up the hill. The old car was looking great, but still acting like an old car. Living in the Hollywood hills tended to turn them real quick from leading vehicle to character transportation. And, of course, in my case it was pretty old to begin with, and between the heat and the smog and the hill, near boiling was routine. And by the way, can anybody really say coolant does any cooling at fucking all?

Things didn't get a whole lot better when I finally did reach home base. The kitten was howling like it'd been totally betrayed, abandoned, and left to starve. In the event that wasn't actually the case, it'd also left a cute little dump beside the litter box to teach me I was supposed to change the stuff from time to time. I knew, of course, I hadn't left the lights on and/or the door unlocked. But I also knew if we were talking serious harm, whoever was in the den wouldn't've been quite so open about it. Turned out, it was Cifelli.

I told him I hoped I hadn't inconvenienced him by not being there any old time he felt the mood to drop by. (Actually, I sort of said sorry I wasn't in and hope he made himself at home.) He said it was okay, he enjoyed looking at the view and it afforded him a chance to get away from the pressures of competitive everyday life and take a small breather. Though he did feel, if I didn't mind a little constructive criticism, I could stand to upgrade the quality of my scotch, blends not saying much for the state of my refinement.

"I hope the ice was okay," I said, taking a chance on a little light sarcasm.

"This brown stuff? I think you ought to give some thought to filtered water."

He was actually right. Though you'd think the city . . .

"What can I do for you, Mr. Cifelli?"

"Well, first off, I think you better feed your cat, it's starting to nibble my Ferragamo crocodiles."

Which turned out to be some Italian alligator loafers you could of bought a small house for. I picked the little guy up and headed for the kitchen. Cifelli came with, the while tickling Sven by the ears and making coochy-coo noises. I guess forgiving. He was also wearing some kind of nice cologne, not too strong, very laid back—talking capo, not cat. This man was a very long way away from sweat.

"I don't seem to be getting any reports from you," said Cifelli, watching me put cat gunk in a saucer on the floor. "Better add some water to the bowl," he reminded me. He was right, it was close to empty. "Water's very important, more important than food. Humans, too. Did you know a person can survive for upward of a month without food if he has water?" I knew that.

"Did you know," I replied, figuring I ought to show some things I knew, too, "the origin of the word *wop*?"

He didn't seem to change any expression when he answered, "Yeah, some guy got tired living."

"Wrong," I said. "It means With Out Papers. It was about immigrants didn't have like a green card."

"Thank you for sharing," he answered, somehow leaving me the impression I might of done better leaving well enough alone.

"I found it in a book, *1001 Things You Never Knew*. It was one of the ones I never knew."

"Right. The reports?"

"I haven't given you any reports because there hasn't been a whole lot to report. I'm sure you know the picture's a go again, with Laszlo Nagy replacing Fortunata directing. Everything else is more or less stet—not sure about the screenwriter. Which I get the feeling doesn't probably matter."

"I don't care about those details. What I need is some sort of hook to deal with Nash."

"I'd be happy if I could help, Mr. Cifelli. But you know that's not exactly my line of, uh, expertise."

"Never too old to learn something new. 1001 things. I thought we had an understanding you were going to nail Nash doing the murder."

"Of Fortunata."

"Right, of Fortunata."

"Well, I been sort of distracted. Would you like me to give back the money?"

"No, I'd like you to do the job I'd like you to do. Maybe I should explain something to you."

I had the awful feeling he was going to explain the nature of pain and my upcoming relationship to it.

"No, you don't have to. I promise you, if there's any way I can link Nash to this, I'd be more than happy to do it. I personally owe him—he had two of his guys do a number on me just because I talked to you. So it's not I don't want to help."

"Well, then you will. I have every confidence in you. Look, Rayford . . ." (Uh-oh, "Rayford"—anybody calls me Rayford they're not my buddy) ". . . let me background you a little. Fortunata was a gambler. I'm a gambler. We did gambling together. Happens I do it a little better. Bottom line, he was in to me for two hundred and eighty thousand dollars."

"Uh-huh!"

"As you know, I like to work things out. I suggested, when he seemed unable to repay, that instead he permit me to help produce his picture for a few modest points. Twenty-five. Nothing greedy. I was even still gambling— the show had to make a profit for me to collect. So we achieved a measure of agreement."

"But along came Nash."

"Along came Nash. Whatever his in, I don't know. I suppose Fortunata needed some actual cash. Hey, I'm not an unreasonable man—you work with me, give me a way to come out, I'll certainly listen to reason. But Nash, you know how it is with short people . . ."

I didn't know how it was with short people, except a lot of them were good dancers.

"The midget just didn't want to listen. I gave him a call— he gave me a dead Angelo. Is that reasonable? Is that the way civilized people do business?"

"Absolutely not, Mr. Cifelli. I'm totally your side."

"So I'd like to see you get a little busier on the job, some more concrete and immediate results."

"Ah-hah."

And then he did that semi-awful thing with the eyes when

the light sort of goes out and you can tell the human part left with it. "Capish?" he said.

"Right. Total capish. It just was—personal problems, all that. Got a little behind. But you're number one as of now, I promise."

"Good," he said, patting my cheek, handing me a bunch more money, petting the cat, and letting the light back in behind his eyes. I don't know why it is I keep worrying about him, he's a really fairly okay guy. So far.

"I didn't hear from you so I thought I'd drop by, maybe we could go grab a bite or you weren't up to it, send out for something," I said to Francie through the crack in the door.

"I don't want to," she said. "Anything else?"

"Well, work."

"Work. Right. I checked the deutsch marks thing you told Mark about, rate of exchange? I guess you were thinking Billy Zee might match up to that hundred fifty-three thousand something—"

"Well, I got the notion it was such an odd amount in dollars, one fifty-three eight forty-six, maybe it was even in something else."

"Yeah. Anyway, the exchange the week of the murder was one point six six to the dollar." She reached into her bathrobe pocket and came out with a slip of paper. "Which worked out to two hundred and fifty-five thousand, three hundred, and eighty-four deutsch marks."

"Not exactly a fit."

"While I was at it, I also checked on pounds, in case it was somebody English blackmailing or something."

"Francie, could I come in?"

She just kept the door barred, went on. "But I don't suppose it makes much difference now, Nigel Hampton being the only Englishman on the scene and him dead."

"Just for a few minutes. We could talk?"

"Anyway, for the record, the exchange that week was roughly one pound for a dollar seventy-four. So one hundred and fifty-three thousand, eight hundred, and forty-six dollars also comes to an odd amount in pounds." She again checked her notes. "Eighty-eight thousand, four hundred, and seventeen."

"OK. It was just a shot. Thank you."

"If that's all," she started closing the door.

"Wait, wait. Francie. Why are you shutting me out like this? I want to be in on it."

"You were in on it."

"Yeah, but not alone. Come on, you're my girl, woman, chick, whatever the hell it is you folks are these days. Lady-love, how's that?"

"I think not. I think maybe this is a good time to let it go."

"Look, you don't feel well. You're depressed. You don't want to see me right now. All right. I think you're wrong, but all right."

"I'm going to close the door now."

I stepped back. What could I do?

She closed the door.

Didn't even ask me was Sven okay.

On the corner of Fountain and La Cienega I stopped at the gas station and used the phone.

"Bradley, you're home, you're out. Good."

"And how. Quelle ordeal."

"Yeah, swell deal. So, Penny's lawyer got you out?"

"No, actually it was Brian riding to the rescue."

"Ah, good. Right. Listen, I'm near your neighborhood. I thought maybe we might grab a bite together, bring each other up to date."

"Aw gee, I'm sorry, Goodman. But Brian and I have plans. We're going to Eureka."

Whatever the hell that was.

"Oh, well, sure. I was going to check out the Swoop group today, but it didn't work out. So I thought maybe we'd pop over tomorrow morning and get going on some more interviews. We could be working the book and the case the same time."

"Sounds like a plan. Should I tell Francine?"

"I don't think she'll be up for it. Want to, even."

"Oh, I'm sorry about that."

"Well, she's a little moody. Probably be okay."

"I'm sure."

"So, I'll pick you up, ten okay?"

"Ten's good."

"And give my bes—say hello to Brian."

"Will do."

Hung up. Said good-bye first. Only on TV, the movies, people hang up without saying good-bye. Good-bye is very big in real life.

I cut back down to Beverly Boulevard and back east a few blocks to pick up some chicken at Golden Bird. They were out of business. Couldn't believe it. The best chicken ever was. No Chicken Delight, no Colonel Sanders, no Pioneer, ever touched Golden Bird. This old black guy, had two of them, wouldn't franchise. Satisfied he had enough, my understanding. Made the absolute best. Gone? Jesus. So many good things . . .

I popped up to Sunset, grabbed a five-piecer at Kentucky Fried, secret herbs and all, went home, cleaned up the new dump by the litter box—I catch on, cat—watched some crappy TV, flaked out.

Sure was exciting being a Hollywood private detective.

22

Mark Bradley

We did, of course, first return home for me to bathe and shave and Quik-Tan away my prison pallor. I bedecked myself (very few people I let do my bedecking) in my new Burberry double-breasted pinstripe gangster suit from Saks. I'd finally had it with trendy Chelsea Road charging such outrageous prices for such poorly made glitz. Not that I'd gotten exactly frugal. With the striped cotton Charvet shirt from Paris at a hundred and eighty dollars, the cravat from Battaglia I bought in lieu of feeding a family of four in Bangladesh for a week, and the one pair of Gucci loafers I'd found without either their colors or logo, I was a major movie coming to theaters everywhere.

With Brian similarly accoutred (he'd taken a more tolerant view of my overspending at Chelsea), we popped into the Beemer and drove, keeping to neutral subjects, to the wilds of Santa Monica and the oasis that was Eureka—Wolfgang Puck's newest adventure in trendiness. You had to hand it to the man. Probably no other chef and/or entrepreneur in California could have managed to erect an outlandishly expensive restaurant in an out-of-the-way, lowish-rent spot and draw the chicest, up-to-the-minute crowd. Well, sort of correction. It wasn't exactly the show-business insters of Spago renown. More an incredible number of well-heeled yuppie couples, with wives mostly in outlandishly expensive clothing, husbands in undistinguished shirtsleeves carefully–casually turned back to feature gym-enhanced forearms. The wives were without exception young and long-haired, the men almost young and almost always with the dry, sparse hair that seems to go with financial derring-do and over-leveraged stress. The waiters, young, cute, and gay, exchanged hugs with the yuppie wives—being Sports Connection buddies. The men looked pale and overworked, with strained smiles, somewhat relieved to be partially off duty (even if with business associates) inasmuch as the devastating din made deal making out of the question. It was a very beautiful place, packed with people extraordinarily grateful to be allowed in, about half of whom were at the bar sampling Wolf's new brew. The place was, essentially, or maybe superficially, depending on its success, a brewery, created from scratch to make his own designer beer.

The food was extremely spicy California cuisine, but as usual served with Puck's great style and panache. (I found the panache a little overseasoned.) Additionally, like most new places Eureka seemed to have been aurally designed by someone long deafened by decades of top volume rock 'n' roll. In the words of my partner, Ray Goodman, on another such occasion, "Hearing's becoming a lost art."

Thus in the superficial Sturm und Drang, we were successfully able to postpone our showdown fight, arguing in relatively less vested self-interested areas, to at least keep our chops in order (in the sense of emotional embouchures). Mostly it went along the lines of:

Me: "How can you order veal when you know what cruelty they're subjected to during their brief lives, living in tiny pens, unable to turn around, scarcely able to move, fed some antibiotic mush that causes constant diarrhea—"

He, interrupting, able simultaneously to flirt with a marvelous-looking waiter: "I suppose you think chickens and turkeys spend their weekends at Aspen?"

Me, determined to stick to the subject, or the non-subject to avoid *the* subject: "At least they should be allowed to run around free till that awful time comes. I'm really verging on vegetarianism."

He, not meeting *my* eyes, for sure: "Good luck. I hope you never find out broccoli's got feelings." Then, an original signer of the Declaration of Independence, to the waiter: "I'll have the parmigiana."

I've had better times.

But I, too, like the trendy and in and the hip, and it was definitely happening at Eureka. So, somewhat mollified by the prettiness of it all, and the good food, and the lack of hard liquor, I felt the stress of the day gradually loosening its grip on my molars, and got to the point where I could leave off rehearsing mentally the arguments yet to come. What also got me off the subject was noticing L'Ermitage's

Tiffany Kestner at a table along the far wall, in the company of Freddie Forbes, the set designer. Of course, he with the carved cheekbones, who spoke like a Hanna/Barbera cartoon only with the barest lip movement to avoid wearing out his facial parts (or drawing another panel), would have recovered from surgical enhancement at her establishment. The old queen was, as usual, wearing the high, stiff collars he affected. What with the taut, parchmenty cheeks and the starched neck, he looked like nothing so much as a petrified florist. Be that as it may, when he rose from the table and headed for the men's room, that being the closest to his gender (you may gather, I really dislike swishers), I got up quickly on a hunch and interrupted his progress just short of what sounded like an English soccer crowd waiting at the bar.

"Freddie! Freddie Forbes!" I called.

He turned, wondering if it weren't an auditory hallucination in all the din.

"It's me, here, Mark Bradley," I said, closing in and pulling him gently to one side (relieved I'd gotten to him before the rest room). "I see you're with Tiffany Kestner."

"You're, uh, the writer. Claudio's writer."

"Correct. We met at his house the day he, uh . . ."

"Bought the country cottage."

"Yeah."

"Well, nice running into you. Why don't we lunch one day?"

"I'd really like that," I said, investigative reporting requiring the occasional lie. "I was just curious about Tiffany. She okay?"

"Of course; why not?"

"Well, I mean, her—whatever—the attempted rape, I gather . . . the thing with Terry Coyne."

"The thing with Terry Coyne?"

"He was arrested, I understood, because of a complaint by Ms. Kestner."

"Oh, yes, but not for rape. For stealing a Fabergé egg."

"A Fabergé egg? I wouldn't imagine Terry would even know a Fabergé egg if he saw one."

"Between you, me, and the light source, I don't think Tiffany would, either. I'd bet a coon's wage it was not a Fabergé egg but an incredible simulation, you get my drift."

"So, wait a minute. Terry Coyne was arrested not for sexual assault, but stealing a phony Fabergé egg?"

"Life's little ironies."

"Just one question—why?"

"Because young Terrence is a kleptomaniacal sexual compulsive constitutionally unable to keep his hands to himself."

I suddenly got a flashback picture of Terry pocketing Claudio's lighter, back at the house.

"It's either snatch some snatch or something else," Freddie continued. "I'm sure he started out wanting dear sweet Tiffany's no doubt desirable body parts, but ending up instead with a figurative Fabergé egg on his face—the horrid heterosexual deviate." With which psychological evaluation the staid pillar of normality concluded his gossipy character assassination and with a—spare me—wave of the wrist, continued on to the rest room.

"Being only an amateur psychiatrist, it was always my understanding," I was saying to Brian on the way home, "that kleptomania and sexual compulsion were two separate disorders."

"Yeah, so're acne and baldness, but that doesn't mean you can't have both," he replied. I *know* I don't have acne, and whatever slight loss of hair I've experienced falls well within the range of normal atrophy.

"What makes you out of a clear blue sky choose acne and baldness?" I couldn't help asking, trying very much not to sound defensive.

"Because leprosy and bad breath were taken," he replied, settling nothing much. "Actually, I find it pretty funny that they came up with sexual compulsion as a disease nowadays you're supposed to get treated for. Can't you just see someone going in for therapy: 'Help, please, you've got to help me stop getting laid!' "

"True, it would top most people's list of Diseases I Can Live With. But the other thing is interesting. That Terry's a klepto."

"Yeah, I guess."

"I mean, it opens up some options that could explain some things."

"Like what he sees in that dumpy Maurissa Burroughs?"

"Maurissa Burroughs is hardly dumpy. You're talking about America's sweetheart."

"I thought that was John F. Kennedy, Junior."

And so it went. You can think of a lot to talk about if there's only one subject you daren't.

But finally we did arrive home. We talked about the evening's festivities, we talked about my experience in jail . . .

"Tell me about that penal code again," said Brian. "And stop pulling at your nose."

I'd been peeling skin off it ever since getting that awful sunburn aboard the *Last Rites,* or whatever it was, committing Claudio's ashes to the seas.

"Everybody in jail kept asking me to share the cocaine I didn't have. It got ugly there for a minute."

"Were there any cute fellow felons?"

"You'd be surprised what an unattractive crowd you get to meet in jail. No wonder Sean Penn was so at home."

"Can you believe him? Madonna must have been mad."

Which gives you an idea the lengths to which one can take avoidance.

"All right, let's talk about it," I said finally.

"Talk about what?" asked Brian not so innocently.

"We have to, Bri."

He sighed petulantly. "All right. Talk."

"What's going on?"

"Nothing's going on. Life is going on."

"Not life as we've come to know and enjoy it. What's changing?"

"Mostly just I'm bored. I'm young, I haven't done a lot of things. I want to . . . party."

"That's my impression."

"So? What's so terrible? You want me to say it, I'll say it—I want an open relationship."

And it was said. An open relationship being the equivalent of going to a marriage counsellor—the beginning of the end.

"Two reasons no."

"And my line is, which are?"

"One, I want a commitment. And (B) I want to go on living."

"And what you want is what we get. You know all about it. Your needs are more important than mine. Your knowledge is superior to mine. You're better at everything than I am."

"No, not everything."

"Oh?"

"You're better at sarcasm."

He smiled. He did have a sense of humor. You can get away with an awful lot if you have a sense of humor. But not everything.

"I'm sorry, Brian," I said finally. "It's not going to be that way."

"Then what happens?"

"What do you think happens? You go and do that exciting life you seem to want."

"How?"

"Not my table."

"But I don't have a job, I don't have any money."

"I guess you'll have to do something about that. I'll help you get started."

"Help? I expect a lot more than that."

"Why? Because you gave me the best months of your life?"

"I just, I think you should—do the right thing by me."

"I'm doing the right thing—not living a lie. I said I'll help you; I'll help you. I won't go on supporting you."

He took quite awhile thinking it over. We had time to get undressed, into nightclothes, and think about where everybody was going to sleep, that's how long.

"Well," he said finally, "maybe I made the wrong choice."

"I have no doubt you did. But you also did make the choice."

"No second thoughts allowed?"

"Not for the reason you're having them," I said. Then added, "You can sleep on the couch for a few days till you get yourself organized."

"You're sure?"

"I'm sure," I said, to my distress in a somewhat quavery voice.

"I'm used to seeing grown men cry—I go to Clippers games."

I gave him a wan smile. He took his pillows and a blanket. I figured, really, there was no law said you had to cry. The phone rang, postponing the decision.

"Hi, Bradley?" said Goodman.

"Yeah, hi."

"I'm not interrupting anything?"

"No." You can't interrupt something that's over.

"Thought you might be interested in something."

"Yes?"

"Forint."

"Forint."

"That's Hungarian money. You remember I asked you to ask Francie to check on Deutschmarks? Which didn't work. And she checked on pounds, which didn't work. I finally figured maybe something else."

"You're talking about the exchange rate?"

"Yes, the mysterious $153,846 Fortunata paid to X? Well, I know this lady over at City National Bank, and I asked her what was Hungarian money and what it traded for last week. Turned out forint, sixty-five to the dollar."

"And one-hundred fifty-three thousand and whatever turned out to be what?"

"One million forint."

"This where I say bingo?"

"This is where."

"Laszlo Nagy."

"The new odds-on favorite."

Phew.

"Good work, Goodman."

"I thought so. Pick you up ten in the morning."

"Right," I said, intellectually aware one didn't actually die of a broken heart. "See you in the morning."

23

Rayford Goodman

I woke up being suffocated by a wad of cotton pressed against my nose. I yanked it away, gulped air, bolted straight up—and tossed one scared little cat to the foot of the bed.

That's what it was going to be? Little cats sitting on your face at six in the morning? He hung there frozen, all four legs out straight, looking like an early American doorstop. I reached down and picked the guy up. Critter fit the palm of my hand. A shaking, purring, fluffy thing, big wide eyes. I found I wasn't particularly mad.

I did all the regular morning things, which now featured first feeding the kitty. Then I shaved, showered, washed my hair got dressed, and made a good breakfast. The last was courtesy Francie, who'd stocked the icebox. Usually, it'll come as no surprise, I had a tendency to run out of things. My icebox usually looked like the Antarctica display at a small town museum—icy and empty, give or take a stuffed penguin. Now, different icebox. I suddenly wondered was I the last person in America called the refrigerator icebox? There was a while I called it Frigidaire, but that got lost when Frigidaires started getting named logical things like Hot Point and Whirlpool. Icebox wasn't any dumber, come to think of it. She'd filled it with healthy foods for me, and good-tasting ones for herself. I figured the least I was entitled to was unhealthy eating. Made myself two fried eggs, bacon rare, cream cheese on a bagel, real coffee (what's the sense drinking coffee you take the benefit out?), half-and-half (already a compromise), and a real sweetener not made from petroleum by-products called sugar. Measure me for a casket.

It was still only a little after seven, so I used the next couple hours to make a start opening my last month's mail. It looked so awesome. But once you threw out all the catalogs it was mostly just appeals for charity. And since that'd clearly developed into a scam where the charity was just a product for the money raisers to profit on, all that left was bills.

Nobody, of course, wrote letters anymore. Which was just as well. What few letters did get written spent half themselves bawling out the other person not answering last time. Anyway, nobody wrote me.

I even paid some of the bills, then watched a little morning news on television. Or what passed for news—I won't go into that. And it got to be about nine-thirty.

I called Francie.

The answer machine went, "You have reached a person no longer in service. Don't leave a message, I won't get back to you. At the beep, give up."

Not a promising beginning.

"Listen, Francie, if you're home and can hear. We can talk about our personal problems anytime you want. We can even not talk about them, you want. But we do have business together. I still need to know what was in Fortunata's will, so go pick me up a copy. Then get fifty dollars from Penny, or petty cash, or I'll reimburse you. Put it in an envelope and take it to the county coroner's office— that's 1104 North Mission Road. Give the envelope to a Franklin Alonzo Skeffington, he's in Records. He's a skinny guy wears a lot of talcum powder and looks about half dead himself. Basic type cast. I want him to find out was it the same gun killed Nigel Hampton as Fortunata. I'm picking up Bradley at ten, and we'll be over at Fox to watch them shoot interiors on the picture. Maybe we can find out something." Which seemed to cover things.

Or almost.

Or not quite.

"I love you. Case you didn't know," I said, just beating the beep.

Girls like to hear that.

Bradley was waiting for me corner Kings Road and Willoughby, picking dead skin off his nose. Not the most attractive thing I ever saw him do, but I guess it passed the time.

I noticed he looked a little down in the mouth as he got in the car, and he didn't do much small talking as we drove on. I wasn't exactly top of the world myself. But he seemed worse off.

"I figured you had your own plan for the book and could keep on doing that while I worked on the case," I said, to get the ball rolling—not exactly new ground.

"Right," he answered. Which was I think the same as last time I said that.

"Mostly, naturally," I went on, "concentrating on zeroing in on Laszlo, now we know he got all that money out of Fortunata."

I cut down La Cienega, both quiet again.

"Of course, the thought occurs to me," said Bradley with a sigh, back to life, and back to complicating matters, "if Laszlo was blackmailing or extorting money from Claudio, he'd be the last one who'd want to kill the goose that laid et cetera."

At Wilshire I turned right, taking it out to Century City.

"I was hoping you wouldn't notice that," I answered. "Possible, too, though, that Fortunata said, 'Enough's enough, I'm gonna blow the whistle.' "

At Avenue of the Stars—what'd you think they were going to call it, Avenue of the Bit Players?—I turned south.

"But if Claudio was paying off before, for whatever reason, whatever new reason would there be for him to risk exposing whatever it was then, now?" said Bradley.

I didn't know. But I had to feel we were making progress, since there were so many more questions we didn't know the answers to than when we started.

At Pico, I turned west, past the Hillcrest golf club on the left, and on to the Twentieth lot a few blocks down on the right. I turned in, drove around, and stopped at the guard house—old Checkpoint Charlie. I recognized the guard.

"Norbie," I said. "Norbie Hunt. I haven't seen you, whew, must be fifteen years."

"Longer," he answered. "I'm Neil—Norbie's son."

"Right!" as people always say, as if they were grading someone instead of being corrected. "I'm Ray Goodman. I knew your father." Clearly. "Good to see you. You got bigger. So, you work here now." I wasn't getting a lot wittier. Get on with it. "What stage is the *Fell Swoop* company?"

"You expected?" he asked, consulting a clipboard.

"Ray Goodman," I repeated, since he apparently hadn't heard.

He continued to look. The phone rang, he went to answer. It was a good time to drive on through before I covered myself any more glory. We'd find it. He didn't shoot at us or anything.

In the movies or on TV, whenever they showed a movie lot there were always lots of Indians and guys in armor and Frankensteins walking around. Real life was a lot of guys with beer bellies you couldn't believe who did this and that and goldbricked till it was time to retire and pass the job and the belly on to their kid. I asked one of them where *One Fell Swoop* was shooting and he told me Stage 12, which I guess was enough work for this morning as he immediately sat down and lit a cigarette. Another guy came over to help him.

Stage 12, where I'm sure they made *Casablanca* or *Captain from Castile* or something loaded with history and romance was a warehouse you entered through a foot-thick freezer door into a holding hall facing another foot-thick freezer door with a cop light on it telling you don't go in if it's flashing. It wasn't flashing.

Inside, it didn't look like it'd be flashing for a long time, as four thousand people milled around doing what looked like not much of anything. By a lighted set we spotted ex-cameraman new director Laszlo Nagy talking to I guess *his* new cameraman. He was making a frame of his fingers and aiming it at some furniture on the set. It was the director version of the painter looking at his thumb. He then squinted through a viewing lens hanging around his neck and aimed that at the set. That didn't seem to do it, either, because then they both went and looked at a script in a leather cover with his name printed on it, lying on top a high captain's chair with his name painted on that, too. I guess directors had trouble remembering their names.

Bradley and I edged our way over to the fringes out of the hot lights around which everybody was hanging out. Maurissa having her makeup retouched, Claire and Barbara—I still hadn't talked to Barbara—and Sherry Cohen head-to-head with Vernon Charles. Head-to-head being mouth to ear. Sherry's mouth.

"I don't care why he's not here. He's not here, and not being here is costing us thousands of dollars a minute."

Vernon motioned Claire over.

"What's the latest?" he asked, clearly passing the buck. "Is Coyne out or not?"

"I have it on the highest authority Terry was released on his own recognizance about a half hour ago," said Claire, I guess his agent, too. "He'll be here any minute." That's what the Texas/Alabama lady said. What it sounded like was, "Ah hev't awn thighst awthahty Teh's relissd bou hef oweh go. He be he mos in min."

"If we had just about five minutes less in the can, I'd fire his sorry ass in a flash. It's what Claudio intended to do," said Sherry, not leaving much doubt who was the new boss in town. "The oversexed little bastard."

"He's not oversexed. And his ass is not sorry!" said Maurissa protectively.

I turned to Bradley. "You have to figure she knows the inside story," I said.

"From everything I've ever seen," agreed Bradley.

I couldn't help being thankful we were on a sound stage. Being made for sound, you could comfortably listen in on most any conversation anywhere, just by tuning in.

"So, you hear that?" I continued to Bradley. "Fortunata was going to fire him."

"Yeah. Is that a big exclamation point I see over your head?"

"Well, it's certainly a motive."

"Don't you love the way we keep narrowing things down?" he said.

Meanwhile, everyone was just hanging around loafing. Which was different from the way they hung around when they were working. Though it looked much the same. "Well, can't we shoot around him?" Sherry was asking Vernon.

"Can't we shoot around him?" Vernon asked Laszlo.

"Why not we shoot around him?" Laszlo asked his cameraman.

"We could shoot around him," said the cameraman. "Do Maurissa's reaction shots."

"All right, pipple. We're going do Maurissa reaction shots," said Laszlo to the company.

"Attention, everybody, we're going to do Maurissa's re-action shots," said the assistant director. I think the movie business has a lot of people hard of hearing or slow to catch on.

"Where is that?" said Laszlo, thumbing through his script.

Sure would be great if it was page 107—and missing (being I had 107 in my pocket, lifted off Hampton's body).

"Ninety-four," said the A.D., not too hip to the laying down of clues in the proper sequence.

Laszlo took a peek, then left the script on his chair. "OK, let's get the show on the film. Someone get Maurissa."

Someone went to get Maurissa. Turned out to be the A.D.

En route, the A.D. spotted us, decided there was a possibility we ranked even lower on the totem pole, and took a shot. "You people. This is a closed set, no visitors."

"Publicity," mumbled Bradley. "It's all right."

"It's not all right till I say it's all right!" The smaller they are, the smaller they are.

"Where is Maurissa?" shouted Laszlo. "How must I to wait for my actors?" He was nicely into being a director—already a Nazi. The A.D. scurried off. All being pretty dopey since Maurissa was only a few feet away and must have heard the whole thing. But it was a ritual. Tradition. Stupidity.

"Why don't you," I said out the side of my mouth to Bradley, "meanwhile go see what you can get out of Claire? I'll take a shot at Barbara, I been meaning all this time."

I could see the wheels turning in Bradley's mind. Was it because gay to gay I wanted him to question Claire? "Since you already talked to Barbara," I reminded him. "And I didn't yet."

He closed his part-open mouth, nodded instead, and together we crossed over to Claire and Barbara.

"Uh, Miss Aronson," I said. "Barbara? Could I have a word with you?"

"About what? If it's about the book—"

"Not exactly. It's more about trying to find out who killed your . . . friend."

"Isn't that the police's job?"

"Well, yeah. Also every responsible American citizen, too. Right?"

"I'm not going to tell a whole lot of personal things."

"Fine," I said, seeing she'd already committed. I maneuvered us slowly off to a side, out of the light, and away from Claire. "I just know there're things you could help with. Stuff only you'd know. You happen to be a very important figure in this case. Real unique."

I could see she didn't have a whole lot of objection to being called unique.

We settled over in a corner. She took out a pack of cigarettes and lit one. The smoke drifted my way. I could almost taste it. I'd given up smoking, but I didn't want to miss out on a chance for any possible rapport I might get, so I asked for one, too. I considered asking for one for later, too, but I had a little trouble justifying that in my mind. I lit up, then edged into business, starting easy. (Boy, it tasted good.)

"You actually live out at Fortunata's house."

"Well, I have been. I'll have to move now, of course."

"Take your meals, more or less have the run of the place?"

"Well, more, naturally when we were going together. But even just on a work basis, it wasn't just in the office, it was wherever."

"So you know the house, and you'd know the kinds of things he might or might not have."

"Why don't you just ask me what you want to ask me?"

"Does he have a gun?"

"Did."

"Did? What happened to it?"

She shrugged. "Gone."

Killed with his own gun? "When did you notice that?"

"Right away. The day he was shot."

"Who would have known where it was?"

"Anybody with eyes. He kept it on his desk. As a paperweight."

Which narrowed it down nicely. To anyone who'd ever been in his house. It didn't even have to be planned. Could have been spur of the moment, impulse. Argument, angry words, there it is, pick it up—bam.

No. Because whoever did it had to have hidden, or we'd have seen him. And not only after—before. Making it premeditated.

"Anything else?" asked Barbara.

Think later, take advantage now. "I just heard Fortunata was going to fire Terry off the picture. That true?"

"Yes, it's true. The dailies hadn't been all that great, and Terry's not the most endearing person you'll ever meet."

"Anybody else about to be canned?"

"Not that I know of."

"But you would know."

"True."

"So, Terry was the only one. Nobody else. Not, say, any other actors."

"No, firing actors is always the hardest because you have to junk whatever film you have they're already in."

"How about others? Set designers, dressers, whoever."

"Not that I know of."

"Say, Vernon Charles, the producer?"

"Why would he fire him?"

"No idea, it was just a for-instance."

"Well, I can assure you, if there was one person who was not—at any time—in the remotest danger of being fired, it was Vernon Charles."

That was interesting its own way. Why so sure? It was about then Terry Coyne arrived. Or Rocky Balboa. A lot of noise. About as underplayed as Cleopatra entering Rome. Which did it for interviewing Barbara, again. Everyone gravitated to the noisy, center stage–grabbing star.

"You wouldn't fucking believe what they fucking did to me," he commenced, dialogue by Tom Lasorda. "I haven't had that much attention around my asshole since I changed agents."

Which is when a none-too-pleased Maurissa joined the group. "Just answer me yes or no, is it like true you raped that L'Ermitage lady?" she demanded, no dancing about the shrubbery.

"Maurissa, how could you even think such a thing?" said Terry, all outraged innocence. "She just got pissed off because I wouldn't."

"Why wouldn't you, was she like physically deformed?"

"No, she's beautiful. Hey, babycakes, I wouldn't because I and you are fucking going together."

True love is sure touching.

"After all I've like done for you," said Maurissa.

"This is certainly very fascinating," said Sherry Cohen. "But since we're already two and a half hours behind schedule today alone, could we hold the romantic specifics till lunch and perhaps get on with making the picture?"

"Who the fuck's this?" said Terry. "I'm talking, lady."

"Uh," said Vernon Charles. "Terry, I guess you don't know Sherry Cohen?"

"No, I don't know Sherry Cohen. And I don't want to know Sherry Cohen. And I don't give a rat fuck about Sherry Cohen."

"Yeah, I think you do," she said. "You just don't know it yet."

"My boy," said Laszlo Nagy, putting his arm around the star. "Maybe you would like it to say hello the new president Fortaco Productions?"

"Sherry Cohen?" said Terry.

"Sherry Cohen," said Sherry Cohen.

"You're fucking gorgeous," said Terry, who I felt sure always knew which side his bed was buttered on.

24

Mark Bradley

While the world champion sucking-up contest was under full steam, I had other metaphors to fry. After first ascertaining Goodman's assignment to interview Claire wasn't just stereotypically setting a gay to catch a gay (not unlike the newscasts, where Hispanics always interview Hispanics, and blacks blacks—"This is Seamus O'Hoolihan reporting drunk from just inside the Shamrock Bar and Grill . . ."), I immediately cashed in on it.

"So, Claire, didn't I see you and Barbara at the Gay Pride parade the other day?"

"Prolly. We wuh awn the Muthers and Uthers for Lesbin Rahts flo'." ("Probably. We were on the Mothers and Others for Lesbian Rights float.")

"Uh-hah. But I thought I heard somewhere she used to go with Claudio?"

"Evuhbody used to go wi' someb'dy. Nob'dy starts out a full blown—you should par'n the 'spression—lesbin. Truth b'told, Clawdo turned her out. Not on purpose, a course."

"He treated her badly?"

"He wadn't her favit puhson."

"Still, she kept on working for him."

"Look lak."

That meant something. There was a clue in there somewhere. But I had to be careful. I didn't want to spook her into clamming up. (Beginner's gumshoe jargon.)

"You folks fixin' t'put me in you all's book, too?"

"In all probability. You're one of the players." Ah-hah, the old ego-stroke key to the door.

"It's, uh guess, alus good for bidness."

There was a little flurry of noise, a definite increase in hubbub volume. Similar to but different from when Terry showed up.

"What's goin' on?" said Claire.

Out of the corner of my eye I could see that Nash and Heather had come onto the set. His arrival seemed to have added to the undercurrent of tension. Understandably. His entire little being radiated danger and implied threat.

"Nash and Heather Hansen," I said. "Over there, by Vernon Charles." I noticed Barbara leave Goodman and cross over, too. "Goodman was telling me he saw Barbara having lunch with them at the Ivy the other day."

"I wouldn't be surprised."

"The day they were strewing Claudio's ashes."

"Yah."

"Well, I'd have thought Barbara would just naturally go to that."

"I tole you, it was all over 'tween her and Clawdo."

"It was all over between everybody and Claudio. I'd still expect her to go. I mean, even so, unless of course she hated him."

"You askin' writer-wise or detective-wise? Because if you're tryn make something out of her not bein' on the boat, you're jumpin' to conclusions."

Being a person who usually just hops to conclusions, I noted her desire to tell me something here. "And she wasn't _not_ going somewhere—"

"Right, she was _going_ somewhere—to lunch with the man'd become her new boss even befoah, Barry Nash."

Ah-hah. Whatever significance there was to that. Across the way I could see Vernon Charles leave Nash and Heather and go say something to Laszlo Nagy.

"So let me understand, Barbara's working for Nash? Has been for a while? Even when she still worked for Claudio?"

"Look, whatever you may think of him, Barry Nash is right generous with money. The pay is goo-ood. And that's another thing Clawdo stiffed her on. He figgered allowin' her the pleasure of his body was enough."

"I still don't see why she stayed."

" 'Cawse fo' a bit, it was enough. Till he, mannuh of speakin', spread it around."

"And now?"

"Old Barb's done went and gone alternate life-style."

"So I gather."

"Which ah puhson'ly view as one small step for womankind."

Then there was a lot of shouting of "Quiet," "Quiet on

the set," "Everybody quiet!" Which I could see indicated some actual impending production. Claire crossed in to watch, and I did the same, sidling (I'm especially good at sidling) up to Goodman.

"Get much from Claire?" he asked quietly.

"Not a whole lot. You?"

We exchanged intelligence separately gathered. Until more current business was about to commence.

"Quiet!" the A.D. thundered to no one in particular. Just on general principles. Tradition.

"All right, now, darling, in this scene," Laszlo was telling Terry, "you find out the woman you trusted so much your whole future been going around and fooling around this other guy, worse, your enemy."

"The cunt's no good," said Terry.

"With shadings," said Laszlo. "But I don't want, you're letting her *know* you know. So you act like it's normal everything, but it's no longer normal everything—a tightening of the lip, a coldness from the eye."

"She's a cunt."

"Got it," said Laszlo. "Now you, darling," he said to Maurissa, "got your own reasons. It's not all black and white. No man's a villain to himself."

"Never mind the man, what about me?"

"I mean you—man, woman, the same. Nobody says it 'Look how bad I am, what a rotten person.' Everybody thinks they're right, everybody's got inside an excuse."

"Ah, my like motivation!"

"Your motivation."

"And besides?"

"Besides, the other guy gave you a big bunch money."

"Works for me," said Maurissa.

We watched as they rehearsed the scene. Laszlo was working confidently, and to my less than expert, yet sophisticated eye (I *had* seen most of the movies ever made) doing a more than competent job.

Goodman, I noticed, used everybody's preoccupation with the scene to amble over toward Laszlo's director chair, on which still sat his director's script. Meanwhile, to my surprise I saw that Harvey Pitkin was somehow, unobtrusively (he majored in unobtrusive) on the set. Did that mean he was back on the picture? Must be. Which also meant he benefited from Claudio's death. The man Claudio'd publicly humiliated and fired off the picture was now both reemployed and (coincidentally or otherwise) avenged. That'd bear looking into.

And speaking of looking, I now noted Goodman looking at me from just outside the ring of light, at the director chair, indicating with a sideways tilt of the head to join him. Which I did, super casually, covered by the diversion of the director directing.

"So now, Terry, you're going to enter the room, look like nothing's changed, but showing a little something's changed, and go up to Maurissa sitting by the fire and say your line."

"Hi, honey, I'm home."

"Right. That's the line?" To the script girl, "Hi, honey, I'm home?" The girl nodded.

"Wouldn't it be better," said Terry, "if I said, 'I bet you'd never believe what happened to me today, honey, hi, I'm home.' "

"No," said Harvey, "the 'Hi, honey, I'm home' is satirical, deliberately cliché."

"Right," said Terry. "It's cliché. 'I bet you'd never believe what happened to me today, honey, hi, I'm home.' That's original. Whatta ya think, Laz?"

Laszlo affected to be seriously considering this wonderful suggestion. All the while his eyes examined the rafters and carefully avoided taking official note of Harvey walking off the set. We, meanwhile, took the opportunity this diversion afforded to sneak a peek at his script. On the pages opposite the dialogue were all the notations similar to, or maybe identical with, those which had been in Claudio's—camera setups, angles, notes. It seemed to me I even remembered some remarks verbatim.

"Looks like the same script," I whispered to Goodman.

He quickly flipped to page 107. It wasn't missing, but the 107 that was there looked suspiciously virginal—no notations at all on the back. Then he closed the script and reopened the leather binder to the first page—which turned out to be the original cardboard cover. There was a water stain in the shape of a circle—where Goodman'd set his glass down when it was still in Claudio's outer office the day of the murder. It was the same script.

"That means Laszlo's the son of a bitch who hit me over the head!" I said.

"Unless it was Hampton."

"Hampton? How Hampton?"

"Well, he was the one, after all, with the original page 107. How did he get it and *when* did he get it?"

Now my head hurt all over again from remembering being zonked and trying to figure out what Goodman'd just said. But mulling time was running short as I heard Laszlo's voice. "Let me take a look," he said, presumably in response to Terry's brilliant addition to the dialogue. I looked up to see he'd turned and was headed our way. Goodman, meanwhile, quickly replaced the script in the position we'd found it, but whether quick enough or not was hard to tell.

"What're you pipple?" said Laszlo. "Supposed to be a closed set."

"Don't mind us," said Goodman. "We're not here to interfere with the picture."

Laszlo humphed (middle-Europeanly), took his script, and went back to the lighted circle.

". . . we're here to solve a murder," concluded Goodman sotto voce, evidently too sotto to get a rise.

I motioned for him to follow me farther away from the action, where we settled behind some packing crates.

"Let me suggest something," I suggested. "When I was in jail Terry gave me the distinct impression Laszlo was a lot more than just Claudio's cinematographer. That he was the one who actually did the creative work, planning the shots, the setups, characterizations. Essentially a ghost director."

"Which would explain the million-forint payoff," said Goodman, nodding. "It didn't have to be blackmail—it could have been simple payment for his services. We might even be able to find, either in other scripts they worked on together, or bank records, that there were other payoffs like that."

"Right. Which would ordinarily tend to make you think he'd have a vested interest in keeping Claudio alive, to trade on his special relationship. But maybe, just maybe instead, the understudy finally got fed up with waiting for the star to get sick and created his own opportunity to get onstage. There came a time the money wasn't enough, he wanted the glory, too."

"And if Hampton knew that, and could prove it by producing the payoff note from the script . . ."

"Then he'd have to go, too!"

"Good thinking," said Goodman, allowing me about a second and a half in which to bask. "Only one flaw," he went on. "How could he have known once Claudio was out of the way *he'd* get the job?"

"That's the only flaw," I agreed, hearing the steady hissing of busted balloon.

"Quiet! Who is that talking?" thundered Laszlo, immediately followed by several guys screaming "Quiet! Quiet on the set!"

And when it was absolutely, totally hush, dead still quiet, the A.D. added, "Shhh!"

We watched Terry come through the door, cross to Maurissa, and say, "Hi, honey, I'm home" many, many times. We heard, "Hi, *honey*"—with menace, with awareness, with contempt. We heard, "Hi, honey, *I'm* home"—signifying if she expected the duplicitous lover, she was in for a disappointment. We heard, "Hi, honey, I'm *home*"—giving just a hint of what their place of residence meant and what she stood to lose. And one final take, in deference to his nuisance value, of Terry's version—"I bet you'd never believe what happened to me today, honey, hi, I'm home." Which he wanted to do again, not sure he'd gotten all the deep subtext and implied wealth of meaning. Laszlo gave that suggestion due consideration, came to a decision.

"Lunch!" he said.

"Lunch!" shouted the A.D.

The actors and crew swiftly dispersed. Lunch was important. For Maurissa it meant either a time for confrontation with Terry or, more likely, a time for consumption of Terry. And vice versa. For the crew it meant surcease from idleness, a chance to move about, go eat something, drink something, smoke something. For Barbara it meant reporting to Nash—we could see his beady eyes look upward in our direction, then narrow unpleasantly. Claire stood off to one side, waiting for Barbara to finish her finking.

"I think this might be a good time for us to get out of here," I suggested to Goodman.

"You may be right. Although one of these days, I'm going to have to go one-on-one with that Hansen woman. She knows I know she was the one at the Ermitage. That can't make her too comfortable."

"Maybe she feels you'll give her professional courtesy—since you're both in the same business."

"We are not in the same business. I'm a good guy," replied Goodman indignantly.

"Well, I meant in the adversarial sense—the chasers and chasees. Whatever," I finished lamely.

In the very short while it had taken to discuss this, the stage had virtually emptied. The workers were gone; the actors were gone; the director, producer, A.D., script girl—we were suddenly very alone with just Nash and Hansen, the former eyeing us in his steely way, the latter listening and nodding, also eyeing us. It made me distinctly uncomfortable.

"More and more I think we ought to get the hell out of here. Lunch would be good—someplace off the lot, for example," I said.

"Face. You gotta save face," said Goodman, staring back at them. "You can't ever blink, show fear or nervousness."

"I suppose that rules out running?"

At the very moment Hansen started slowly toward us, a delivery boy, in uniform, entered noisily and crossed over toward Nash.

"Goodman?" he asked. "Letter for Mr. Goodman. You Mr. Goodman?"

"Not only ain't I Mr. Goodman," said Nash, indicating us, "but you better get to him right away, or else it could be very hard to make any kind of delivery. To Mr. Goodman. Or his associate," he added, an addition which didn't contribute a lot to my day. The delivery boy came over to us as Hansen retreated back to Nash, and after a brief consultation, both left the stage.

"Letter for Mr. Goodman," the boy said. "Sign here."

Goodman took the envelope, signed. The boy didn't immediately depart.

"Tip?" I whispered.

"He's a professional," said Goodman. "It's what he does for a living. He gets paid a salary. This man doesn't want a tip."

"No, what I want is your fucking philosophy," said the boy, still lingering.

Goodman, unperturbed, opened the envelope and extracted its contents, a single page.

"From Francie," he said. I gathered we were to be denied

the pleasure of her company. "She says she talked to my man at the coroner's . . ."

"And?"

"And I owe her fifty dollars bribe money."

"And?"

"He said a comparison of bullets from the bodies of Fortunata and Hampton revealed both were shot by .22's."

"Yeah? I'm beginning to feel like a straight man—a feeling I haven't had since puberty."

"And that both were fired from the same weapon."

"Which means what? That's good, right?"

"In a way."

"Which is?"

"One killer."

"So, what's bad?"

"One of the people—or two of the people—Maurissa and Terry, mostly Terry . . ."

"Didn't do it because they dumped their gun after Claudio's murder but before Hampton's! At least it rules them out."

Progress.

"It rules out they did it with that gun," said Goodman.

Very little progress.

"Doesn't it rule out anything?"

"Yeah—a simple solution."

I was afraid of that.

Meanwhile, the delivery boy remained.

"What the hell is it?" said Goodman.

"There's also another message."

"Yeah?"

"Verbal. From a guy outside."

"Well?" demanded Goodman.

"Let's see . . ." said the kid pointedly, as if trying hard to remember. I couldn't stand it anymore. I reached into my pocket, came out with a five.

"Here," I said.

All this, of course, took a bit of time. Which is why by the time he actually delivered the message, which was, "Get out, fast"—it was almost immediately followed by an explosion, which ripped the camera to pieces, the set to shreds, and the lights to a thousand points.

25

Rayford Goodman

We were really lucky. Or semi-lucky. Total lucky would be the dopey kid gave us the message he was supposed to right away. It never occurred to him, "Get out, fast" might mean *fast*. The semi-lucky part was we were behind the packing crates, pretty much away from shit zero.

Still, while I didn't seem to be hurt in any way, and I could see Bradley and the kid were both all right, I didn't seem to be getting up. It felt like some kind of beam had fallen on my chest, like I was sort of lying there with a big hunk of something on my chest. But after I started to feel the nausea in my neck, at the sides of my throat, and the great bursts of sweat pouring off me, I knew it wasn't the explosion, it was your basic angina attack—full out.

"What is it?" I could hear Bradley saying. "You all right?"

I meant to answer. It was a direct question. I didn't want him to go worrying.

"You're not all right. You hit by something?"

"Pocket. Nitro," I replied, I thought helpfully.

It got a little vague after that. Were the firemen paramedics? Were they just studio firemen? Was it a studio vehicle taking me to, I guess, the hospital?

It was the hospital, that much got clear pretty soon. I'd been, looking back, given a shot of something. Otherwise it would of been clearer, since it wasn't the first time this happened. Though not exactly an old friend. I remember telling Bradley not to forget Francie's memo—I didn't want anybody else to see it—and him telling me not to worry about things like that. What'd he want me to worry about, dying?

Another thing I remembered before taking, I guess, a nap. The whole thing wouldn't've happened the goddamned messenger hadn't hassled us for a tip.

* * *

The decision I made, though why for chrissakes they brought in Luana, I can't imagine. We were divorced, after all. But that didn't stop her calling in specialists and consultants who were going to charge an arm, a leg, and part of a heart. We were not going to "shoot for open-heart surgery." They wanted to try another angioplasty, okay with me. More than that, no way.

Luana strongly felt I should "have it fixed, darling, once and for all." But once and for all didn't strike me too reassuring. Plus, it was hard to feel a woman who'd cheated on me, walked out on me, left with another other guy, then taken me to the cleaners to pay for all that action, necessarily had my best interests at heart, no pun intended.

So then, she wasn't there after a while, and while I was still nice and doped, in came the lawyers or lawyer doctors to stress me out with informed-consent shit. "You may die. You may become paralyzed. You may suffer a fatal heart attack. You may have a stroke. In certain rare instances, you may turn into a wounded wallaby. Sign here."

I hate that shit. How can they subject you to that kind of anxiety just before a medical procedure?

Then there's the other crap you have to sign. If you really read it you'd never have anything done, any time. It says you assume all the risks. That even if they're dumb, negligent, malicious, and try and/or succeed in killing you, tough shit. You relinquish all claims now and forever by you, your dog, and anybody you might ever know in this or any afterlife. I sign because the doctor says I need the procedure. I sign because I basically believe no matter how many lawyers can dance on the head of a pin, if they do something really gross—like leave a clamp inside you—no jury's going to pay any attention to what you signed. You're going to get awarded eight million dollars. Which, of course, you won't collect. Because they'll appeal. It'll be knocked down to eight hundred thousand dollars. The lawyer'll get half, the rest will be hospital bills—and you'll get to keep the clamp.

When they do an angioplasty, they keep a continuous stream of fluids being pumped into you intravenously. The same stream comes continuously out your dickie. You have a choice of ignoring it, just peeing it on out, which tends to leave you in a soaked bed to recuperate, or they put on a condom. (They have a third option, which is a catheter, but I can't imagine any man in the history of medicine ever opted for a catheter.) You choose the condom. But the fear of death and or turning into a wounded wallaby is so pervasive, you shrink to the size of a thimble and the condom slips off. So you wind up anyway in the recovery room in a soaked bed. I tell you these delightful details because I don't understand why they can't at least make you comfortable post-op. Part is it's easier for them to lift you from the procedure table in the sling/sheet, whatever it is, in one move, onto the gurney. Then dump the whole package, sling/sheet and you, onto a bed. I guess it's easier on the help. The upshot is you're stuck lying in the wet for eight hours or so. Not so oddly enough, what I remember most.

The procedure itself is a lot like an angiogram. They stick a needle through your groin, and I think simultaneously an arm, and work a wire or wires up into your artery. At the end of which is a balloon. They inflate the balloon, to push aside the fatty deposits and this feels exactly like a heart attack. Because they are stopping the blood and air and what-all (I don't promise to be totally scientific) from reaching the heart. It hurts. It really hurts. They do it over and over again, and you have these feelings of a heart attack over and over again. And it's fantastic, because you almost the minute it's over feel better.

And I was in a soaked bed, feeling very uncomfortable, even though by then it was practically clear water.

But I hadn't turned into a wounded wallaby.

I stayed in the recovery room for what seemed to me, anyhow, many, many hours, during which I wasn't allowed any visitors. I wasn't up for reading, there wasn't any TV; I wasn't in much pain. So I thought.

If all the mayhem and carryings-on was of a piece, it certainly tended to look like a Cifelli gang number. He had the motive, being stiffed out of the money Fortunata owed him. Then, with a chance he might have recouped with his piece of the picture, even Fortunata out of the picture, getting aced out of that, too. And being Nash was the guy not only stole his piece, also killed Angelo. But wasn't he out before Fortunata was iced? Right. So, as Rosanne Rosanadana used to say, "Never mind." I learned one thing, though. Don't try to solve mysteries in intensive care. Your mind's not totally on your work.

* * *

In the tiny, tiny room they moved me to, the first visitor I had was Armand Cifelli. Speak of the dickens.

"I know you might assume, from various circumstantial situations, that this might be me," he said.

I wasn't so sick I didn't know to keep my mouth shut.

"It was not me. That I could be capable of wreaking vengeance on my adversaries isn't an action beyond my purview. Is that the correct word, *purview*?"

He was asking the right guy.

"I am capable of that, but I want you to know I was not responsible. I would certainly never place anyone on my side in that kind of jeopardy."

"Even you warned him get out fast?" I choked out finally.

"You do suspect me."

"The thought sticks in my mind."

"You know me, if nothing else, as a practical man."

"All right."

"What's to be gained? The set is destroyed. Does that end the picture? Does that even seriously impede the picture?"

I had to admit it only stops things a day or two.

"Right. Which is covered by insurance. So no one is hurt."

Then why was I in the hospital?

"But what was the intention? If not to kill you—I assume your associate wasn't the target . . ." (I always loved the way they called everybody associate—"Meet my associate, Vinnie; my associate, Augie; my associate, Mom.") ". . . you were. But if the object was to get rid of you, why then, as you recall, warn you by sending a message to get out?"

I was tired. I was in a post-op situation. What did he expect from me, serious thinking?

"It was to scare you off. And of all the people who might have an interest in scaring you off, I rank lowest. Since I'm the one scared you *on*. You work for me. If I changed my mind, I have only to tell you and stop paying you. So I wanted you to know, when you felt up to figuring this out, you could start by eliminating me."

Which was, in its own way, a nice bit of attention. It beat a horseshoe of flowers anyway.

* * *

An angioplasty isn't open-heart surgery by a mile and a half. These days they hardly want you to stay longer than it takes to get the bed dry (I was in a new, clean bed, thank you). You're up before you know it and walking, and arguing about the bill in no time flat. A word about which, by the way. The trouble with doctors (and lawyers, for that matter), they've got a vested interest in not solving your problem. The less they solve it, the more money they make. The minute they solve it, the paying stops. Now, the Taoists of old China had the right idea. They only paid their physicians when they were well. If they got sick, the treatment was free. That's an incentive.

I learned that once from a bartender in Chinatown. Or maybe it was a B girl on the next stool.

Be that as it may, I hadn't got to that yet. Arguing about the bill. What I had got to was being able to think about the whole situation. Cifelli was right, and it was also nice of him to care enough to let me know. Anyway, nice or not, I was working for the man because working for him was the easiest way out. And because it happened to be we had the same interests. And also it paid.

The second visitor I had was Bradley. He got as far as the door to this little room with the glass windows all around. I could hear the nurse telling him no one was allowed visitors when in intensive care. Which made me think two things: why hadn't Francie at least tried to come, and (B) did I dream Cifelli?

I knew I didn't dream Cifelli. He'd been there, visitors or no visitors. The regular rules just didn't apply to the likes of an Armand Cifelli—any more than the Frank Sinatras or Jackie O's of this world. You don't tell those people anything about rules.

But if you weren't Armand Cifelli or Frank Sinatra or Jackie O and you wanted to get in, needed to get in, had a reason to get in, what then? Then, cliché had it, you did the doctor thing—sneaked a white jacket and a stethoscope, and pretended you were a doctor. If you were a man.

The reason I was having these thoughts at this particular time was the back of that nurse I could see, carefully keeping her back to me, the staff, anybody who passed, was scary familiar. Because if you had to get in and were a woman, you'd dress as a nurse. And if you'd done it before, say at L'Ermitage, you'd even have your old uniform ready to go.

Heather Hansen finally got her moment when there was no traffic around and turned to face my room. And even though I'd suspected it was her, I still like to have another coronary on the spot.

I had a slight advantage being I was in the dark and she was in the light. But I couldn't get out, because the glass door was the only way, and that faced her right on. I could feel my heart beating wildly in my chest. I looked at the monitor and saw the peaks peaking higher and more irregular. Heather took a few steps and started toward the room. There was no way out for me, and no weapon I could improvise any match for a gun. I looked around desperately, but I knew there was no place to go. I couldn't even roll off the bed with any hope of hiding. I didn't have that much mobility.

I could see her peering into the gloom in my room, the glass probably reflecting back at her. But she had to know it was my room. It couldn't be any accident. An orderly or someone started by. I considered calling out, but then whoever it was would come in the room and no doubt turn on the light, making me an even better target. By which time, anyway, the moment was lost as he kept on wherever he was going. Heather took another few steps, was now just about five feet from my room. I felt my heart beating even louder, even faster. When she peered into the windowed door to be sure it was me, I had a flash of all the movies I'd seen where the good guy had the foresight to put a bunch of pillows in the bed instead of himself. Then there'd be the *ptu-ptu-ptu* as the dumb killer shredded the goose down. I hadn't had that insight. Instead I lay there, watching the door slowly open, feeling my heart beat so loud and hard I was sure it would burst through my chest as I saw it was no doubt Heather, and no doubt a very large .38 in her hand.

I took one last breath and held it, as the fleeting chauvinist thought passed my mind how embarrassing I was about to be killed by a goddamned girl.

26

Mark Bradley

The first thing I did after the explosion was find out I was
OK. I'd certainly read many times how in emergencies others have unhesitatingly turned to the care and well-being of
their fellow folk. So I guess I wasn't a hero. Though the
thought did occur heroism might involve a certain amount
of stupidity, or perhaps a genetic lack of basic survival instinct. I will say this, I didn't concentrate *long* on self-
preservation. Partly this was due to an almost immediate
feeling of elation to find I'd survived, and to the virtually
simultaneous realization my partner was in serious trouble.
There are degrees of non-heroism.

As directed, I located a small bottle of nitroglycerin tab-
lets in his side pocket, and slipped one under his tongue. I
could see his face was a solid sheet of perspiration, his
breathing extremely labored, and I hadn't a doubt he was
suffering a cardiac attack.

To my enormous relief, the nitro quickly began to restore
him. I was doubly happy not to have to give mouth-to-
mouth CPR, as I'm reasonably certain in the fullness of
time, on recovery, he would have come to regard it as a
sexual overture. He should be so lucky.

Anyhow, once he was safely ambulanced to UCLA Medical and his personal physician summoned, I turned my attention to the immediate circumstance. The set was a
shambles. But evidently, nobody else'd been hurt. I couldn't
really tell who was suspiciously absent or merely at lunch.
Sherry Cohen was around, slightly dishabille, in company
with Terry (they sounded a lot like a vaudeville billing—
Sherry and Terry, Tops in Taps), who I'd venture to guess
had been solidifying relations with his new employer in his
dressing room trailer. I looked for Maurissa, but she either
wasn't there or was keeping a low profile, perhaps to avoid
confrontation. She had a new employer, too. Barbara and

Claire I didn't see, either; nor Heather Hansen and Barry
Nash. Harvey Pitkin was around, maintaining his usual air
of betrayed depression. Vernon Charles, I expected and
spotted. ("I needed this. Everything wasn't bad enough,
going to cost a fortune in overtime.") I had him pegged as
the kind who would have brought his lunch from home,
both as most cost-efficient and to be on the scene for just
such a contingency. Had to be a Virgo. Freddie Forbes, the
set designer, seemed genuinely distressed to have lost his
set. But actually, he stood to profit a lot when they rebuilt
it. A vague motive, were he feigning chagrin. Highly doubt-
ful. And of the various guildsmen, grips, prop men, best
boys, gaffers, carpenters, electricians, sound men—all the
fat middle-aged practitioners of these and other arcane
movie arts and crafts—I saw no one who immediately in-
voked my suspicion.

The messenger was missing, I noticed. But it wasn't remotely possible he'd had anything to do with it.

I found the memo Francine had sent over, strangely—
in light of the cyclonic explosion—right next to its original
envelope. I picked them both up, tucked the memo in the
envelope, the envelope in my pocket, and made tracks the
hell out of there.

Things had been getting the merest bit out of hand, it
seemed to me, and with Goodman hors de combat, it would
behoove me (always a good behoover) to take care of business—before business took care of me.

To that end I had hied myself hence, to the office.

Now, hours later, having managed to elude Penny—evidence in favor of a deital existence—settled quietly in my
office, I continued to pursue serious mulling and musing.
The instinct to get something down on paper (or on computer) remained strong. But the need to make some sense
out of it all first even more compelling. So I went around
another time.

Who the hell would want to blow the set up? Why? Superficially, Cifelli. He was odd man out. He was, really, an
injured party. But there was no profit in it. And Cifelli
was not a man for idle gestures, even violent ones. In my
experience he never did anything on sheer emotion. So for
the moment, rule out Cifelli. The only other person I could
think of who might do such a thing was Nash. But he suf-

fered a loss from it. Or if, because of insurance, no loss, at least a delay, and certainly no gain. Unless he wanted to make it appear Cifelli was responsible. But even that didn't offer a profit. Still, of course, Nash *was* the sort who operated on emotion. And there was no one else I could see who'd remotely profit. Plus, if he could make it look like something Cifelli had done *and* be rid of us, at least Goodman, who I guess he knew worked for Cifelli, that had to be a gain from his point of view. Best fit I could work—for now, anyway.

The other piece we had was Francine's memo—and where the hell was she, by the way?—which I took out of my pocket. I reread the results of her interview with someone named Franklin Alonzo Skeffington in Records, at the county coroner's, apparently a contact of Goodman's, to whom she'd given fifty dollars. Here, in typical Francine fashion, she appended a voucher for business funds expended on behalf of Pendragon Press, under "PURPOSE" describing it as "Bribe to county official to illegally reveal information about confidential details of a pending investigation."

As I recalled, the memo said Fortunata and Hampton had both been killed by .22s, the same weapon.

Goodman and I had started to talk about that before the roof fell in, so to speak. It meant Terry and/or Maurissa couldn't have shot Hampton—and at us—with the gun I saw Maurissa bury in the briny. Which tended to let them off. But then why were they dumping the gun, and what gun, altogether?

Then I got it. Before the blow-up, Goodman had told me he found out from Barbara that Claudio had a gun, which he kept openly on his desk, as a paperweight. We knew Terry stole things. Even Forbes knew Terry had a problem. (I could just imagine Goodman's definition: "No problem, he's a fucking thief.") So, either because that's what he generally did, or out of pique that Claudio was considering firing him—assuming he knew, and if Claire, his agent, knew, he would have—he stole the gun. But when Claudio turned up dead, he got understandably nervous to have the gun in his possession. Even if it wasn't the murder weapon, it was stolen from the scene of the crime, at the time of the crime. So, helped by Maurissa, he decided to deep-six it. I liked that. Nice and neat. Rang true. I was getting the hang of this. Which is when the door opened, and a bedraggled Francine shlumped in.

"Hey, nice of you to honor us with your presence," I said, by way of avoiding talk of the big A.

"Go fuck yourself," she replied noncommittally.

"You, uh, OK?" I immediately crumbled.

"Wonderful. Terrific."

Dance, ballerino, dance—I cautioned myself.

"Good, then maybe we can get some work done around here first."

"First what?"

"Before we go to the hospital. You did hear about Goodman?"

"Yeah, I heard. It was on the radio, and on my telephone—a lot."

"Well, from what I hear he's doing all right. The angioplasty went fine, so they didn't have to do a bypass. As of half an hour ago, he was still in intensive care, no visitors, but expected out anytime now."

"Swell."

"So I thought we'd get a little work done and then go together to the hospital."

"I don't want to go to the hospital."

"The man had a heart attack!"

"Which he survived. Evidently nicely."

"Your concern is really touching."

"Hey, I happen to be a little off Mr. Goodman at the moment."

"Yeah, I've noticed that. Is it that Mr. Goodman forced himself upon your protesting body, and in contravention of your expressed desires refused to use protection, thus impregnating you as a result of his brutal and unrequited lust? Would you say that's a fair representation of the facts, missy?"

"Would you go balance your rectum on a hot poker?"

"You're not going to visit him in the hospital?"

"No, and would you fucking get off my case?"

I took several deep breaths, tried to remember she was really my friend and he was really the pain in the neck. But at the moment she was making it a little hard for me to keep my relationships in order.

"OK, then work. What've you got for me?"

"I got a copy of Claudio's will, per your buddy's instructions."

Now it was my buddy.

"Which revealed what?"

"The bulk of his estate, exempting specific behests, goes to his ex-wives in equal amounts; separate smaller but also equal amounts to his children."

"Which is how much?"

"That isn't specified, but it's a lot."

"How do you know?"

"Well, the houses, the cars, the boat, the income from participation in the profits of old films yet to come—a lot."

"Opening up an awful lot of suspects, then—theoretically."

"Not really. Because while an awful lot, wives and kids, benefited a lot, they'd been taken care of all along anyway. They do maybe a little better, but it's split a lot of ways."

"*And* they'd have no reason to kill Hamilton Cohen and Nigel Hampton."

"None I could tell."

"OK, what are the specific behests?"

"Servants, usual, customary, generous enough, but not spectacular."

"Right. And?"

"Charities taken care of in separate trust."

"Get to the people I know."

"Billy Zee got twenty-five thousand."

"Which would be enough to put a hefty down payment on a Cadillac Seville, as I understand it."

"But not enough to murder for, in Beverly Hills terms."

"Unless he thought he'd get more."

"Why would he? He was just someone Claudio picked up in Germany on location and took a liking to."

"OK, I guess a pass on Billy Zee. Who else?"

"Barbara Aronson—one hundred thousand."

"Which she'd more or less alerted us to. Again, not a whole lot by movie standards, and considering her long association.

"She's also executor. Trix?"

"Paid?"

She checked her notes. "Without fee."

"What about shares in Fortaco? Who gets them? Or is that just part of the estate?"

"There's no mention of Fortaco per se."

"Anything else?"

"There is a provision of five hundred thousand dollars for Laszlo Nagy." And here she referred to specific language in her Xerox of the document, "my great and loyal co-worker, who has been a continual inspiration and help in my work."

"Um-hum, uh-oh, and ah-hah!"

"Wait. It gets deliciouser. There is a codicil."

I mentally rubbed my hands together.

"Which says," she went on, "that the aforementioned behest mentioned in F, above, sub-paragraph VIII, is hereby amended as follows: inasmuch as I have since provided during my lifetime suitable compensation for his assistance and support, I hereby delete the paragraph pertaining to Laszlo Nagy, and leave him only the additional sum of one dollar, as token."

"A falling fucking out!"

"But did he know and when did he know it?"

"And did knowing provide another motive, or get him off the hook for the one he had?"

"Hey, I'm just a dumb, recently knocked-up researcher, what do I know?"

"Just one thing, Francine," I said. "Are we going to dwell?"

They told me they had no updated information at the hospital. While he wasn't currently listed in intensive care, he also had no room number assigned. I asked them what that meant. They said they didn't know, they were only human and the computer had no information.

I decided to give the computer a chance to catch up on things before riding out to Westwood and seeing for myself.

Francine was just sort of moping around.

"Nice work on the coroner guy," I said by way of trying to cheer her up. "Finding out Claudio and Hampton'd been killed by the same gun."

"All in a day's corruption," she said. Then added, "Plus, of course, Hamilton Cohen."

"Hamilton Cohen what?"

"Killed by the same gun, too, I threw that in on my own."

"Wow, that's really interesting. Don't you get it? We know Heather did Cohen (and by extension, Nash). No idea in the world why, but there it is—Goodman saw Heather at the Ermitage. So if everybody was murdered by the same gun, we've got our killer! I gotta tell Goodman."

I called UCLA Medical again. Again, no record. Was it possible he'd already been discharged? Didn't seem likely. On the off chance, I phoned his house, got the answer phone, hung up.

"I think I'm going to drive out to UCLA and check it out," I said, sort of hoping she'd say me, too. "That's what I'm going to do."

"Go do," she said.

"Hey," it suddenly struck me. "What about your cat? He'll be hungry."

"You want the keys?"

"It's your cat."

"At his house."

"So?"

"So I guess it'd be a good idea if you went and fed it."

This wasn't one of the times it was easy to be her friend. She took a key off her ring, tossed it to me, almost reaching my shoe.

"The operation took a lot out of my arm," she explained.

I didn't think it was exactly the moment to comment on girls' throwing arms.

I popped into the BMW and drove west toward Goodman's house. I didn't mind a whole lot delaying going to my place, since Brian was still there ("You can't just find a place overnight") and the air was frosty.

I turned up La Cienega, got hung—who hasn't, every time—at the top of the hill at Sunset, where I rode the clutch and watched my thermometer climb, finally got the signal, turned left and over to Sunset Plaza Drive. I turned up Sunset Plaza, past the hideosity they'd erected on a tiny triangle of land overlooking the chic stores and across from the single dwelling that'd replaced the irreplaceable Sunset Plaza Apartments of early Hollywood fame. The guy who tore it down intended to put up a hundred-unit condo. But his plans were thwarted by an alert citizens group who successfully campaigned against its erection, you should pardon the expression. But it was only a pyrrhic victory since in the interim he'd destroyed the landmark they fought to save. Stuck with an expensive lot, he opted to build himself a mansion instead, then suffered an ironic comeuppance when *his* view got blocked by the aforementioned hideous condos, which were slipped in while the powers-that-be told the citizens group they'd gotten their way once, what more could they want?

I continued up Sunset Plaza, bore left into Rising Glen, turned left at Thrasher and the bird streets, and continued on up to Goodman's house.

I rang the bell, just in case. But as I expected, Goodman wasn't home. I stuck the key in the lock and opened the door. The cat would sure be glad to see me.

The cat wasn't glad to see me. The cat was dead. Brutally, hideously dead. I made it to the door, threw up, and cried like a baby.

27

Rayford Goodman

"What happened," I was telling Bradley ("once out of the pit"), "when she stepped in the room and I got a load of that big gun, instinct took over. I'd like to take credit being so inventive about staying alive, but it was more on the order of shit luck. I threw my arms over my head, pulled up my legs, and turned my back, in a full fetal frenzy. But it turned out when I rolled over, I fell off the bed. What that did, it ripped out all the monitoring probes and electronic crap I was attached to, and set off a bunch of panic alarms. They clanged and buzzed and beeped, and in nothing flat came the pounding of feet and the rolling of equipment from the Code Blue folks. In galloped the medical cavalry, and out slunk the Indians. With all the activity, and in her nurse suit, Heather easy slipped away. And half an hour later, so did I. Waiter!"

We were discussing this at the bar at Le Dome, where I'd already put away a matched pair of vodka rocks.

"But should you be out of the hospital so soon?" said Bradley.

"Compared to staying in and dying?"

"I see your point."

The out-of-work actor portraying a bartender answered my cue. I ordered another vodka rocks, and Bradley said he'd just finish the beer he was drinking first. I know that type. They act like they're drinking with you, but they're not really drinking at all—they're keeping score of you.

He'd been standing outside my house, rearranging the dirt in the garden and for some reason washing off my leaves, when I drove up. He told me not to go in. I said why. He said I didn't want to go in. I said why. He held on to me not to go in. Naturally I went in.

The fuckers.

Bradley had walked me outside and made me sit on the

steps. Then he went back in, called I can't imagine who to come clean up the mess (Yellow Pages, under Awful, Terrible Jobs Nobody Else'll Do?), then phoned and told Francie. After which, with good common sense, he piled me into his car and drove to the nearest bar. In this case, Le Dome, if you didn't count a couple of the fruity sidewalk café numbers along the way.

"OK," I said when I'd got most of the next vodka down my gullet, "we're talking war."

"I don't suppose you'd consider it might be a job for the police?" he said.

"And Chief Broward's going to take my side?"

"Against Heather and Nash, could be. He *is* the cops, and they are the robbers."

"You forget, time to time he's the robbers, too. Plus it being me, and even you now—no way he's going to help. I'll find my own way, in due time. But it'll have to be back burner till we finish the case."

"We could be a lot closer to that than we thought," Bradley said. "Turns out when Francine checked your coroner connection on whether the same gun killed Claudio and Hampton, she ad-libbed Cohen, as well."

"Ah?"

"And it turned out, it was the same—for all three!"

"And since I know Hansen was at the Ermitage, saw her with my own eyes going in and out Cohen's room, she must have done them all!"

"My thoughts exactly."

Yeah.

Not that complicated. Straight ahead. That's what it turned out to be.

So why wasn't I satisfied? Why didn't I get that little click and the goose bump thing when you knew?

"I still can't imagine why they'd blow up the set," I went on. "The cat, I suppose to send me a message. Get off Nash's back. That being the case, though, then why send Hansen after me at the hospital? Flip side, if they were going to kill me, why bother with the cat?" Which all of a sudden wasn't just a word. "That was such a cute cat!"

Oh, Christ, I couldn't goddamn be going to have a crying jag? I'd never had a crying jag. I couldn't stand guys had a crying jag. I guess I looked it, too, because Bradley said, "Go ahead, it's all right to cry."

That stopped it cold. I'd be all right. I just had things to do. One of which was have another drink I felt pretty sure.

Somewhere in there Francie showed up and was sitting at the table holding my hand.

"Oh, Jesus, Francie, I'm so sorry."

"I'm sorry, too," she said.

"I tried to take good care of Sven. I really did."

"I know, Ray. I know you did."

And I had another drink, and they did some talking, and it got to be later, and part of me was feeling no pain, but another part was feeling a lot of pain—physical pain. I didn't exactly know was it from the angioplasty mostly or falling on the floor. At least some of it was falling on the floor—the part in my shoulder and upper arm.

"I'm hurting," I said.

"We all are," said Francie.

"But we're not all hurting in our shoulder and arm," I said.

"Oh," said Francie, "I've got something for that."

I guess I raised an eyebrow because she assured me she wasn't talking serious drugs.

"Ibuprofen," she said, giving me a pill said Rorer on it. I got the feeling she still wasn't back to honoring her pledge to give up drugs and seemed to remember vaguely Ibuprofen shouldn't be coming out of a prescription bottle. But by the time it finally registered what she'd really given me was a Quaalude, somehow I didn't seem to mind all that much. Then somewhere before I finished what turned out to be my last drink, I heard her say, "Now all we gotta do is call the auto club to come tow him home."

And that was sort of all I remembered before waking up in my old familiar bed, with my old familiar hangover.

I wasn't feeling what you might call sprightly. Or half human. Every bone in my body ached, every muscle, every sinew, every nerve end. My hair hurt.

Which is why it was surprising my mind worked clear enough to all of a sudden remember Hansen entering the recovery room and pointing the big gun had something wrong about it. The big gun! It wasn't a .22, it was a .38! Big, ballsy gun for a big, ballsy lady. But not the murder weapon.

Which, of course, didn't mean positively she hadn't killed

the others. She could have a second gun. But it did raise
the question why, if she was the shooter, change weapons
now? On the contrary, since the thirty-eight didn't have a
silencer, wouldn't be any light-sounding pop like a twenty-
two. It'd make a hell of a lot more noise. Drawing more
attention, and making escape a lot harder. Not too logical.

Problem was, give or take a change of gun here and
there, it still looked like Hansen had done them. Meaning,
too, Nash. But there were so many reasons that would have
been a dumb move I just couldn't really go with it. On the
other hand, it would sure solve a lot of my problems it was
the way things actually went down. Being it was also the
way Cifelli wanted them to go down. And not giving Cifelli
what he wanted was a whole other health hazard at a time
I wasn't exactly peak form.

Enough theorizing. Time for some legwork.

While I waited for my coffee to drip through, I picked
up the phone and called Francie. Answering machine.

"I'm not here; sometimes I think I've never actually been
here. You want to chance it, leave a message."

At the beep I said, "Stop it, Francie, answer the phone.
We've got business!"

She picked up. "Hi, I'm here. You feeling as bad as I
think you ought to feel?"

"Not at all," I lied. "I'm fit as a fiddle and ready for
love."

"Fit as a fiddle?"

"Before your time. Listen, what was the messenger service you used to send over your memo to Fox yesterday?"

"Um, Speedline—on La Brea. Want the number?"

"Yeah." I held the phone, wondering how long we could
continue being so damn impersonal. She came back on,
gave me a phone number and an address. "You wouldn't
know the kid's name?"

"No, sorry—but I'm sure they'll have a record. What are
you after?"

"I'm after the name of the guy who latched on to the kid
just outside the set and gave him a message for me to get
out fast—right before the explosion."

"You want me to run it down?"

"No, I'll do it myself."

"Anything else you want from me?"

I could do without straight lines, I thought. My coffee

was starting to boil. "No," I said. "I'll get back to you later. Thanks for yesterday."

"OK. Sorry about Sven. For both of us."

"Yeah." Sorry about both of us, too.

Heavy dead air.

We said good-bye. It felt like neither of us wanted to, but that there was nothing to keep us from doing it. And we couldn't figure out how not to. Good-bye.

I hadn't gotten over being beat up by Moke and Poke, Nash's boys—at Bradley's. I hadn't gotten over these little "cardiac episodes"—as the doctors so damn cutsey put it. And I damn sure hadn't gotten over my hangover, which felt like someone was trying to pull my eyebrows up through my skull from the inside.

It was getting harder to play with pain. Harder to make believe I was just a little temporarily out of shape. I was, very definitely this morning, getting older. And I was doing it in one of the worst businesses for it, in one of the worst places for it. I better fucking punch somebody out soon.

The Speedline Messenger Agency on La Brea had a definite policy against giving out the name and address of its employees. They would not—ten dollars—tell me his name was Christopher Redden, and absolutely refused—ten more—to specify the location at 4603-1/4 Laurel Canyon where he lived. I'd rather have punched than paid. But it seemed somehow wrong, given the near blind old woman was so fat she hardly fit her wheelchair. Christopher Redden lived in one of those big Laurel Canyon single-family homes built in the thirties that now had about ten or fifteen sort of apartments in it, each with a number ending in a fraction. He was the one through the open-ended bathroom on the fourth floor, in the back side room with a scenic view of the garage roof. I didn't see the garage roof right away. First off, I had what I sincerely hoped was a stitch in my side, instead of a leaky heart valve I didn't know was there. I found myself gasping for breath. Another reason I was gasping—and didn't see the garage roof—I had to first plow through a thick cloud of pot smoke in back of which sure enough was Christopher Redden sitting on a bed, mellowing out. Being his day off—of a likely life off.

"Christopher, I'm the guy you brought an envelope a day before yesterday at Twentieth Century-Fox."

That didn't particularly galvanize his attention.

"Yeah? So?"

"I want to ask you a few questions."

With the surliness that's such a feature of his generation, he took a shot: "What if I don't want to answer?"

"I only wish," I said.

Maybe there was something in my face.

"Go 'head," he said. "What can I do for you?"

"Before the old dung hit the wind machine, you brought me an envelope. Remember?"

"Yeah. Sure."

"And after you gave me the envelope, you said you had a message from a guy outside."

"You say so."

"You don't?" I said, a little louder than I intended.

"I say so!" he answered, quick.

Better.

"Let me open a window, here," I said, starting to feel the fight semi-leave me.

"Why not leave it closed, I'll give you a toke," he answered, offering me a lit joint.

"Thanks just the same," I said, taking the joint and butting it out in a coffee can ashtray, and opening the window. Redden looked like I had insulted his mother.

"Let's get back to the guy," I went on. "With the message? Remember?'

" 'Get out, fast.' "

" 'Get out, fast.' "

"Not fast enough, right?"

"Right. Tell me about him. What'd he look like?"

"I don't know. A regular guy."

"Tall, short, thin, fat?"

He shrugged.

"You're not trying to piss me off?"

"No, man, really. He was, I don't remember anything special."

"Did he look like he worked there?"

"How would I know that?"

"Mustache. How about a mustache?"

"Couldn't say. I don't think so, but you know—could've."

Possible I could still get to punch. But he was so skinny and so stoned. I have some pride. Instead I merely said, "You're not being a lot of help."

"I'm really trying, man. You don't feel maybe I ought to get paid to help. Just a little?"

"All right." I took out a ten. "Talk to me."

"I mean, for what I already said," he said, taking the ten.

"You have nothing else to add?" I said, getting loud again, considering shoving the ten down his throat.

He thought again. It didn't look like thinking came easy. "Well, does it help at all, he wore glasses?"

Maybe. "Designer glasses?"

He shrugged.

"Frames?"

He shrugged.

"Tell me you don't mean sunglasses."

"I don't mean sunglasses."

"Then you can go on living," I said, cutting my losses.

On the other hand, small gain. Whoever set the explosives, I knew before it wasn't Nash. Too tight a time frame. Now I knew it wasn't Cifelli, either. Neither he nor any his boys I knew of wore glasses. In fact, maybe it was an image thing with gangsters. Because in my experience, was it Dorothy Parker said, "No hard asses ever wear glasses"? Maybe *Robert B.* Parker. So what it meant, we had a new joker in the pack.

I climbed back down the stairs, back down the hill, stopped for a minute while I swore I really was going to stop smoking now and pay some attention to getting back in shape, and got in the car.

Halfway down, I pulled into a parking lot by a convenience store (convenience store meaning you could conveniently pay twice what everything ought to cost because you were too poor to go shopping at a supermarket and stock up). I got out to make a phone call, which I figured ought to go at the regular price.

I checked in with Bradley to see what was happening, and he told me to get a newspaper.

There was a row of vending racks outside the store selling semi-porno publications, semi-Christian tracts, and one for newspapers.

On the first page of the metro section there was a major

article about the explosion on the set. In the middle of the article it said Barry Nash, with alleged underworld connections, had been brought in for questioning. Listed as an executive producer on the picture shooting at the time, Nash remained under suspicion, pending further investigation of the apparent sabotage.

Since I was about ninety percent sure he'd never put himself in a position where if he got hung up another sixty seconds he could've been killed, there had to be another explanation.

The other explanation was someone was trying to frame Nash and maybe force him off the picture, and out of the picture.

28

Mark Bradley

Francine told me Goodman had gone off to interview the messenger. Theoretically, I was free to start writing the book. I should start writing the book. It was getting late to start writing the book. But it was so hard to tell the Claudio Fortunata story when we not only didn't know who killed him, we weren't even sure why he died. I didn't begin to have an approach. A handicap publisher Penny found difficult to credit.

"Tell me again why I'm not getting any pages?" asked Penny after I'd failed to sneak in past his always open (to spy) door.

"Because I haven't found an approach, a narrative hook. A style, even."

"Because you haven't started work, you mean. You find your approach when you approach your word processor and turn it on. Your narrative hook comes to you when your rent is due and your checks stop. Your style is high-fashion fear. Get fucking going!"

He had such a way of cutting through all the higher values, past the savoring, eating, and digesting, and right to the shit.

I didn't really believe I'd be able to get much down on paper until a whole lot of questions were answered. It was the method of any self-respecting investigative reporter to get the facts, find the underlying reasons, organize the material. It was also the best way to avoid actually writing.

And one of the ways to do that was to keep current on the media, which is when I'd read the papers, seen the semi-bust of Nash—brought in for questioning—gotten the call from Goodman, and told him. He called back and told me his reading of the situation—that someone was trying to frame Nash for the explosion, which added to his feeling he just couldn't buy the Hansen-Nash scenario for the whole schmear.

"Not that I give a damn about any bust. Whatever they got on him he'd deserve for forty-seven other reasons anyhow."

"Still," I said, "if you're right, it behooves us to use whatever breather this gives us to solve the case."

"No argument. I've been working my way through the list of other suspects, and I think it's time we had a little talk with old Harvey Pitkin."

The screenwriter, fired, now back on the job somehow. Gotcha.

"Makes sense to me," I allowed. "Where do you think he's at? They can't be filming, I don't suppose, till they get new sets."

"You don't know the movie business. They don't shut down for things like that, they just change the schedule. And according to my contact at Fox, the *Fell Swoop* group is on location at the old Mercer Hotel, downtown."

"You have contacts at all the studios?"

"Well, *all* is not that much anymore. But I used to, when there was Republic and RKO and Selznick, and Hal Roach."

I could see Goodman was about to wax nostalgic on me. (And I really wasn't up for waxing at the moment.)

"So who's the contact at Fox?" I hurried on.

"A lovely lady named Lillian Bernhardt. Used to be Lillian Hart when she was a starlet. Now works in production."

"And Lillian Bernhardt, née Hart, was once famous?"

"Semi. She was mostly famous for having a terrific set of hooters."

"Big deals."

"One time it was, when a bosom was a god-given gift, and not something came from duPont. Anyway, she fell on hard times, so to speak, when gravity overcame her talent."

"Hollywood's a very unforgiving town."

I heard him sigh over the phone, yearning for the time when the tinsel was real.

"Anyway," he said finally, "I think we ought to go see how the shooting's coming along and have us a chat with Mr. Harvey Pitkin. You up for that?"

I felt fairly certain that wasn't a sexual reference, so I allowed as how it sounded like a plan to me.

The Mercer was an old hotel, built in the twenties, during a boom. It was very solid and very European, constructed before California realized it had a style of its own.

The company was located in the basement, shooting a chase of some sort in, out, and around some very impressive plumbing. Of the sort I feel certain they don't even have anymore. It looked like the boiler room of the *Lusitania*, I imagine. Just now it was also tricked up with a lot of hissing, steaming, and boiling going on to add zip and zing (attorneys at German law).

Terry was being, you should pardon the expression, terryorized by a band of either Ninjas or a wild pajama party. After an extraordinarily complex choreographed fight (the end of which we saw), he'd broken loose. Now they were setting up for a chase through the maze of pipes and machinery. Which of course would be filmed in tiny segments from a variety of angles, to maximize the excitement, the intrigue of which always eluded me anyway. At the moment, various charges were being primed to simulate where the bullets would hit and ricochet. Laszlo and a host of technicians were walking through the paces, and it looked to be a good long while before anything would recommence.

When Harvey had satisfied himself that there was some likelihood they would be following his script, he detached himself from the group and ambled over to the catering table. This was a long affair, with sectioned offerings of various esoteric viands, the best I could determine a combination of French cooking and soul food. A sign discreetly placed at the far end informed us the caterer was probably an imaginative black. It read, "BON EATS FROM UPPITY CAFÉ" and below, the informative promo, "NO FETE'S TOO BIG."

We watched as Harvey got in line behind a couple of production people, Jennifer Charles being the only one I recognized, and started filling his plate with a mess of grits and what, heaven help us, might be chitterlings. People in show business would eat anything free, I noticed.

"Care for a snack?" I asked Goodman.

"You don't catch me eating colored greens."

Trouble was, I didn't know if he meant it.

"Help you gentlemen?" asked a tall, mocha managerial type behind the counter (Monsieur Le Bon Eats). But before we could answer, a large gray-striped cat leaped onto the table and grabbed a pork chop.

"Hey, scoot, man!" yelled the caterer, taking a swipe at the offending feline with a heavy wooden spoon.

"Don't do that," screamed Jennifer, quickly sweeping the cat into her arms. The cat, alarmed by all the noise and sudden moves, took a swipe at her arm, zipping out of both arms and sight before any blood rose to the surface.

"You scared him," she admonished the caterer, immediately setting out to find and soothe the beleaguered animal.

"You notice I didn't say *scat*," said the caterer. "That's a word I reserve for Ella."

Which arcane exchange seemed to amuse Goodman, and at least take his mind off cats.

"What can I offer you?" asked the man.

We each settled on a mug of coffee and a piece of cornbread, and followed to where Harvey had settled at a few picnic tables set up in a corner.

"Hey, Harv, mind if we join you?" said Goodman, sitting down.

"No, yeah. Sure," said Harv with his customary mixture of defensiveness and hostility.

"How's it going?" I began the rally.

"Yeah, okay. Getting there."

"Don't see Nash around. Wonder if they're still holding him," said Goodman. "They didn't strip him of his executive producer stripes by any chance?"

"I don't know. Certainly didn't help."

"But he's still on the picture?" I asked.

"I don't really know. The bad press couldn't've enhanced his position."

"Who could fire him?"

"The money. The studio. We all have morals clauses, or some damn clause they could break a contract over if you happened to delay production by blowing up the set."

"Think he did that?" asked Goodman.

"I can't imagine who else has that exact style. Good stuff; you're not eating?"

We just shook our heads noncommittally while exchanging covert looks at Harvey, really digging in. He'd turned surprisingly friendly and forthcoming. Although maybe he was just starved for companionship. He didn't have the sort of personality that invited conversation.

"We were at Fortunata's the day he got killed," said Goodman. "The day you got fired."

"I didn't get fired, I quit," he corrected us quickly.

"Right. I guess you weren't exactly sorry when Claudio met his maker," I added.

"Hey, I didn't like the guy, I admit. And I wouldn't care if he did the *mambo* with his maker, the bastard folded on me first time that twerp Terry started changing my lines."

"So you quit," said Goodman. (After being fired, I remembered.)

"Fucking A," said Harvey, machoing it up.

"But you allowed yourself to be rehired," I persisted.

"Well, second thoughts. You know."

"Which you had the option to have, evidently, once Fortunata left the scene."

"You don't suspect me?" he asked, mid-bite on something frightening.

"You had some motives. You were pissed at Fortunata," said Goodman. "That's revenge, one motive; you could change your mind, for money, your salary—that's two—"

"In addition to which you had a piece of the picture, for three, depending on getting credit," I added.

"Plus a pro rata share of Fortunata's once he was gone," Goodman threw in.

"Not exactly."

"What not exactly?" asked Goodman.

"The pro rata kicks in on the talent and above the line on the end fifty percent."

"I don't understand," I said, not understanding.

"My piece gets bigger if Terry's out, if Maurissa's out, if Charles or Nagy're out."

"But not if Fortunata?" asked Goodman before I could.

"No, his share went to Hamilton Cohen. Cohen and Fortunata split fifty percent, sixty-forty. Survivor take all—after the wife."

"But Fortunata was divorced. Technically, he had no wife."

"Right. But Cohen did. That's what he traded the extra ten percent to Claudio for—his wife's inheriting his share."

"So you're saying Sherry Cohen had a very big motive for both killings," I asked.

"Is that what I'm saying? Yeah, I guess so. What exactly are chitlins made of?"

"I don't think you want to know," I said.

"Good," he said, chomping on those pig intestines, a very long way from observing dietary restrictions.

"Just one more thing," said Goodman, after a long pause when we watched him be remarkably undisgusted. "What happens if there are no survivors of the Cohen-Fortunata deal?"

"Then that half gets thrown into the kitty, too."

"Fifty percent more to split?" I asked, getting the feeling of rising excitement I guess Goodman was feeling, too.

"That's right," said Harvey.

Goodman got up. I got up.

"Thanks, Harvey," he said, turned to go, then, doing his little Columbo turn. "Oh, by the way, is Sherry Cohen on the set?"

"Sure. She's the boss. I think they set her up with a temporary office on the second floor, with the other production offices."

Goodman was moving pretty fast for a guy who'd just gotten out of the hospital. I had all I could do to keep up with him.

But by the time we got to the second floor and found the office in a converted hotel bedroom, haste wasn't an issue.

For the record, it was another of the *neat* killings—.22 to the temple.

29

Rayford Goodman

I got us the hell out of there fast. While Chief Broward wouldn't get the initial squeal, it being L.A. and not Beverly Hills, he'd certainly get the news fast enough to poop on my parade. The least we could expect a very big hassle just on general lack of principles, for being there. Again.

Of course, all sorts of other people were there. Again. I'd seen Terry and Maurissa, Vernon, Laszlo, Forbes, Jennifer, Harvey—and of course, Sherry. Who had an alibi, being the corpse. I didn't remember seeing Claire or Barbara. And Billy Zee I hadn't seen since soon after he became an heir. And neither Nash nor Hansen, either. Though stood to reason they were doing a hit they wouldn't be showing their faces a whole lot. And while it wasn't exactly an ideal time to be making radical moves, being already under suspicion on the bombing, still Nash *had* survived all this time. And he had done some very strange numbers to do so. I couldn't count him out.

"It's getting very hot," said Bradley suddenly. Out of the blue.

We'd been driving along in my car, on the Hollywood freeway, which we'd, as they say, accessed at the Broadway on ramp, heading north.

"Want me to put the top down?"

"I'm talking about murder," he said. "As you very well know. When is it ever going to end?"

Some crazy bastard in a Pontiac sedan cut right in front of me. They just never let you have a space between cars. A car length for every ten miles was the rule of thumb. On the freeway you got three lengths, somebody always cut in. I'd been ready for it. I always drive like everybody's crazy. Because they are.

"I think it *has* ended," I said, answering Bradley. "Unless you consider you and me as possibles, being, I'm sorry to say, still somewhat at risk. But that's Nash and company. The other murders I believe are over."

The Pontiac—whatever they're calling them this year— after all that aggression now decided he wasn't in such a hurry. Used to be they spent a lot of money to promote a brand name so you'd come back to it again and again. Now the name of everything got changed all the time. Maybe so you'd forget who to blame. Anyway, now the Redskin, or the Arrow, or the ZX422 (Xes and Zees and numbers are big for car names, too) pulled right, and slowed down. I passed him. I noticed the windows were tinted. Which seemed sort of extravagant in a mid-priced car. One of the rear windows was cracked a few inches, and I could see there were two other guys back there. Car pool, I guess.

"You really think they're over?" asked Bradley.

"I really do," I said as now the sedan cut back in behind me and quickly caught up. In fact, they were tailgating me. Another my favorites.

Bradley was thinking about how I knew the murders were over. I wasn't ready to tell him yet why I thought that. Because so far I only thought it, I couldn't be a hundred percent positive.

The XT9042i or whatever was really becoming a giant pain the ass. He wasn't just tailgating, he was practically on top of me. Since I wasn't looking for a confrontation with that kind of maniac—especially since folks took to pot-shotting each other on the freeways—I made another move. We were coming up on the quarter-mile marker to the Sunset Boulevard exit. I edged right, to the right-hand lane. Sure enough, he followed me. The words *followed me* suddenly began taking on more than just casual meaning. Instead of slowing down, I speeded up. He speeded up. Now I was just at the edge of the off ramp when I suddenly swerved left, back into the main traffic flow. He zoomed past me, slammed on the brakes. But I could see through my rear-view mirror he couldn't back up and get back on the free-way because other cars had followed to exit, blocking him.

I zoomed on, Bradley blissfully unaware, then took the off ramp to Hollywood Boulevard, where I turned left.

"Where're you going?" Bradley asked.

"To Musso and Frank's. I thought we'd have some lunch."

"I don't want lunch. My god, how can you think of lunch?"

"We could just have a drink."

"I don't want a drink."

I sensed he was growing testy.

I ignored him and kept on.

"Come on, we'll have a bite to eat. You'll feel better."

"I don't want to. I have to get home."

"Why, what's the hurry?"

"Brian moved out this morning."

I guess it was just like a real couple. Hurt the same way. "When you prick us, do we not bleed?" Bad choice of words.

"Hey, I'm real sorry," I said.

He nodded. "I'm in the middle of converting a couple of my closets into a laundry room."

"Yeah?"

"So I ought to be there to let the contractor in. He's starting work today, now that we got the permit."

"That's it!" I said, keeping right past Musso and Frank's, slipping into high, and taking off in a thunder of hoofs and a hearty hi ho, Silver.

"Now where're we going?" asked Bradley.

"I'm taking you home."

"And then what?"

"Then I got to look into something. If I'm right, I'll have a handle on how to go from here."

"To get the murder person or personettes?"

"Right."

"And what do I do?"

"Sit tight."

He digested that for a while, as I cut down La Brea and down to Franklin, then west toward Kings Road.

"I suppose I could clean out my closets and rearrange things. Now that I have more space," he said.

"Or start on the book," I suggested.

"Let's not get ahead of ourselves," he answered.

I left Bradley at his condo and headed back up, making rights and lefts and rights, going east and north and east. It was my day for wasting energy resources, as I now had to get back on the Hollywood Freeway. But speaking of energy, '64 Cadillacs not being among your mileage winners, I had to stop for gas. Which was another thing seemed strange. California was growing by jillions every year, all with cars, and more and more gas stations were going out of business. When it was nineteen cents a gallon, there was one on every block. Anyway, finally found one, tanked up, had the cap back on, paid, and was back in the car—when I saw the Pontiac slide in behind me. By the time I had the motor running, the driver had yanked my door half open, stuck an arm on my shoulder and said, "Hold it. Police."

He slowly released my shoulder, took out his wallet, and showed me his badge.

"What is this? You're the guy's been chasing me, nearly got me killed on the freeway."

"Didn't nearly get you killed, I was trying to catch up to you. I have a warrant for your arrest."

"Yeah? Let's see it."

He reached into his pocket and pulled out the warrant.

"You're to come with us to headquarters."

He tried to open the door the rest of the way. I held on. "Just a minute."

"Don't give me a hard time, Goodman. I got backup in my car."

It didn't feel at all right. For one thing, no Miranda. "Just let me look at this," I said, glancing at the warrant.

He relaxed his grip, stepped back just a bit, but leaned down to keep an eye on me. I kept my eye on the warrant, then quickly and with all my might threw my shoulder against the door, banging it against his head. I caught him just right and he went to the ground. I threw the already running car into gear, stepped on the gas, and zoomed out onto the street. The warrant had been addressed to "Raymond Goodman."

And we all knew who always called me Raymond.

By the time I hit the corner, the other guys—who I could see were Moke and Poke, the twosome from Bradley's condo—were out and had their "associate" up and back to the car. He slipped again behind the wheel as the others piled in. I didn't see any more as I was giving getting away my fullest attention.

I caught the light turning at Fountain and La Brea, took a sharp left at the last minute, figuring that ought to hang them up. But by the squealing of brakes and honking of horns, I knew they'd gone through the red and were still on my tail. I'd started out with several cars between us, but after I turned and the next couple continued on, they'd managed to gain. They kept pace with me to Sunset, where I turned right. The traffic assured more or less they couldn't actually do me on the city streets. On the other hand, it also kept me from giving them the slip entirely.

I didn't think this was a situation where you got a split decision with a tie. And driving till one of us ran out of gas, given my basic seven miles to the gallon, wasn't going to work my favor. So with the on ramp to the freeway coming up at Van Ness, my planning on going that way the first place, I decided to gamble. My theory was the big old Eldorado, with its eight cylinders and hundreds of horsepower, had to be faster than the new tin cans.

That was the theory. The reality was he parked on my tail pipe. Still, weaving in and out of traffic at upward of seventy miles an hour had a fair chance of catching the eye of some cop's radar gun. Plan number two that didn't work.

I did manage, for a bit, to get a car between us, but when he started tailgating that, the guy chickened out and pulled over. Now I was in the fast lane, clear ahead, and hitting eighty when they started shooting. They were going for the K.O. here and now—no more abduction and a remote spot for the kill.

It was the strangest thing. As I felt a couple bullets thud into my trunk, I started being pissed off the damage. I'd just had the car fixed up, dents all out, new paint, the works. It hadn't looked this good new, and here the bastards were breaking my car! The one through the window reset my priorities. I totally floored the gas, inching up to ninety. They fell behind just a little, but not enough for me to really pull away, then quickly regained position, almost bumper to bumper. There was a flash of what I guess said "LANE CLOSED AHEAD," but I passed it too quick to read. Actually, it wasn't till I was almost on top of the caution truck mounted square in the lane with its flashing lighted arrow pointing to the next lane right that I thought it might be a break. My car being a big old sixty-four, theirs being a recent midsize, I sat a lot higher, and there was a chance I was blocking them seeing the sign.

Anyway, it was the move to make. I had to swerve hard to avoid it myself, at ninety-two miles an hour. Whether they ever saw it or swerved at all, or just plain plowed straight into the truck, I'll never know. I knew the guy wasn't that much of a driver the first place, having faked him out before, plus getting clonked on the head couldn't have helped his reflexes a whole lot. Or you could say dumb luck. The crash was enormous. Though I was a little disappointed there was no big ball of fire, like in the movies, I still thought it played pretty good.

They say the separate parts of a car are worth three or four times the whole assembled car. This one was worth eighty times. Ka-boom!

I didn't have a minute's remorse. I gradually slowed down to fifty, by which time I felt my heart beating fast enough and hard enough to scare the hell out of me. But I was very soon back to normal. Wondered, Would the insurance company have some sneaky cop-out excluding bullet holes? See?

I went about my business downtown. After Hollywood and Beverly Hills, downtown L.A. always seemed like some strange city didn't belong in California. It could have been Cincinnati. And of course, dealing with public servants was the same everywhere—drive you crazy. There was a time we traded off civil service—gave them permanent security in exchange for lower pay. Which after the Great Depression, they were damn glad to get. Then came good times, they organized, got equal pay, and now permanent security meant fuck you, I don't have to do a damn thing, including being civil.

I managed not to get into an actual fight and to find out what I came for. But I paid a fifty-dollar bribe and took a lot of lip. Someday. (The list grew longer.)

When I showed up for a late lunch at Madeo's, on Beverly Boulevard, Armand Cifelli was already there. That was how I knew which was the number one table. He had about five waiters filling his water glass, opening his napkin, polishing his silverware, rearranging his plates. Maybe more. Maybe one was taking a leak for him.

When he saw me, he waved me over.

"Hey, Ray, how's the boy?"

"OK, Mr. Cifelli. Thanks for coming," I said, sitting down, two guys holding the chair.

"Thank you for inviting me," he said graciously. Immediately a captain who looked like he'd bought a new tuxedo just for the occasion showed up with a tray of drinks. "I took the liberty of ordering you a drink," Cifelli continued. "Tanqueray Sterling vodka with Perrier, wasn't it? But since the Perrier thing, I thought maybe Calistoga."

"Thank you, wonderful," I said sincerely, swallowing down half a glass in a gulp.

"Moderation, Rayford, moderation," he cautioned. "Life is to be savored—slowly." With which he sipped a glass of Valpolicella poured from the most gorgeous bottle I'd ever seen. I knew was going to cost me a bundle. "Wonderful wine," he went on. "Thank you again."

And it went on like that. There was a protocol to follow with Cifelli. You didn't come right out and say what you wanted or what was on your mind. You dined, you asked after each other's family. You addressed the problems facing your country and the world. You regretted the loss of finer times, better ways of life. And when you did finish the lunch; when you did accept the zabaglione (with the management's compliments, thank god), and polished it all off with a small sip of Sciarada—then and only then might it be time to *hint* at why you were meeting.

"Mr. Cifelli—Don Armando, if I may—with the deepest respect."

He nodded, not insisting on a euphemism.

"It is now part of the lore of the land how one can come to someone such as yourself, under whose protection I surely must be—seeing I work for you?"

He nodded.

"And ask for help in solving a serious problem."

He nodded.

I told him about being roughed up at Bradley's condo by Nash's boys. I reminded him of the explosion on the set, which almost killed me. About Hansen at the hospital. I told him about the death of my cat. And finally, I told him about the attempted abduction, then the out-and-out shoot-out on the freeway by Moke and Poke, and whoever Doke was.

"Now it's true," I went on, "you had previously decided not to war with these people. That is your decision, for your own business. But I now have an ongoing problem. I have suffered and continue to be threatened. So, if it must be that it's not for your own interests, then I wish it for mine."

"You would like a solution."

"I would like a *permanent* solution."

He was silent for a long moment. He drained his glass of Sciarada, which was quickly refilled.

In the silence I went on, nervously: "I know the lore also has it that once a favor is done, the favoree is in debt. And one day he will have to do a favor in exchange. I accept that."

Cifelli drained his glass. Then he reached for his napkin, patted his lips, pushed the chair back, and stood up.

"Thank you for a most excellent lunch," he said.

And left.

30

Mark Bradley

Even using those areas now accessible due to Brian's departure, I seemed in no danger of having excess closet space. (Bradley's Law: Stuff accumulates to fill the space available for it.) And with the rearrangement of my worldly goods, and the lack of blank spaces, it was as if he'd never been. Oh, yeah, and there'd never been lyricists, either—the mere idea of you; the longing here for you . . .

The contractor had made an appearance, to pick up his check, but also to knock down half the wall and start making the premises unlivable. With the dust of shredded plaster still unsettled, he then laid the news on me that further examination of the site had revealed certain unanticipated difficulties that could well render the job undoable. I told him I had budgeted for just such a contingency, and suspected the undoable was doable, just not at a reasonable price. He—having been a contractor longer than I'd been a contractee—told me that it might be possible—at double the price. I told him, with a certain smugness, I had anticipated that, and was prepared for double the price. He reeducated me that what he meant was double the double everybody mentally budgeted for. I, of course, had a choice—I could forfeit the deposit and consider the bits of lath and plaster and exposed cross sections as some avant-garde sculpture, or submit to the extortion. I told him to go ahead. He said fine and made to leave. I asked if today weren't a working day. He said he'd see me on Monday. This being Thursday, I found it a mite unsettling. Was he, perhaps, an adherent of some esoteric religious sect that observed weekdays as sabbaths? He allowed such was not the case. It was simply that he had such integrity that he couldn't possibly disappoint the other, prior client he'd promised to finish a job for two weeks ago. A man of honor, the while folding my check in neat quarters, he'd have to complete that first. I let him out and popped a Xanax.

By now it was a little after three, an awkward time. Too early to quit for the day, too late to start anything meaningful. Still, there were some preliminary chores I could do. I went to my computer and started setting up files for potential chapters. We'd discussed doing the making of Claudio's Oscar-nominated films, his relationships with leading ladies, the travails and triumphs vis-à-vis the studios, and wives and children. Money might be another good one, I thought, and set up a file for it—how much he'd made, how much he'd spent, on what, whom, etc. Naturally, biography on this level didn't entail the sort of dedicated research one might do on, say, Franklin D. Roosevelt—but more than, say, Barry Manilow. I hadn't settled on a title. *And Action: The Autobiography of Claudio Fortunata* was out, of course, with his demise. I stopped, constitutionally unable to continue working on an "untitled." I could never be a painter— "Untitled Book Number Four." However, I could settle on a maybe—and that's what I came up with. *A Man and His Movies*. (All of which was totally speculative anyway, since Penny would probably retitle it something like *The Naked Megaphone*.)

I think I was missing Brian.

I know I was missing Brian.

I would try not to distort the memory till it came to be the greatest loss anyone ever suffered in life. Cute hadn't cut the *moutarde*.

Francine checked in to ask if I had anything specific I wanted her to do in lieu of getting blasted out of her skull.

I said she could come over if she wanted, and I'd hold her hand. She said she was in the throes of founding an order whose sole requirement would be a prohibition against physical contact of any sort.

"You could come over and not hold hands," I said.

"Yeah, but even then I'd have to relate or at least momentarily abandon my total concentration on self-pity."

"Aren't you taking this a little to extremes?" I asked gently.

"Yep," she said. And hung up.

A Man and His Movies. It had a certain ring. This week the *New York Times* Book Review nonfiction listings, number 6, *A Man and His Movies* by Mark Bradley. Mark Bradley—with Rayford Goodman, I remembered. Not fair. The man wasn't going to write line one. *A Man, His Movies, His Biographer, and a Freeloader*. I was really missing Brian, I could tell.

The intercom buzzed. He was crawling back. He'd be meek, apologetic. What should my attitude be? Aloof? Regretfully removed? With just a hint of the possibility for reconciliation?

If I wanted him back, I wouldn't have let him go in the first place. Remember, remember—it didn't work. But I wouldn't hide.

I pushed the button. "Yes?" The TV monitor, per usual, was totally fuzzed out.

"Goodman," said the person who wasn't Brian at all. "Can I come up?"

So much for soliloquies. I buzzed him through.

I waited at the door and watched as he virtually waltzed down the corridor. The title *Cat with Canary Feathers* came to mind.

"You're looking mighty satisfied," I said. "I gather you found out whatever it was you intended to find out."

He nodded, grinning.

"You haven't actually solved it?"

He assayed a gross Mona Lisa smile.

"You have?"

He said, "You're not going to invite me in?"

I invited him in.

"You know? You really know?"

"You're not going to offer me a drink?" A two-hundred-pound tease.

I offered him a drink. It was clear he was going to take his own tantalizing sweet time, so I might as well relax and let it take whatever it was going to take.

"The drink is to your liking, sire?" I inquired as nothing noteworthy was forthcoming.

"It'll do."

By which time I'd decided I was not going to beg. I was not going to implore him to spill his ample guts. "I have news," he said finally, offering his glass for me to refill and following me into the kitchen.

And news he had, indeed. I was startled and astounded to learn of the determined attempt on his life. Till now it had been sort of suggestive of potential mayhem, shot in the direction of, exploded near—but this was out-and-out. People had been shooting to kill. And the same people who'd followed when I was in the car, blithely unaware. (I'm good at blithe.)

He told me of their fortuitous dispatch, with car and futures totaled. But I knew they were only foot soldiers, and their end wouldn't end the threat—not incidentally, to both of us. To be at such jeopardy for a collaborator who didn't write a line!

I was a little confused he'd be so elated. Relieved, I could understand, but not quite this air of amusement.

"That's not even the big news," he went on, and I had an inkling my first perception had been correct. He'd made a breakthrough. He then proceeded to tell me what he'd learned in Los Angeles' venerable Hall of Records, with its musty archives containing, obviously, all sorts of interesting intelligence. Very interesting and informative.

"But what prompted you to go this way?" I asked when he'd finished.

"Well, the old process of elimination."

"The Metamucil Method," I said. He just looked.

"Forget Angelo, Cifelli's driver—that was clear gang shit. Leaves us Hamilton Cohen at L'Ermitage, which we'd already suspected wasn't a mistake; Fortunata at his house; Hampton at the Beef and Barium; and Sherry at the Mercer Hotel downtown. Cohen, Fortunata, and Hampton we all know killed by the same gun. My bet, Sherry too. Also lots of people had access to all of them. God knows lots of motives, and lots of opportunities. But only one murder had an offbeat angle—Fortunata's. And that was he was killed with us practically there on the scene—at the very moment it was done—and no escape for the murderer. Whoever killed him couldn't of got past us. Which we didn't concentrate on at the time since we figured lots of people were in the house. But it turned out wasn't so. After I left, you stayed right there. You were still there when the police came, and after they sealed off the area and searched the premises."

"Yeah, okay, so we already suspected he/she/they were still in the house, nothing new about that."

"Right, but we didn't figure how."

"Ah-hah." Which is when he told me his theory. Which made sense.

"So you know how."

"Think so."

"And . . . who?"

"Ah," he said, offering me his glass and following me back into the kitchen while I refilled it. "I have my suspicions."

"But you don't know?"

"Well-l-l, they're strong suspicions."

I filled the glass with Absolut—be damned if I was going to stock his brand—and added a dash of Ramlosa.

"So where do we go from here?"

"You're going to love it."

I waited.

"We're going to get everybody over at Fortunata's house and do 'I suppose you're wondering why I've asked you all here.' "

I loved it.

"Not totally everybody," he allowed. "There are some we can eliminate."

"Such as?"

"Start with Terry and Maurissa. He had a good motive, because Fortunata was going to fire him. Which would have meant losing not only his salary but his percentage in Fortaco. But we know it wasn't the murder weapon Maurissa threw overboard because there were more murders afterward. We can just about be sure that gun was the one got swiped from Fortunata."

"Which did place him at the murder scene, more or less at the time of the murder."

"Well, with all the fits and starts, the motive, the opportunity, technically you can't rule them out, but yeah, you can," said Goodman.

"Based on?"

"They're just not capable of this kind of stuff. Make it a judgment call—it's not Terry and Maurissa."

There was a high color to Goodman's cheeks now, which I preferred not to think of as high blood pressure but rather excitement. He began pacing, exuding a kind of confidence I hadn't seen before. It was contagious. I started to get the feeling we *were* moving, it *was* beginning to happen.

"Right, cross off Terry and Maurissa," I said, taking his glass back to the kitchen, this time filling one for myself as well. "Who else?"

"Claire Miller represented the package," Goodman went on, following me in. "So her commission would remain the same no matter who replaced who, long as the picture got made. Pass on her."

He leaned against the refrigerator, dislodging a magnet-held photo of Brian I'd forgotten to take down. There'd be lots of pictures, I thought with a sudden sharp pang. Enough.

"OK," I said brightly. "Anybody else we don't invite to the party?"

"I think the ex-wives. They all were promised specific and equal amounts, which they all got, but which weren't a big improvement over how they'd been doing, plus had the downside of eliminating the golden goose from making more."

"And they'd hardly have motives for any of the others."

"Right."

"OK, who else can we eliminate?"

"Tiffany Kestner, for sure. I'd like to include her because she's so good to look at, but I can't make any possible connection for her to be involved. Agree?"

"Agree."

"Freddie Forbes, the set designer—no reason."

"That I can see."

"Pass on him," said Goodman with a straight face.

"Who else?"

"The gangsters."

"Really?"

"Really. Cifelli didn't have any more than a passing motive for maybe Fortunata. But even there, dead, he'd never collect what he owed him. And revenge against Nash, it was all too oblique. He wanted to get Nash, he'd get Nash direct."

"But what about Nash? He stood to make more money on his picture deal with some of the victims out of the way."

"Yes and no. True, he'd get a giant cut of their cut. But who'd make the picture? He needed a director; he needed a producer; he needed someone in charge of the business. He wasn't equipped to make the picture himself."

Made sense.

I was starting to feel my drink, so I suggested we go back inside and sit down.

Goodman threw another few ice cubes in his glass, and

some soda, but no vodka, I noticed. I guess he liked to take a break before cocktail hour. He followed me back into the living room, where we settled down on my fluffy sectionals.

"So we've eliminated Terry, Maurissa, Claire, Tiffany, Forbes, the wives, and the gangsters from the party. That leaves who?"

"We're going to invite Harvey Pitkin, Barbara Aronson, Vernon and Jennifer Charles, Laszlo Nagy, and Billy Zee."

"But we can certainly eliminate one or two of them," I felt pretty certain.

"Yeah, but we need them for window dressing, to set up the real killer."

"And, of course, you have a plan."

"Is a bear Polish?"

"Which you're not going to tell me now."

"You got it."

The son of a bitch. "Harvey, Barbara, Vernon, Jennifer, Laszlo, and Billy," I repeated. That really did narrow things down.

"And of course, Chief Broward," Goodman added. "Invited, not suspected."

"A fine cast of characters. Now tell me, just how do you propose to get them there?"

"That's where you come in. You and Billy Zee."

31

Rayford Goodman

"Naturally, they're not going to just show up because I invite them," I explained to Bradley.

"Naturally."

"And they're not even going to just show up because I tell them they're under suspicion for the murders."

"I would," Bradley said. "Just out of curiosity."

"That's 'cause you didn't do it, and don't have to worry about getting tricked into someone proving you did do it."

"True. Although if I had done it, I'd have done it so cleverly I'd show up just to show them I had nothing to fear by showing up."

"Look," I said finally, losing patience a little. "This is not about how you'd behave or what you'd do. All right?"

"All right. So how do we manage this?"

"We use Billy Zee. As a special friend, it's not surprising Fortunata would trust him to hold a sealed letter, in case something bad happened."

"Yeah?" said Bradley, filling the spaces nicely.

"He had plenty good enough reason to be afraid. To protect himself, or at least get revenge, he wrote down his suspicions in a letter, to be opened in case of death."

"Really?"

"Which he left with me to give his good buddy, Billy Zee, the designated best friend."

"And how did you know about this?"

"Billy Zee told me."

"He did?"

Sometimes Bradley was a little slower than you might expect.

"He didn't really," I finally had to say. "This is just the line."

"But there is a letter?"

Bradley!

"There will be, once you write it."

"It's a trick!"

"Ah-hah, you catch on."

He started nodding his head, catching on. Swift. "And the letter will help catch the murderer?"

"We'll see. What it will do first of all is get all the remaining suspects together where I want them to be."

"Fortunata's."

"The scene of the crime. One of them anyway."

He seemed to like that. "And when?"

"Tomorrow night, say nine o'clock."

"That way they'll know it's not for dinner," said Bradley, who I guess thought of things like that.

"And give you time to write the letter," I said. Plus me time for a few things still needed doing.

"We're not going to collaborate?" asked Bradley with maybe just a touch sarcasm.

"Sure. I'm going to tell you what to write."

"An 'as told to' letter." I gave him a look. "Kidding," he added. "So we do this letter."

"Right."

"And Billy Zee's going to be in on it?"

"Not necessarily. No reason he has to know it's not the real decoy. I just say Fortunata left it with me for safekeeping."

"Beautiful," said Bradley, first time showing some admiration—which he quickly took back. "But why do we need a letter altogether? I mean, a real letter. As long as everybody *thinks* there's a letter, they'll come. Isn't that the idea?"

Writers really hate to write.

"Plus the letter's to open up some areas," I went on. "You'll see."

"You don't really know who did it."

"You'll see," I repeated.

"All shall be revealed in the fullness of time?" he asked.

"If you consider that a better way of saying 'you'll see.'"

He sighed. I could tell he was frustrated. I enjoyed that. So the next order of business was get Bradley started on the letter, line up Billy Zee, and get the word out to the various guests. Once that was all set up, I'd figure how best to get Chief Broward on board.

* * *

I spent the rest of the afternoon going over with Bradley what to put in the letter. I called it writing; he called it taking notes.

Before leaving Bradley to do the easy part, putting the words down, I had a call to make. I reached Billy Zee on the car phone in his new Seville. While the reception faded in and out (was I the only one noticed that?), I told him I'd been entrusted with this letter from Fortunata he wanted Billy to read for certain friends and guests at the estate.

Billy naturally asked what was in it. I told him it would be unethical for me to read the letter (and a little tough before we counterfeited it). I hadn't the slightest idea. But it was what Fortunata wanted, and I was sure Billy'd respect that. Especially since, who knew, it might say there was some additional money or stuff coming his way. That quickly turned it into a sacred obligation. He said he'd be there with bells on. I said to dress casual.

Then I called Francie, who was still at the office, and asked if she couldn't meet me for dinner. She said she didn't much feel like it. I said it wasn't entirely personal, there was some business she had to do for us. She said in that case come to the office.

"Look, I have things; I can't get to the office," I said, a little annoyed at this tooth pulling. Then gentler, "Why don't I pick you up your place seven-thirty and we go to Michael's in Santa Monica? We can do our business and have dinner, too."

"It's all business?" she asked.

"No, it's not all business," I admitted. "But it's enough business we have to get together."

She tried a little hanky-cranky to weasel out, which I found more than a bit annoying. She wasn't feeling all that well. She was behind in her work. She wanted to wash her hair.

"It's not that big a sacrifice," I said with just a touch of temper. "To go some place it's a hundred-dollar-a-plate dinner."

"What did you do, win it?" she said.

Some things I wouldn't dignify. All honesty, it wouldn't necessarily be that much, we didn't have wine.

"All right?"

"All right, only I'll meet you there," she said. "I want

to have my own transportation." Going the extra mile. Oh, yeah.

"Fine, might be a good idea. Michael's, at eight o'clock," I said.

I was at the door, just about out, when the phone rang. Bradley got it, held up a finger for me to wait.

Turned out it was a Sergeant Kleindeist, Chief Broward's administrative assistant. Evidently Bradley'd found an admirer. That happened a lot, I noticed. Lots of real good-looking women finding him real attractive. Most, I guess, didn't know—and some wanted the honor straightening him out. He tended to find it amusing. This case, looked like she found him attractive. Real attractive. Enough to compromise an ongoing investigation by warning him Broward had just sworn out a warrant for his arrest—and incidentally, mine too. Bradley thanked her and agreed yes, it would be nice, they got together one of these days for a drink.

So we'd have to keep a low profile until tomorrow night, since being pulled in by Broward wouldn't exactly expedite matters. Which is why we moved our base of operations to the Bel Age Hotel on San Vicente, where Bradley registered us under the name of the brothers Grimm, Jakob Ludwig for him and Biff for me.

Once or twice in my life the men's room somewhere was either closed or flooded or somehow out of action, and I had to go real bad. Once or twice what I did, I scouted out the ladies' room and found a moment nobody was there. Even doing my business fast as I could, with the difference of textures and smells, there was a guilty sense of breaking taboos. Like trespassing a harem. That was the way I felt getting a haircut in a beauty salon.

But ever since my barber retired, it seemed like there weren't any new ones going in the business. Whoever did, most of the money being in women's hair, they became women's hairdressers. Only on the side doing a few men. At least, Beverly Hills.

Anyway, this was an important night to me, so I went to get my hair cut. I was already used to not hearing any good jokes anymore and not being able to get a shine. I didn't think I would ever get used to everybody being so blatant. All the whooping and hollering and doing a lot of "my dear" while betraying confidences I didn't want to hear about people I didn't care about.

One thing I really liked about Bradley, he wasn't a professional gay. He was a writer, a person, lots of things. With most of the others, I always got the impression being gay wasn't just a sexual preference, but a full-time job they seemed to spend all their time and energy at.

Anyway, having escaped with my virtue intact, and my hair "styled," I went to the cleaners and picked up my good suit. In the days when money was tight I'd developed the habit storing my clothes at the cleaners. It avoided having to lay out cash before it was absolutely necessary, and saved closet space. Plus I always had something cleaned and pressed and ready to go on short notice.

I still thought my guy, and all cleaners, looked like some kind of degenerate. They all seemed to be skinny, with tight skin over high cheekbones, wispy dead black hair. I wouldn't be surprised to find any of them turned out to be a mass murderer or did something awful to small animals. I do believe it was the fumes got them. The people worked there, too, always seemed to have a guilty, oppressed look. Like they'd signed on for a cruise turned out to be a slave ship. The places never seemed to be air-conditioned, and there was always a lot of noise and steam and sweating. I half expected someone to slip me a note saying, "Help, I'm a prisoner in the stain-spotting department."

I went back to the Bel Age, checked that Bradley was coming along on the letter, got dressed in my best duds—due to the pressure dodging the police, my only duds—and made tracks to Santa Monica.

Michael's was a beautiful restaurant, on Third Street just north of Wilshire. Near the ocean in Santa Monica. But definitely not a waterfronty kind of place—except like I imagined Cannes and Nice would be waterfronty.

It was set in a magnificent garden you'd have to be half dead not to appreciate and looked like Princess Grace might have kept a locker there.

The waiters were sort of Bobby Short clones. They were all kind of cafe au lait, semi-society types, looked like they might be rehabilitated junk-bond brokers.

Francie hadn't arrived yet, so I told the woman at the desk my name and asked would she please escort my guest to my table when she came. The woman said she would be

happy to do so, and I said thank you, honey. I got a severely dropped smile for that one.

Try as I might, I keep saying "honey" to serious lady
libbers. I don't mean to. It's not that I'm unaware of their
sensitivities, or sensibilities. But I keep doing it. Like I say,
"Nice to see you" to blind people, and things like "Keeping
you on your toes?" to folks in wheelchairs. As if my brain
decides what would embarrass me most and overrides my
control.

So to apologize, I said, "I'm sorry, dear."

Cutting my losses, I headed for my table and took a seat
facing the front—though the setup there was nicely balanced
and didn't penalize the guy by making him face a wall half
the time (one of my few pet peeves).

It was still light this time of year, and softly warm, with
a beautiful, gentle smell of flowers. I was about half in love
and I was all by myself.

One of the ex-junk-bond dealers came over and asked
did I want something to drink while I waited. Which of
course wasn't such an outlandish idea in a restaurant,
though somehow people took one look at me and tended
to ask did I want a drink even if I was at the shoe repair.

I asked, kidding, what did he recommend in a vodka. He
answered straight they were impressed with a new offering
called Denaka, from Denmark. I took a chance.

Denaka turned out to be (he brought the bottle for me
to see) a good-looking package, a black enamel bottle which
you couldn't see through (I guess you'd know it was empty
when nothing else came out) at a modest 101 proof! That
topped any entry I'd come across before. I figured I'd joked
myself into a seven-dollar-a-shot drink.

Which didn't stop me from having two by the time
Francie showed up.

She was wearing her "lady clothes"—a dark blue chiffony
dress cut nicely above the knees ("Nobody in the history of
the universe ever looked good in a midi"), showing off her
good legs. Though no sylph, she did have very shapely legs,
which was somewhat of a rarity these days. Because while
there were zillions more literally heart-stoppingly beautiful
girls than there ever used to be, with bodies not the most
famous movie star ever had in the past, most had relatively
unshapely legs. For whatever reason, I don't know, even
though very long, today's beauties didn't seem to have too

much knee and ankle definition. You might gather, I am a leg man. On the other hand, the new breed had long waists with very shapely midriffs, which—there is a God—they'd been showing a lot of, too.

Anyway, there was Francie, dressed in her blue soft silky number, featuring legs and also starring some major milky cleavage. All of which had to be considered a good sign. Add to that she was smiling, and I was getting more good vibes than Lionel Hampton.

"You're certainly looking lovely," I said, rising, suavely reaching for a face to kiss and only knocking over one of the water glasses. "Which you can see, has me all thumbs," I added.

"And a couple of lips," she answered good-naturedly, taking the seat opposite me. Always a tough choice, did you want to look directly at the person, or half at in exchange for a little body contact?

"What're you drinking?" she asked.

"It's a fresh little number the sommelier came up with, a Danish vodka." I showed her the black bottle.

"And it's lightproof to protect the delicacy of the potatoes?"

"Something like that."

"I'll have a go," she said to the broker hovering nearby. "Take three cubes of ice formed from a clear Canadian brook, deposit them lightly in a six-ounce Baccarat crystal, and without bruising, pour gently to the top with this designer booze you're touting. Merci."

All systems appeared go, I couldn't help noting hopefully.

We downed another couple of killer mood-enhancers, then faced off with Gregory, who would be serving us tonight. He delivered himself of a long offering in menuspeak, after which Francie elected pasta with seafood and Chardonnay cream sauce. Neither being in the mood to pig out, I added, in the words of gourmets everywhere, "I'll have the same."

"OK, so what's the story, Richie," bringing us to part of the business at hand.

I told her about the projected showdown on the morrow, and what I'd need from her to bring it all off. First, how I wanted her to contact the principals. They were Barbara Aronson (whose cooperation would be needed in any event, being still her home ground as Fortunata's executor—but

asking whose support would serve as a good cover to divert
suspicion away from her); the Charleses, Vernon and Jennifer, he because as line director he knew more about the
day-to-day operations, and use or disuse of funds—his wife
for reasons I'll get into; Laszlo Nagy, for plenty of reasons
and because whatever he wasn't in on he'd likely know
about; and Harvey Pitkin, because he had a good motive,
opportunity, and exactly the sort of smarts to create the
kind of plot this would need.

"Meaning you suspect him?"

"Meaning I can't rule him out."

I told her I had already taken care of getting Billy Zee
there.

"I like him," she said.

"You like Billy Zee?"

"For the murderer?"

"Well, like all of them, I can't rule him out, either. I'm
also going to invite Chief Broward."

"You don't think he did it?"

"No, I don't. But I think one of these people did, and I
think I'm going to be able to prove it. Plus, if I don't,
Broward won't have so far to go to nab me."

Again, Francie's job would be to frame an invite that told
everyone Fortunata had left a letter behind with specific
instructions to have it read before them all. She should suggest sensational revelations to come and possible benefit to
the recipient. I told her to send each invite by hand-delivered messenger (I suggested Speedline, for nostalgic
reasons—if you can be nostalgic about someone who goofed
up warning you an explosion was about to wipe you out)
and to get written assurances from each he or she would
attend.

She'd been taking notes furiously, and now concluded.
"Wow, sounds exciting. Can I come, too?"

"You'll have to," I told her. "Because there's one other
thing I'll want you to do." And I told her what that was,
and how we'd go about it.

It was only after I'd finished the details that she excused
herself to go to the ladies' room.

Her going to the ladies' room, of course, always made
me suspicious. But the good news was, it was the first time
tonight.

The in-between news was she was back in a very few

minutes and both there'd been no change to her makeup I could tell and hardly enough time to've actually gone to the bathroom. I tried not to look for telltale signs on her nose.

Business officially taken care of, we ate our food—which was really good. Hard to say was it worth what it costs (though I understand they'd recently lowered the prices by about a third—which meant, way I saw it, they admitted they were gouging the first place; not like they'd instituted savings), but since nickel candy was fifty cents to a dollar, and the food here was about as good as it gets, I guess I'd have to say it was worth it. Given the present world.

I was very encouraged by the way Francie was looking and acting, and it seemed to me we were back to let the good times roll.

Looked like a job for Charlie Charm, so I put on my lopsided, cute-codger grin, and took a shot.

"I've been wondering," I began over Irish coffee. "How come we don't hear anything about the G spot anymore?"

"I think that may have been because only one guy ever found it."

"Well, in the interests of science, I thought maybe we might—you should pardon the expression—take a crack at it."

She laughed. But instead of letting me know everything was OK again, she said, "Excuse me." And went again to the ladies' room.

I told the waiter to bring me another Irish coffee, hold the coffee.

This time she was away longer. And when she returned she'd redone the makeup. At least powdered her nose, inside and out.

"I've been thinking," I said finally. "Since you don't seem to want to give up dope, and it's very hard for a boozer to relate to a doper, I'll do it with you." I held out my hand. "Give me some."

"Don't be a smartass."

"I'm not being a smartass. I'll join you. Let me, I'll do it with you."

"You're being ridiculous," she said. "You can't do coke; you've got a heart condition."

"So do you, just yours hasn't arrived yet. Gimme."

"And what if you like it?"

"Then we'll have something in common."

"Cute. The basic guilt cure."

"Well, you have to admit it won't work one of us doing it."

"I admit."

"Would you consider quitting?"

"I already considered."

"Even if not quitting means the end of us?"

"I don't know where you've been. I'm under the impression we already broke up."

"Well, I thought that was just the, you know, abortion thing."

"I suppose it triggered things."

"You know, it's not like it was exactly totally my fault. I had a hand in it, so to speak—"

"I know. And I know I haven't been reasonable. But something—it just changed for me."

"Well, why don't we have another go? Why not we take another shot? You can even put off about the drugs—till you're ready."

"Rayford . . ."

Uh-oh.

". . . it's not fair, it's not reasonable. But it's over."

Which is when the stockbroker came over and asked if there was anything else I wanted. I told him I'd had just about all I could stomach.

32

Mark Bradley

By the time Goodman returned to the Bel Age from his date with Francine, I had a draft of the letter ready, but he was in no condition to read it. It didn't take a lot of intuiting to conclude things hadn't gone well. Still, I figured I ought to say something, it was hard to ignore.

"How was dinner?"

"Actually, dinner was very good. Service excellent. Ambience s'perb. The vodka was a lil presumptuous."

"And the company?" I ventured timidly.

"If Siskel and Ebert'd been there, it would of made three thumbs down."

"Sorry," I said. And, changing the subject: "On the brighter side, I pretty much took care of things on the home front."

"Yeah?"

"I contacted Barbara and used your line about the letter possibly offering potential further gifts, et cetera, and she agreed to hostess the get-together tomorrow night. Actually, she wasn't all that enthusiastic. But I reminded her as executor she had certain duties to perform besides just picking up her inheritance and cadging free rent at the mansion pending probate."

"Good-o," said my partner succinctly.

"I also sent out the invites to everyone on the list."

"Nifter."

"Plus, I finished a draft of the letter, if you'd like to look it over."

"You cover ever'thing I said?"

"I think so."

" 'Kay."

"You don't want to check it out?"

"Hey, you're the writer." I guess things had gone worse than I thought—the man's spirit was seriously damaged.

"I'll check it the morning," he reconsidered. Then, in that terribly exaggeratedly neat way some inebriates have, daintily undressed, hung up his clothes, brushed his teeth, combed his hair, and went to bed. As a roommate, old Biff wasn't all that bad.

We had room service send up breakfast. Since it was highly unlikely they had egg substitutes and artificial bacon, Goodman treated himself to a cholesterol-be-damned heaping of the real thing, followed by pancakes lathered with butter and maple syrup. When he noted my raised eyebrow he ventured in defense, "You notice no Bloody Mary." Virtue comes in many sizes.

If he was outraged at the cost of this breakfast, he was considerably mollified by the realization our hiding out was on the expense account and he wouldn't have to pay. (The premise being, of course, that we had to stay free in order to write the book.) It pleased him, too, that all the foreigners, being the only ones who could afford to stay in major hotels today, were the principal victims of this outrageous gouging.

I checked my home answer machine, but there was nothing from Brian. I told myself that was all to the good. There wasn't much sense to a break that was only partial, I told myself, but I found I hadn't been totally convincing.

When I said I'd be calling the office, Goodman started telling me what I should say to Francine.

"Look, that's not going to work," I told him. "I don't want to get involved in any of that 'tell her I said' and 'tell him I heard what he told you to tell me he said' crap. Whatever your personal problems, you have a business relationship to maintain."

"Right. I'll get them to fire the bitch."

That got me.

"Kidding, I'm kidding. I know Francie's a very valuable member of the team. And she could always change her mind."

I called the office. I was just about to tell Goodman not to expect a change of heart when I heard myself asking Francine if there'd been any calls from Brian.

"No," she replied, "but there've been several from Chief Broward's office. Getting heavier and heavier."

"He can't seriously be thinking of us as the alleged perpetrators."

"I don't know. Ridiculous as it seems, it's starting to look like that. Unless he has some enormously convoluted plot in mind to flush out the real culprits."

The thought of Broward having any plot more convoluted than that necessary to promote a free dinner was hard to swallow.

"I guess it's sheer desperation. What'll we do?" I asked Goodman, on the extension.

"I plan to invite him to the party tonight. We'll either nail the real killer, which is certainly the gist of *my* convoluted plot, or we might as well go back to the clink with him and let the lawyers suck some of Penny's blood."

Francine was to confirm the attendance of everyone on the list and meet us at Claudio's by eight-thirty to check the arrangements and be on hand for Goodman's briefing on her part in tonight's mystery theater.

With that, Goodman himself called Billy Zee, reminding him of the engagement. Billy hadn't forgotten.

Then he went over the letter I'd written in Claudio's name, satisfied himself it had a fair chance of serving our purpose, and pronounced himself ready.

"What about Broward?" I asked.

"I think we ought to let him know we'll be available for questioning tonight after nine."

"But not where," I said.

"Oh, no. Where we'll tell him later, so he can't get in the way."

And that about covered it for the time being. Oh, one thing more. Goodman called his buddy Franklin Alonzo Skeffington at the coroner's office. He chitchatted with good old Skeff long enough to bet him a new hat Sherry Cohen had *not* been killed by the same gun killed all the others. He seemed happy to lose the bet.

According to plan, at eight, Goodman and I arrived at the massive gates to Claudio Fortunata's estate. Also according to plan, Goodman hid on the floor of the car, out of sight of the monitoring TV security system, as I was buzzed through.

I was to go in alone, see that the door was left on the latch, distract Barbara by asking to be shown a safe allegedly hidden in the pool house which I had reason to suspect might have some bearing. She would, of course, disavow any knowledge of such a (fictitious) safe, but I would insist on seeing for myself. Goodman would then have time to sneak in and proceed to Claudio's study, where he wanted a good twenty minutes to search for what we were really seeking. If he found it, our lives would be infinitely easier, and the bluff of the letter less absolutely necessary. We would see.

By twenty-five after, I'd conceded there was no safe in the pool house and allowed myself to be taken back to the main house. A few minutes later Goodman "arrived" at the main gate, in company of Francine (with whom he'd rendezvoused, per plan), and was buzzed through.

The Charleses showed up about ten to nine (producers tended to be on time), he in a nondescript suit, with sleeves too long, she elegantly accoutred in what looked to be eleven thousand dollars worth of cowboy duds (incredibly including sequin chaps). They were followed shortly by the affable Laszlo Nagy, exuding goodwill and confidence—what a difference a contract made. Then Billy Zee, in a splashy new deal-maker wardrobe. Given the new car and the Rolex alone, he must have gotten a sizable loan based on his impending windfall. Then, in the same clothes I'd seen him wear on every occasion our paths crossed heretofore, the never dapper, ever harried Harvey Pitkin. And the players were all in place.

Goodman, as ringmaster, allowed an air of expectation to build up: first asking, on behalf of their departed host, if anyone cared for drinks before the evening's business commenced. Everyone did, and Francine, on instructions, accompanied Barbara to help prepare them and monitor their quality.

I took the opportunity to ask Goodman "how things were" and by his barely perceptible shake of the head I knew his quest had been unsuccessful, which was not unexpected. He excused himself to make a call (I knew, to Broward, telling him where we were).

And finally all was ready, drinks were served (I noted with interest Goodman had abstained), and it was time to mount the production, in local parlance.

"I have here," said Goodman, taking an envelope out of his inside coat pocket, "a letter from Mr. Fortunata which he left with me the day he died. He told me then in case anything happened, give it to Billy Zee for him to get in touch with all of you. But since he didn't give it to Billy, but to me to see Billy did that (no offense, Billy) I figured I have an obligation to see his wishes carried out. Which is why I decided the best idea was publicly give it to Billy and let him just read it out loud. That way nobody can claim any kind of tampering, and we'll all find out whatever it is at the same time."

"Excuse me," said Harvey, the writer. "Didn't you say it might be in our financial interest? How'd you know that if you didn't read it ahead of time?"

"Good question," said Goodman, I could see stalling for time.

"Didn't you tell me," I leapt to the rescue, "that that's what Claudio indicated when he gave it to you?"

"Yep, that's what I told you. OK, Harvey? OK. Now, if there are no other questions, or even if there are, Billy—here's the letter. You're on." With which Goodman went to sit in the only remaining chair, a heavily upholstered number at the far side of the room. He tried to pull it closer to the group, but it was so heavy it resisted his efforts. So instead he merely leaned forward to help bridge the distance.

Billy went over to a standing floor lamp, which was lit, though in fact it was hardly necessary, light from the recently set sun still nicely streaming through the open window. He opened the envelope, extracted the letter, cleared his throat portentously, and commenced reading.

"This is a letter to my friends and co-workers, and the one among you who is not (friend, anyway). Clearly, if this is being read, it's because my fears were justified and something the far side of dire has happened to me. As to who I think did this, I'm not going to say just yet because I'm not exactly positive. But I think what I have to say, in the hands of a professional, will point to the guilty party. That's why a copy of this letter has also been delivered to the police."

At which point Billy stopped, looked at Goodman—as did everyone else in the room.

"That's right," said Goodman. "They ought to be getting it any minute now. Go ahead, Billy."

Billy took a deep breath, continued. "All you'll have to do here, then, is hang on to the guilty party till the police arrive. It's a good bet I contributed to my own downfall in a number of ways. I suppose it wouldn't do much good to say I learned my lesson?"

Billy stopped for a moment, to allow the room a chuckle. Score one for the dead comic.

"OK, here goes. Most of you know I'm not the most conservative guy. Besides being what the scandal press calls a womanizer (how come they don't call the more active ladies 'manizers'?) . . ."

Goodman gave me a look. I'd done a little punching up since he'd last read it.

". . . I'm also, unfortunately," continued Billy, "somewhat of a compulsive gambler. And while the former vice has gotten me into a few tight spots—thank god!" (another look from Goodman) ". . . the latter is probably what eventually did me in."

Mumble, mumble, mumble—they sounded like extras told to make crowd noises.

"By the time we went on hiatus during the filming of *One Fell Swoop*—to get additional financing, and me to get a little facial nip and tuck—I was into hock to the bookies for two hundred and eighty thousand bucks. And while it's a lot of money, it wasn't an amount I couldn't handle, given time. But unfortunately, 'Time is money' never carries greater truth when the time has run out on money owed to combination shylock/bookies. So, to settle the debt and ease the pressure on myself, I agreed to 'sell' an interest in the film—twenty-five percent, to be exact—for my outstanding debt to Armand Cifelli, loosely disguised as Sorrento Ventures. Technically, I couldn't exactly do this, but I figured as long as it wasn't cutting into anyone else's points, no harm done."

"But it was," interrupted Laszlo Nagy. "True, we each had our points spilled out—spelled?—but it's also we would get whatever wasn't given, in proportion."

Which provoked a brief outburst of indignant agreement from the others, most of which was directed toward Billy. "Hey, don't argue with me," he said finally. "I'm just reading a letter."

"Right, let the guy read," said Goodman, who seemed to be monitoring everybody's eyes.

"Then I made another mistake. I only claimed to be a great director, not a businessman. I met Barry Nash. He seemed to know about my problems, being in the problem-making business himself. He said he could help me. Which turned out to be like trying to get Mussolini off your back by turning to Hitler."

Goodman gave me another look. I thought it was kind of clever.

"Anyway," continued Billy, "he said he knew Cifelli and felt he could get him to ease off and wait for me to pay after I got my salary from the picture—a service he would perform in exchange for only ten percent of the picture's profits. He said there would be no problems. There were problems. First off, there was a gangland-style murder of someone who worked for Cifelli. Which I strongly suspected was Nash's doing. I still hoped, because I wanted to believe maybe it was a coincidence, or didn't have anything to do with our particular business. But then Cohen got killed at L'Ermitage."

"Which was a case of mistaken identity, right?" said Vernon Charles. "Being in bandages, whoever killed Cohen thought he was killing you, him being in your room and all," he directed at Billy, as if he were actually Claudio.

"Don't ask me," said Billy. "I'm just reading."

"Read," said Goodman.

"When the police, and everyone else, thought it was a case of the wrong guy at the wrong place, I thought so, too. I thought Cifelli was behind it and simply ordered the hit to pay me off for welshing on him. Later on, I realized that wasn't the way it was at all."

"Why, how? What made you change your mind?" said Barbara. Then she, too, suddenly realizing it wasn't Billy talking, it was Claudio, became embarrassed. "I mean—sorry."

"Go on," I said to Billy.

"But first, when I got out of there and went home—the day we all met, actually—"

"The day he was killed," added Goodman.

". . . I was in the middle of a conference with Mr. Goodman and Mr. Bradley when I got a phone call. It was from Cifelli. He told me just because I'd made 'other arrangements' didn't free me from my obligation to him. In fact, having insulted him and shown what he considered a 'lack of respect' I'd gotten him mad. Therefore, if I was cutting him out of the picture, I was more or less cutting my throat as well. You can imagine how comforting that was. He was calling the debt. I'd either come up with the entire two hundred and eighty in twenty-four hours or else. The 'or else' was spelled out as 'failure to comply would impact on my continued residence on the planet.' Which I'm sure you'll all agree was as nicely worded a death threat as one is likely to encounter. Which didn't make it any the less terrifying. So there I was, now involved with two mobsters instead of one and in worse trouble than ever. Remember, at the time I still thought Cifelli had murdered Cohen, thinking it was me."

Mumble, mumble, crowd noise.

"But then almost at once I stopped and reconsidered. Cifelli was far too good a businessman to kill me and lose any chance to collect all that money just for vengeance. Which brought me to another conclusion, to wit: Hamilton's murder hadn't been a mistake, it'd been on purpose. So, who? Who benefits? The people I assume are here listening to this. For while Cohen's murder wouldn't throw his twenty percent (forty of Fortaco) back into the pot, since it would come to me, there was one thing it would do. It would set *me* up. If after that *I* got killed, the whole fifty percent (our combined ownership of Fortaco) would get thrown back into the pot—and that could be worth millions."

"He was forgetting Cohen's wife, Sherry, inheriting his share," Goodman added, it seemed for my benefit. Go keep track of all that biz-biz. "Which, of course, the killer didn't," he went on. "Forget. Bringing us back to the central fact that everyone here—except Barbara, but including Terry and Maurissa—stood to gain a whole lot. Motives for all of you. Big, big motives. We all got thrown off the track for a while, reasonably enough. First, it was Nash who suggested to Fortunata he change rooms with Cohen. Then, always looking for ways to get at his rival, Cifelli, Nash sent over Heather Hansen, who happens to be a professional killer in case you're interested, to take out Cohen—figuring rightly Cifelli would get the blame. But Hansen actually got there too late. Not only because Cifelli'd hired me to protect Fortunata—I was too late, too—but because somebody else'd already killed Cohen. Billy?"

"The letter goes on," Billy went on. "So, if Nash slash Hansen didn't kill Cohen, who did? Clearly one of you here, all of whom benefit enormously, now that I'm also gone. Who? That's the big question, who . . ."

I'd figured Claudio would have milked the moment; the man *was* a director.

"Well," said Billy, reading, not possessed of the best sense of dramatic timing, "I've pretty much figured that out, too. And I've passed that additional information on to Mr. Goodman, who will now, in the great time-honored tradition of detectives everywhere"—Goodman gave me another look—"proceed to name the culprit."

At which point, I noticed Francine slip casually out of the room. I knew what the plan was, but I could see the timing was going to be off, and the whole setup was in danger of collapsing if she acted prematurely. I made a move to intercept her, but when it caught Laszlo's eye, I was forced to back off.

"Wait," said Jennifer Charles. "Before you get into all that, why don't you let him finish the letter?"

"OK," said Goodman. "Finish the letter."

"Submitted for your consideration," said Billy, reading, "yours truly—and it's signed 'the late but still great Claudio Fortunata.' "

During the course of the letter reading, as the hour grew later, Goodman and I had gone around, turning on various lights, so the room was quite bright.

"So now what's supposed to happen?" asked Laszlo.

"Well, I'll tell you," said Goodman. "I'm going to solve the case."

Mumble, mumble, mumble.

"Since we know—or I do, anyway—Cohen, Fortunata, Hampton, and Sherry, too, were all killed by the same gun, we don't have to solve all of them to find the murderer—just one. And the one I think we know about is Claudio Fortunata."

Meanwhile I was trying to pantomime to Goodman to look out the window, but I seemed never to be able to catch his eye. Each time it seemed to be someone else in the party, making me look nutty.

"Forget all the other murders, forget all the clues. The one biggest distinction about Fortunata's is it was contained. Meaning, we know who was here and who was not. At the time, the one thing we overlooked was that the one who did the murder had to have still been here afterward, after everyone had gone, but while Bradley was still here, while Hampton was still here, while Barbara was still here, and while the police were still here. Since Hampton was himself a victim later, and since we have other evidence absolving Barbara, that meant the killer, one of you here, knew of someplace in the house in which to hide, someplace he or she wouldn't be found where they could wait it out. And that person is going to jail, because I know who and I know how and before much longer, I'll know where."

I almost couldn't bear it. But there wasn't going to be any stopping him. As I watched with mounting horror, Goodman crossed to the doorway and, simultaneously giving a prearranged signal to Francine, said, "Ladies and gentlemen, the name of the murderer is . . ." (I *think* it was Goodman—or was it just the echo of a thousand actors in a thousand movies?) Francine, true to the plan, pulled the main electric switch. The idea was the guilty party, realizing flight was the only way to escape prosecution, was going to take advantage of the darkness to go to the secret hiding place—after which we'd see who was missing and know the culprit.

That was the plan.

The reality was, when the lights were suddenly doused and all the lamps went out, nobody moved. That was because we were still left with the clear and quite adequate natural light remaining from outside.

We'd totally overlooked the advent of daylight savings time.

33

Rayford Goodman

I'd have to say that rated as one of the worst moments of my life. It was certainly right up there with heart attacks, divorce settlements, and your odd war. It may just be we've all seen too many movies. I still can't get used to hitting a guy in the face—doesn't sound like a mallet hitting a grapefruit, or however the hell they make that sound in pictures.

"Why is it," said Harvey Pitkin after a bit, "I have the feeling something was supposed to happen just now and didn't?"

"Because that's what we wanted you to feel," I said, desperately trying to figure how I could save this mess.

"I'm willing to bet it was a case of dramatic premature ejaculation," he went on. "You were setting something up and the timing went wrong."

"You can't know that," I replied, I admit weakly.

"God, it's like a director rewriting," he said.

And then it was Laszlo picking up on it. "And why it is I have the impression," he said, "was not Claudio wrote that letter in the first, second, or any place?"

"All in good time," I said, stalling, looking out the window—seeing the Irish wolfhounds lying around. Didn't seem all that broken up over losing Fortunata.

"Wait a minute," said Billy. "I'm supposed to be getting something here. Ain't I supposed to be getting something?"

"No," said Bradley, finally pitching in, "we only said there might be something in it for you."

"Well then, shit," said Billy. "I'm out of here, the hell with this."

"Just—a—minute. If you will," I said. "You're dead right. You're all just too sharp for me to keep trying to con you. You busted us. We did have a little scheme in mind. And it did lay a little egg."

Mumble, mumble, mumble.

"But," I went on, "that doesn't mean I don't know who killed Fortunata and the rest. That doesn't mean I don't know the basic whys and wherefores."

"What does it mean?" asked Vernon Charles.

"It just means I'll have to prove it another way."

Another look out the window.

"And I'm supposed to keep serving drinks and fixing hors d'oeuvres?" said Barbara, a little cranky.

"Hey, it's not K.P. Just give me a few more minutes of your time. Aren't you all curious? Don't you at least care?"

Mumble, mumble, mumble.

"OK, just hold it a minute. Give me a minute!"

With which I called a hasty confab with Francie, Barbara, and Bradley. It was desperation time, and to try a far-out Plan B.

Mumble, mumble, mumble.

"OK, try to follow me on this," I said, a last bid for attention. "Let's start with who didn't do it. Though Maurissa and Terry, like all of you here, except Barbara and Billy, were in line to gain when the various victims got preempted from the picture deal, they didn't do it. It looked bad for a while because my partner saw Maurissa throw a gun in the ocean during Fortunata's burial. But it turned out that wasn't the murder weapon, since the murders kept on happening after. Addition, we all know Terry's a thief, and it turned out that was Fortunata's gun, which Barbara told us got stolen before. Plus for other reasons, take my word—they were off the hook."

"You are really going to take it all night?" said Laszlo.

"No, but I'm going to take it as long as it takes it. Second, Barbara, though a woman scorned, managed to find . . . other sources of comfort." That was a nice, sensitive way to put it, I do say so myself. "Plus she didn't profit from the murder. Well, yes, some—from Fortunata's will. Actually, fair amount some places, but not enough Beverly Hills-wise; plus didn't have the opportunity or the motives for the other ones. Strike Barbara. Who also has my confidence," I added.

"And me, you already said didn't have a motive," reminded Billy.

"Well, of course you did, a little, since you, too, got something in the will. But considering the future potential if Fortunata lived, you're actually a net loser."

"I wouldn't put it exactly that way, but OK."

"The others who aren't here, the Claires, the Freddies, the Tiffanies, all for one reason or another—pass."

"What about the most obvious ones of all," said Jennifer Charles, "the gangsters. Either Cifelli or Nash?"

"Yeah, well, I must say most things tended to point to them most of the time," I went on. "The murders of Cohen, Hampton, and Cohen's wife, Sherry—all very professional. All .22s, all neat, clustered shots—no extra fuss, no wasted effort. The double *X*'s in Cohen's cheeks. Definitely looked like one or the other of them responsible. Add to that the explosion on the set—again a terrorist move, again the sort of thing we'd expect from gangsters. Too good. Too much signature. And, everything but motive."

"What about," said Laszlo, "if was Cifelli. He had motive, getting to even from Nash."

"Yes, in a way. Though I know from personal assurances and his character, he didn't. Plus he had reasons to protect me, not harm me, and I was endangered there. Nash, on the other hand, was a definite enemy of mine. He did want me—I know from other attempts—out of the picture."

"So could be Nash, right?" said Laszlo.

"No, not him, either, because somebody *warned* me just before the explosion. Somebody knew it was going to happen, but didn't want me hurt. All that somebody wanted was to have it *look* like Nash was responsible."

"For what reason?" Barbara asked.

"To get rid of him. Force him off the picture. To be able to exercise the moral turpitude clause, and eliminate his piece of the action."

"But all of us left would profit from that," said Jennifer.

"I know," I answered. "So that didn't pin it down, but it did eliminate Cifelli and Nash."

Bradley, I noticed, all through this hadn't said hardly a word. Clearly, he was still mystified. Even having heard the new plan—or the setup for it. Yet in many ways he'd been key to my figuring it out. Even if sometimes unconscious.

"So what you are saying, if it's correct I am reading you," said Laszlo, "the suspects are down to Mr. Charles, his wife, Jennifer, Mr. Harvey Pitkin—and myself?"

"R-r-right!" said Bradley suddenly. And I knew the sun had broken through—he *knew*.

"So who else didn't do it?" asked Harvey.

Bradley looked at me. Smiled. I nodded. "You're on."

"You didn't, Harv," said Bradley. "Oh, you had motive, too. With Cohen and Fortunata both dead, you not only had a shot at getting your job back, but stood to have your share considerably increased—depending, it's true, on getting credit on the picture."

"That's some 'depending.' How would I know I'd be re-hired on the picture?"

"You knew I'd hire you," said Laszlo. "You knew I'd get Claudio's job. You knew I knew your real value from the picture, and you knew me. A new director, chances pretty good I'd want everything the way it was, not to shake the boat."

"But how would I know he'd be the new director?" said Harvey.

"You'd know it, the way everybody would know it," said Vernon Charles. "It's part of my character, to take the conservative way. If the picture went forward, I'd produce. If I produced, I'd keep the same personnel. No waves from me. To 'shake' the boat, either."

"So, wait," said Harvey. "You," indicating Bradley, "start off by saying it wasn't me, then everybody piles in with all this crap designed to show it was me. Are you accusing me or absolving me?"

"We're just all discussing the possibilities," I said, taking over again. "Let's move on. Let's concentrate for the time being on Fortunata's murder. That one tells us a lot."

Mumble, mumble, mumble.

"The others—Cohen before, the rest after—were all clean, surgical, professional. But Fortunata's was gross, a bloody slaughter. The word overkill. It might of been planned, but it was still a definite act of passion."

Ooooh, mumble, mumble.

"Which turns us to Mr. Nagy," said Bradley, indicating Laszlo.

"Right," I went on. "All those years doing the actual work. All those years being the actual creator. It had to hurt real bad."

"You bet," admitted Laszlo.

"The world praising the wonderful Claudio Fortunata, him taking all the bows, making most of the money, you doing all the work, while he was totally dependent on the genius of—"

"Laszlo Nagy," said Laz. "Absolutely. But I didn't kill him."

"Still, we have proof of his payoffs to you—one million forint, maybe every time—in addition to your official salary. And that proof at first turned up missing from Fortunata's script, the script he kept all his notes in, about everything."

"But Nigel Hampton knew about the script," Bradley interrupted, on the hunt now. "He'd seen Fortunata daily make all sorts of entries in it. Maybe he'd even read it; he must have read it to cut out the one most incriminating page, on the back of which Claudio'd noted your payoff."

"For what purpose, Hampton?" asked Laszlo.

"Who knows? To blackmail you? To get a part from Fortunata?"

"But once Claudio was murdered," Bradley went on, "it was a whole new ball game. He didn't want any part of that. Now he saw his page of script less for income than insurance—to protect himself from the killer."

"Meanwhile," I picked up, "his still being there kept the killer trapped. It wasn't till Hampton left that the killer had a chance to run, but by that time Bradley'd returned from Barbara's office. So he got coshed. Only it was too late, the cops were already on the way."

"Then Hampton contacted us later," Bradley took over. "But before he could tell us who he suspected, *he* was murdered."

"I suppose you think I did that, too?" said Laszlo.

"You were the one who stole the script, except the one page."

"Yes, I did that. Both I was going to need it for to direct, it already had many of *my* notes. Plus, I admit, I didn't want you to find out the forint. Don't mean I killed him. Frustrating, yes. Unfair, yes. But I was making a good living, too, don't forget."

"Right. Except for one thing. It looks like you knew once Fortunata was out of the picture you'd be in. And if you knew that, you would have a motive—you'd have revenge, justification, and the glory. But the trouble is: how *could* you know that? No one even knew the picture was still going to get made. At the funeral everyone thought it was all over. Everyone but one . . ."

"I have a feeling we're getting down to me," said Vernon Charles finally.

"Well, as some politician once said on a day he must have been in the clear, 'Let's take a look at the record,' " I went on. "Right from the beginning. Cohen gets killed. Now, since we learned what a big interest he had in the picture, we assumed it was on purpose. But let's go back to the original idea. Let's say Fortunata *was* the intended victim. Let's say you, Charles, for the sake of argument, went to the L'Ermitage to kill Fortunata."

"Which I wanted to do why, again?"

"Both because you stood to benefit financially from his not getting credit on the picture. You, of all people, knew Laszlo could do the job, had been doing it really. So there'd be no loss there, and potentially a lot of gain."

"Conjecture, conjecture."

"Logic, logic."

"You said 'both because'—what's the other part of the both?"

"Maybe even the stronger one. One day when I was talking to you, Barbara, about various people either getting fired—like Terry was in danger of—or possibles, I mentioned Vernon. Remember what you said?"

Barbara remembered: "I think it was along the lines of, 'If there's one person who's not in the remotest danger of being fired, it's Vernon Charles.' "

"Exactly. Well, Vern, it stuck in my mind. Why were you exempt, why were you the only one who never, under any circumstances would be fired? I didn't even have to ask, it was obvious—because that would piss off your *wife*! And why would Fortunata care about not bugging your wife?"

Bradley nodded, I'd have to say sagely. "How she cried and cried at the hospital when we talked about Claudio. She just went on and on! Crying and crying. It wasn't an ordinary reaction to the death of a husband's co-worker."

"No, no husband's co-worker. Fortunata cared about not bugging her because he cared about *her*, because he was also humping her. Isn't that right, Jennifer?"

"Conjecture, conjecture," she said softly, not terribly convincing.

"Well, I say—conjecture, conjecture—the day your husband went to write fade-out to Fortunata's career, the man was actually AWOL, actually with you, in another part of the hotel. Doing the dirty deed. Then, with Cohen dead—even by mistake—killing Fortunata made even more sense now. He'd get rid of not only his rival for his wife's affections, as they say in the papers, but a guy with big points in the picture. Only that murder—messy because he was involved emotionally, hated the man—led to the others. Hampton because he had disappeared from the house, showing he knew something, might very well have known the key something. And when he saw Hampton, clumsily disguised, talking to us at Forest Lawn, figured he was going to tell us something—that something presumably being he knew who the murderer was—and maybe even how. So he followed Hampton and shot him outside the Kit and Caboodle."

"The what?"

"Just my partner's colorful way of describing the Whip and Surrey," Bradley put in. "When we showed up before he'd gone, he pinned us down with some random firing and made his getaway. Then, when it turned out Cohen's share hadn't got thrown into the pot but went to Sherry Cohen, she had to go, too."

"Very fanciful, very colorful," said Vernon. "And where is the least shred of evidence?"

"And what on earth did you intend to result from making up that letter from Claudio?" said Jennifer, idly looking out the window at the sound of the dogs barking. Finally.

"I have a lot of evidence," I said, daring to take a breath.

"Right," said Vernon with regained confidence. "And you think this is Perry Mason and all you have to do is throw out a few hints and I'm going to stand up and confess. Forget it."

The barking got more insistent.

"Are those Claudio's dogs out there?" asked Jennifer, pointing out the window.

"I suppose," said Barbara from her chair.

I knew they were. Because besides seeing them right after the lights went out, and the *light didn't* go out, I'd sent Francine to fetch them and place them exactly there, and make sure they barked. (Plan B)

"The poor darlings," said Jennifer.

"Has anybody been feeding them?" I asked innocently. "They look positively emaciated."

"I would guess the cook," said Barbara, as she, too, had been quickly cued. "Well, the cook's gone, actually. Maid, too, now that I think of it—I've been using a cleaning crew."

"So nobody's been feeding these doggies?" I said. "All this time?"

"Gee, I really don't know," said Barbara, as good an actress as Fortunata had said.

"That's outrageous," cried Jennifer, really upset. "I'm going right out this minute, this very minute. They've got to be starving!"

"They waited this long," said Bradley, a slow starter but a good finisher. "They can wait another five minutes."

The dogs barked again. Piteously. Perfectly.

"Please, Mrs. Charles," I said. "Just another few minutes."

She was visibly disturbed. Good.

Now, howling. . .

"I can't . . ." And started for the door. Bradley barred her way.

"Just a minute? I'll hurry this. So all right, back to you, Vern—you want to know what my evidence is? The one thing that set the Fortunata murder apart from the others was we were dead sure the killer stayed in the house after the murder. But how? Where?"

"How and where, indeed," repeated Vernon.

"There had to be someplace, didn't there? There had to be a spot, known only to the killer, where no one could find him. How could that be?

"Well, I had my first clue when I learned you, and the missus, were the previous owners of this place. The second when Fortunata was discussing it, how it'd been built in the fifties, then of course, redone, and redone again. The fifties—you and the fifties. And what was so special about the fifties? The Cold War. Conservative—you called yourself conservative. Bomb shelters. A house like this, time like that—absolutely. But where? No evidence now. Which meant it'd been redone somehow.

"That sent me to the Plans and Permits department, and sure enough, there was a permit for alterations in the study here. But no plans. A contractor would file a plan."

"But a do-it-yourselfer might not!" piped Bradley.

"Exactly. And we know how old Vern here likes to do it himself—he's told us that. He even volunteered the delicate job of rebuilding Fortunata's latrine—"

"Vitrine," Bradley corrected me.

"Whatever. So there had to be a secret place, somehow made from the old bomb shelter—and it had to be on the first floor here, of course. In fact, it had to be in this room."

"But I'm sure you looked for that," said Vernon smugly.

"Yes, I did."

"And you didn't find it."

"No, I didn't." Cue the dogs, Francie. Quiet. Damn.

"But then, say such a thing even existed; somebody else might have known about it. After all, I haven't lived here in many years, but a lot of other people have."

"That's right. I thought about that. In fact, it helped me eliminate some people. Barbara might have known, but I knew Barbara hadn't done it. Billy Zee might have, but I didn't see a reason for him, either. Harvey, not likely. Nor Laszlo. See how it kept narrowing down? And who that was left benefited most from the killings? Why, the Charleses, surprise, surprise."

Now some great barking.

"I want to go feed those dogs," said Jennifer. "I don't care about all this theorizing. There's nothing you can prove. I don't know anything about all this. And I'm sure Vernon doesn't, either. Meanwhile, there are hungry animals."

"Oh, there're a lot worse things than hungry animals. There are abused animals, there are murdered animals. Why, would you believe it, Jennifer, my own cat was horribly cut up, horribly murdered, left to suffer and die, its fur all bloodstained, its little bones all—"

"Stop, stop!" she screamed. "I don't want to hear it. I can't stand those things." She started for the door. Bradley restrained her.

"Right, I forgot. *Your* cat—Fluffy, wasn't it? Didn't I hear once, the very same thing happened to your cat? Didn't I hear it died a particularly horrible and brutal death?"

She stopped struggling, but her body remained rigid.

"My little cat. What kind of a person would do a thing like that? What kind of man?" I went on. "Sure, it looked like Nash, it was supposed to look like Nash," I went on. "But it wasn't. They didn't want to scare me, or punish me—they wanted to *kill* me. And you don't bother murdering pussycats when you want to murder private detectives.

No, it had to be somebody else, someone not only capable of doing something that awful, but probably somebody who had *done it before*."

Still, she remained frozen, unmoving.

"So, could it have been Vernon? Vernon the line producer, Vernon the cuckold (what a great spot to operate from if you're really Vernon the mastermind). Or was it simply Vernon, good old reliable Vernon—the animal abuser, the brutal, heartless animal killer."

"Vern . . . ?" she said in the tiniest voice.

"Don't fall for it," he croaked unconvincingly, removing his glasses.

"What a plan, he gets practically all of it. With Nash, the alleged cat-killer and set-blower-upper aced out of his cut. And who, by the way, would have greater access to explosives from, say, the special effects department than the inconspicuous, nonentity line producer?"

"Yes, by coincidence, we do get it all, my sweet, my expensive sweet," said Vernon, willing her to silence.

"And you go on living with the man you know, in your heart of hearts, not only stole from all the people who trusted him, not only murdered four people—four!—but . . . what did you say the name of your cat was? Mine was Sven. My poor dead little pussycat was Sven . . ."

I motioned Bradley to ease off, step out of her way. And now, almost in a trance, Jennifer started across the room.

"Don't . . ." said Vernon.

"His little broken bones, his bloody fur—"

"Stop!" said Jennifer. "I understand. I agree!" And she continued to the far wall. God, she wasn't going to pull out a book and make the wall swing open . . .

No, she reached into the arm of the the plush reading chair I'd vacated and found some sort of lever. The chair, rigid when I tried to move it—I'd thought the damn thing was bolted down—popped free. She swung it, I guess on a hinge, to one side. A spring trapdoor underneath opened upward, revealing a staircase leading down. She stepped back.

In that instant Vernon dashed across the room and leaped down the stairs. I started after him, but she stopped me.

"It doesn't go anywhere. There's no other exit," she said.

And so it was. Vernon coming back up.

"OK, you found me out. You found my secret place.

Later, take a look—it's still totally provisioned. There's still enough stuff to last for years down there. Outlasted the Cold War. It was masterfully done."

"I'm sure it was," said Bradley, hoping for an easy conclusion.

"But surely, you didn't think I'd outfit a room for every possible contingency and not think to stash a gun?"

He showed it to me. Right, he would have thought of that. He was a producer! It was a big gun, too. Colt .45 Not the murder weapon, I noted automatically. So now he climbed all the way out again and backed cautiously toward the door.

"I'm going to leave now," he said.

"I don't think so," I said. "You killed my cat. You fucking killed my cat!" And the dumbest thing I ever did, I just ignored the gun and ran over and bashed him in the face.

And the dumbest thing, he let me.

Which is when good old Chief Broward stepped in from the small study next door.

"Just as I figured," he said, taking out the handcuffs.

"You were here all this time and you didn't step in?" I yelled. "He might have killed me."

Broward looked me right in the eye. "That was a chance I was willing to take," he said.

34

Mark Bradley

They, of course, took Charles away. He attempted to threaten a lawsuit based on infringement of his rights and slick trickery, but it was hard to sound authoritative with a broken jaw. Jennifer's involvement, if any, other than what had to be some peripheral awareness, couldn't be reasonably established. I remember the quizzical look on her face as they cuffed Vernon and she turned—not to Broward, which annoyed him plenty—but to Goodman. He was exceedingly kind, I thought, perhaps mindful of the emotional pain he'd had to inflict in order to get her to reveal the whereabouts of the secret room. His oblique apology was inherent when he said, "The dogs really were fed. If you'd like, I'll show you."

And she said, "No, you're the enemy." Though without a lot of conviction.

He nodded understandingly. "Point of view," he said. Then tacked on, in case it'd slipped her memory, "He did kill your boyfriend."

"I know," she said, and started out.

We watched her through the door. And to me, sotto, "Not to mention Fluffy."

I sighed. The Fluffys are ever with us. I suppose even the chicest of the chic have their lapses. I wonder if even Mrs. Paley didn't have a Muffin or a Whiskers in her storied past.

There were other details. The statements. Reviewing the basis for some of his conclusions. And last, a few recriminations.

"Don't think I'm forgetting you were trying to pin this shit on me and my partner here," Goodman told Broward.

"Just an old police trick to motivate your best effort."

They exchanged a couple of looks that made clear mutual admiration wasn't a part of their relationship.

"Well, listen, if we're going to go around solving all your toughest crimes," said Goodman after a bit, "we ought to at least get some kind of consultant fee."

"I'll drop the charges, how's that?" said Broward.

Penny, of course, was in hog heaven—or whatever the publisher's equivalent is. Hog heaven sounds about right.

"So when do you think we'll have the manuscript?" he asked, not before, not after, but instead of "Are you all right? Did anyone get hurt?"

"I would say, working together with Goodman, about three months."

"Jesus, you got to be kidding. I want this *out* in three months. Can't you do better?"

"Working alone, I can have it in six weeks."

Penny was a lot of things, but slow wasn't one of them.

"But he gets credit," he said, accepting the condition.

"He did solve the case," I had to admit.

"So it's equal."

"It's equal, me on top, of course."

"Don't get sexual. He's the bigger name."

"I don't care. No go. It's the least."

"We'll work it out."

"No, we'll settle it."

"OK," said Penny, pulling a coin out of his pocket. "Call it," he said.

He flipped it high.

"Heads," I called.

He caught it and turned it over on his wrist (wherever *that* originated). "Tails," he said, showing me. "Get writing."

I sighed. Well, at least it wasn't "as told to."

By which time he was through the door and turning toward his office. "They always call heads," I heard him faintly muse as he ambled down the hall. Could the son of a bitch . . . ?

I told Francine that Goodman and I were celebrating solving the case by having our traditional wrap party at Chasen's that night.

"What do you mean, 'traditional'? You did it once."

"Hey, this is not a country long on tradition—we tear down buildings built in the fifties. So you do something twice, it's virtually a way of life. Anyway, the point is, you're invited, seeing as how you're an integral part of the team."

"You don't want me there," she said.

"I want you there."

"He doesn't want me there," she said.

"He wants you there."

"I don't want to be there," she said.

I didn't have much of an answer for that.

"Anyway," she said, "I've got a lot of research to do, and follow up, and checking."

"Which has nothing to do with it."

"You noticed."

I don't know why the breakup of this ill-matched couple, whose union I had opposed all along, should be hitting me so hard. Unless it had to do with my losing mine. And faith in anybody's. And the gaping emptiness of the years ahead . . . . . . Nah.

I put on my Ungaro putty-colored double-breasted suit, a white generic sea isle cotton shirt that cost a hundred and thirty-five dollars even without a designer label, a beige, brown, and black Bolgheri tie, and my tan and beige Cole-Haan killer shoes that Fred Astaire couldn't have lived without. I looked like the feline's sleepware.

I stashed my car in the garage at the Beverly Center and waited on the corner diagonally across from the Hard Rock Café, opposite a Cedars Sinai "artwork" that even I had to concede looked like nothing so much as a junkyard for discarded railroad ties. (Harry, we coulda bought a cat-scan machine, you crazy?) There wasn't even time to find out if this was an area conducive to cruising before Goodman, at the helm of his huge Cadillac, turned the corner and moored the bygone behemoth beside me.

He was wearing one of his new blazers, this one with a heavily embroidered crest that seemed to establish membership in something having to do with either yachting or bowling, it wasn't clear. We exchanged greetings and I got in. The tape was playing something aggressively blarey, which I guess I reacted to because it prompted the following mini-blowup: "Stan Kenton. I know you probably never heard of him, he goes way back to the brass age. While you're probably used to more artistic stuff from punk rock groups called Proud Poultry or Pap Smear, or something like that."

"See, it just shows you how you prejudge," I replied. "It happens I do know who Sam Kenton was." Which seemed to end that conversation as he continued the few blocks west to Chasen's.

I was very pleased he didn't try to park in the Hughes market lot across the way but seemed willing to pop for the valet parking provided by the restaurant. Or maybe he just didn't want to risk his new paint job on a left turn against the traffic.

Inside, we ambled to the front room, which housed the celebrities, some of whom I was surprised to find still living.

Sitting at what I was reliably informed was Cary Grant's table (still?) was none other than Armand Cifelli, who gave us an effusive greeting by raising his usually hooded eyes and looking at us directly and at some length, without a threat. Implied or otherwise.

Julius, the maître d', not only recognized us (Goodman, really) but seemed actually glad to see him. I know it couldn't be from the lavishness of his tipping.

"Good evening, Mr. Goodman," he said. "Your table is waiting."

Goodman, whether by a peripheral rating in the pecking order or by choice, I didn't know, didn't sit in the front. But as the bar room to which we were led was also filled with many notables, I took it to be a matter of preference.

"Your booth," said Julius.

"Thanks," said Goodman, unbuttoning his blazer and treating me to a glimpse of satin kelly green lining. "This okay?" he asked me.

"Fine," I said, sliding in. He nodded to Julius who, in either event, had departed.

We were seated only a moment when drinks were set before us, large tumblers of vodka on the rocks, with a bottle of sparkling water of some sort.

"Compliments of the gentleman at the bar," said the waiter.

We both looked up to see not exactly a gentleman, but Chief Broward perched on a stool, executing a slight finger wave.

"Thanks," said Goodman as the waiter departed. "Some 'compliments'—he don't even pay for his own." With which he nodded an acknowledgment to Broward, who pantomimed an indication for Goodman to come over.

"I'll go see what he wants. Otherwise he's liable to try sitting with us and *we'll* be stuck for his tab." (To say nothing of his company.)

In Goodman's absence, I looked around the famous room. I did like it here. It might no longer be quite so in—in the sense of a trendy, now, happening restaurant—but it retained a monumental residual Hollywood class. The walls remembered. The booths remembered. What a Hollywood it had been. Since Goodman was still occupied, I decided to go to the men's room and take a pee in Clark Gable's urinal.

When I returned, Goodman was back at the table and there were four glasses on it. In front of him, an empty and a full. In front of me, two fulls.

"Drink up," said Goodman. "You're falling behind."

"The evening's young," I said.

"Yeah, but you're a writer. I never met a writer yet didn't drink."

"That's because the only writers you meet are in bars—not home writing, like the rest of us. What'd Broward want?"

"He wanted a line on where he could find Barry Nash. Or even Heather Hansen. For questioning. Seems they're looking into the whole mishmash of Fortaco Productions, whether there might not have been some money laundering going on."

"Might not?"

"Whether provable stuff, or at least local bites on the news. Elections coming up and all."

"I thought he was going to retire."

"I expected him to. Maybe he sold short on oil."

"So what does that mean—he can't find Nash and Hansen?"

Goodman shrugged. "Who knows? He says, 'It's as if they disappeared from the face of the earth.'"

I opened my mouth, let it pass.

"Let's have a look at the menu," said Goodman, either not noticing or hungry. He snapped his fingers (don't you hate that?). Evidently the waiter did, too, since he ignored him for a good three minutes. By which time he was ready for another drink. I demurred, instead examining the menu.

But I found it a bit hard to concentrate. How bizarre life was. Here I was, dressed to the nines, my lover gone, dining in luxury and style with my, I guess I have to admit, partner, dressed to the fours—*his* lover gone. So two guys, with what you might call a love/hate relationship, hold the love—locked in a forced social embrace. If life got any funnier, I'd kill myself.

It didn't come as earth-shattering that Goodman perused the bill of fare at great length before coming up with the surprise entree of "New York steak, medium rare, extra fries, burnt. Any vegetable that a person would *choose*—none of your kales, or seaweed, or elf's breath."

"And you, sir?" asked the captain.

I couldn't believe what I heard—myself saying, "I'll have the same."

"And for an appetizer?"

"Salad, house dressing," said Goodman.

I nodded. In for a penny.

"Oh, one thing," said Goodman to the captain.

"Yes, sir?"

"Would you give me Mr. Cifelli's check?"

The captain nodded.

What was this?

"They make a nice drink," said Goodman, taking a big swallow, clearly not telling me.

"*They* make a nice drink? Who do you know doesn't make a nice drink?"

"Look, pal. If I don't criticize your way of life . . ."

I took a deep pull at my glass. They did make a nice drink.

"So the whole thing hinged on your finding the secret hiding place?"

"Hey, they could of taken the place apart and found it, or someone, somewhere, would know. No, the whole thing depended on getting someone to show they knew where the secret place was."

"Well, you pulled it off. More power to you. And it will make a good book."

"Looks like we're a team," he said as I found time hadn't hung all that heavy and somehow I was actually into my second drink.

"I wouldn't go that far," I ventured. "This is only two."

"We don't have to get married," said Goodman. "I just meant, I don't know—it seems to work out pretty good we work together."

I, who hadn't even been able to plan a stable relationship that lasted longer than a year and a half, certainly wasn't about to commit to a working one for any great length of time. We'd see.

The next thing I saw, besides a mysteriously appearing third vodka on the rocks, was our salad.

The second next thing was Armand Cifelli, standing over our table.

"Ah, Mr. Cifelli," said Goodman.

"I wanted to thank you for your graciousness in picking up my check."

"My pleasure, Mr. Cifelli," said Goodman. "I thought of it as returning a favor."

"Nice try, Rayford," said Cifelli. "I thought of it as you paid for dinner. The favor we'll worry about another time."

Goodman smiled, evidently what he expected.

"Nice to see you again, young fellow," said Cifelli, and left.

I was about to ask what that was all about when the realization hit me I didn't exactly want to know what I wasn't exactly ever going to be told.

Some partners are more silent than others.

I found I had a real good appetite for the steak.